I0742863

Two Fishes

from the

River Nile

By

Prophet Allyson Michael D'Espyne

WORKBOOK PRESS LLC
187 E Warm Springs Rd,
Suite B285, Las Vegas, NV 89119, USA

Website: https://workbookpress.com/
Hotline: 1-888-818-4856
Email: admin@workbookpress.com

Ordering Information:
Quantity sales. Special discounts are available on quantity purchases by corporations, associations, and others.
For details, contact the publisher at the address above.

Library of Congress Control Number:

ISBN-13:   978-1-953839-78-7 (Paperback Version)
                978-1-953839-70-1 (Digital Version)

REV. DATE: 09/14/2022

TWO FISHES

FROM THE RIVER NILE

BEGINNING IN 2010:

In the winter of 2010, after a long hard day of dishwashing at a local company, whose business was to provide food for the seniors of the ''Meals on Wheels Program,'' I fell asleep on a park bench. A few hours later, the Lord Jesus woke me up to go to my janitorial job, which I did in the evenings, three (3) days a week.

The next day when I arose, the Lord Jesus spoke to me. He told me that he is giving me four things:

1. Jesus is giving me a home.

2. Jesus is giving me two (2) fishes from the River Nile.

3. Jesus is giving me two (2) luxury cars.

4. Jesus is giving me money.

At nighttime, I would peruse the local newspapers looking feverishly for a house with the option to buy. Reminiscing as the hours went by on the awesome Word of Our Lord Jesus Christ.; his fiery eyes piercing me through and through with a gentle kiss. Jesus in his Immaculate being keeps using me beyond the limits of my humanity. Sometimes, I feel as though, the world co-exists in another world of its own.

Psalm 8:1 O LORD our Lord, how excellent is thy name in all the earth! Who hast set thy glory above the heavens.

2 Out of the mouth of babes and sucklings hast thou ordained strength because of thine enemies, that thou mightest still the enemy and the avenger.

3 When I consider thy heavens, the work of thy fingers, the moon and the stars, which thou hast ordained;

4 What is man, that thou art mindful of him? and the son of man, that thou visitest him?

5 For thou hast made him a little lower than the angels, and hast crowned him with glory and honour.

I remembered one of my best friends Harris would consistently go to Super 1 Food market, to do his grocery shopping. As he walked the aisles paying attention to the voice of Jesus, as he selects the food that is essential for the season of the moment. We on the other hand, would take a pushcart and listened to our minds and our taste buds.

We would not stop to read the amount of calories that are written on the cans, boxes, vegetable wrappings, or even the brown paper bags that houses the foodstuff. At the same time, we are too busy chatting with our children and our better halves, as we push the cart through the lanes of the supermarket. Some of us are on the cell phone talking to someone, taking their grocery list that even Jesus cannot get in his word to us. We are oblivious of what is happening around us. We live only for the moment.

Invariably, Jesus keeps me posted and focused on his itinerary. Jesus knows that I love to read, so he physically takes me by the hand to the nearest library. This one was situated on Greenwood Road, opposite the Capitol One Bank. It stood on the corner and occupied about three to four acres of land.

Jesus in his wisdom took me to a small reference book that dealt with root word and its beginnings. Every afternoon,

Jesus would direct my path to the library, though small, to continue studying this profound book from A to Z. Did I knew, what Jesus was doing? No, I did not. Did I question Our Lord Jesus Christ? No, I would not ever do that.

Studying with Jesus is like wrestling with the wind, as it keeps blowing your hat off your head, no matter how hard you try to keep it on your head, until you firmly hold it against your side. Jesus keeps you wanting more and more and more. Whatever you want and it is in his will you will one day receive your joy; no matter where you are in life in the world of statistics.

Jesus never wrote you off. Your school teacher wrote you off. Your professor of music at the university wrote you off. Your father wrote you off. Your mother wrote you off. Your brother wrote you off. Your sister wrote you off. Your church choir wrote you off. Your son wrote you off. Your daughter wrote you off. Even the general public wrote you off. Jesus is still standing

Take a look in the mirror; tell me what you see? Yes, you are standing perpendicular. You are like a prism reflecting light vertically and horizontally and even forming circles because you can roll yourself into one. Jesus gives you a talent to take to the mountain top. One thing that is required of you to do is to keep your eyes focused on Our Lord Jesus Christ.

O LORD our Lord, how excellent is thy name in all the earth! Math school teachers must bear in mind of a gift given to them to really show Jesus off in their classrooms. Far too often, they have allowed the devil to trespass against Jesus in the classroom. This is not about statistics. If only the teacher would listen to the cries of their students and not viciously pelt the duster at the student, who is not attentive.

When students have to deal with teachers of this temperament, as I had in years gone by then it affects the progress of the student, who is presumably not distinguished. Teachers who are cocky and will always be cocky would not see an improvement in the classroom. Teachers who are self-confident would not see an improvement in the classroom. Teachers who are self-assertive would not see an improvement in the classroom.

Every year since I have been in America, it has been plastered all over the media about the failings of our students in the world standings. To this day we "Americans" have never been in the first ten countries of the entire world. Scholastically we have failed as a Super Power. Yet we boast of the love of Jesus. Jesus is the genius. Keep your eyes on Jesus!

At the library, Jesus would allow me to take notice of the children age 13 and under. They would always be heading to the computer section designated for them. Most times their parents would not be with them, as they play their favorite games on the internet. Parents must bear in mind that their children would not be the ones, to have to give an account of their stewardship. This is the sole responsibility of the parent.

Children who are accompanied by their parents are oftentimes found in the aisles with their parents selecting books of their choice. These parents are avid readers that take their time carefully choosing books, as they peruse the contents of the books. Some of them may or may not pay attention to the testimonials written on the back of the cover of the respective book. And like the river that flows, they are often at the library borrowing books with their children.

Jesus is ready and waiting to teach you something. Are you willing and available? It is often said that the sky is the limit. There is no limit in Jesus. The library is there for you to come and borrow books that somebody has donated, to the institution of the love of the hand of Jesus. The library is there for you to come and borrow CDs and movies that somebody has donated, to the institution of the love of the hand of Jesus.

People have not realized that when anybody falls asleep whilst reading a book that, that was the hand of the devil. People have not realized that when the page or pages are torn out from the book by your hand that, that was the hand of the devil. People have not realized that when you have to circle a phrase or sentence for remembrance that, that was the hand of the devil. Jesus never forgets.

Jesus loves a cheerful giver. The library is a cheerful giver. You do not have to buy a membership to join the library. You do not have to be forced by anyone to join the library. You do not have to sell your dignity to join the library. You do not have to be a member of the green party to join the library. You do not have to be democratic to join the library. You do not have to be a republican to join the library. You do not have to be an American to join the library.

The library is an institute of learning. Freely come, freely go! There are many, many countries all around the world that do not exercise this freedom. These countries are like some people, who will go in the line for the homeless and receive a cup of coffee and a sandwich. Then they will come outside and pour the coffee in the canal, and wrap the sandwich in tissue and throw it in the dumpster.

Or they will leave the breakfast shelter in a rage and lift their heads to the heavens and use all the profanity that they can think about. Jesus is only reminding his children who withstand the arrows by day and by night that Jesus is alive. Somebody has to take the torch to the mountain top. Somebody has to take the torch to the mountain top for it to become a beacon of hope for the hopeless ones. Somebody has to take the torch to the mountain top for it to become a beacon of hope, thus forming a prayer to the angels and the saints.

At the library there is solitude which is the state of being alone, though surrounded by many voices that break the silence of Jesus. Some people walk out into the wilderness to read their favorite book. The clouds above their heads are racing at a terrific speed to form darkness. The sun is shut out, but your eyes keep eating the reading off your special story in the dimness of the light.

In my silence of memorizing the root of the word, Jesus is showing me the wisdom of mortal man. I recalled my apprenticeship back home in La Trinity. I had just been transferred from the Bookbinding section to the Compositors' Work section. I supposedly fell in love with the assembly of single-metal type character faces. Taking each letter from the case and placing them in a stick, which is placed in your hand brought me great joy and peace within. The reading of the word was upside down.

It took centuries to reverse the order. If only we can stay in five minutes of immortality, then and only then, our wisdom would be accelerated with tremendous speed that we can catch the falling light. The computer is not the answer to the question or the replacement of the single-metal type written book. The wisdom of Jesus far exceeds mortal man. In other words, we ain't see nothing yet.

Jesus is waiting at the end of the line to see all who is going in and coming out of the library. Jesus is waiting at the door of the house of the Lord to see all who is coming to serve him. Jesus is waiting at the entrance of the Hall of Justice to see all who is ferociously fighting the lion in the den. Jesus is waiting at the entrance of the hospital to see all who is coming to visit the sick. Jesus is waiting at the entrance of the prisons to see all who is coming to pay a visit to an inmate.

In my moment of silent reading, I will hear footsteps running through the lanes, and as soon as my eyes make contact with the eyes of the little one, the running will cease and the child will quietly return to his mother. Jesus is showing me that the child is fully aware that he must not run but walk in the library. Jesus also is showing me that the parent has misgivings and shortcomings in the training of her child.

It is not about parents shouting and screaming at the top of their lungs. It is about our faithfulness and our adoration of Our Lord Jesus Christ. Jesus does not need your help. Jesus wants to show you, that it is imperative for you to keep your eyes on him. The failures of your parents, grandparents, and great grandparents are things of the past. It is your responsibility to rewrite the wrongs.

The reading of books brings you knowledge. And precisely, what is knowledge? Acquaintance with facts, truths, or principles, as from study or investigation; acquaintance or familiarity gained by sight, experience, or report. Jesus wants to prepare you for the future. Jesus wants to prepare you for the future, so that you will become the future for your children.

There are authors who have written books inspired by Our Lord Jesus Christ. There are authors who have written books of inventions and innovations given to them by Our Lord Jesus Christ. There are authors who have written books about their wartime escapades and the way Jesus used them on the battle field of a ruthless world. There are authors who have written books about the lives and times of a few phenomenal people of the world.

Jesus job is to develop in you a listening ear to hear him, when he calls you in service of the Lord. When you sit in the quietness of the library, you will hear him speaking to you no matter what is happening around you. When Jesus has given you a job for you to do, he teaches you how to get the job done.

As soon as family hears that Jesus is now working with you to bring about a new work, jealousy begins and all hell breaks loose. The Bible says that God is a jealous God. Yes he is. Jesus is intolerant of humans' unfaithfulness and rivalry. Who are you to tell Jesus, what to do?

O LORD our Lord, how excellent is thy name in all the earth! Jesus pays everybody a visit in their lifetime. Most times people are reluctant to go do the will of the Lord. Since it does not meet their ego; they put it aside and continue their life as usual.

Everybody in life cannot and will not become a great singer. Each one of us comes with a molecule of uniqueness for Jesus to flower with his breath that circles this unique molecule which will one day proliferate other symptoms of love, when we exhale, as we journey life's emptiness. This void comes along, because of our refusal to listen to the voice of Our Lord Jesus Christ.

At the library, Jesus keeps showing me the reference section, that nobody comes and removes one book a day from the shelf. Nobody will take a book off the shelf, and take a seat and read. These very important memoirs printed in black and white were not put there just to take up space. These were the avid memories of a peculiar people. These were the inscriptions and definitions of the Glory of Our Lord Jesus Christ. Are you really listening?

A few weeks ago, the City of Shreveport, Louisiana, held its annual "State Fair" at the park on Greenwood Road. Everyone had to spend money to buy tickets to have fun time in the fall. The event was packed out for the few weeks that it lasted. Millions of dollars were spent at the event. To study by reading is not fun time for the average family in

America, especially those who are locked in by systematic slavery.

The daily newspapers that come off the press of the various printing companies in the State of Louisiana are stacked on the shelves of the periodical section that most parents and children do not read. Yet they want to be excellent at the gift or talent that Jesus had already put in them, before the foundation of the world. It is about time that parents start speaking the truth to their own children.

Excellent defines itself as possessing outstanding quality or superior merit; remarkably good. Excellent is also worthy, estimable, choice, fine, first rate, prime and admirable. John the beloved, the disciple whom Jesus loved, stood under the cross to show the world how excellent is thy name in all the earth. John did not quiver. The Holy Ghost kept him strong under the cross. Where is your strength?

The parents who are blest with children do have a formidable task. Their first job is to love Jesus at breakfast time. Their first job is to love Jesus at lunch time. Their first job is to love Jesus at dinner time. This is their first love. They have failed in the word of excellence. Jesus gave them a treasure of his love. Now, where is there love for Jesus? Their love is to sit around and do nothing. Their love is to blame Jesus for every wrong thing that happens to them in their lives. Their love is to give up on Jesus.

They lose sight of the fact that Jesus has surrounded them with all these children, who are the eyeballs of Jesus that keep steering into their eyes, when they walk in unbelief. They allow satan, the devil to blind them in their everyday choices. They sing the hymn because something good has happened to them on that joyful day. A beautiful, melodious voice, that has lost its sweetness in the distance.

Jesus shows everybody up at the hour of their need. And

that is why, they faithlessly walk the plank, in the middle of the ocean. They refuse to walk to go run their errands on a daily basis. They must have bus fare. They must have car fare. As soon as things do not go their way, everyone becomes their enemy. Jesus is standing there at your side, especially when things are going wrong.

All you have to do is to take a deep breath to welcome him into your heart. It does not cost you the fare at the state fair. It does not cost you the fare on the bus. It does not cost you the fare for the taxi. It does not cost you the fare for the lottery ticket. It does not cost you the fare for the bingo card. Jesus at all times wants you to know that he is standing there at your side.

O LORD our Lord, how excellent is thy name in all the earth! When a family comes to the library to edify themselves, in the vast depth of the peak of Mount Everest, theirs is the kingdom of heaven. How many homes in anyone's lifetime have you visited and see everybody reading their favorite book? How many classrooms have you seen all the students' eyes reading? How many churches have you seen everybody either reading, singing, or dancing? How many line segments are there in a polygon?

Jesus extends his love by blessing you to give birth to children, who are born gifted in poetry. This is a gift that the whole wide world is lacking of. People are too caught up into themselves that they allow satan, the devil, to rule them out of the necessary gift. The less time spent in trying to read tea leaves to ascertain one's future will become a real solid rock of the triumph of Jesus. To perpetuate truth: you need to understand the true beginnings of the River Nile.

Of course, you need Jesus in your everyday life to take you through the tunnel of your mountain of love. You need Jesus to impassion you with love. The love for word and its volume of meanings can only be brought about by continuous reading. It is said that the leaf does not fall far from the tree. Are you that leaf that is falling under the tree of Our Lord Jesus Christ? Are you overflowing with the love of reading deep down in your soul? Until you get the true meaning of Jesus for yourself, then you cannot be used by him in the future.

A person in the service of another is what Jesus keeps showing the whole wide world and they keep missing the bus at the bus stop. I recalled my deceased mother Phyllis D'Espyne, who was a seamstress and a housewife. At the time, she was making a dress for one of her few customers. It was a time when things were hard and monies to feed her eight children were scarce. After making the dress for her friend, who could not have paid her for the dress, even though she was employed, my mother gave her the dress anyhow.

Jesus is constantly teaching even when we are not looking. Sometimes Jesus puts us in a mode of great expectations. We gather together to go pray for a parishioner at the hospital. As soon as we get there, we become pensive. We get into the elevator to the 13th floor. As we approach the nurses' station, we get hold of ourselves and announce to the nurse, where and to whom we are going to see.

Arriving at the patient's door, we enter to greet her in the spirit of Jesus. In that moment of reflection, we allow Jesus to take us through this service which is humbly His. After praying, singing and dancing in the spirit of Jesus, we still cannot tell whether the patient is likely to be healed or not. Jesus keeps us in our expectations. We will like to say the obvious before we leave, but we just cannot commit unless it is the whole truth.

This spirit of service wears us out to say the least. What keeps us going is the love of Jesus in our hearts. Jesus takes his time to build the house. Jesus is not in a hurry to finish a work that requires the smoldering of hot coals under your feet. During this time, your service goes unrewarded and nobody takes notice of your good deeds. Jesus knows that you are in the desert; you do not know. You keep on going to visit the sick without reservations.

Sometimes we have to do some heroic things for Jesus, even though our fellowmen do not view these things as heroic. It is like a painter painting a picture in the abstract; the minutes, the hours and days are gently passing by unnoticed. As soon as he is finished, he is angry with himself. He cannot see why it took him so long to do Jesus's foolishness that would have taken him less time on his own.

To be in the service of Jesus is a blessing from God the Father, God the Son, and God the Holy Spirit. We take the work of Jesus to casually and not faithfully. We view Jesus as sometimes unfair and not fair. Jesus must weigh in at every call. It is like standing in the rain with your new suit without an umbrella. We tend to see the obvious rather than the face of Jesus in everything that we do because of his love.

Jesus is untiring. Yet he will take us along if only we will let go. It is not how much work that you do for the Lord. It is not how many years that you have been laboring for the Lord. It is not the vast number of good deeds that you have done for the Lord. Jesus hope is that you share it with others with the hope that they share it with others too.

In the year 2010, I did not have any clue that the Lord Jesus Christ was preparing me to write a book far less books. All I remembered vividly is Jesus repeatedly saying to me that we have to learn these root words for you have lost them through sickness. I knew that Jesus is truly right and will at all times be right throughout all eternity. Jesus helps me keep my composure in all my undertakings.

O LORD our Lord, how excellent is thy name in all the earth! Pointedly, Jesus is saying not only to me, but to the entire world not to incline to the so-called gods of the world. Jesus love for us is above the words of mortal men. He knows how to wrap his arms around you and keep you from falling prey to the tricks of the enemy. Jesus knows how to stem the tide of injustices that often overpower us to let satan steal our measure of faith. But the more we allow the recalcitrant gods to sway us in any way; the more we let go of Jesus if only to wipe away the tears with both hands, is the more we have not yet understood Jesus's genuine love for us.

The arms of Jesus are like the eagle who sits on the peak of Mount Everest, in South Asia. At the height of 30,000 feet, the eagle can spot a prey in the middle of the jungle. The eagle descends and captures its prey, a rabbit whose color is black, so, how come we as a people of Jesus cannot come together as an eagle in flight? We are in dire need of sight as an eagle. We are in dire need of the majestic confidence of the claws and the sharp beak of the eagle. These heroic gifts have been eroded by our doubts, and fears, and disappointments in life. Wake up my people!

We are at the library because of the internet. We obviously spend too much time playing with toys and not reading the books that Jesus wants us to pierce our eyes into each day of our lives. The world is spinning on its axis, whilst we are having fun gambling on the internet. Our children adopt our attitudes day in and day out, night in and night out. They give up because we have already given up on Jesus. We are greater and mightier than the eagle. We can reason, and assimilate facts, and figures than any bird that Jesus has created.

Put aside the toys! Affix your eyes in the Word of God which is your Bible. Read your Bible to your children! Train your children to read their Bibles to their children! Equip them with the armor of Jesus which is the Bible! Let them feast on the Word of God! We know that Jesus is the answer. We are very much aware that Jesus can heal all things. We have infinite joy, when we nourish our children with the love of Jesus.

Jesus wants to comb your hair and to style it into the beautiful roses in the garden that you pass by everyday on your way to work only to absorb its scented-flowering fragrance. A lingering scent, which you wish, that you can bottle up, to take with you wherever you may go.

The laborers are few in the vineyard. Are you ready to do the will of Jesus? Or are you waiting for him to call your name? Don't you look to your neighbor for advice! Look to Jesus and enter in! Jesus has a word for you to take to your parents. Jesus has a word for you to take to your siblings. Jesus has a word for you to take to grandpa. Jesus has a word for you to take to grandma. Jesus has a word for you to take to your children.

Jesus knows that you need that brand new car that you keep looking at from the show window. Jesus knows that you need that beautiful pair of golden color shoes that you keep steering at through the corners of your eyes. Jesus knows that you want to build your own house that he has promised you that you will get. Jesus knows that your child has run away from home and only heaven knows, where he or she is. Jesus knows everything.

Jesus knows that some of you are waiting on him, or a preacher to deliver you from the pressures of this world. The oppressed families have given up on Jesus, but, you are still standing. Jesus knows that some of you are tormented and will be tormented by Lucifer, the devil, and will not drink of his blood. Sometimes, they leave you all alone at the house, because you are no longer good company. You talk about Jesus every second of the day, and what he has done for you.

You rely on no one else but Jesus to come and comfort you each passing minute, each passing hour, each passing day, each passing week, each passing month, and each passing year. Jesus is still standing.

O LORD our Lord, how excellent is thy name in all the earth! Purposefully, Jesus is the good news. Unlike the eagle, he descended from heaven, which is millions of miles away from the earth. Jesus came to change the teachings of the Word of God, because nobody had it right. His good news began in a city and the capital of Israel called Jerusalem. It is an ancient holy city and a center of pilgrimage for Jews and Christians alike. Indeed, it was the beginning of the Christian Movement. It was the beginning of the walk of Jesus.

Jesus did not have a cell phone to carry around with him wherever he went. In his hand, he embraced his Bible, which was the unadulterated Old Testament. Jesus depended on God the Father miraculous gifts to spread his Gospel of truth, wherever his feet touched the ground. The angels took the word from the mouth of Jesus to his prophets, who were expecting his coming and took his message to far off places.

Jesus is still walking on the face of the earth in the form of Holy Spirit, but, where are his children to take his word and carry his message around the world? Everybody has dropped the Bible and made the cell phone their god. Some of these homes have no Bibles, but they surely have cell phones. Their pastor is the one giving them advice on the other end of the line. Where is Jesus in the age of the millennia? The church is dying because we do not want to be told by Jesus or anyone else, what to do.

Now, here comes chaos. The blind man no longer has to stand at the corner waiting for one of the children of Jesus to take him across the dangerous highways. Due to the fact that the Christians are too busy running their mouths off on their cell phones. The Christians no longer have to buy a newspaper to see what is on sale. All we need to do is to touch a smart phone and hit Google, and we can have a great day shopping on line. We Christians behave that we are in charge. Really!

Jesus is often taken out of context for far too long. We will always believe the false prophets or pundits as they are called in the secular world that we live in. Jesus takes offence when you dilute his word. Jesus will not stand by and allow anyone to sugar coat his word anymore. His name is Excellent. What is your name? There is no man on the planet whose name is excellent. So tell me the reason, why you are following another god? The only miracle worker is Jesus.

We live in a world of compound interest. Interest computed on the accumulated unpaid interest as well as on the original principal. Jesus is not about the foolishness of human beings. Jesus speaks in terms of miracles. Well over two thousand years ago Jesus had performed many miracles. Where are your miracles? If you do less speaking may be Jesus will one day come along and show you something. We cannot keep still not even for a moment. We are forever living in a vacuum.

Miracles are real. We leave what is real to serve what is unreal. We adore the world of magic and kick the Bible outside the front door. At the university, we bow down obsequiously, at the feet of professors. As soon as we meet so-called important people, we begin to fawn. We use flattery to get anything we want. Sometimes our children are all embarrassed by our flattery.

Jesus is showing that after two thousand years the needle on the dashboard has never really moved. Jesus is showing that the same things that he had overturned in his walk on the face of the earth is now, once again, worshipped and adored. The magician whose performance at the auditorium is sold out week after week with the same stupid act of a bouquet of flowers, and an unseen rabbit still steals an anchor. Where is your mindset?

We are texting and driving as though that is a very smart choice. The accidents and the death tolls by this paranoia does not seem to dawn on anyone. Even the police officers are texting and driving. Drivers do not care about the law and the fines when caught for this crime. Do not text and drive has now become a paradigm! It is the sign of the times.

Jesus is not waiting for humankind to catch up with him. Jesus is not waiting for mortal man to once again to become conscious of his omnipotence. Jesus is not waiting to literally throw stones from heaven on a daily basis and put Homo sapiens in a frenzy. Jesus is still standing.

O LORD our Lord, how excellent is thy name in all the earth! Jesus is worthy. We creatures do not possess this innate gift. A quality that comes only from God the Father to show the world that Jesus is the Only True Living Begotten Son of the Almighty God. A trait that human beings world over is wrestling with, because they believe that one day satan, the devil, will give this gift to them. A gift that satan does not possess.

Jesus is worthy and is worthy to be praised. A triumphant message of hope! Equivocally the library is a message of hope. Writers from all walks of life fill the shelves with their experiences of a life that, they had never planned out for themselves. Suffice it to say, nobody wants to seriously follow Jesus. They want to follow the myths of the world. Even though, they do not believe in the ideologies of the communistic world, they too have become a communist of some sort.

Undoubtedly, the teachings of our Lord are given to his anointed sons and daughters to preach the word in good times and in bad times. Stand for Jesus on the mountain top!

Stand for Jesus in the public square! Stand for Jesus on the highways and the byways! Stand for Jesus at the junctions of your life! Stand for Jesus when there is no one else standing! Stand for Jesus at the four corners of the globe!

The more families that fill the lanes of the libraries all across these 50 states of America accompanying their children, and encouraging them to read as a goal the entire lane of books, the more America will be filled with the wisdom of peace, joy and love. The blessing of freedom shall not be turned into a curse. The blessing of Jesus, whose eyes are on these 50 states will not be here forever, unless you bend those knees in adoration of Jesus. Jesus is still standing.

The stakes and the prize are higher than you foresee, because the truth had never been spoken to the children of Jesus for well over fifteen hundred years, thus saith the Lord. From then on the seeds of catastrophe were planted by the fallen angels. And these are the reasons why the people of the land keep shifting and shifting and shifting far off to the left. Even their faith in Jesus is threatened by satan and his fallen angels.

They will wake up on Sunday mornings with all good intentions of going to church only to be misdirected by a phone call. They will wake up on Sunday mornings with all good intentions of taking the family to church only to be threatened by another religious group that does not share their faith. They will wake up on Sunday mornings with all good intentions to pick up someone that needs a ride only to be threatened by their boss. They will wake up on Sunday mornings with all good intentions to serve the Lord, but on this occasion the car would not start.

Jesus is making it abundantly clear that no one can blame anyone for their missteps but themselves. Jesus already knows all the tricks of the devil and his cohorts. We shall persevere like Jesus through and through, especially when the writing is on the wall. Car or no car, take off your shoes and begin to walk to church. On your way, call your Pastor to let him know that you are on your way.

This is an example of excellence in the sight of Jesus. For we live in a world of tremendous callousness. People are indifferent to you when you do not have a car. They will pass you on the way to church with an empty vehicle and will not stop to pick you up. And have the audacity to look you in the face and say to you that, "they see you and will never stop to pick you up."

In the days of Jesus there were no cars or buses. People had to walk for miles and miles and days just to have a glimpse of Jesus. For the angels spread the love of Jesus throughout the vast lands around. The Holy Ghost kept Jesus standing for hours with his long sermons, for he knew others were on crutches coming to receive his every Word. Women hugging their handicapped sons and daughters, who had fallen asleep on their breasts. The paralyze man held on the shoulders of their brothers coming to receive a miracle from Jesus.

Everywhere Jesus had visited thousands of people gathered around to hear the true voice of the one that everyone had been waiting for. A spectacle that we were not blessed to envisage. But the Bible says do not be dismay for you have been blessed twice, because you were not present to bear witness of the sweetness of Jesus.

O LORD our Lord, how excellent is thy name in all the earth! The psalmist Jesus is saying to all his brothers and sisters to leave everything and follow me. Follow Jesus! As I read through the afternoons, evenings and nights for as long as the library is opened, the light of Jesus brightens and illuminates my mind.

I recalled my first Pastor who resided in Brunswick,

Georgia. His story remained with me to this day. It has been now 18 years ago, but its freshness has not lost its scent. His story began that as a child, about eight years of age he fell into a state of coma. It ruined his elementary school life. He could neither read nor write. Now the good Lord Jesus uses him and has given him the gift of interpretation of his Word.

Many scholars around the world would like to have this gift. Jesus shows the very scholars that this gift is only given to his sheep of the cloth. This is one of the reasons that they would be excommunicated from the church of god. They too have to go to church and listened to the interpretation of the Word of God, as they are fed by a chosen vessel of Jesus. This precedes any university degree of Theology. Jesus had no university degree.

Jesus is excellent, will always be excellent and will always, always, be excellent. And for those of you, who think that Jesus is playing with his Word, just continue to deny him. When Christian folk open their door to give shelter to people who are not Christians namely: muslims, bhudists and those of the same ilk. They must know that they have to be respectful at all times.

When it is winter the library is as empty as the fields and plains of Louisiana. The clatter of feet by children roaming through the aisles of the library ceases immediately. Ideally, this is the time for the children to read more at their homes for it is cold outside. It is a pity that the schools do not take their children by the school bus, to the nearest library in the vicinity. This will profoundly gladden the heart of Jesus.

It takes a lot of labor that goes into the production of books to fill the shelves of this sacred institution. It takes a lot of heart to print the truth that is recorded and dictated in the daily newspapers. Many reporters and writers have lost their lives in saying and writing precisely what they truly saw. Yet we take reading casually, and delight in games with our friends on the internet.

Jesus is pristine. We go to school to become excellent in the gifts that Jesus has blessed us with. Our teachers would tell us and show us the books that we ought to borrow to read from the library. Then our reading and our writing would improve as we continue the road to Jesus. Jesus is continually using others whom he puts in our way to nurture and nourish us into new life.

Some of us are blessed with the gift of music. Our teachers are there to admonish us, and to dissuade us from those, who have given their souls to the devil to become successful in the art of Music. They are there to teach us what to observe, so that when we leave school we would not fall prey to the divisiveness of the ways of satan, the devil. The culture of music is pregnant with evil.

Our schools are put there to remind us of Jesus. Jesus is the ultimate teacher. There will never be another supreme teacher like Jesus. Without Jesus there would have never been schools that anyone could attend freely. That is why there are public schools. It is to show the children that Jesus cares about their education. It is to show the children that Jesus truly died for their sins. It is to show the children that Jesus will never forget them no matter their situation. It is to show the children that Jesus can and will make you wealthy, if only you will surrender your all to him.

Jesus is very much aware, that the powers that be would lie to you, to tell you that it is because of their doings, and their hard work that they have made it possible for you to walk with your heads held up high. Where were they before the foundations of the world? Where are they now to show the whole wide world, that they and Jesus and God the Father is preparing and building a new heaven and a new earth?

O LORD our Lord, how excellent is thy name in all the

earth! The psalmist Jesus is saying that God the Father, God the Son, and God the Holy Spirit is giving and will be giving to all America a reservoir of libraries. Astonishingly, Jesus is sending a wave of people crossing the bridge. Jesus's wish is to provide for the unborn children who will be here tomorrow. Jesus is still standing.

There is a River Nile at the library. It is seen by the variety of backgrounds of authors, who displayed their talents in literary manuscripts, magazines and books to nourish our souls. The diversity of people, who lend their ears to Jesus despite opposition from family and friends, to paint a picture of words without a brush is a splendid color that depicts, the two fishes from the River Nile.

Jesus stood up in front of the congregation of Jews and read his own life, death and resurrection coming out from the book of Isaiah, but did the congregation truly accepted the Word of the Lord? Do we have the strength to do the same as the perfect one? Honestly, no. At the same time, we take Jesus for granted. In that moment, we assume that we can do anything whether right or wrong, since Jesus had already paid the price.

We adopt this attitude wherever we go and sew the seed of the damned. We rush into a state of amnesia suddenly forgetting, what Jesus had already provided for us to take us from zero to the mountain top. The library provides that seat of learning. The library provides us with that distinction of excellence. Jesus gives us those beautiful eyes to eat and absorb the experiences of others.

We cannot allow the enemy to root us out of our heavenly call. We cannot allow the imps of this world to eat our flesh, so that we can regurgitate the vomit of tomorrow. We cannot allow the seedlessness of the spirits that roam our houses with the hope of subjecting us, to their worthless tomorrows. We cannot allow the grotesque of obscurity to walk with us, as we try to read in silence.

Jesus is our sublimity. He did not create us to fall for the ridiculous. We are awe-inspiring creatures, if only we will consistently look deep into our souls and flow with the light of the majestic one. In this light, we will uncover precisely what is the meaning of our sufferings to give light to our future. Jesus did not allow us to be born with a golden spoon strapped in our mouths. Jesus allows us to take on a birth like his of a humble nature.

This birth of rags to riches is to give hope to a multitude of people, who have been robbed of their golden spoons. Yes it is an enormous undertaking. Yes it is an unbelievable rugged climb. Yes it is a no-guarantee task that you will ever come back to finish the tale of your God-given spike to the heavens. Yes it is a fruitless decision, because we all want guarantees of tomorrow.

Jesus did not have to finish his work here on the earth. Jesus would have entered into heaven regardless of the circumstances. Jesus had already existed. We have never existed in the purity and likeness of Our Lord Jesus. Jesus finished his work here on the earth as a pathway for us to freely walk into heaven. When we read the books of awe-inspiring authors, who came from backgrounds as ours, and have fought the battles of becoming a new creature, then we will understand and appreciate the name as no other as the perfect one, Jesus. It is the only name I know.

Jesus is walking a tight rope for us to bring about change in our neighborhoods. In some of our surroundings there would be open-air revivals. This is a time for the sick, lame, cripple, handicap brothers and sisters, who have fallen sick to disobedience owing to the evil of this world, to come to Jesus to heal their bodies and their souls. This is a time for soul searching and a renewing of our walk in the ways of Jesus.

Jesus is not recording our sins in a book. Jesus is not recording our sins on a leafless tree. Jesus is not recording our sins in the hearts of those, who truly love you. Jesus is not recording our sins to throw them back in our faces, when we meet him on our journey on Calvary's road. Jesus is not recording our sins in his head to make you feel uncomfortable as you enter into his presence. Jesus is not recording our sins and etching them on the leaves of 1000-year old trees in the jungles of Brazil.

I sat in peace and quiet reminiscing and going through old manuscripts that had been dated back to the 19th Century. As I had the privilege of seeing and touching history at the largest library in the world located in the City of Manhattan, New York, I can just imagine what the world would have been without that pungent and raucous source.

Jesus is showing me trails of children gathering on the steps of this very library to trace the beginnings of their heritage by their first three letters of their surnames. Nobody wants to grow up in a world as an orphan amongst billions of people. Nobody wants to be robbed of their heritage. Nobody wants to be referred to as a bastard. Nobody wants to be exiled in totality from each one of their siblings, cousins, aunts and uncles.

When we read we must not be forced by anyone to cram for an intending examination. Jesus does not accept this form of teaching by some scholars of the society. This is tremendously wrong and students should report this immediately to their superiors. Jesus gifts are enough for you to profit in this world of gross evil. Reading relaxes you. It is good medicine for your mind as you travel through steep steps and slippery slopes.

In the serenity of the library, you would have opened up a whole new world of knowledge that would keep you always wanting to grasp more and more, in your search of the who you are in this jungle of a world. As soon as you have discovered yourself, now you can say hello to Jesus. You see Jesus wants to sit in your eyes, so that he can read together with you through the sleeves of roll up printed paper.

If Jesus wants you to become a detective, you will be reading all of the books that fall under that particular author's name of the one that you are presently engage in. It is your humble duty to find out every conceivable book that that author had written in his entire life. You have to familiarize yourself and furnish yourself with each copy, because you would know or be able to perceive or conceive the mystery.

Human beings must learn to accept that the gift that Jesus hid in their bellies have to be unearthed by him, or a Prophet in order for them to obtain peace and to finish the work at hand. Otherwise, they will be living a life of continual torment and misery. Whether rich or poor there will be no peace. Whether physically strong or physically weak there will be no inner strength. Inner strength is what we need to do the will of Jesus.

If Jesus wants you to become a scientist, you will be reading all of the books that fall under that particular author's name. In this case, you can also read other writings and follow closely the experiments as shown in their illustrations. To get ahead in this field of physics, one must take on the mantle of Jesus. The higher the calling; the greater the risk. This is one of the reasons why some people to whom this field of endeavor had been given to, eventually stopped their walk abruptly.

Jesus does not want young scientists to feel disheartened or disenchanted, especially when experiments take too long to give a result. This is a time for you to quietly spend with Jesus in quiet contemplation. You shall bear in mind that your gift is firstly for the children of Jesus, who have lost their way because of strife and terror from totalitarian and fascist dictators.

If Jesus wants you to become a hymnist, who is awe-inspiring, then Jesus will take you along a road of silence. Firstly, in your walks to the library, he will give you the music and pierce your soul with the lyrics, as you walk with him on Calvary's road. After committing the words to your memory and making the hymn your own, Jesus will allow you to write the name of the hymn and the chorus and the verses to let you know that it is now yours. The music Jesus will keep for you forever.

If Jesus wants you to become a military person, you will be playing and be fascinated by military games. You will have fun reading geography and history books. Maps and illustrative figures and drawings you will master by just looking at them. As soon as you enter the forest you will never forget the pathway of entry. Rivers and streams will always be your fascination. The older you get, the more your life will be spent outdoors.

If Jesus wants you to become a pioneer, you will be spending all of your free time exploring sights or new territory, that has been created by volcanic eruptions. Life for you will be robust and full of excitement. Discovering new things will be your first goal. You will become passionate and drawn to Jesus for allowing you to behold and stepping on a new creation.

If Jesus wants you to become a choreographer, you will occupy the road of excellence and take on the persona of Our Lord Jesus. You will be endowed with the gift of creativity, not just in movement, or an arrangement for ballet. But Jesus will gift you in usurping and taking an epic stance, as a mark of humility to show satan that he is not responsible for procuring your gift.

Besides, the arts are plagued with the spirit of the Antichrist. Jesus danced his way into the hearts of his fellowmen, whilst delivering the Word to the populace. Dance is important, once it is done in the typical manner of the likeness of Jesus. The angels dance, the saints dance, the cherubims dance, the seraphims dance and delights the heart of God the Father, God the Son, and God the Holy Spirit.

Jesus stands in his Ivory tower of excellence to show the world that they shall in all fairness to their own children, do the right thing and speak the truth about their frailties and their misgivings. It is something that parents shy away from, thus leaving the child to believe that they are perfect. Judges, lawyers, police officers, soldiers, especially those who wear embroidered hats, shall let their sons and daughters be aware of their weaknesses.

Truth is like a two-edge sword. It cuts deep into your soul.

3211 MILTON STREET:

A great big, old concrete house painted in white with black painted window frames and glass pane looking out at you, as you view people passing by. The house sat atop an incline with enclosed cellars below. Beautiful living and dining room enough to seat as many chairs and couches to lie on. High ceilings and an eating kitchen occupied the back of the living room. On my left, two large bedrooms with a full bathroom separating the two bedrooms in which there were a beautiful clothes closet. The last room at the rear, I placed my gas dryer and hooked it up on the gas pipe.

I moved into this house in and around the early winter of 2011. For some remote reason, the winter was like summer, so I did not have to use much heat for that time of the year. The grass was tall all around the house, for the house was unoccupied for a long time. On weekends, I would roll up my sleeves and with a hoe in hand uproot the grass, that felt like cement, as I rooted it out. It took me about six weekends to see some light.

Jesus is saying that we expect him to come down from heaven with his angels to do the work that is expected for us to do. We often tend to forget that Jesus is not only our eldest brother, but more importantly he is our Lord. He is our voice in heaven. We need his voice to interpret our every word when we pray. Jesus translates our thoughts, actions and vows, when we choose to make a promise to our best friend, who stands beside us.

Our thoughts rule us in our everyday decisions. We cannot look left or right with our thoughts, before we cross the street in heavy traffic. It is a time for us to stop and have a seat to think through our mind process, as we gather ourselves to make a conscious and earnest decision. Challenges would consistently come our way for the most part to block our blessing that is on its way. Satan is in these challenges; all we need to do is to hurdle the evil or climb over the back of the enemy. Jesus is still standing.

Anything that comes your way as easy is never, never, good. There is no justification for the evil. We get in the way of Jesus, due to some fool, who came along and brainwash us to believe that this evil person, we could change. The philosophy is that out of evil cometh good. No, no, no. Evil begets evil. Thousands of years ago Jesus said that there are many sheep in wolves clothing. This is precisely what he meant. False Prophets!

Some of us would not adhere to this teaching. The reason was that, we knew someone, who was evil is now a change person and a perfect gentleman in our midst. Be it as it may, this Christian soul was struggling with the evil both inside and outside of his body to confront and fight the evil no matter what. The change came as soon as Jesus entered deep within his body and root out the enemy, who had him in a stronghold.

At the universities, the students that occupy the classrooms are between the ages of 18 and 25 years of age. Their experiences of life are like smoke before the fire. Their presumptuousness are SAT scores that are held to the highest. Jesus is bemused by academic scholars, who pride themselves with so-called charismatic gifts, which are truly given to men of the cloth.

Jesus is like the remote control in our hands, we subjectively depressed a button that took us into the living rooms and bedrooms of other countries. Quite happily, these people do not see us looking at them. Then we vicariously believed to ourselves that, we have revealed the plot only to find out our cultural differences. People in faraway places do not need your lens to determine the result of their backyards.

As I pulled the grass up with the hoe, I stumbled over ants' colonies that festered and took over the very walkway that surrounded the parallel sides of Exposition Street. Impulsively, we would destroy and annihilate the very wise creatures that never stops working. A few bites here and there would make us real angry thereby inhibiting us from real and surreal things of life.

Maybe some of us need to learn that cleanliness is next to Godliness. We pride ourselves on keeping our clothes clean and tidy without realizing the love of Jesus for his vulnerable creature the ants. Our eyes are glued to the TV and the internet and not on the wisdom of the ants. Jesus does not have to tell or command the colony what to do. Jesus does not have to shout out aloud at his small fragile children of the earth. Jesus is still standing.

2 Corinthians 5: 10-11 For we must all appear before the judgment seat of Christ; that every one may receive the things done in his body, according to that he hath done, whether it be good or bad

Knowing therefore the terror of the Lord we persuade men; but we are made manifest unto God; and I trust also are made manifest in your consciences.

Jesus is wisely looking at us through his window, which is his crowns that sits atop his head. Jesus does not need the internet. As I wield my hoe through the tuft grass with gloves to prevent me from getting stuck by the thorns that runs off vines, it tells me to this day that the society does not want to wait on Jesus. Human beings must sit and think through their perceptions or discernments of fleshly desires.

It is easy to come up with fraternalistic ideas that came out of a referenda. It is easy to go along with the moralistic views or aspects of traditional so-called values. It is easy to follow the dictates of any religious movement. Be reminded that Jesus shall be your first choice! Is Jesus speaking to you right now? Go follow him! There will at all times be an uphill battle.

Since when your principles are in total agreement with the instruments of God the Father, God the Son, and God the Holy Spirit. The twelve apostles were directly schooled by Jesus. Are you schooled by Jesus? Adam and Eve were schooled by Jesus. Noah was schooled by Jesus. Elijah was schooled by Jesus. Moses was schooled by Jesus. Are you schooled by Jesus? Jesus is still standing.

We pride ourselves on following our innermost thoughts that vehemently guide us through the day. Yet we struggle to do what is truly just. For we are consciously aware of the Ten Commandments of Jesus, that had been dictated to and written by the Prophet Moses. These Ten Commandments, that we seemingly break everyday of our lives; sometimes without thinking. Making a conscious effort to do the right thing is not as effortless as Jesus. Saying to ourselves that we got it and failing tomorrow are not the right teachings for our children.

The thorns of life would succinctly get us, as they hid themselves amongst the tall grass of life's uphill battles. The sweat pouring profusely from the top of my head to the soles of my feet is enough to wear out the soles of shoes of men that own no cars. Jesus teaches you each passing day. Every day is a new day in the eyes of Our Lord Jesus. His message is the same today. Please do not allow others to lead you astray!

Lifting my shoes up to examine the ground under my feet sometimes; making sure that I am not standing on an ants' colony, as I wiped away the sweat from getting into my eyes. It is astounding and hilarious, as you keep laughing to yourself on the outpouring of the wisdom of Jesus. The quickness of the passing of time makes you wonder, when Jesus overwhelms you with his presence. The overriding unbelief of a peculiar people that are showered by the Holy Spirit, but really do not care about the next day.

The wisdom and beauty of the tireless tiny ants, whose ways we care not to follow, working feverishly all day and all night long, bearing its load on its head through hills and valleys of a moonless night makes me shudder at the sight of tolerance. Jesus teaches me not to destroy these sunny-tireless creatures, but to dig them out with a shovel and toss them over the mountain side, which is to say that you are not welcome on my terrain.

Displacing them from time to time taught me that when they are disturbed by human hands, they would leave and free you up with an antless footpath. Yes they are there to remove the carnage left behind when you have killed a bug or a small tree lizard. But more importantly, they are an eye-opener letting us know to pace the floor at night with an open book, to prevent us from falling asleep in the middle of an intriguing story, so that we would not want to run the risk of losing.

Jesus harasses us from time to time, as a child harasses his parents. It is the way of Jesus being intimate with his children, as they painstakingly undertake great risk in combating the evil of a ruthless world. Jesus harasses us in our thought process. Jesus harasses us in our sermons. Jesus harasses us in our deliberations. Jesus harasses us in our songs of praise.

Conscience is the part of the superego in psychoanalysis that judges the ethical nature of one's actions, and thoughts and then transmits such determinations to the ego for consideration. At the house, the Lord Jesus would deal with me on the question of morality in high places: sadly, those seats were often taken by the clairvoyants of the world. Jesus is the only bridge between heaven and earth. Mediums have no place in the sight of God the Father, God the Son, and God the Holy Spirit. Jesus is still standing.

When a peculiar people of God allow the Sigmund Freud's of this world to overtake their inner selves, Our Lord Jesus has a big problem with these mediums. Jesus is not playing in that year 2017. Jesus will be doing a new thing: which will mainly consist of uprooting the roots of satan in high places.

These roots were already formed in the House of Representatives, and in the House of the Senate. They use their gifts of clairvoyance, when they run for the offices of the hierarchy. They are often tricked by the narrative of sensational topics, that plays into their emotions. Prolific writers become sensational speakers and these are two fine examples of two fishes from their river Nile.

1 Timothy 5:8 But if any provide not for his own, and specially for those of his own house, he hath denied the faith, and is worse than an infidel. In the summer of 2011, the intense heat ravaged and burned the grass and made it much easier for me to hoe the entire yard and the pavement in front of the house. The temperatures were staggering well over 115 degrees on any given day.

On these weekends, I would refrain from cleaning the yard, because these dangerous temperatures drained my body to the pulp. Whatever weight I gained during the winter season, soon fell off in the first month of summer. Jesus is showing me the old curtains left behind in the living room, the kitchen, both bedrooms and the added on washroom. These thick drapes kept the house extremely hot and replacing them would have brought me penniless.

Sometimes, I wonder about the impoverished people of the city of Detroit which stands in SE Michigan on the Detroit River. A river in SE Michigan, flowing South from Lake St. Clair to Lake Erie forming part of the boundary between the U.S. and Canada. Founded by French settlers in 1701, Detroit was a city famously known as the US automobile industry in the 1900s.

These beautiful people became destitute from the standpoint of economics, that benefitted the one per cent of Michigan. These families slept on the steps and sidewalks of the wealth of a golden city that vexed the soul of Our Lord Jesus Christ. These scarred families through no fault of their own had to bear the same fervent heat of summertime, which I had to bear, when I too slept in the open air for years in booming cities all across America. Please remember Jesus is still standing!

At nighttime, I would sleep with the inside front door open to prevent me from utter dehydration. Even though, the fan would be on full speed, the air would still be humid. Minimum wage would not suffice to say the least. Jesus shows himself to thousands of Christian people in high places, who became timid and stingy in their giving. They would not give for fear of losing their peers.

The windows though many were like cemented in the walls. They could not move up or down. The only one that was movable housed an air-condition unit. Jesus is often showing up America to the rest of the world as a people of great charity, but then charity begins at home first and not the other way around. You cannot love the people of Turkey more than the people of Detroit.

My neighbor Debra would always be smiling when she

saw me cleaning the yard adjacent to her garage. The short brick wall that separated the two properties was really put there for a great reason. I came to find out for myself, that the colonies of ants that lived there over time became a menace to her family's well-being. So the wall was erected by her husband George and herself to keep out the little creatures. And, when this did not work to keep the ants out, the pest control personnel were called in to spray her surroundings. This was done at least once a month.

But if any provide not for his own, and specially for those of his own house, he hath denied the faith, and is worse than an infidel. We believers, in Jesus in our earnest quest to win souls for Our Lord and Savior Jesus, pontificate his Word on pulpits around the world, reassuring our followers of the rewards of heaven.

Jesus does not play the games that the children of America do to poison the hearts and minds of their fellowmen by believing in magic, but yet, reward themselves as proponents and propagators of Christianity. At the house, Jesus would take me through this burdensome life to teach me precisely, what is wrong with America. We say that we love the name Jesus; where is our love? Are we really seeking his face with real purpose?

We become very satisfied even in our mediocre situation. We look up in the sky aimlessly doubting and doubting and doubting that we would never ever make it, don't care how hard we try. Jesus has blessed us to see another day, another day that has passed us to no avail. We lie to ourselves daily. Next year will be an eventful year. Playing Jesus. Faking it to make it.

Jesus has left you a long time ago, but you keep lying to yourself. Jesus has left you since you cannot tell the evil one to get out of your house and go, right now. You enjoy the evil that exists in your surroundings. You enjoy the evil comments from your so-called husband. You enjoy the swearing and the dirty words that come out each other's mouths. You enjoy the filthy movies and magazines painted on your walls. You tell everybody that life is great when you are always broke.

The very first thing in the morning, you have to look up those Lotto numbers to see if you have won any money. Consequently, you call your friend to transcribe every single detail of a wounded loss. Now you have given advent to a pity-party that has lasted for hours on the cell phone. For the rest of the day everyone becomes your enemy. Even the cleaning of the house or the yard is no longer a priority.

Jesus is showing me a broken house complete with broken windowpanes whose cellars are open to all the rodents of the world. Precluding, but not excluding stray dogs and stray cats. We all want to have a better life. We all want to own nice things. We all want to drive a better car. We all want to travel the world. In all of this, we forget one thing. His name is Jesus. There is no happiness without Jesus.

How could you invite you neighbor over to your house when it is dirty? How could you sleep on your floors, when they are covered with roaches and rats? How could you enjoy a meal with bugs running all over the table, especially in the kitchen after preparing and doing all that hard work? How could you teach your children cleanliness, when you are not clean yourself? Bathing and changing your clothes everyday does not mean that you are clean.

Jesus cares by showing you how to take care of the little things. After every meal, you clean and wipe the table. Then you turn and wash all the utensils with the help of your family. But what does everybody do; pack all the wares in the kitchen sink and hit the road. On their return, the roaches, rats, mice, ants and the like are on the race track. The spilled juice and remnants of food decorate the untidy floors.

We have to sit and think through our daily duties and sometimes put up a menu of things to do every hour of the day or on the weekend. To combat the devil, we sing a hymn as we go about the business of the day. We do not wait to see him to begin to sing our favorite hymns. Before we begin to sing, Jesus has already possessed us. If we would only avoid the menacing thoughts that beset us, whilst taking care of our household chores, we would definitely see the hands of God. Jesus is still standing.

Our homes are our castles. If we cannot keep the few rooms clean in our houses, how can Jesus give us our earthly mansions? Jesus did not put us here to catch hell all the days of our lives. Jesus is using us if only we would allow him to have his way. Jesus would not force himself on us to bring about any good thing. Jesus would not push us over the deep end. All Jesus wants to do is to show us his love.

But if any provide not for his own, and specially for those of his own house, he hath denied the faith, and is worse than an infidel. A huge number of Christians believe that because they have been born again by Baptism, that they would enter the kingdom of heaven. Jesus is charismatic. Jesus did perform many miracles on the face of the earth. In modern times the word miracles have been excommunicated from this evil world. Jesus is still standing.

Jesus makes it simple every moment of our lives by nurturing us and pushing us forward to do greater things that he did on the planet. But we shy away for want of quiet persuasiveness. We believe and take for granted the three times that Jesus fell, face downwards in the mud, with the cross and open wounds still bleeding and stuck to his garment. Jesus literally pushed himself from the prison to the cross. An insurmountable task for us to swallow.

The cries of human beings are louder than the cries of the animals which are slaughtered in the jungles of Brazil.

Jesus is showing me the broken panes in the windows of abandoned houses in the neighborhood, where I once lived. It was Queensborough, Shreveport, Louisiana. Sometimes on one block, there are at least ten abandoned houses. People, in all the wealth of America, have lost their mind in their giving to one another. Jesus last words to his disciples were love each other as I have loved thee.

There are Neighborhood Watch signs posted on every block in almost all towns and cities of America. Where is the love? These are houses that could have been renovated by the neighbors, and given to homeless families at a reasonable monthly rent. Is this too much to ask for? Or must we wait for the second coming of Jesus to go rush vehemently to do the right thing? Jesus is still standing.

It is grossly disheartening to see the aesthetic beauty eroded by the sight of desolation. Rundown neighborhoods, which once were the talk of the town. Rundown neighborhoods neglected by the powers that be. Rundown neighborhoods abandoned and are now infested by the rats and the vermin of squalor. Rundown neighborhoods, whose real estate values are now diminished. Rundown neighborhoods that nobody wants to relocate.

Sad to say, this is not an isolated case. This is in every black neighborhood in all America. Love thy neighbor as thyself has become cliché. Us Christians tend to throw out the good and let in the bad. We sit and bite our nails as soon as a situation presents itself. We would not call on Jesus first when trouble comes. We would not give Jesus the time of day. We would not allow Jesus to rock us into heaven.

Some of these properties, the grass is as tall as the tallest man alive. They cover from half of an acre to about an acre. This is the perfect breeding ground for snakes, spiders and wasps. On these sites: old cars, trucks and bicycles are abandoned. Jesus is showing me the faces of smiling children that once dwelt in those houses.

Families that did not want to move out of those neighborhoods through no fault of their own were dislocated. Cherished dreams of the good old days were now crushed and buried by the evil of progress. Businesses that fed those families for decades had to move on to other countries abroad. Some people chose to leave with those companies to far off lands and of course were promised a haven.

People must remember that there is no place like home. This is something that families should seriously consider when approached by any business owner to make that dreadful mistake, which ultimately sinks you to the bottom of the ocean floor. Life is too short for one to recover from this dilemma. Friends are lost forever. Being a stranger in a foreign country is not always the better of two worlds.

That is why Jesus took the whippings from a mighty hand for us. Jesus comes around to tell us what to do, but we are not listening to the groans of the Holy Spirit. We often feel that we should not consult Jesus on this particular topic. We believe that we are not culpable. We believe that we got this one. We think that in our moment of twilight we can discern the crown among thorns.

Stray dogs going through yards looking for food are not a glorious sight to encounter in the darkest night. The barking of dogs, echoing in the early hours of the morning of a fenceless abandoned property, is a sure sign of a rundown city that nobody cares about.

But if any provide not for his own, and specially for those of his own house, he hath denied the faith, and is worse than an infidel. God the Father, God the Son, and God the Holy Spirit is not happy in the way the New World treats its most vulnerable children. Jesus is profoundly saddened by the shanty towns of the Western Hemisphere. No more, no more, no more!

The arctic: characteristic of the extremely cold, snowy, windy weather north of the Arctic Circle did not come about for the human race to walk in and steal everything and now leave laughing. Jesus is the creator of the world. It is his house—one he will protect.

One day I filled the washing machine with two weeks of clothing left after a very long arduous fortnight. To my surprise, the commode overflowed and the bathtub was half-filled with stinking water and debris. Apparently, as the washing machine pushed or emptied its water there was an accident. This was my reasoning. Anyhow, I grabbed a bowl and did my best to clean up and tidy the bathroom.

Evil is everywhere. Jesus is poignantly showing his disgust in brotherly love. Homeowners beware for the coming of the Lord is swifter than a two-edge sword. It is all well so you may think to lie to yourself. But to lie to a customer for your own selfish needs Jesus will not forget and in some cases will not forgive. This is like standing in the deep waters on stilts, whilst luring your friends to come on in.

Jesus looks at everything besides the lonely park bench sitting in the sun on a gorgeous day. If we would only take care of each other without thinking or adding the cost—surprise, surprise! We pray everyday, at the present time, Jesus is there drawing us closer to his window of love. We seem to think in that moment of despair, where is Jesus? In a resounding echo, Jesus is right here.

Jesus would really like to teach every one the true meaning of his Word. Can you eat forgiveness and forgetfulness? This medicine is too much to swallow. The thought of having a place of your own is enough to bring forth happiness. Jesus is saying that this is not the yard stick to use to determine happiness. Happiness comes from deep within. As a child you clap your hands to make you happy. As a man you seek the face of Jesus relentlessly.

It is easy to look back on your past memories, especially when it is filled with lots of cake an ice cream. Needless to say, who wants to reminisce on a perilous-belligerent sojourn? When brothers want to take the eyes out of their so-called friends, what do they expect from the likes of their enemies? Sometimes, we go about creating our own antagonists without any respect for allies.

We find ways to make money in the real estate business. So we take our inheritance and buy up a few houses and rundown small apartment dwellings to make a killing and gain respect from our peers. We do not care of its overall condition. We patch and we fix only what meets the eye. Once the bathroom flushes that is good enough for the tenant. The gas can be turned on in the kitchen that is good enough for the new resident. The light comes on as you flick the switch, this is more than enough.

Jesus is saying to the entire human race. You came without nothing; you will definitely leave without anything. Too long have I secretly come to your place of abode to sit and talk to you one on one, about your quest for lustfulness, You will ignore my promptings, even at this very moment to fulfill your own selfish desires. Your philosophy is of days gone by everyone must sit on your table, except the Lord Jesus.

The word "no" is not in your dictionary. You are like spoilt children, rotten to the core. Jesus is repeatedly showing these pitfalls, so that others would refrain from this growing evil in the four corners of the globe. This get rich scheme attitude is tearing the very fabric of the society that Prophets and Prophetesses were sent to regenerate and make anew, as a reminder to believers that Jesus is Lord.

If we would only listen to the music of the wind blowing in the trees, besides the shouting of total emptiness; besides the tiptoeing of ribald phraseologies being thrown from pillow to post, underneath eyelids of drooping eyes, then Jesus is going to say, thank you.

But if any provide not for his own, and specially for those of his own house, he hath denied the faith, and is worse than an infidel. Jesus is showing me of the many faces that are in attendance at fireworks all around the planet. Most of whom emphatically believe that there is a Supreme God. Moreover, do they believe in God the Father, God the Son, and God the Holy Spirit? They clearly do not.

Americans should learn to understand that Jesus is not playing games with his Gospel. The schools built were erected by Christian hands. The hospitals built were erected by Christian hands. The colleges built were erected by Christian hands. The courthouses built were erected by Christian hands. The libraries built were erected by Christian hands. Jesus is humbly saying that I am that I am sends me.

One morning, I awoke with the fragments of the ceiling all over me. Immediately, I rolled out of the bed dusting myself vigorously. I began to roll my eyes around. I noticed, with the sunlight piercing through the windowpanes that were left naked by the drawn curtains; that half of my ceiling was still up there. Yes, but now only time would tell.

With the intense heat scathing through every open door brought with it ladybirds too many to count traversing upside down on the ceiling in the living room. The swarm of ladybirds kept me on my feet. It took me hours each day to get the rid of these colorful bugs that gives off a stench when you killed them. Events like these happen to us from time to time. Jesus is still standing.

The moment we seek God with all our might is enough for

Jesus to stop by and say hello. It shows Jesus that we have abandoned our all to hear his holy name resound from coast to coast throughout the arms of Justice. Jesus has already paved the way for us. We hold on to the strength of the grace of Our Lord Jesus. For he has showered us with his mercy by giving us a very long and lengthy life, and forbidding us not to cling to the affairs of the world, and forging our footprints in the sands of time.

Jesus is showing us his struggles in a ruthless world. We so often deny him by substituting others, as if by substitution, it would make Jesus angry to confront us in the errors of our ways. All these are reasons why we wake up in the mornings, and swear to Jesus to come and kill us right now. We do everything to make others sin against the precious blood of Jesus. We are profoundly fascinated by our success without the help of Jesus. Yet during the night, we keep pacing the floors for want of sleep.

Every nail that pierced the hands of Jesus is an utterance of peace. For it took peace to ascend the cross knowingly knowing for the hour to be shown by the seraphs. These celestial beings took the lead in directing Jesus throughout his earthly tenure. They kept him up all night long with their songs of Praise. Jesus's timing was never of the earth. The seraphs, he alone can see.

From time to time, things would appear to be succulent. These are the times to be watchful. Satan, the devil would at all times be very ostentatious. In the spirit of happiness one needs to be humble and grow more humbly for the sake of saving souls even at the threshold of their blessing. Jesus is showing me the doors of families, shut tight, owing to the refusal of saints to persevere for others, who are not of their ilk.

It is about time for the human race to stop hating one another. To hate is a disease of the mind. Jesus is all about love. You shall love God with all of your mind, heart and soul. You shall love your neighbor as thyself. Jesus teaches us in so many simple ways for us not to forget the cross. He gives us neighbors to be loving and kind to. He gives us children to play with other children. He takes his sweet time to teach us these simple but profound ways to love, though somehow, we digress in wantonness.

Jesus is slowly shaping us to build a future unimaginable. We keep falling no matter what we do. Most people tend to hold on to their past, especially when they have lost something dare to them. Oftentimes, they are caught sobbing and speaking to themselves in melodious voices. These variables undercut the nails that pierced the feet of Jesus. We got to hold on to Jesus"s unchanging hands.

But if any provide not for his own, and specially for those of his own house, he hath denied the faith, and is worse than an infidel. Jesus is somewhat revered by his esteem friends in the Justice department. Time and time again they are faced with the responsibility of executing the law. And time and time again they keep falling and failing, Jesus in two areas that would put them at the pinnacle and seat of the Almighty God. Jesus also is showing them and is counting the cost.

Anointed men of God the Father, God the Son, and God the Holy Spirit have resoundingly criticized same sex marriage, and death by hanging, electric chair, or any other means other than the natural course of life and death. These learned men who are held in high esteem by their peers, and the general population that they seek to represent should be very careful in accepting these offices, when not given to them by Jesus.

Elected officials should not be swayed by the agendas of the status quo. We are in the 21st Century. Jesus is no longer playing games with anyone especially one who holds a high or a very high seat on the face of the earth. Jesus will be making examples of his Word in the ensuring years. Make no mistake of his presence! This is Jesus world. And he will prove it to you each day. Jesus is still standing.

In my neighborhood, I observed same sex couples, who are raising their children in these relationships which ultimately twist the minds of the children. For the children they play with comes from couples of the opposite sex. These children see pregnant women that they would challenge with the quest8ion of how this baby really came about? This is called practical experience.

No one needs to go to High School to be taught the fundamentals of childbirth. The very twelve-year olds are giving birth to children next door. So the children do not have to look far for an answer to the rights and wrongs of a perverted society. Sometimes these babies are born out of incest. Is this what the society has already come to? Are these innocent young ladies guilty of incestuous relationships, and are they hiding behind the fence? Jesus is still standing.

You reap what you sow. The Bible does not tell a lie. Why keep fooling yourselves? The animals mate right in front of the children. The birds of the air are seen mating by the children; eggs are laid and the offspring are produced. There is no human being that is not shaped in iniquity beside Jesus. Jesus already knows that you would be swarmed by your friends and families. Everyone would be coming after you to change your mind, even your own Pastor. This is precisely what Jesus is saying to the whole wide world. Just do the right thing!

Having a gay son does not give you the right to marry him off to another gay person. Having a lesbian daughter does not give you the right to do the same. Having a sex change does not give you the right to marry someone of the opposite sex. Cross-dressing does not give you the right to marry someone of the opposite sex. Whatever you see at birth is who you are. Your emotions have absolutely nothing to do with Jesus.

Jesus loves every creature that he has created since the foundations of this world. He gives life and he takes life. When there is a situation at the house either a Prophet or a Pastor is called to quell the fears of the family. If someone is sick at the house, either a Prophet or a Pastor is called upon to heal the sick. Sometimes the man of God may have to overnight. Sometimes the man of God may have to spend an entire week interceding, before the throne of grace.

Since all the birds of the air and of the earth could not teach us family life, then we are the most stupid people on God's earth. Since all the animals of the earth could not teach us family life, then we are the most stupid people on God's earth. Since all the fishes in the seas, rivers, lakes and oceans could not teach us family life, then we are the most stupid people on God's earth. Jesus is still standing.

It is about time to empty our closets and to face the music of redeeming grace. It is about time to level with our families and friends. Jesus is forever in the praying and forgiving business. Jesus came to save our souls from eternal damnation. There is no big, medium or small sin. Sin is sin. Thank God for the saving grace of Jesus.

But if any provide not for his own, and specially for those of his own house, he hath denied the faith, and is worse than an infidel. Jesus is eremite. This the world has used and abused over centuries. Jesus is non-religious. The life of Jesus on the global front, is not the whole truth and nothing but the truth. Jesus remotely speaks to me as if caught in flight millions of miles away.

Summertime in Louisiana could be extremely hot and languid. It could last for six months in one given year.

The season brings with it wasps of different species that would attack you, as you are engaged in cutting the grass. Landscaping the property took enormous time in shaping it the way you would want others to view Jesus in the distance.

As soon as you undertake a job given to you by Jesus, the devil would intensify his intrusion to stop you at all cost from bringing about the good work of Jesus. This is to say that we brush off the opportunity attributed to us by Jesus to settle for mediocracy. Oftentimes we wrestle with Jesus petitioning him to get what we want. We would not accept it any other way. Once given what we asked for we turn away to boast about our insistence in having it our way. We fail to see satan in the midst of our weaknesses.

Joseph got engage to Mary, a virgin. One day he discovered his bride pregnant. Joseph knew that he was definitely not the father of the unborn. Clandestinely, he divorced his bride to return to carry out his own agenda. Jesus in the form of the Holy Ghost spoke to Joseph to return to his bride for what you have borne witnessed to is of God the Father.

Joseph promptly returned to his betrothed without his insistence that he is not the father of the unborn child. How many of us have never questioned the Lord Jesus? How many of us would be obedient to Jesus unto death? Jesus had already given you the desires of your heart. It would become visible in the future. Christians do not have to show proof. Jesus will show the proof for us in his Word.

For centuries, we have allowed the devil to show us off in furnishing us with fine clothes, jewelry, mansions and expensive cars. It is about time, we strongly and firmly reject, with the help of Jesus, all forms of trickery used by the devil and his cohorts. The birds of the air continually take their time to build their nests. The animals cry out to Jesus for help to stop the poachers and the slaying of their families not just for ivory, but for respect to God for his creatures here on earth.

Jesus puts us into situations to show us the value of patience. Meanwhile, our ears are fed with music plugged in, as if this would affect the voice of Jesus speaking to us from his heavenly throne. The music would be changing, but the voice of Jesus changes not. The script would be changing, but the voice of Jesus changes not. The distractions would come your way to kick you out of gear, but the voice of Jesus changes not.

Jesus spends more time teaching us patience than anything else. When we are outside cleaning the yard, we give ourselves a time to complete the job. Jesus gives us a command to go do something. Jesus does not put a time limit on us. Whilst we are working, we have already given instructions to our children to say things like, "we are busy working in the yard."

Likewise our time to pray in solitary. We shut out all the noise in the house, while simultaneously preparing ourselves for undistracted sovereign prayer to Jesus. Our neighbors would be playing loud music, as they traversed along the street to their respective homes. Sudden loud voices would be heard from children playing nearby. Or friends meet friends to carry on a conversation right outside your sanctuary.

What is Jesus doing? Jesus is simply teaching us patience. We do not have to secure a particular spot in the house for prayer. We do not have to create utter silence. We do not have to set the alarm clock. We do not have to tell someone to call us back at an appointed time. We do not have to tell someone that we are about to have pray with Jesus. We do not have to be robust.

But if any provide not for his own, and specially for those of his own house, he hath denied the faith, and is worse than an infidel. A person who does not accept Christianity as their faith is an infidel. The coming of Jesus that marked the end of B.C. and the beginning of A.D. is tantamount. God the Father proves everything. Anno Domini: in the year of Our Lord gives credence to the truth that Jesus is truly the Son of the Almighty God the Father.

There is no church on the face of the earth that Jesus did not stop by to let the church know that it is preaching the wrong doctrine. We can run but we surely cannot hide for the coming of Jesus is real. The Bible has already foretold us that these End Times would be treacherous. What more are we waiting for? The signs are at our doorsteps. We do not need to look further anymore.

Jesus teaches us how to become vigilant. Until we begin to harmonize our thoughts, efforts and sharing the Word of God closely with each other through reading passages of our Bible at break periods, which will end our frustrations, as we walk hand in hand through these dangerous times.

In my backyard, the children in the neighborhood would ride their bicycles in and out of my garage enjoying their childhood, as I enjoyed mine. Children have to be reared in an atmosphere of comradery. There are challenges in the unforeseeable future that would one day come their way. A healthy upbringing would afford them the distinction in arriving at a pertinent conclusion. Children have to play, but could only do this in the neighborhoods that watches over them.

You do not have to know the parents of these children, because the children have painted a picture of every household in their vicinity. They could equally write a thesis of each family in their surroundings. They could safely say whose been good or bad to them. Their memories record every single event like the computers of the world. Their minds come equip with spell check and innovations of our present-day electronic data machines.

It is amazing, if we can only listen to the voice of Jesus, what we will be able to achieve in a world of variables? Jesus is constant. We need to pool ourselves behind Jesus to individually find out, what we have to do for our Lord? It is something that we must not be afraid of. Everybody wants to make a mark in life. Seek Jesus! It only gets harder when we procrastinate.

Jesus is not a web site. You cannot e-mail Jesus. You cannot instagram Jesus. You cannot twitter Jesus. Every child needs to know the truth about Jesus. Parents be advised that your children will have a better future if only you will release them to Jesus! On the other hand, their future will be obscure. They need to be free to tell you everything that is affecting their very lives.

You need to listen to their silence especially when they are not looking. You need to listen to their conversations, when they are engaged with their peers. You need to listen to their lyrics in their music. You need to listen to their murmurings at night, as soon as they fall asleep. You need to be there for them in every decision-making whether good or bad. This is what Jesus wants you to do for your children.

Love is proof at the end of the darkest road. Whatever challenges you have faced in your life would be greater in your children's life, so do not try to change the course. Have faith in Jesus! Do not stir the pot until he tells you to! Do not discourage your children in asking Jesus for any single thing, which are the desires of the heart! Do not attempt to shape their future around your future goals, just to make you feel good!

The Jesus in you wants you to acknowledge the Jesus in your children. When the roof on the house is shredding for you to know that there is a leak in the roof, Jesus does not want you to patch the leaking area. Jesus wants to treat you to a brand new roof.

Your front porch is in shambles. Normally you would change the boards in that area. Jesus wants you to tear down the entire porch and erect a brand new porch with seating for everybody in your immediate family. This would send a message to the devil, a very clear message, that you truly love the Lord. You and your children are not second best. You and your grandchildren are not second best. You and your great grandchildren are not second best. Jesus is still standing.

But if any provide not for his own, and specially for those of his own house, he hath denied the faith, and is worse than an infidel. Jesus is only going to fight your battles, when you have denied the satanic spirits that you play with even on the internet.

You put signs up on your front doors to remind the general public that you and my Lord will serve the Lord. Yet on the inside you keep playing games with the enemies of Our Lord Jesus. You stop speaking to your neighbors because they have been blessed by Jesus with a brand new car. You stop speaking to your neighbors since you have found out that all their children have been blessed to attend LSU. You stop speaking to your neighbors for no other reason than they are foreigners.

Jesus is very much aware of the big why in your life. Did Jesus tell you what he is going to do for you in this coming New Year? Is this important? Yes, it is. We cannot allow our neighborhoods to shape us in the ways of Beelzebub. These spirits dwell in the four corners of our jurisdiction. Whether we are walking or driving do not make us alienated from the minions sitting on the window silts.

The sidewalks are filled with broken pieces of bottle

together with faeces scattered everywhere, is a sure sign that the enemy is here and is creating havoc in the minds, hearts and souls of the homeowners of this neighborhood. We take things too lightly, especially when they are naked and brutal.

Jesus is not blindsided. Jesus does not need blinders over his eyes. Jesus does not need a yoke around his neck. Jesus does not need a prescription from any earthly doctor whatsoever. Jesus is as solid as the rock that sits atop Mount Everest.

We keep making wishes as soon as we behold a fallen star. Instead of desiring for ourselves, turn the tables around and long for a greater blessing for our children. In this way, we slam the devil to the ground, now Jesus comes into our hearts and open up the windows of the still-born in the wombs of our childless children. Jesus wants our minds to be like the perimeters of the four corners of the planet that twirls and signals the brightest stars at night.

Jesus is creating a revolution in the souls of architects to pursue the course of the river nile in our inner cities, whose sole purpose are to change the appearances of antiquity that runs the risk of killing the bodies of the impoverished sons and daughters. The human race is fed up with the deceitfulness of the one per cent of the wealthy few. This is not to say that the other 99 per cent are all gullible.

The fire of Jesus is climbing every mountain in the Middle East, whose livelihood is to seek out and prey on the most vulnerable in each town, city and seaport. Jesus is not about crippling economies for the ambitious few. Jesus is about changing the whole spectrum of the literate global minds. It is not okay anymore for you to call the shots. It is not your place to tell Christians world over what to do. Are you really listening to the voice of the true living son of the Almighty God the Father? Jesus is still standing.

In 2017, Jesus is opening up the windows of the human head, to hear every single word that cometh out of the mouth of heaven, thus saith the Lord. For there is no one besides you, who is Jesus the Lord. The hills in the horizon are jagged and dangerous. The Word of God is a thousand times ten thousand. It breathes new life into the nostrils of the oceans' floor.

Jesus is the weeping eyes left behind in abandoned houses. Jesus is the abandoned children left behind in those broken walls. Jesus is the hungry children still looking for their parents that would never return to the sanctuary of the house. Jesus is the survivors of the torn down house that once was the talk of the town. Jesus is the city children, whose voices were once heard coming from the dispossess storied-buildings of inner cities.

In this New Year, Jesus is rolling down the windows of the Prophets and Prophetesses, who are blinded by the spirit of torment in their lives. The job of Jesus is always to strengthen you to face up to the atrocities of the earth. Jesus time is now; Jesus will not have it any other way.

The arms of Jesus are wide enough to take each family up the staircase from earth to heaven. No one could enter heaven without the Word from the mouth of Jesus. No one could hide in the midst of any family unentering heaven. The door of heaven is like the eye of a needle. Its height, width and depth one cannot see. When you live for Jesus everything will be alright.

THE WRITING OF HYMNS:

Mathew 26:30 And when they had sung an hymn, they went out into the Mount of Olives. The writing of my hymns began in 2012. One morning during the winterish month of January, most likely around 3 a.m., I was jogging on the sidewalk, when the music to my first hymn came to me. Then the words followed and I began to sing the hymn. It took me a while to get accustomed to this new phenomenon, which is another spiritual addition in my life. Jesus never told me before that this day would ever come. After a few days, Jesus literally took me to the store to purchase a note book to write down the hymn.

In the afternoons, Jesus would humanly take me to any restaurant to compose hymns. Normally, he would sit me down with pen and paper and rehearse the chorus in my mind. After a while Jesus would give me the title to the hymn. Jesus who has a great sense of humor would be giving me jokes, because he knows that I am dependent on him for everything. I am the first in the family to be blessed with this awesome charismatic gift. A gift I never asked Jesus for, but one he graciously bestowed upon me.

The tears would roll down my cheeks to remind me of the beautiful name of Jesus. Pointedly, the river Nile is now rolling down my cheeks. Of course, we are not going into the Mount of Olives as it were in those days. It is interesting to note that all hymnist should be anointed, before they partake of the fruit of the spirit. Alarmingly, nobody cares about what they compose in these times of perish. The wall is falling on them, but it is to no avail.

How in the world do we want to speak the word of peace, when there is strife? How in the world do we want to obtain peace in the family, when there is a measure of hate among family members? How in the world do we want peace at the dinner table when there is gross resentment with each other's beliefs? How in the world do we want peace in our children's lives, when we cannot obtain peace within our very selves?

The door of the church is always open to all. Though some of us might feel, that Jesus has slighted us, because we were not called for such a high, priestly office. Jesus is present in his hymns. It is a trail that we must follow, until we get to the mountain peak. A trail that we should adhere to, for it is a trail of Jesus, as we lift each other's foot one by one up the slippery slope to paradise.

Isn't it ironical to believe that Jesus is near, though far away from us Christians? Clearly, Jesus is showing that he had already begun to open up the book of Revelation, whereas churches are still struggling in the closure of the other books.

Simultaneously, parishioners are taking deep breaths, hoping that the unveiling of the apocalypse would not saturate them with its truth. Jesus is not buying time. You need to shake off the dust from your shoes every time you ignore the call of Jesus in your life. You need to stop pointing fingers at the outpouring of the Holy Spirit, in the mouths of Gospel singers, who are presently engaged in breaking the door down of a ruthless world.

Jesus is showing that everyone is not accepting the lyrics in these new compositions. Especially those from a religious upbringing that do not want to shout, clap and stamp their feet in the presence of our Lord Jesus. Also Jesus is shaping and molding the hearts of Holy Spirit children to sing out vociferously, thus emptying their gifts in the hearts of the congregation.

Too many singers are not doing their part in teaching others through their music, the power of the Holy Spirit in lifting up the holiness of the Word of God. The writing of the song is one thing, but the singing of the Word is absolutely different. The words take on the eagle in flight. Too many singers especially anointed singers do not need to sing in a dead church or a church playing church. Jesus is still standing.

Jesus is and will be in attendance right now. For it is the name of Jesus, who you are lifting up to the heavens from the earth beneath, so that others will ascend with you. Jesus is and will be in attendance to guide you in song, so that you shall get out of self to be taken to a beautiful mountain in heaven.

We must bear in mind not to be afraid of Jesus lifting us up in the power of the Holy Spirit. We need Jesus to take us through the fire of the baptism of the Holy Spirit. We all need Jesus right now.

And when they had sung an hymn, they went out into the Mount of Olives. Jesus is transparent. Wherever Jesus walked he generated light. It is imperative for a hymnist to become electromagnetic. Your movement in song should be surrounded by the awesome charismatic electrolytes of a moving star waiting to give birth to another song. A hymn begets another hymn. Jesus is saying stop the stealing!

Jesus does inspire anointed preachers, prophets, ministers

of music and some singers of gospel to write and sing their own renditions carved out by Jesus. These anointed voices of God would at all times be changing and fine tuning songs to elevate his church. When we stumble, we fall. It is the duty of the congregation to accept all new material without exception.

There is an awesomeness with Jesus when he is putting word to the particular song. Be it an ode, praise or worship hymn. Jesus is in no hurry to complete the song. Firstly, you got to be focus. Secondly you got to be listening to the voice of Jesus. Thirdly, you got to be possessed by God the Father, God the Son, and God the Holy Spirit. Fourthly, your love for Jesus must be audacious.

Sometimes, the Holy Spirit would roll you over at night to pen a song of praise. It might be 1 a.m. As a man of God, your response shall be to get up right away, to do the will of your eldest brother Jesus. This is no time for tardiness. This is no time for procrastination. This is no time to look at the clock to see how many hours of sleep you are losing, while staying awake with Jesus. Jesus is still standing.

In retrospect, I remembered my favorite hymn, "When Jesus Comes." In totality Jesus returned me to my visits to the infirmary, hospitals and the blind institute. This I did some forty years ago. Jesus would create a song that you have already created in your heart without your knowledge of doing so. It is the same way that you have been blessed, to receive so many things, simply because it was given to you before the very foundations of the world. Jesus work in the aftermath of his crucifixion is to bless you twice, for your eyes had never beheld him face to face.

It is the highest honor given to a human being in allowing Jesus to teach you how he truly operates in his universe. By doing so, you could differentiate between the good and the evil compositions in song. You could without reservations teach your children and your children's children the truth of Jesus, which is watered-down or diluted to please the majority of the Christian world.

Jesus is not pugnacious. He is sweet Jesus. A hymn is not a toy that you play with just for the fun of it. Its true meaning is hidden deep inside of your belly. You can only regurgitate the song, if only you would relax in faith for the seraphim to come strengthen you. All this is taking place as a sequence of joy trailing down from the dew drops of the springs of heaven.

In everybody's life, there is a glimpse of truth, which Jesus takes to put together to write a song, or a hymn, or a national anthem, or anything to fill the soul with Jesus. The hymn will be a continuous flow of joy connected to peace, thus lifting up in voice to get to worship. Lyrics like no turning back would not be a song of worship. Jesus is creating a world choir of songs of worship.

People are going to church hopefully to become a new creature. Anointed singers of God, when not interfered with by any member of the church, shall be used by Jesus, in a mighty way to add lyrics, or speak out while singing to heal the broken-hearted.

Jesus is showing me anointed singers of Jesus, who are sent to join choirs are being rejected by the very members of these choirs. Being conspicuous is not a trait of Jesus. Jesus does not tolerate ostentatious behavior. Jesus does not relegate power in the hands of dubious-minded Christians. Jesus is constantly breaking new ground for another evergreen plant. Whilst the world of evil grows in significant numbers to choke the hardworking saints of God the Father, God the Son, and God the Holy Spirit.

And when they had sung an hymn, they went out into the Mount of Olives. Jesus is forever blest. Jesus shows himself in the writings of his hymns. Jesus is not about who gets there first. Jesus is about his given Word. Jesus is using his anointed voices of song to sweep the world of hate under the fire of love. Jesus is shifting the sun upward, so that the rays of the sun will not scorch anyone.

The earth will definitely make progress, as Jesus enters the hearts of men to do a mighty work in them in order to bring about a newness of life. Jesus is the only one to confer gifts or fruits of the Holy Spirit upon the human race. There are a starvation of hymns of worship, which will draw others unto God the Father, God the Son, and God the Holy Spirit. To obtain these gifts one has to be devoted to the Word of God.

Some people do not like to fast. They want to achieve great things without any evolution in their thinking. Your conscious is your guide. You shall be aware of the promptings of his Holy Spirit. For the promptings grow into words, which forms sentences to complete a line or chorus in song. These words grow deeper in meaning, in measure to the amount of faith that you possess in Jesus.

Your faith has to climb mountains in order to sing for the eagles that sit on the highest peak. This is not easy to attain. Jesus speaks to everybody. But sadly, we fight Jesus in the initial stages of our development in the writing of hymns. Jesus will give you the title of the hymn. On the other hand, your self-will gets the better of you; now you do not like the title. This is your first biggest mistake. Do not forget that Jesus is Holy! Jesus does not do anything wrong.

You do not have to try to sing the hymn in the timing of the hymns of these times. Whatever Jesus puts into you in music you follow that throughout. Success will follow in Jesus's time. The more you write the higher you will have to climb the mountain of God. This is not a dream. It is a reality. And the reality is the exception to a great hymn. Forging ahead is a tumultuous task. Jesus is still standing.

Your head becomes Jesus's world. Anytime, Jesus wants you to sing that song, he will put you in the mood that he wishes for you to sing the hymn in front of the congregation. This is not what you think it is. This is a molding of the song in your heart to reach out and touch somebody in the midst. You are an instrument of the fruits of the spirit, besides Jesus there is no other.

We need Jesus to take each fruit of the spirit to mold us into that fruit in song. To let go of self brings humility in song. Immediately Jesus starts to move you in his passion of love. In front of the mountain of love stand four lions with eyes all around their heads. As you ascend this gigantic mountain, you will meet elephants to salute you on your way to achieving the golden crown from the hands of Jesus.

Jesus is the answer to our every prayer in song. Jesus needs us to wait patiently for him to come to anoint us with a double dose of his love from his mountain of love. Jesus wants us to relax in the midst of torment, as we ascend in song through the dark tunnels of the lives of the downtrodden.

Afflictions are everywhere. All these things are and have become a necessary burden. Obedience in song selection is a prerequisite to the healings of the minds of the children of Jesus. Anointed singers of Jesus must allow Jesus to have his way anywhere he takes them. You will not know precisely the time of Jesus entering your soul to bring about a miraculous work that you have never begun.

Jesus works of miracles happen faster than the eyes could see. Perhaps Jesus wants to bring about a miracle in a slow process of healing. Undoubtedly, the world is moving faster in the doings of evil than the doings of good. Jesus in his risen body cannot come down from heaven to pay churches a visit at a time of enormous doubtfulness. Jesus wants to richly bless the world, if only they can hold on to the outpouring of the Holy Spirit. The world had been made in six days and Jesus rested on the seventh day.

And when they had sung an hymn, they went out into the Mount of Olives. The resurrection of Jesus into heaven marked the beginning of Praise singing. The beginning of End Times is the time for all Christian houses of worship to sing hymns of worship. Take it or leave it the church is lagging behind! Jesus is not waiting for the church to play catch up. Catch-as-catch-can is a perfect example of our emptiness.

We keep running a race that has already been finished. We keep hiding behind the blinds of success for there is none. We keep speaking words of optimism knowing fully well that we must first remove our negative attitudes. We keep laughing to ourselves only to find out without accepting our dysfunctional selves. Society has put us on a pinnacle besides the blessings of Jesus.

All these are reasons of a broken church. We need the Holy Spirit to stir up the roots of songs which lay deep inside our bellies. We believe too much in ourselves. We seek the face of Jesus only at a time of calamity. We disappear in crowds, as soon as we have seen someone who would discipline us. We carelessly think to ourselves in remembrance of the grace and mercy of Jesus.

In happenchance, we play games with the living word of Jesus. Jesus sees this reflecting in our hymns. The repetitiveness of the same melody is almost generic in every composition. Even the lyrics say the same thing and tell the same story. Moving on to ascend the mountain peak is somewhat far-fetched to say the least. Pugnaciously, the enemy throws us in a stronghold.

The clock on the wall would speak to us if only we would

listen to its chiming. The rivers that flow into the Atlantic Ocean would bellow a new song as like the Pacific Ocean. Jesus is extremely calm, but is more ferocious than ten thousand roaring lions. The more we listen to Jesus the nearer we are in defining the hymn that is worth more than a thousand books. Jesus is still standing.

We treat Jesus's hymns less than the soap operas on the television set. We treat Jesus's hymns less than the action movies displayed at the cinemas in the movie theaters. We treat Jesus's hymns less than the Oscar awards given out on that celebrated night. We treat Jesus's hymns less than the Tony awards given out on that celebrated night. We treat Jesus's hymns less than the Grammy awards given out on that celebrated night.

Hymns are like the central nervous system in our bodies. Each nerve ending is a line in a hymn. To put it together in song, you need Jesus. To touch the very souls of man in depths of feet below the ocean floors, you need Jesus. These gifts are not easy to acquire. These gifts come from Jesus, for only Jesus alone can fix it. Poignantly, Jesus wants to sharpen us sharper than a razor blade.

The miracles of Jesus in song will not be like his miracles on the earth. One must bear in mind of the time of the miracles of Jesus. One must not forget the awesomeness of God the Father, who used Jesus to bring about this epic show of the mysteries of heaven. Heaven and earth will pass away but my word will stand. Miracles will be of a difference. God the Father, God the Son, and God the Holy Spirit will be showing a newness on this planet.

This new thing will be much more spectacular than the fireworks that I have seen in San Francisco to bring in the New Year. This new thing will be much more hair-raising than the great Moses, who parted the Red Sea. This new thing will be much more breathtaking, than climbing the

North Pole. This new thing will be much more thrilling than putting a man on the moon. Jesus is still standing.

People are fed up of waking up every morning to see what earth calls, "the dawn of a new day." Without Jesus there will be no new hymns. Each hymn that comes from the breath of Jesus is like your favorite birthday, the one that you would not ever forget. It is not alright to sing those dead hymns that spew out of magnificent cathedrals world over. Some of these songs have become outdated.

Until we get to worship in song, we would have become as dead as the Dead Sea. Jesus is showing me the whole spectrum of his universe. It takes light to enter heaven. It takes light to see the presence of Jesus in the form of Holy Spirit. We need the light of Jesus to capture our imagination in song.

And when they had sung an hymn, they went out into the Mount of Olives. Jesus in his transfiguration shows up in his transformation of song in this New Age which is the Apocalypse. These new hymns of worship are to nourish the roots of Jesus. The narrative in these times will change to the narrative of the movement of change in music to fulfill the void left behind by the decapitation of Prophets before the advent of Jesus.

It is a known fact that Jesus will come around in the bodies of his younger brothers to bring about this song of worship for his heavenly father. To God be the Glory! This newness of life is a dawn of a new tomorrow. This wave of hymns will sweep the snow off the Arctic. Jesus will become the Mount of Olives in their lives. For to know him is to allow him to embody himself in you. Jesus is still standing.

Everybody would categorically share the philosophy of being beholden to looking at the bright side of everything. Well, precisely what is everything? You need Jesus in every singular decision. A church breathes new hymns into the bodies of their congregation. The size of the congregation does not matter in the eyes of the saints. The ethnicity of the people does not forge the beginnings of the saints. Jesus is the rightful justification of change.

The harp is a musical instrument created by Jesus to show the human race how to bring about the mysteries of Jesus. Jesus is the one that the human race searches for but never finding. Besides searching for Jesus there is a fixed agenda hidden deep down in the souls of wicked souls. Mortification is not the answer in overcoming trepidation by being disobedient.

The crushing of the head of satan is exactly what this is all about. One's belief in luck is not the answer to worshipping God in spirit and in truth. The choirs in heaven are waiting to inspire mortals with crescendos of love. Yes God says that he is immutable. Jesus also says that he alone can fix it. The choice of doing good or evil is yours. Depending on the choice you make causes an action before the metaphysics.

The baby falls sick at the house, yet Jesus says, leave it alone! You are not accustomed to hearing the voice of God in your life, but for some reason you did what was required for you to do. Within hours the child returns to normalcy. You have just felt the true power of Jesus. In that moment you believe that everybody listens to the voice of Jesus. Really.

The world is forever changing its aspects even in praise and worship. It is always all about the money. Jesus does not care about whether or not his music or lyrics are highly appreciated or not. All Jesus cares about is his music flowing throughout the River Nile of the whole wide world. This is not an action pack movie. This is a reality. We need to fix our eyes on Jesus.

Are we ready to do the work of the Lord? Can we stand

still in the moment? To love him is to serve him. There is a turtle in our lives often pricking us between the sheets of time. Jesus is already suckling his young to feed a starving world that is filled with hate, defiance, and mockery. Jesus is still standing.

Jesus is showing me the destruction of forces *vis-a-vis* the human souls, who are doing everything to disrupt the solidarity that will come about through new hymns of praise and worship. The human soul is beyond the comprehension of the genius of any mortal man. The human soul is beyond the metaphysics of a laughable world. The human soul is just a stripe less than Adam, the first human being to be created by God without the shape of iniquity. His world was lost to the entire world when sin was committed, for his world was the Mount of Olives.

And when they had sung an hymn, they went out into the Mount of Olives. Jesus is throwing out the dust from the cave of Adam and Eve. In essence, Jesus is alerting humankind to come to grips with the reality of a thousand years that had already passed for the human race to be bounded by satan, the devil. These thousand years of the damned had basically been turned over by the workings of the Prophet Daniel.

History will consequently prove by the hand of Jesus that all is well in the kingdom of heaven. Jesus will beat the earth with tempest of hail to let the world know *via-a-vis* the mercy of God. As soon as one builds a house on the earth his authority heightens without love for anyone. Hymns are borne out of humility. The opposite will forever be hate. The wind will blow wherever it may, but now the tempest is over for the freedom of the painted brushes of time.

Jesus will in earnest surprise the doubters, who incidentally chose to follow the beliefs of other stereotype religions throughout the planet. By doing so, Jesus will augment the music through inspirational lyrics that will increase the appetite for the kingdom of heaven. These lyrics will consume the souls of believers, as they listen more attentively to the wisdom of God.

In Jesus there is no besieging in the gospels of the Lord. Where Jesus is taking you no man has gone there before. It takes fortitude to draw others in song to the feet of Jesus. It takes unswerving patience to stand before the enemies of Jesus whilst delivering the word in song, before a congregation of mostly disbelievers. Jesus's appetite is to search for the one who is brutalized only because he is faithfully taking the scourging at the front door of a business about to be close down.

Jesus is putting together the signs of the times to come in music, so that the world will not be trying to figure out the true meaning of the Book of Revelation. The few preachers that are anointed by Jesus to bring the Word will be very creative in writing as well as in speaking. Jesus is showing up all the nuances given in the form of rhetoric via persuasive speaking, writing, dancing and singing. All these subtle differences will reflect in the lyrics of hymns.

The truth will be enshrined in musical hymns. The eagle in flight looking for its prey through valleys of thick forests, which through its big golden brown eyes will circumvent to ensure the capture of a rabbit feeding from the springs of a dimly creek. Music is Jesus. Music does not belong to the evil one. You can raise all hell to be saturated with music, for all hell will do is to curse your family for generations to come.

Hymns are the meeting of the minds between God and man. It is joy beyond compare. The dress for music will change as Jesus draws his sons and daughters to the sound of music. Jesus is addressing the signs of times for to know him is to love him. Some people have already written down in cement the meaning of the book of Revelation. Some people persuasively have written a book about the happenings of the Apocalypse. Jesus is saying that only a fool takes to the streets without first looking up and down before *via-a-vis* the traffic signals.

How could you translate something without first consulting the writer of the Word? You cannot see into the future unless the blinders of satan are remove from your eyes. The writing of hymns are not noticeable. So how could you get ahead of Jesus? A church without hymns is a dead church. A church without new hymns to suit its times is a dead church. A church without melodic sequences in the style of the seraphim is not a church taking its congregation to heaven.

Jesus gives direction to those who are blessed with patience. It is a virtue that is tremendously lacking in the house of God. Every chorus in a hymn needs the blood of Jesus to cement the word in your heart. Jesus shed his blood not just to save those who were present, but on the contrary, to save us that is coming behind at this appointed time. For these are terrible times, where there are no worship, no adoration, no love, no respect, not even for the crucified one. The people of Jesus are being knockdown one by one, because of the defeatist attitude of a Christian world besieged by Radical Islamic terrorists.

All these religious movements came about to prove that the entire book of Revelation is totally wrong. Nobody talked about new hymns and new music crescendos from the bowels of heaven. Jesus puts out a book for only a few anointed brothers and sisters to translate. Just as Jesus assembled twelve disciples in the city of Jerusalem; Jesus is once again assembling only a few. Jesus is still standing.

And when they had sung an hymn, they went out into the Mount of Olives. Jesus is showing me great mistrust in the leadership of the ministry of music. Humankind should seek the Lord before accepting a hymn from anyone because hymns could also bear the number 666 in its title. Jesus does not care how good the music sounds? Jesus does not care how great the writer is? Jesus does not care how great the Pastor or the so-called body of the blood of Jesus Christ Movement is? All Jesus cares about is that we do as he says.

The hymns of Jesus are to build confidence in the souls that are prepared from the earth to their glorious home in heaven. Jesus says that the poor will always be with us. These terrible times are the true meaning of the poor in spirit. Jesus is profoundly misjudged by church scholars in a world of hype that tears at the very foundations of the world. Hymns are the rivers of waters that flow from the seraphim.

Jesus is pouring out his spirit of boldness into the hearts of the children, whose pleasures are the whisperings in silent song of worship offered up to Jesus to help them combat the killings of innocent children around the world. These happenings are real. We live in a time of utter chaos. We are in dire need of inspirational hymns to embolden us amidst terror.

As ministers of music and writers of hymns, we have an enormous task ahead of us to undergo the necessary surgery from God the Father, God the Son, and God the Holy Spirit to stay encourage, so that others can see the silver lining of light, which leads to heaven as the River Nile.

Jesus knows every country that is headed by a fallen angel. Jesus knows every city small or big that is overtaken by a fallen angel. Jesus knows every evil device that is used against the children of God. Jesus's time to destroy or annihilate these fallen angels has not yet come. Meanwhile our duty is to love each other as Jesus is teaching you how to love yourself.

It is easy to sing the song, but can you stay pressing on

the trade winds of the planet? Jesus consistently works in an easterly direction. Human beings try their very best to clamp down Jesus without virtually any success. Jesus is not a math problem. Jesus is not a physics equation. Jesus is not a symmetrical figure. Jesus is the apple of your eye. The Mount of Olives is in your part. Just step up to the foot of a tree to pick a leaf.

It is disheartening to feel that Jesus has abandoned you. It is troubling to assume that Jesus has deserted you. If Jesus had placed you in the fire of the open desert: this means that he loves you. This also means that out of you will come fiery voices to fill the air with joyful sounds. For it is not that he has abandoned you, Jesus just left you there for safe keeping.

Sometimes, we feel like an orphan in a motherless home. Mother is dead. Now you are left all alone with your father. Dad is trying to fulfill both roles without any measure of success. Jesus knows that you are an understanding child filled with remorse and sadness. At the church you sing the song with a heavy heart only to find out that Jesus is near. At the weddings Jesus moves you in song that whispers the spirit of everlasting love.

Jesus is never compromising. Whatever hymn he gives to you ask him for the gift of humility? Watch and see him work as you worship him in song. There is no greater gift than to worship him. There is no greater gift than to adore him with thanksgiving in song.

Hymns are the eyeballs of God. Jesus wants you to know that his resurrection though disclaimed by the enemies of Our Lord Jesus Christ, have brought the world to this crisis. It is time for us Christians to pick up where our faithful servants have left off to continue in furtherance of the walk to paradise. It is time for us Christians to lift our heads up high to receive the blessings of the singing saints in heaven.

It is time for us Christians to take the hand of each other up the whirlwind of the Mount of Olives.

And when they had sung an hymn, they went out into the Mount of Olives. Jesus in his humility comes to us from time to time to ensure that we stay on the road to paradise. Some people sing a hymn whilst engaging in work on the job. It is amazing how they get through their work on a daily basis. They are there dancing. They are there singing. They are there smiling. They are there acting. They are there praising. Jesus is still standing.

All this emotion is shown in song in offices high. All this feeling is exuberated to an unknown audience. All this overflowing of enthusiastic-joy is given to a people, who chose not to turn back the clock. The churches are empty. Moreover, the savage action of the Roman soldier, who had pierced the side of Jesus with a lance that went straight through the heart of Jesus is still overflowing with water, because we are not listening to the promptings of the Holy Spirit.

Jesus is constantly molding people to as it were, do the right thing. As soon as Jesus turns his back, the good is forgotten instantly. Jesus knows the importance of just one talent. At least 80 per cent of the world has not achieved the crown. Why go chasing after somebody's talent when you have not achieved or fulfilled your very own? Singing for Jesus takes you to worship.

Some people Jesus have given the title of a song together with the chorus. Then Jesus disappears in the wilderness. Don't get mad with Jesus! Whether he returns or not is not your business. Jesus is proving to a world filled with deception that he is the same today. Do you look the same? Only Jesus looks the same. Could you pick a leaf from the olive tree of Jesus? Jesus is still standing.

Some people Jesus have given the title of a song, all total chorus as well as verses. Today the song is hidden only in their mind. Somebody told them that that song needs rewriting. Did Jesus told you so? Jesus is the only hymn writer that never lost a fight. Jesus is the only hymn writer that never asked anyone for their advice. Jesus is the only hymn writer that can generate songs to make you happy until Jesus comes to take you to heaven.

The hymns of Jesus are not to be taken lightly. They come in waves as generations come in waves. The eggs are broken. The youngsters come out. They run to their parents athirst for food. Likewise you must stay the course through the valleys of wantonness to one day have a seat beside Jesus on his heavenly throne. Jesus is not about camping out. Jesus wants to show you off.

Jesus is showing me hymnist tearing up songs of inspiration. They feel that Jesus music will not sell. They are praying for Jesus to allow them to put their own music and nuances to his lyrics. If Jesus wants you to be wealthy you surely will. Jesus wants to use you in a mighty way. His secondary purpose is to awaken your family whose been sleeping far too long.

The pinnacle of any hymn is Jesus. Until you get to the acme of the crown of Jesus you cannot replace the eye of a needle. Jesus in his magnificence wants to take you to places to show you what it means to be called a child of Jesus. The nights are long but Jesus is still waiting, waiting, waiting for a new vessel to undertake the journey to place the crown on his head that awaits him at the summit.

The zenith is yours to behold which is placed atop the tree on the Mount of Olives. Musical geniuses have died trying to get back what they had achieved *vis-à-vis* the entrance to the Mount Of Olives. No human being can rival against the God of heaven in his quest to dine with Jesus on his throne.

Music is in everything but everything is not in music. You turn the switch on beside the looking glass; the lights come on; you freeze when you see a reflection in the mirror. This piece of drama did not happen perchance. Jesus is inviting you out into the deep to take you to an unknown place known only to God the Father, God the Son, and God the Holy Spirit.

Jesus will not take you there if you did not harass him 24/7. The birds will welcome you on entering the Mount of Olives. Jesus does not have to give you a litmus test. A crucial; revealing test, in which there is one decisive factor. Jesus is well aware of your imperfections. This is not a requirement for Jesus to come pick you up to take you to the throne of Grace.

And when they had sung an hymn, they went out into the Mount of Olives. Some Christians on their return to Jesus do not have to extinguish the fire first before they take up the offer. Looking at Jesus to see if Jesus is looking at you will not augur well for the future. Jesus is in the rollercoaster business. Jesus's job is to pick you up from wherever you are to pitch you into prosperity.

Jesus is showing me the trampling of feet. Jesus is showing me the disfigurement of bodies. Jesus is showing me the dismembering of arms. Jesus is showing me the dismembering of feet. Jesus is showing me the loss of an eye or eyes. Jesus is showing me the total disregard for the sanctity of human life. Jesus has never stopped showing me things. We did not create this world. We were not there in the midst of Jesus together with his heavenly Father. Every word in the chorus or in the verse or verses has a distinct meaning to a command given from above.

Loving Jesus is a triumphant loveliness exploding in him. Going out into the Mount of Olives is the serenity in music that the world has been missing since the death and resurrection of Our Lord Jesus Christ. The hymnist needs Jesus to inspire him with music that uplifts the souls of every race. The lyrics shall be polished by the hands of Jesus. All these things intertwined with each other are like the clock on the wall that keeps ticking all day long.

Jesus is in his vernacular. A language when spoken we cannot understand. It is not so much that we cannot comprehend the language of heaven. To understand him is to know him. Music takes us through the fiery furnace of heaven. Music keeps us in the fire until we have been burnt in the baptism of fire. You cannot think music. You think Jesus. His love for us is enormous.

Music is devotion. The leaves of heaven will in no way resemble the leaves on the earth. Jesus is the leaves of heaven. His music given to you is like a painting with you clutching him with all of your might. You need him much more than you can put in the words of a hymn. His voice will at all times be young and crisp whilst yours will be screeching sounds coming from a sidewalk on a rainy day.

Music is profound conviction. It is not how good you sing the song to a listening congregation, that falls asleep, as soon as the Pastor begins to preach the Word of the Lord. For the Word of the Lord comes from Jesus through the Pastor directly to you. Jesus does not want you to overlook his Son of the House, who is his representative in the body of the Lord. Sometimes order is broken, when the congregation wants to participate in music more than the Word of God. Jesus is order.

When one is deeply moved by the waves of music coming from the sounds that encircles him this is a time of stillness, so that Jesus can use him in a deliberate manner. The congregation comes to the house of God to be healed, or delivered, or saved, or expecting a miracle in their lives. Anointed voices of Jesus need the Lord to sanctify them in song. Anointed voices of Jesus need the Lord to deepen their anointing.

You cannot do the job until Jesus becomes the driving force in your life. He must be number one in every facet of your life. You want to do greater works. Jesus had already given you the power to do exceedingly good works of wonder. Jesus had already ushered you into the promise land. But you keep allowing others to take you to places that Jesus will not take you.

You relish empowerment, whose power are you seeking? The power of the devil will never ever get you to fame in worship. The power of satan will never, ever get you to the throne of Grace. The power of satan will never, ever get you to the seraphim. The power of satan will never, ever turn your water into exceedingly good wine.

The true wine of Jesus is to love him in the deep valleys of your music. These valleys are your frailties that show up in the hymns that Jesus keeps giving to you to feed your congregation of ignorance. When your congregation rises that is when you have risen to. The greater the gift taking you to greatness in spreading the Word of God through the hills especially in these trying times, the tougher your training will be in clothing your choir.

And when they had sung an hymn, they went out into the Mount of Olives. All it takes is one leaf to clothe a choir to fill an entire auditorium with the sweetness of Jesus. That one leaf is equivalent to 0.001 per cent of an ounce of uranium. The fire of Jesus is his love. It takes fire to move anything on the earth. It takes fire to block out the workings of the transgressors of evil. It takes fire to take you up the scale of music.

There is blindness in music. This comes about where there is suicide in an attempt to steal the fame of Jesus. The shedding of the blood of Jesus on the cross produces blindness in the hearts of men, who go around stealing music from their choir members without paying them for their musical input. These are troubling things in these troubling times.

The atmosphere in the church is its music. It is critical for the musical director to find Jesus in a mighty way. It is not how many hymns you sing. Your choice of hymns will take the congregation to the River Nile. Jesus is changing the atmosphere in the church. Too many churches have already collided with the icebergs of the evil found in the world. Too many churches have been split into two unequal parts. The damage done is immense. Jesus is moving on with his end times Sons of God.

Jesus is leading his church up the lateral sides of the Mount of Olives. Jesus is anointing his sons wherever he leads them to pontificate his Word in song, thus alleviating the strongholds of the stench of sin. Jesus is straightening the ties around the collars of his sons to let them know that now the decision is theirs alone. The atmosphere on the planet is one of doom and gloom. Jesus is still standing.

The roots of heaven are in the souls of his musicians to orchestrate the music of Jesus in an environment of love. The roots of heaven are in the portals of the flowers of the olive trees put there by Jesus to illuminate the eyes as they make their downward steps along the sides of the Mount of Olives. Jesus is executing his armor laterally showing the human race that the time is now.

Jesus is eliminating the elephant on people's backs. The musical chairs that we play in church trying to negotiate with the Ministers of God to bring about the necessary changes that we shall have in the music of the day thus denying the zenical right of Jesus. The feet of Jesus are truth indeed. Whereas, the feet of humankind in musical hymns are thrown in all directions especially, that of the sphinx.

Jesus is distributing his spirit of joy found in the hearts of innocent children, who love to perpetuate his name in music amidst the dragon-trailing devil along the sides of the hills of China. Suffice it to say, that the people found in servitude cling to Jesus stronger than those born in Christian countries around the world. They are patiently waiting for the coming of Jesus in song.

Russian Christians, whose Sons of God have to preach the Word for fear of decapitation from the looks of the eyes of the Politburo are still marching on to victory in Jesus. Their hymns in these perilous times come directly from their souls. Their worship takes the form of dancing and singing all in one. They are not afraid of the darkness of evil. Their singing of hymns brings tears to the eyes of Jesus. Their attendance at the house of the Lord is growing in populace day by day. Jesus is still standing.

The hymns gushing out the wounds of the sides of Jesus are not easy to hold on to in these turbulent times. These hymns will pick you up and throw you in a whirlwind to heaven. If you are not ready do not go near the worship hymns of these times of terror.

Christians, who are held in Islamic religious terrorists' strongholds throughout the Middle East, are growing in strength as they hold on to their measure of faith. These feet of Jesus are covered with sores, yet still they tarry in song. The Sons of God are singing their hymns from within to keep them from falling asleep on a very cold concrete.

Isaiah 66:1 Thus saith the Lord, the heaven is my throne, and the earth is my footstool: where is the house that ye build unto me? and where is the place of my rest? Jesus is allowing his Ministers of Music to build him places on the earth to house and store his music for generations to come. These sanctuaries of music will be like building blocks of prisms throughout the land.

Jesus who is sublime is reaching out to the Body of Christ to teach them how to venerate him in his Holy of Holies. Jesus is taking the necessary steps to bring about a newness of grandeur among his anointed voices of song. This lofty sound of music is a built-up of his resplendency. Jesus is about growth in the misunderstandings of a careless few. The love of Jesus has to well up with the fire of Jesus in your heart. Otherwise nothing will never get done.

My Daily Diet:

In the summer of 2001, my daily diet changed from three meals a day to one meal a day. I remembered walking to the marketplace to purchase whatever Jesus wants me to eat on that given day. The prices were fantastic as I shop around for my meal of the day. Jesus would overpower me to direct my thoughts. The marketplace was like a breath of fresh air. Fruits and vegetables were stacked high on long tables.

When Jesus is taking you out to show you something he will not say much. All you know is that Jesus is with you like no other. No one can see him talking to you or carrying on a conversation with you. You will be conversing with him on the inside. This conversation could last from five minutes to hours on end. The time is going by without your knowledge.

Aisles of people flock these open-air places. The smell of fresh fruits makes your mouth run with saliva. We often wonder as a child what heaven is like. Well, here is a glimpse of heaven on earth. Jesus only stops by to deliver his Word to those who wishes to receive thus.

On this particular day, the people stood motionless as I rolled my eyes around to see precisely what the Lord would have me to eat. Slices of watermelon caught my eyes, but Jesus would not have me freely taste it or purchase it. Meanwhile the Jesus in me would usher me on. Jesus is saying that some people were told by the Lord exactly what to go to the marketplace to purchase to eat, but would eat all that fresh, sweet, watermelon first, before acknowledging the true Son of the Living God.

Some people would tell Jesus to his face that he says in his Word that we must forgive each other seven times seven. Mind you, this includes Jesus also. The bad news is that the gift that Jesus was developing in you; you have just lost owing to your own conceitedness. Anointed preachers of God have to tell their respective congregations about their total disrespect for Our Lord Jesus, whenever they fall into diverse temptations. The church shall come to order in the name of Jesus.

As the crowds lessened Jesus took me to the banana section to weigh three to five pounds of his delight. I ate bananas all day long until I fell asleep. We can all evolve into something special, but we would rather settle for mediocrity.

In my whole life I have never eaten one thing in the way that Jesus led me to do this thing. Your mind is the mind of Jesus. Our Lord Jesus does not want you to play with anyone's mind. It is astonishing to others, when you speak the truth. Jesus speaks the truth to you in his Word. Jesus does not care how others interpret His Word. Jesus will come to you to show you the truth about his truth. Speaking the truth is not a practice. Speaking the truth one does for the love of Jesus.

Anything that the Lord Jesus tells you to do is for a wealthy and treasured reason. It is not for you to think about; just do it! As soon as you do it, something will definitely occur. Whether it is pleasant or not, you did the right thing. The Bible says that Jesus hour had not come when his mother came to him to ask him to perform a miracle at the wedding at Cana. Immediately in obedience to his mother, he changed water into wine.

How many of us have been told by our mothers that the Lord Jesus told them to tell you what to do to change your situation? Yet to this day, we have not done what our mothers had told us to do. Our lame excuse is that Jesus should have told us first. Are we greater than Jesus? Then why are we still sucking our teeth? It is about time to mortify our bodies

Jesus teaches by example. Whatever Jesus tells you to do, he already did. The following day, Jesus tells me to buy a bag of raw yellow onions, mustard, two cans of sardines and a can of roasted salt peanuts. It took me two hours to eat one raw onion with mustard. As soon as I was finished eating the onion, Jesus was laughing and standing at the side of me. These visions of Jesus are like a movie. That day was Sunday.

Questioning Jesus was never my forte. I would hear what he says and automatically move into doing what he says to do. His speaking to me did not scare me, for whatever Jesus did to me was faster than lightening. All that I remembered was that I longed for him for over forty long years.

That Sunday I ate another raw onion, before I ate the sardines and the peanuts. The next morning I rose to eat another raw onion with mustard. Jesus is showing me now that these things will one day come to pass, but will only be revealed in another book.

I remembered having a meal of steak, rice, beans, cabbage, lettuce, broccoli and a slice of chocolate cake. Before I could take my seat the Lord Jesus says to me to eat only the cabbage, lettuce, and broccoli. The rest you will give away. The world is lacking in hindsight. The floods come and go and come again. But we do not see the eyes of Jesus looking at us. The tragedy is plastered all over the news media.

Jesus is building a new earth. Something we absolutely do not believe. To believe it we must see it. Jesus is not one for showing anything in the absolute. Jesus says, you do as I say do! It is utterly amazing how a world could be that naive. It is somewhat stupendous not to believe now that we have entered End Times. Jesus is saying, that the Word ""End Times"" is choking the living daylight out of us.

The people of this world have become so obsessed with life here on earth, that they feel that there are no tomorrows. Every time a new born baby comes into the world: that is a sign of a new tomorrow. Every time a flower blooms: that is a sign of a new tomorrow. Every time you have a meal: that is a sign of a new tomorrow. Every time Jesus speaks to you: that is a sure sign of a new tomorrow.

Jesus is looking at the wasted opportunities given to us. At birth, we are breast fed by our mothers. This milk constitutes all the nourishment that the scientist cannot provide for the health and well-being of our child or children. We in essence follow the rudiments of our young scholars, the doctors, to teach us what Jesus is consistently giving us from generation to generation. Jesus has never changed his recipe. We have.

Some of us rush the baby into weaning. Jesus will never leave you alone not even for a moment. Jesus is at all times around you, but unnoticeably in your sight. Mothers' milk kept the children with a well-balanced diet. As soon as we have to prepare a meal for ourselves, here is where the classroom comes in. Yet the teachers are constantly falling sick on a daily basis. Your doctors are falling sick to cancer. Your nurses are falling sick to disease.

Jesus is consistently, consistently, showing himself to his children to bring his Word out as a showpiece to a stubborn world. It is well to say that Jesus put you in these high offices of life, but now, who are you fooling? The dietitians fall sick as everyone does. How could you be in a field of healing, when you are continually falling sick? You can run but you cannot hide. Jesus is still standing.

You need Jesus to keep you healthy each singular day of your life. Jesus is your well-balanced diet. In the morning Jesus will tell me to drink a hot cup of black coffee. I will drink it without question the world will have a question or two before the coffee is drunk. Jesus does not care about the decaffeinated-world. Jesus cares about God the Father, God the Son, and God the Holy Spirit. Jesus is not about leverage.

The world has gone decaffeinated, so too are their bodies. In the morning is orange juice. Lunchtime is orange juice. Nighttime is orange juice. Jesus ate olives from the olive tree, how many of you are eating olives in your diet? Do not take this as a surprise, but a whole lot of you surely are not eating and living right! Every time you turn around you have to put a pill in your mouth. Wake up!

The medicine cabinet is overflowing with all kinds of pills, where is Jesus? Jesus is right there. First thing in the morning are a handful of pills followed by a glass of water. You do not need to begin your day on drugs. As a baby you began your day on milk. Why on earth are you beginning your day on drugs? Jesus is right there looking at you. All you need to do is to call his name out loud. The writing is on the wall. All you need to do is call his name.

All that medicine are not good for you anyhow. It is about time you stop lying on Jesus. Jesus never told you to go to the doctor in the first place. You awoke one morning not feeling well, before you know it; you were off to see the doctor. You never stopped to think, or to ask, or to call on the name Jesus. You treat Jesus as a Sunday meal. This is a grave mistake that a whole wide world is making come Sunday mornings.

Jesus is not a Sunday morning meal ticket. Coffee is a widespread bean given to the whole world. Simply relax: enjoy one of God's earthly treasures. Is this too much to ask from a people, who have deserted the name of Jesus? We feel that we know everything. Jesus is the one who knows everything. Jesus is the one who died on the cross for me and for you. Jesus is our Savior.

Bread constitutes almost every ingredient under the sun. In the days of Jesus bread was eaten without baking soda. Bread was not baked in modern-day ovens. Bread was baked in mud ovens. The Lamb of God is Jesus as a shepherd leading his followers into the promise land. Where is the Jesus in you? Nothing in Jesus happens by chance. No man has come to the knowledge of Jesus by share luck. Bread is sustenance.

We live everyday of our lives searching for this bread of life. Searching, but not finding. The universe has one owner, who is God the Father, God the Son, and God the Holy Spirit. We keep mixing other things up that are not of Jesus. We keep trying other methods that are not of Jesus. We keep fighting with our Pastors, only, to our own detriment. We keep yearning for the Word of God to be melted down and wilted to suit our own endeavors.

Jesus is not the one to help you when you keep putting Jesus aside in order to pursue your own flamboyant agenda. Moses had to put aside his richly, audacious garments, so that Jesus can come to him to anoint him for the job he's been called to perform. Could you put aside all that you are doing right now to follow Jesus? Could you listen to one voice all the days of your earthly life? Jesus is still standing.

The voice of Jesus is our friend throughout all eternity. The voice of Jesus is a gentle voice. To find him is to love him. To find him is to share him with others every moment that he gives to us. Jesus is shared in our giving to each other. This bread we take literally for granted. When we give, we shall give lovingly from the very depths of our hearts. We shall give of ourselves freely.

Far too often we tend to hold back in our giving. We keep a check on everything that we do for others; not forgetting to put a price. We would not lift a hand, if what was promised was not forthcoming. We turn into a ravenous wolf as soon as a payment was not on time. We walk with a list wherever we shall go. Jesus is showing me a long handwritten list. It is not how much money that you give or lend to someone? Jesus is looking.

We came into this world naked. What we see is what we get. The river ebbs; the river wanes. Jesus is our fountainhead. Jesus is our only source to heaven. There is no other way. Our nudity is our humility, a humility we do not see.

We have to eat of the bread of Jesus in order to make healthy decisions. Situations come; situations go. Strongholds are when we get caught in a trap. Life is too precious to allow the enemies of Jesus to sway us into the floods of darkness. We walk the streets with hoods over our heads. We make movies with hoods over our heads. We sing songs with hoods over our heads. We do choreography in dance with hoods over our heads.

Jesus, who is the bread of life, keeps showing me the reluctance of generations to come to live for the name of Jesus. We tend to agree that good things come to those who wait. But,is this just for conversation? Or is this to be rooted in the souls of the human race? You better believe it! Jesus is still standing.

We must hunger for the body of our Lord Jesus, if we want to do well in this world. This strong desire for the Lamb of God is missing in our daily diet. We must pray with a fervent heart. We shall not yield to anyone, but the Lord Jesus. We shall strive purposefully to enunciate that Jesus is the only mediator between God and humankind. This is our primary prayer: the lifting up of our heart to Jesus.

Lunchtime is very important. Jesus is saying that Jesus is solely your meal ticket. How many people spend their time reading the scriptures, whilst having a meal of green leafy vegetables? Too many times we fall prey to being a follower of the status quo. The news media dictates a whirlwind of very important news at 12 noon. We have become so indoctrinated to the news at this hour. BBC (British Broadcasting Corporation) carries its top-breaking news at 12 noon each day of the week.

The lighting of candles can be seen as a ritual throughout the world. Many religious churches burn candles on their altars as a form of worship. These churches have indoctrinated a vast number of the earth's devoted followers at their vigils. These ceremonies became fixed in their minds, which tended to sway the congregation in the wrong direction. Huge numbers of followers or membership do not make it right.

Jesus knows that the outcry of the youth, who were fenced in by the doctrine of predestination tattooed on the walls of great Cathedrals is a reminder of Jesus himself, as he had walked talking against the politics in fundamentalist religious churches. Jesus is the Supreme Being who administers Justice for all. Jesus is saying that your lunch hour shall be kept sacred and set apart.

Did Jesus have a lunch hour? Yes, he did. Jesus would walk through ears of corn to have a bite in the middle of the day. Jesus would help himself to olives from olive trees at 12.00 o'clock. Jesus would stop by the house of Lazarus to have lunch with the family. There are a lot of things that Jesus did that cannot be recorded for it would make too many books for bookshelves.

The life and times of Jesus must not be taken for granted. Jesus went fishing in the river. After catching a fish he drew a coin out of his mouth. It was lunchtime when Jesus fixed himself a meal. Your lunch hour is a time for thanksgiving.

Breaking bread among six to twelve friends or brothers is a wonderful thing to do at 12 noon. Some people from time to time forego breakfast for lunch.

Also, there are some people whose first meal begin at lunchtime. Jesus is showing me three tents. One tenth is filled with enquiring people. The other tent is filled with ordinary laid-back people like southerners. The final tent is filled with people who care less.

The primary tent is the one that Jesus would give less attention to. The Bible says that Jesus must not be questioned. An enquiring mind will ask questions repeatedly ignoring the Holy Spirit. Jesus never questioned or had ever questioned his heavenly Father. Jesus is holy. Humankind has fallen short on being holy. You cannot allow Lucifer to put you in a stronghold.

The other tent of easy going people reminds Jesus of himself. These people take life in stride not missing anything or forgetting something to do. They work like electricity. Be ye perfect as your heavenly Father is perfect is another way of looking at this side of the peak. Forgetfulness is not found among these people. These people grow to old age with a perfect mind. Satan is the one that makes you forgetful.

The final tent is the people headed for hell. They are the ones that at all times will be looking good. They are extremely showy and flamboyant. Nothing goes unnoticed. They seemingly work long hours without breaks. They project the image of wealth in a fashionable way. They spend money lavishly. At restaurants, they are served obsequiously by the waitresses. Much attention given is their greatest asset. They roll into money as sheets of tin are rolled into silver tops as coverings for cans of goods.

Lunchtime for Jesus is a time to spend talking to his heavenly Father, whilst enjoying his goodness of providence distributed throughout the earth. Be reminded that God the Father and his Son Jesus created the earth! Jesus is showing me the apples, grapes, bananas, oranges and ice cream are the earth's favorite food around the world. At lunchtime, either one or all these things are eaten on the planet.

We all want Jesus to speak to us each day of our lives, but what are we doing about it? Absolutely nothing. We follow our so-called leaders, who do nothing for the love of Jesus. Lunchtime they sit in their ivory towers having meetings that got absolutely nothing to do with the name of Jesus. They sit there with their friends shaking champagne glasses as though Jesus does not exist.

We walk like them. We talk like them. We shake hands like them. We celebrate like them. We dress like them. Are we walking like Jesus? Are we following his every meal that he ate in his Word? We love to be a follower rather than a leader. Were there ever a time, that you filled up your trolley, with only foodstuff from the vegetable section of the supermarket? Now you are wondering why you are sick. Jesus lives. Jesus eats the same food from the vegetable stand. Jesus is well. How are you sick?

Jesus is talking to you, but you are not paying him much attention. Jesus is giving you your daily diet, as he slowly anoints you for his daily work. If you would acknowledge him as your Lord and Savior, now you would behold him face to face. The ice cream needs quite a number of ingredients, before it becomes the ice cream. So you do need a variety of vitamins and minerals to become the most beautiful rose in the garden.

We do not want any help from the Lord Jesus to bring us to fruition. We want to try, try, try, try, try, try, try, try, and try again. Our accomplishments must be borne out of ourselves. Our achievements shall be self-willed. Jesus must not take credit for anything. He is our eldest brother. Then why are we sick? Jesus is saying look at the sun; see how it disappears as night steps in. Jesus is still standing.

We all need Jesus to show us the way. The more that we think we need him, the greater will be our perseverance. Jesus is our only shield and buckler. Jesus is waiting on us to step aside for him to enter. We take forever to make one movement. We keep taking our briefings from the horoscope.

We have four seasons. In spring, our lunches will be different. We definitely cannot eat the same thing daily. The sweeter the fruit juice, the more of this type you will drink. Some people eat the skins off the mango. If you can digest the skin eat but just one mango. Jesus gets extremely bitter when someone lies on him. God the Father does not relent.

In summertime, one can drink water or lots of varieties of sodas. This also is a great time for tea lovers. Lunchtime will consist of potatoes, sweet potatoes, cauliflower, green figs or green bananas, plantains or the like. You can mix it up with rice or beans of any kind. Lettuce will be the best choice for summertime. Cucumbers will be your second choice.

As the weather changes into autumn, so do you change your diet. For lunch you will have fried chicken, French fries, soda, cabbage, eggplant or anything of like ilk. As the trees gradually breaks down to a skeleton, so will your body become, if you do not know precisely what to eat. Jesus is shedding some light on this subject, because no one cares but Jesus.

Winter can empty you out in a flash. The harsher the winter, the more meat and vegetables you eat at lunchtime. It is a time for coffee lovers. Black only. The black bean is medicinal. You need your central nervous system ticking like the clock on the wall. The ripping of the harsh winds at night, when you are walking the streets can cause or give rise to walking pneumonia.

Jesus knows it all. Why don't you come worship him?

Menu for the fruit lovers is at 12 noon. Two bananas, one peeled orange, one mango, a container of watermelon pieces, mixed with pine apple pieces. Any mixture of fruits along these lines are welcomed. Jesus is showing me a multiplicity of illnesses that fresh fruit can cure. If people would do right, Jesus can come to the church to perform his supernatural gifts.

Beware of artificial flavoring of fruits in foodstuff! God the Father, God the Son, and God the Holy Spirit created all varieties of fruits for humankind consumption. But in modern times, the scientists have grafted almost every natural fruit on the face of the earth. It is imperative that families familiarize themselves with organic fruits throughout the world.

Jesus is showing me a tempest: a violent snow storm of hail. Jesus wants the planet to know that the fruits of the Holy Spirit are a necessity in a world swimming in chaos. People of all ethnic groups are desperately fleeing to other nations that are willing to shelter them from the ravages of the jaws of Satan. The world needs a healing of peace, so that it can still spin on its axis.

Jesus is saying that the pendulum swings to and fro. We experiment far too much with the natural elements of the earth. These tests are done or rather conducted in the earth's atmosphere, or in the wilderness by our so-called scientists. Thus penetrating the environs with elements that will cause further erosion to soil—the result being low food production of any kind and sickness.

The apples no longer taste the same, some twenty years ago. The luster of the grapes glittering in the sunlight has lost its brilliance over time. The myriad of foliage all around the planet are affected by these tests done for want of power.

Life expectancy deteriorates as the day goes by. Jesus is saying that the enormity of destruction will be felt from the year 2020—2070.

The world takes the erosion of the planet with a pinch of salt. According to the adage: "Business as usual." This would not affect their life style in anyway. Needless to say, some people definitely do not have breakfast or lunch on any given day. Well, how about this, some people would prefer to have meat or meat products all day long for the rest of their lives.

Lunchtime is not for shopping or making groceries. Meditating on Jesus in the middle of the day is like being lost whilst wondering in the city at night. The sudden loss of the sense of direction, geographically, tears out a page of wisdom from the annals of the city's direction. Jesus is predominantly lifting up the world on his shoulders. Jesus is never absent. Jesus is present at lunchtime.

The world can take off anytime to have fun. Vacationers can be seen scuba diving in the seas enjoying the rough and choppy waters of the Atlantic Ocean. Researchers swimming underwater in their quest to fulfill unanswered questions, that the scholars on the earth have blatantly denied. Jesus is waiting to till the soil of the ocean floor. Jesus is preserving the Dead Sea for tomorrow.

Iridescent is the colors of the rainbow. This is a gift from Jesus given to humankind especially, when seen in the middle of the day. Where is all the laughter? Where is all the joy? Jesus is safely taking care of his children, who are stuck in the middle of the road at lunchtime. Jesus is praise. Where is your faithfulness? God the Father, God the Son, and God the Holy Spirit is looking for his love.

The Ark of the Covenant was visible in the sight of Moses, as he engaged his enemies in battle. During the battle Jesus allowed the enemies to torment Moses by stretching his arms out wide. Whenever Moses hands fell, the Jewish people would begin to lose the fight. Ultimately, whenever Moses hands did not fall, the Jewish people would not lose a man at battle.

Jesus is showing us by demonstrating the power of prayer culminating his diet at lunchtime is the answer to a long, healthy life. Make no mistake about it, time waits on no one. Jesus wants us to effervesce in the liveliness of our communities.

Nothing is wrong in forming prayer groups during lunchtime. Nothing is wrong in sharing a watermelon during this time. Nothing is wrong in sharing a morsel of food with each other, something very appetizing like tidbits. Nothing is wrong in the breaking of bread during midday. Jesus is sheltering his flock from the enemy from 12 noon to 1 p.m. We keep on harassing Jesus with our enquiring minds. Sometimes Jesus will leave us alone to climb the mountain top.

Christians worldwide have a responsibility to care for each other on a day-to-day basis. Prayer is omnipotent. Jesus shares his Word only to those who will stop to listen to his Good News. Keeping it real at lunchtime is like an eagle in flight swooping down on its prey. Jesus is saying to his multitude to look at the stars above. Do tell me, what do you see?

Yes, they are thousands and thousands of miles away from the earth. It's also the same for you too. Jesus is not asking us to do anything that basically, we cannot do for ourselves. Hiding from Jesus is not the same as running away from Jesus. Playing that you hear him and not doing the thing that you hear him say, go do! All these are mountains that lie between you and Jesus.

Looking up into the sky surely, you do not see the great, big mountains. These majestic situations are put there to blind us into gross submission. Having a hot cup of coffee, with fresh butter on two toasted slices of sandwich loaf, are not enough to keep us until lunchtime. We seem to think that Jesus is some light years away. Thanks to science some 5.88 trillion miles away. We believe in science over the risen Lord Jesus. Jesus is still standing right at your side.

We keep looking over the shoulders of Jesus in oblivion. I know that you cannot see him. But I know that you can surely hear him. He is speaking to you, whilst on the other hand you want to touch him with your desired hand. Jesus is Holy, something that you do not care about. As far as you are concern, Jesus is Holy for others, but not for you. Jesus belongs to me alone.

We keep not believing in his name. We keep fighting over his name. We keep doing everything except what he asks us to do. Jesus is our every, everything. Jesus wants us to slow down just for one minute to catch our breath. Jesus wants us to take a good look at ourselves from another perspective. Jesus wants us to rely on him alone. This is something that we cannot do. We pride ourselves solely on our own merits.

There is confusion with the love of Jesus. A discord created since the fall of one-third of heavenly angels. Jesus came to make men free. Jesus created symmetry even before the foundations of the world. Yet humankind is very reluctant to bend the knee in submission to Jesus. We say that we love him. How are we showing the rest of the world that we really love Jesus?

We have to spend time with Jesus. More time than we care to. We have to call his name, as we break bread with our brothers and sisters during our midday meal. We owe it to ourselves to stay focus on the name of Jesus. There is no other name held in high esteem. Jesus is making it crystal clear that to love him is to serve him.

Dinnertime: a chicken soup with potatoes or sweet potatoes covered with cauliflower, cabbage, carrots or the like. Some families are very happy to be surrounded by their siblings at this very hour. For those of you who are at the house at this time, there will be meaningful conversation.

At the end of the working day, there is time for reminiscing on checks and balances. Jesus is not about playing games with the minds of Christians in a world of chaos. My daily diet is not in relation to anyone's diet. It changes with the utterances of the Holy Spirit. The spirit of Jesus dwells in me. Do you have the Holy Spirit? If you do not, now is the time to seek his face.

In my sharing, I am conversing with the Holy Spirit. Someone I have grown to know in an awesome manner. Christians take the love of Jesus for granted. Christians take his death and crucifixion for granted. Christians take his resurrection from the grave to heaven for granted. Christians take his return to show himself to his twelve disciples along with his siblings, friends or anyone that the Father had blest to see a phenomenon, for granted.

Jesus wants you to have dinner on him. There is a silence in the ocean where angels meet to sing a song for Jesus. There is a serenity on the Pacific Ocean racing through the ripples in the morning dew. There is a beating of waters on the rocks that will break your silence in the night.

Jesus is running around heaven all day waiting for someone to mail him out a post card. Valentine's Day has come and gone yet nobody remembered to send Jesus his valentine's present. Jesus did provide all the cocoa to make that good tasting chocolate. Did you remember Jesus when you were enjoying that sweet, tasting, delicious, milk chocolate? Did you remember Jesus when you were enjoying those sweet-smelling, beautiful, red roses? Did you remember Jesus when you were devouring that chocolate cake?

It is amazing how quickly we forget the goodness of the Lord. It is astonishing how we view Jesus after all he has done for us. It is striking to say the least, how we blatantly lay platitudes on ourselves. Some of us believe that Jesus is non-existence. This fallacy we uphold. This myth we encourage. We walk the streets at night holding hands in unison of love. We walk down the aisle exchanging glances with the hope that Jesus will bless our marriage.

On some occasions, Jesus is seen dancing in the night. Jesus is forever happy. Jesus is saying that we do not want to cherish the one we love. When was the last time you took out your best friend for dinner? When was the last time you bought him or her a new suit or a new dress? When was the last time you have been to the movies? Jesus loves a cheerful giver.

How many of us before leaving the church are ready to tip Jesus. God the Father, God the Son, and God the Holy Spirit does not ask anyone to give him a tip. But since we are a society of very generous people, shouldn't we also tip Jesus, as we tip the waiters at the restaurant? Humankind likes to wear the same color shoe on each foot. Jesus is not about shoes. Jesus is about God's Glory and his infinite goodness.

Reservoirs all over the world are filled by running streams in its pathway. The rain falls on the earth thus adding additional waters to its tributaries. The reservoirs are all cleaned by the very workers of these said cities. If contaminated the population dies. Take another look at cancer spreading itself vastly throughout the land! Perniciously destructive: not in the ways of men's persuasiveness to discover a cure; but, in his efforts to obtain fame by selling the idea of giving a monthly donation to help a sick child. Where is Jesus in all of this?

Of course, where is Jesus? Jesus is the light of the world. Follow him! As soon as dinner is over, here comes dessert. Jesus is not particularly happy with the parents' knowledge of what is the gender of the child. Read the Word of God and get it right! Jesus is in our everyday menu, yet we throw him out of our conversations. Jesus is constantly looking at the price of gasoline in all America.

Parity is given to all American women in the United States of America. One must understand that when something is given by God the Father, God the Son, and God the Holy Spirit to anyone, or to everyone: this is indeed Holy. Women must embrace this sacred hand of God. Lots of families have dinner together. Jesus is saying that dinnertime is sometimes precarious.

Could you imagine biting a nail in your food; equally swallowing the food together with its remnants? In this case, the last meal is greater than the first meal. What comes after dinner, bedtime? The Holy Spirit is seeking out the remnants of the earth. Who are these remnants? The ethnicity of people of all walks of life. The ethnicity of people, who are excluded from all three distinctive original races. The ethnicity of people, who are precluded from the accolades of life.

This is absolutely what we get in the world after dinnertime. Jesus is showing that these people shall not be used as spare parts in the society as a whole. It is all good to jump around. It is all good to sing a song. The remains of any society that have become a remnant will continually be the most revered in any given society. It is for some a hard pill to swallow, but for Jesus who knows every thought that emanates out of the heart of humankind; creatively changing them into deeds of holiness is truly a remarkable gift to behold.

There is no one that came into this world with a spare part. There is no animal that came into this world with a spare part. There is no tree that Jesus had created that came into this world with a spare part. There is no ocean that the Triune God created on the face of the earth that came with a spare part. There is no sea that the Holy Ghost created in this world that came with a spare part. There is no river on this planet that Jesus had created that came with a spare part. There is no water fall that the Triune God had created and is still creating that came with a spare part. Jesus is still standing.

My daily diet at that time was either breakfast or lunch or dinner. Most times it was lunchtime. And this continued until 2008. Some people Jesus would have a wrestling match with on the subject of fasting. Or is it much more deliberate than trying to push the buttons of Jesus, to see if he would at least listen to his girl for a moment. Jesus is about cleansing the mind. How do we cleanse the mind?

Cigarette smoking does not cleanse the mind. Having a cold beer first thing in the morning does not cleanse the mind. Taking a shot of 100 per cent Rum or under does not cleanse the mind. Smoking a stick of marijuana does not cleanse the mind. Snuffing or puffing on coke or crack cocaine does not cleanse the mind. Overnighting at the casino does not cleanse the mind.

Satan likes to attack the mind of God. Satan knows that when he attacks the human mind, this would ultimately draw a real confrontation between Jesus and himself. A human being reasons: a basis or cause, as of some belief, action, fact, event, etc. Why is satan's first choice, the choice of reason.

It is clear to see that satan, the devil's daily diet is reason. Human beings from Eve to all babies throughout the world would always be troubled in their reasoning. Scholars born to parents that have never made it past Middle School would constantly question their own heritage. Scholars born to kings, presidents, prime ministers, and ayatollahs grow in constant fear in identifying their true birthright.

Jesus is saying that too much emphasis is placed on the fear of satan than the fear of Our Lord Jesus Christ. The burning of coals blowing over the bridge, where there is a mountainous cloud of a spiral whirlwind, as though stationed unmoved by the arms of a most brilliant artist, patiently waiting for the voice of Jesus to direct its path along the road of a golden few. Standing atop the mountain is an old cross beaten up by the many changes in the atmosphere.

The time for conjecturing about breakfast had longed been done with by God the Father, God the Son, and God the Holy Spirit. We all need Jesus to keep us strong as the day passes from day to night. Is anything missing in our daily diet? Of course, there is something missing in our daily diet. Individually, search your heart! Individually, search your ego! Individually, search your pride and compare it to the Lord's Prayer!

Jesus is constantly giving us something to do even before the dawn of a new day. We silently dismiss our thoughts by rolling in the sheets, or the covers, to try to continue our sweet morning dreams. Needless to say, that our daily diet might have been a wrestling match with the judge at the courthouse. We keep washing the dishes, before first, cleaning out all the rice, beans, and meat therein.

Jesus is putting the flavoring on the top of the ice cream cone. Whatever you see is what you will surely get. It is a true test of self. We read the Word daily hoping for a miracle to come to change our rotten ways. The time passes by as winter had just ended.

It is now springtime, but are we rendering our hearts. Jesus is forever looking out in the afternoon gatherings of animals left to pasture. These animals take on the pride and joy of their owners. Their owners shamefully walking away from reoccurred liabilities.

Are you still asking Jesus for something that Jesus had already given up on? Exactly, what is your beef with Jesus. You got no daily diet. You got no seed planted near the grave of your best friend. You got no hope for the future. You got no song in your heart. You keep starting things but never finishing anything. Some of you have done more harm than good to the church.

Jesus has placed a seed of hope in every child that comes out of the womb of man. Your job is not to allow anyone to trespass against the Word of Jesus. Your job is to procreate. Persevering in the love of Jesus is a must for every living creature that can reason through the breath of fresh air. It does not take a lot of faith to move the mountain of despair. All it takes is a mustard seed of faith.

On the cross Jesus turned to one of the two thieves that were crucified alongside him saying today you will be with me in paradise. This thief daily diet was one of stealing everything that he can put his hands on. In this case, he appropriated funds for himself from the tithes and offerings of the members of the church. Stealing from God the Father is indeed a very wicked thing: it is a curse with a curse.

Inventors, who allow satan to be praised by awards given to them through their innovations, would be held accountable for their nebbish behavior. They have lost their eternal daily diet. To God be the Glory great things he has done. Jesus never says to satan be the Glory. Jesus is making his sons aware of the tricks of the armies of satan. The reality is only a few children will be obedient to Jesus unto death.

Jesus is saying that to touch the eye of a needle is to reach into heaven and have breakfast with the Triune God. Only a few saints that have lived on the face of the earth have accomplished this phenomenal feat. Only a few of these brothers/sisters had an enormous heart of gold. To accomplish heaven is no small task. To alert the saints in heaven is to keep calling on the name Jesus.

Jesus is showing that crime is man's daily diet. They sit outside of coffee shops pretending that they are having a gorgeous day, when in reality they are spying on every manager that take a trip to the bank. In their fun time they forget Jesus. They look at their sinfulness as nothing. They say to themselves very cunningly that God the Father is not here. He is somewhere up there.

Their trend of thought is wavering as they read through the daily news only to find more gossip, more fuel for their languishing souls. They are the meat and the potatoes of human bondage. They crawl into the corners of their homes peeping through windows as their neighbors make their way to work. At evening time, they occupy the very same corners of their homes to flip the script at the end of the day.

Jesus is about my daily diet which is Jesus. Jesus is not about your mood swings pretending to be one thing in the morning; another in the evening; another at night. Jesus gave his life for all of us to have an eternal tomorrow. These End Times are not game times. These times signify the end of evil transcending to a life of purity. All the evil that you are seeing will one day come to a halt. Jesus is still standing.

It is about time for people to strive in the dew-forming hills of their tomorrows. It is about time for people to begin to reward themselves for being born to and in a Christian family. It is about time for people to find their families wherever they may be. It is about time for people to downside weaknesses. It is about time for people to cherish their better halves for a better tomorrow. It is about time for people to keep the light of Jesus burning in their dreams for a better tomorrow.

Jesus is the one to choose for the asking. Too many people are seen visiting places in far-off countries to take care of their daily diet. Waving good-byes to your dearest ones does not mean anything to Jesus. Telling them, "see you when I get back" does not mean anything to Jesus. Showing them all the tears does not mean anything to Jesus. Making promises to them does not mean anything to Jesus. Jesus had already given his life for everyone to be successful. Jesus is everywhere.

Are you asking Jesus, only Jesus for your needs and your wants? The answer is no. if it was yes, then you would have had everything by now without exception. The reason that it is no, is that satan beat you up in your reasoning. It is not about you doubting Jesus. When you pray the Lord's Prayer on a daily basis, you have fulfilled your daily diet. Could someone provoke or stand in the way of the gifts of Jesus? Only satan can, once Jesus allows it.

You take a walk in the park on a bright sunny gorgeous day. You are a woman alone enjoying the atmosphere of this beautiful day. During your walk you pass children playing. Joggers pass you by soaked in sweat. Couples jogging slowly pass you by mumbling good evening to you under their breath. In total you walk three miles. You get to the house to take a shower. There is a knocking on your door which you answer. Did you hear loud screams in the park? Your answer is no.

Ignominy in the writing of books penned by scholars is in the forefront of the: *To Do List* held by Jesus. Their craftiness of word has become their daily diet. Their garbage eaten by the followers of the left are turning heads in the direction of the fallen angel. Meanwhile, the unveiled Word is ignored by a dying world. People have become less interested in the lives of the handicap. Absolutely no one is really interested in the dumbfounded.

The perplexity of life still troubles the minds that are caught up in the fire of consuming Jesus in their daily diet. People are still wondering as to why we must have prayer chains. People are giving their ten per cent as a ransom. People are worrying every single day, whether their children will join them in heaven with all the evil that exists in the society. People are of the belief that satan will win the overall battle.

The biggest problem with prayer chains is that at least 90 per cent of the people have never fasted one day in their lives. Some of them never went door-to-door evangelizing for Jesus. Some of them never went over to their neighbor's house to pray with the family. Some of them never said a kind word about their neighbor. Jesus remembers each one footprints left behind in the sea sand.

Yes, it is good to stand in the gap for your fellowman. Jesus is saying that this is a dying sword that is used to pierce satan from troubling the children of Jesus. This is often seen in child molestation. Fathers becoming intimate with their daughters on a daily basis at the house. Fathers and step-fathers becoming intimate with their sons each day at the house. Brothers becoming intimate with their sisters at the house. Sisters becoming intimate with their sisters at the house. Brothers becoming intimate with their brothers at the house.

Jesus is saying that your daily diet should resemble his daily diet until Jesus chooses to change it one on one. It is all well and good to wake up in the morning to thank Jesus for seeing a new day. But did Jesus speak to you this day? Or are you presently doing a good work for the Lord Jesus? Jesus knows precisely what you are going through. With patience, Jesus will take you by the hand, to show you the deep rivers of waters that he has just brought you out of, to make you taste freedom from a life full of doom and gloom.

Jesus is not about the mockingbird. Jesus is about the

world paying close attention to the book of Revelation to view Jesus one day in their lifetime coming down the steps of heaven wearing his Golden Shoes. Jesus is about two of us, not me and you, or both of us, or your peers and us, or your girlfriend, yourself and Jesus. No this is about you becoming one with God the Father, God the Son, and God the Holy Spirit. Jesus is still standing.

THE PREPARATION OF GIFTS CALLED THE TWO FISHES:

Matthew 2:11 And when they were come into the house, they saw the young child with Mary his mother, and fell down, and worshipped him and when they had opened their treasures, they presented unto him gifts; gold, and frankincense, and myrrh. Jesus is rolled into gold, frankincense and myrrh.

As a child fresh out the womb, my parents took me to the priest to be christen. This also means to be received into the Christian church by baptism. Simultaneously my name was appropriately given at this ceremony. Without the gift of baptism, the Lord Jesus would not have been able to begin the process of building within my soul, the gifts called the two fishes. It is indeed a most humbling experience to recall only by trusting through conversations with the Lord Jesus.

I vividly recalled my mother saying to me and my brother Gene that the priest said, "something about them two boys." To date my brother Gene is now a Minister of Music. Sad to say, that our mother never lived to see us both becoming Ministers in our 40s. When a preacher's word never falls to the ground he or she is a true prophet. The question is: did anyone ever told me what is happening to me now before it actually took place? The answer is No.

Jesus had already begun the process of molding me even as a child. At seven years old, I was in first standard. My teacher had given us an end of term Math test. During the test he took my paper and pencil away from me and told me that, "I have been cheating." I immediately got up and left the classroom totally disgusted and headed for home, which was a few minutes away. My mother a housewife brought me back to school instantly. Of course she believed my story over the teacher's lie. I eventually took over the test and scored a 100 per cent.

At eighteen years of age, I had begun visiting the sick at the hospital once a week. My visions had just begun to flow like a river. I visited the sick at the Port-of-Spain General Hospital. Every Wednesday after work as an apprentice at the Government Printing Office, I would make my way to the hospital. People could visit the sick from 4.30 p.m. to 6.30 p.m. I left my job at 4.30 p.m. it took me 15 minutes to walk from work to the hospital.

As I entered the ward on the third floor, I would make my way to the first patient that I believed needed prayer. I would take out my New Testament Pocket Bible and read the prayers selected for the sick. In retrospect, I was boldly undertaking a task without an anointing. The love of Jesus must preempt you before you enter his Ministry of the Sick.

Jesus is not about how human beings view things. Jesus is teaching a few of his children to take care of a broken-down brick wall that has lost its footage. Jesus keeps showing me the daily lives of earthly people. As soon as something breaks down, everybody including business CEOs start using foul language. Most times it is exhibited in front of Jesus's little children. And some grown-ups have the audacity to say that, "they would live to be a 100 years."'

The third floor was like ICU (Intensive Care Unit). It was noted to house patients that needed the most care and attention. Sometimes, I would lose myself by making it my humble duty to visit all five wards on the floor. For these patients hardly anyone visited them regularly. By this time the nurses had grown accustomed to seeing me every Wednesday.

Most times I would exceed the time by as much as four hours. Because there were patients with hardly any visitors to stop by their bedside and even to say, "hello." The spirit of torment came after me, since I became heavy laden and all caught up in the sufferings of people, who have made wrong decisions in the course of their lives. These constant stabbings in my soul almost cost me my life, one late night, driving some fifty miles from the hospital to my new home in Couva, Trinidad.

That night I would never ever forget. I visited the hospital at 4 p.m. I left the hospital very tired and weary at 10.30 p.m. I know that I am very tired, but I believed that the Grace of God would protect me on my way to the house via dangerous highways. Suddenly I fell asleep only to have been awakened by the hand of God, to keep my eyes wide open and praying on the inside for the next twenty miles. Jesus never ever forgets.

Easter is a time when Jesus sows seeds in the belly of his children. So the preparation of gifts continued in furtherance by and with the hand of Our Lord Jesus. Jesus in his display of humility knew that I was very forgetful, so he would automatically take me to the hospital in rich silence.

The day Wednesday would become like a miracle to me. Both consciously and subconsciously I would literally be at peace with everyone in any given situation. My workload at the office would be on zero. A lot of work given but there was peace deep within. In that moment of deep silence, I knew that it was Jesus. As soon as the bell was rung, Jesus would take over my being on the inside, without a word said, yet maintaining power directed me to the hospital.

Some people would ask me to pray for their beloved ones on my visit to the hospital. They would furnish me with the names and the ward numbers. They would not question me the next day. This bothered me for a while, but I always knew, in that moment of silence, when Jesus took it. Jesus who became a human being, so that he could teach us the way that we should go just did not have to do anything at all.

God the Father, God the Son, and God the Holy Spirit does not allow you to break your neck in the face of your good intentions. Jesus is often blame for every wrong thing that happens or have happened or had happened to us in our entire lives. This does not affect the love of Jesus that burns in his heart for us all. Jesus prepares us for all eventualities. There is nothing new or old under the sun.

Perseverance in Jesus is a must, especially when questions have no answers. Needless to say, we prefer to ride on a bandwagon of fools just like us. We must learn to step out in faith; let Jesus in! If you cannot love Jesus, then you cannot trust in him either. Whatever gift or gifts God has put in your belly, Jesus has to stop by, to stir the spirit up, for use in the future. Jesus takes his sweet time to complete the job at hand. Preparation of gifts could take from one year to forty years.

Jesus has assigned each person an angel to watch over you at your very birth. This angel you cannot see as he watches over you. The reason for this is that one day you would have to make a decision to follow Jesus our Savior. This is indeed an individual requirement. God the Father, God the Son, and God the Holy Spirit forces no man to follow him. For no man should boast about his success. When you boast,

boast about your loving Savior Jesus. When you boast, boast about all that he has done for you. When you boast, boast about Jesus-- the crucified one.

Jesus affixes a name to everything. There is nothing under the sun that Jesus did not name. God the Father, God the Son, and God the Holy Spirit names everything. Name or names are ultimately very important. Without a name nobody knows you. Without a name nobody trusts you. Without a name nobody follows you. Without a name nobody wants you. Without a name nobody including the angels of Jesus would surround you.

Jesus knows that these three elements that he has been rolled into will become extinct long before the end of the world. These elements stirred up the gifts in Jesus to do the almighty things that were recorded in the Bible. The heavenly angels knocked on the doors of Jesus to prepare him for an almighty long arduous journey. It is easy to criticize your creator for he is slow. It is easy to run the streets than to stay home to seek the face of the Lord.

Preparation of gift or gifts requires utmost obedience to his every word. This is time consuming. This is walking a tight rope. This is keeping focus on the purpose or the main purpose of your call. This is putting Jesus first at all times. This is paying attention to one voice only. This is not letting satan in even for one split second. This is staying awake with Jesus all night long. Jesus keeps you, yes he will.

Some people have failed Jesus even in their preparation of a gift or gifts. The failure of a gift results in no power. Some development of a gift results in little or no power. For those who have cross over hills result in some power. The completion of gifts result in a Crown on your head which requires you to move mountains and to duplicate Jesus in healings, miracles, walking on water, raising the dead, freeing the captive, giving sight to the blind, removing curses and the like.

In the year 1991, I began my search in New Jersey to continue visiting the sick. Now living in East Orange, I decided to walk the neighborhood hoping to find that peace that once existed deep within my belly. Well into the second week I came across a house with about fifteen to twenty young people that were sick. I stepped in and had a conversation with the woman in charge. After receiving the green light, I assembled about ten people for prayer. I visited them every Friday about 1 p.m.

We prayed a reading from the Bible and sang a few hymns. Even though the peace that once existed deep down in my belly never returned, I was contented to continue the good work of Our Lord Jesus. Jesus always knows when you are seeking his face. Sometimes, he allows the devil to torment you or to weigh you down with doubts, fears, burdensome thoughts, unwillingness to keep company with the down trodden--Jesus loves you.

Jesus love for us is so divinely intense that he moves us to tears in the wake of a sudden death in the family. What are we really crying for half the time we really do not know? But then in that moment of tearfulness we are asking ourselves is he or she in heaven? A question for the only perfect one who is Jesus to answer. Listening for an answer from Jesus does not come in that time or any other time simply means that your loved one is in heaven. How do I know this? You were on the job working for Jesus. You paid the price for your loved one to go to heaven.

During this time, I firmly believed that I had the Holy Spirit. But the truth is I did not. It took me seven more years to fully understand this wondrous phenomenon. It is an awesome thing, when you have received the Holy Spirit. Jesus takes you back for one reason and one reason only to show you that he is with you always. God the Father, God the Son, and God the Holy Spirit will be with you every step of the way. This is the role of Jesus as comforter.

Jesus is showing me all of Central Asia. Jesus is showing me all of North Asia. Jesus is showing me all of Korea. Jesus is showing the love of Jesus is very small in these highly concentrated Buddhist territories. A billion people who have never experienced the love of Jesus in their hearts. Even though there are a few Christian Churches in these lands, the people are afraid for their lives.

Jesus is the Bread of Life. Satan loves to put people in strongholds. These are places of evil worshippers, where the dragon is dressed up in a red suit at a gala performance. These celebrations draw hundreds of thousands of people at various sites in and around the cities. The dragon is the satanic goddess of the Buddhist religion. The question is not hypothetical. Hell is real.

Jesus is continually raising up men and women of God to go out into the world to preach the Word in season and out of season. Of course, the Holy Spirit has to anoint his Sons of God for this mighty great work. These gifts have to be developed in the bodies of the Sons of God. Jesus pays careful attention to every fibre in the body. The process involves some heat before the fire is applied.

When the Holy Spirit begins to speak to you in very clear concise words, this means that he is equipping you for the future to undertake a mighty work that is not readily revealed to you at this present time. Jesus keeps you focus. The rain is falling; you are soaking wet; it is past midnight but you are walking for miles whilst still talking to your blessed Savior.

It is all futile to think that Jesus is not doing anything after reading the daily newspapers. The jail houses are overcrowded yet crime has not dropped in major cities. The rate of murders have stepped up tremendously, as statistics show more deaths in black neighborhoods. And yes, there is racial profiling. What people fail to realize is that God the Father already knew of this happening. Jesus had already told you about these imprints on the walls of Daniel.

This is not shocking to the three in one. What is surprising is that social media knows no end. Christian folks who have no faith will go into a panic, because of constant playing of the news both on the radio *vis-a-vis* television. Jesus is not moved by a sudden unreasonable fear. Jesus depicts calmness in the midst of panic. Jesus controls his emotions in the middle of highway I 95N. Jesus is allowing the abstract painting of the world to come alive in these times so turbulent.

There is no such thing as an unsolved murder. When a crime is committed, the Triune God together with the devil bear witness to the murder/s. Jesus is showing me large sums of money crossing tables as in a circle with men posted at the entrance of the building. Cars chauffeur-driven come to the entrance one by one to pick up their man of business. Beautiful sophisticated women sit in the lobby discussing things of paramount importance.

Cameras are in surveillance of the building as large sums of money are handed out to various people. Jesus equips his Sons of Obedience with the wherewithal. Jesus leaves no stone unturned. Patience is not just a virtue, it is a uniquely divine gift that Jesus administers to his Sons, who he will keep on the face of the earth until all is done. It is to show the human race that Jesus cares.

Jesus is rolled into gold. Jesus is rolled into frankincense. Jesus is rolled into myrrh. This is to depict the life, death and resurrection of Jesus. Jesus preparation of gifts had just begun. Jesus at 14 years old left his stepfather's house to go do his heavenly father's will. Jesus's gifts took 14 years to be prepared. Though fully developed in wisdom at 12 years old brainstorming the scholars at the park. I am the Bread of Life says Jesus. For those of you that chooses me over the devil would not hunger or grow hungry again. This also means that Jesus has to come into your belly for you not to go hungry again.

How many times must Jesus say the same thing over and over again. God the Father, God the Son, and God the Holy Spirit has gifted you not the devil. Jesus has to teach you what he has put inside of you. Jesus has to prepare each person for the future. It is not a popularity contest. It is not a fact. It is in the absolute. We keep begging for bread in the form of nakedness. When the church is full of the power of God there is no nakedness.

Is there nudity in the house of the Lord? Yes there is. No gifts. Dead churches. Dead Pastors. Dead preachers. Dead ministries. When Jesus tells you to go do something and you stop in your tracks to try to figure out what Jesus just told you. The devil had already taken your clothing away from you. Then you start questioning the voice. When you should have gone to do what was told to you to go do.

Is there clarity in the house of the Lord? No there is not. There is doubt and confusion in the house of the Lord. The Old Testament is kicked out of the house of the Lord. Or there are some books that are still questionable. When you did not eat the scroll then Jesus cannot spread the Word out from your belly. When you have never fasted for one day in your Christian life, then Jesus cannot feed you for the rest of your life.

We all need to eat from the loving hands of Jesus. We all need to drink from his Holy Spirit. No weapons form against us shall prosper. This is said everyday of our lives, but yet we are in the same position as our yesterdays. We know the Word, the devil also. We walk the streets everyday dreaming as we go along. Where are the fruits of these dreams?

We go to bed every night dreaming dreams of our tomorrows. We take the lights out at night hoping that there would be a new day. We must know in the absolute that there will be a new day. Jesus says that when you love your neighbor as yourself there will be no need to take the lights out at night. For there is no darkness in heaven. There is no light to turn on in heaven. Hell will be your place of utter darkness.

Jesus is your only key-hole to heaven. The whippings from your neighbors as you leave your homes for church are worth more than a thousand tracts given out by any Christian on the sidewalk. Jesus is about sharing his love on a daily basis by a pleasant smile, a kind word, a firm handshake, a how do you do, a word of encouragement--Jesus loves you.

Jesus is about a warm embrace. A simple hug to someone goes a long way. The tension or stress of the day goes away. Worrisomeness is a mocker that leaves and goes the other way. Joy steps in to fill the warm embrace. Pleasant words are exchanged. Good memories are recalled. Jesus fills you up to turn your day into a wonderful day. Jesus keeps showing his love. Are you there to receive his love? Or are you engaging in foolishness?

The body of Jesus is gifted that every turn that the Lord made whilst on the earth resulted in the healings of the congregation. Every look in any direction resulted in a deliverance. Every smile resonated in the stirring up of the fruit of the spirit of joy in someone's body. Every gesticulation was a very strong warning or a word of encouragement to persevere on the path of righteousness. Every walking stick left behind was taken out and burnt. All crutches were taken outside and burnt by the apostles.

Testimonies were given on spot. This outward expression encouraged by Jesus helped strengthen the disbelievers. The working of miracles swollen the crowds everyday as

Jesus preached the Word daily. Jesus is saying that we have not seen anything yet. Even a few days ago, I was given a vision where I saw snow catapulting and rolling down a hill at a tremendous speed. The sight put me in a state of wonderment. Jesus is saying that it can still be done.

Jesus is real. Jesus expects us to be as real as real can be. We seek mightily to want to hold on to what we want to be over what Jesus wants us to be. We think that we can play with the mind of Jesus. If Jesus asks us to give a hundred dollars to the church, we will first ponder over it, then we will turn and give the church only twenty-five dollars. Like King Saul, we would never speak the truth. We would forever be trying something.

In the year 2002, is when I started to be made aware by Jesus that I have just fasted. The awesomeness of Jesus in keeping you without the knowledge of you keeping yourself. In retrospect, I remembered reading the menu on the glass-pane window: fried chicken with cole-slaw, green leafy vegetables, lima beans and a slice of cake for desert. That morning I had no breakfast without knowing it. Now it is lunch time. Jesus ushered me in the food line to have a meal served for the homeless. As I sat down to eat, Jesus made me eat only the salad and the lima beans, the rest he made me giveaway to my neighbor.

In the eventide, I would not remember to join the food line for dinner. This interpolation continued for several weeks, before the Holy Spirit gave me revelation. During the night Jesus would burst out laughing deep within my belly saying with exceeding joy that I have just fasted. then we both would be laughing. Jesus is full of humor. From time to time, Jesus would remind me that when I had fasted on my own I ate nothing. But now, fasting with him I would eat at least one meal.

Simultaneously, Jesus is showing me children dying by the

1000s in Asia, Africa, the Middle East inclusive of Germany, all because of the atrocities of this world. Gifts that the world would not see. We automatically say to Jesus on a daily basis that we love him. Yet we fail him miserably. We need Jesus to create in us a new mind.

The meticulous hands of Jesus roll me in the midnight oil of the morning's dew. My sleeping time would be just one hour. These careful hands that pay special attention to small details are using all the elements in the early mornings of each day to perfect the gifts that are inherent in my being. Mind you Jesus uses metropolitan cities to blend you among the colors of that city.

The dampness of Washington City in Seattle was used to enlarge my visions. In this way I can see angels descending and ascending. I can see satan split between two mountains. As usual steering at me through one eye. I can see satan entering graves to eat the flesh of dead bodies. I can see the moon touching the earth. I can see satan dancing with his mistress in the eclipse of the moon.

The scorching of the heat by walking through suburbs of rich towns was for the anointing of my face of suffrage. It is good to behold Jesus face to face. You are blest when you can see him at work. It is debonair to see Jesus playing with his seraphim and his teraphim.

Jesus is literally showing me the wide open spaces in downtown Dallas, Texas. These wide gaps of so-called architectural creativity are not from the hands of Jesus, who gave no input in the building of the city of Dallas. Yes there are Christian churches in and around the city of Dallas. But the Jesus who took me there was not pleased with the tone of the city.

There should never be a homeless person in such a wealthy given city. There should never be a hand out begging for bread in such a luxurious city given to the people. There should never be a homeless shelter in that precocious city given to this august body of the city. A city booming is a city blest. A city well lighted up is one given by Jesus to his illustrious people.

The mere fact that you know, that you know, that you know that Jesus has poured out a blessing on your land is enough for you to shout out at the top of your lungs that he is alive. Yes he is. The city of Dallas was used by Jesus to open up my already two big eyes. The walk of a prophet is a dangerous but slippery ascension to the mountain top. The messages you receive from Jesus can be good or bad. Joy dwells in you when you deliver the message.

The workings of Jesus are enormously beautiful in diverse cities. Jesus loves to spread himself out like an open flower collecting snow-flakes in the springtime. It is wild imagination to assume that Jesus will consistently be seen standing at your side, when you hear from him as a breeze whistling in the wind. It is selfish to believe that Jesus should love you more than anyone else in the entire world just because you go do his will. It is a wonderful thing to say to someone that Jesus loves you when that someone has lost his limbs in wartime.

Some of us have had the pleasure of knowing someone whom Jesus did transformed into a new creature. Yet we stand trembling in front of Jesus. Old cities have been transformed into new cities. Still we allow anxiety to step in. What is all this fear about? Can we please sit down in the name of Jesus? We need to relax.

Jesus has to come in to prepare our gifts for the people that is to come our way. Jesus shall steer us in the right direction. Jesus shall teach us how to show mercy. Compassion is needed in the church. it is a gift that is lacking among preachers. There is a line in the Lord's Prayer that culminates the true meaning of compassion. On the cross Jesus says Father forgive them for they know not what they do.

It is about time that we free ourselves from becoming slaves to gambling. There is no one on the face of the earth who is gifted in gambling. It is a disease of the mind. We love to show each other that we are better than one another. That is why we are shaped in iniquity. Jesus is about molding us into the gift or gifts that he has put in our bellies. Jesus is the only one that can forgive sins because he died for us. There is no excuse when we have become prolific gamblers.

When we have become the gift in us, now we can ably provide for our families. Then we can truthfully say that, "Jesus gave this gift to us." The world hides their gifts in Satanic Cults. The world hides their gifts in grave yards. The world hides their gifts in sphinxes. The world hides their gifts in craftiness. The world hides their gifts in wizardry. The world hides their gifts in magic. The world hides their gifts in sorcery. The world hides their gifts in the drinking of the blood of animals.

Jesus is constantly speaking to you through situations that you would fall into, as you climb the steep mountain. Always remembering, that one accomplishment leads to another gift to be opened up. These are the bedtime stories that Jesus wants you to tell your grandchildren. These stories are guaranteed to make them wise. There is no substitute for experience. There is no substitute for a teacher, who has come face to face with the cross.

We tend to give Satan the benefit rather than ourselves. Sometimes, we take too long to make an avert decision. We allow the enemy to get to the door before we can count one two three. Jesus is the Lords of Lords. We cannot see this happening in our lives, unless Jesus can prove it to us. There are many things that Jesus have to prove to us, but not very many things.

The preparations of gifts also will include all ministries. These ministries which are given to preachers, some of whom would become Pastors of great churches. This continuous work in progress, which constitutes transformations, would ultimately become a great movement for the Body of Christ.

The ministry of speaking in tongues is not completed unless you have the gift of the interpretation of the language that you are speaking. Many Pastors that are gifted in speaking in tongues should seek Jesus for the gift of interpretation. This will obviously help the congregation to rightly understand what Jesus is saying through the Pastor or preacher. This gift is extremely lacking in the House of the Lord.

Jesus, the creator of all languages on the earth, is presently raising up preachers in luxuriant places for the sole purpose of reassuring all men that all that glitters are not gold. Jesus is rolled into gold, heavenly gold. Jesus walk on the face of the earth took him to places of many different languages. His walk as a missionary took him world over. Spreading the good news took a lot out of him.

The bowels of mercy are a gift seldom seen anywhere. Christians are taught by Jesus to show compassion everywhere they go. Jesus is saying that in these unequal times, patience in sharing becomes a virtue. It takes time to climb the ladder of success. It takes time to milk the cow by hand. Jesus hands could be your hands, if only you would listen to his every word.

The running of feet by people in the darkest hour of the night, say that all is not well. Where is everybody? Sleeping. No. They are very much afraid. It takes boldness to stand up for Jesus. It is a gift that Jesus will love to give, if only you would repent in earnest. To say, I am sorry, does not mean anything to Jesus. To say excuse me please, does not mean anything to Jesus. Christians have gotten so accustomed to telling lies, that their hearts have been driven some million miles away from the love of Jesus.

There was a time in history, when the whole human race wanted to have a conversation with God. So they decided to build a staircase to heaven. Then Jesus came out of heaven and made them speak in different languages, which halted the job. Now the astronauts are building space ships to get to heaven. Jesus is saying that enough proof by his Sons of God are shown in Christian churches by the breaking of the Bread.

Needless to say, that many human beings are still struggling with the Lamb of God, who takes away the sins of the world. These human beings acquire the steps up the mountain top by worshipping satan, the devil. These acquisitions come in the form of acronyms, which they name companies, corporations, institutions of like ilk. This body of Satanic worshippers are spread throughout the globe, thus monopolizing in the production of steel.

The occults of the planet use the gifts of Jesus to mar his incense by mixing it up with dead fetuses. The vendors of all types of incense are well aware of the evil industry, but as usual nobody cares about the unborn. Jesus is looking at the calendar while scrutinizing the months. It is amazing what Jesus pulls up, as he goes along his route of developing gifts in human beings.

Some has strayed away because Jesus would not listen to their whole story. Jesus is not about your pain. Jesus is about saving little ones that nobody cares about. There are some parents who really, really, really, really, really, really, do not care about their little ones especially, when they are not gifted with a great gift. There will always be a competition at the house to see who is the brightest star. The others will be swept aside; only God knows what will become of them.

Simultaneously, blame goes out to the handicap children.

They must have done God something wrong to be born like that. Astonishingly, Jesus is not surprised. Jesus has read their imprint, as they climb the stairs of the ice-torn mountains. Jesus is not equally perplexed, by the manner in which fathers treat their daughters in the house, in the absence of their mothers. It is shameful to the neighbors when word get out.

Jesus is making it plain, because nobody gets away from the cat-o-nine tail that Jesus walks with from time to time. They will all feel the birch of fire burning on their backs, when they do not quit after a sound warning. Jesus is not relenting from this warning. The world has already been shipwrecked by going the wrong way, not once, but twice. Jesus is allowing the little children to know that he sees all things.

Jesus is writing a letter to a whole world which will begin with the word In. The rest of the letter will be written by the people whose handwriting resemble the handwriting of Jesus. The number of words will depend on their patience in their walk with Jesus.

The whole wide world is expecting the return of Jesus. Pointedly, Jesus wants the world to know that his coming will not be etched in stone, but rather, it will be written in the stars up above. The raven will not be coming to alert anyone to board the flight of Jesus to heaven. Jesus is waiting patiently for us to hold on to his every word. Jesus is forging a word deep down into our hearts for future generations to come.

Promises kept will represent a mile stone in your children, children's lives. In today's world nobody cares about keeping promises anymore. Couples getting engage to be married have become a laughing stock. Nobody cares about Jesus's ministry of marriage anymore.

The world's wantonness has escalated beyond the boundaries of the evil one. Even now, Jesus has not strike back. This is to let us know not to panic. The whirlwind comes to encircle the enemy whilst satan, the devil, tries to figure out the next move by Jesus. The gift of a Prophet is like unto Jesus. The same way that Jesus discerns the devil is the same way prophets can see satan.

The beauty of the gifts that Jesus has put in me, overshadows any architectural or structural or global phenomena that the world considers a wonder of the world. There is a reason why the enemy seemingly stands tall in the eyes of self-will people. There is a reason why existentialism strives in the minds of the unbeliever. The mountain of love that Jesus has in store for his children is not something so difficult to achieve, because it is all in the mind of the followers of Jesus. Just put him first!

There is a reservoir of gifts in Jesus. Just swim upstream and you will reap a harvest. There are times that Jesus will come to you to speak a word of encouragement. But in the same breath, satan will be allowed to stop by almost simultaneously. Then a chill comes over you and you become afraid. Jesus is saying to preachers do not interrupt especially, when you already have seen Jesus.

Jesus is showing me pictures. These are pictures of deceased children, who have lost their lives in shoot-outs all over the country. This means all America. People are asking Jesus to gift them to find these recalcitrant assassins, who have murdered their loved ones, to bring them to justice. Prophets are gifted to heal and uncover everything hidden. Always remember that everyone did not believed that Jesus was more than just a prophet.

I remembered walking the streets at nights, only to find out that I was sleeping in the middle of the highway. In that moment of time, Jesus was rolling me into gold. Why gold? Black is also gold. A color that Jesus wore both day and night. A color that satan, the devil cannot get past. A color that is always ready to deliver someone from the jaws of satan. A color that rules a whole universe. A color that is not transparent. A color that is always ready for spiritual warfare.

When Jesus takes you out for long walks: journeying through tiny towns, small towns, large towns, this is a perfect definition of a gift to help soldiers in the armed forces. Soldiers come home brain damaged. Some of them unfit to work in any environment. Jesus is saying that the walk of a prophet is a quiet moment in heaven, but a disquiet time spent on the face of the earth.

Jesus is repeatedly showing me photographs of the faces of young people. Yes, prophets are even gifted to find missing children. How does the prophet know that he is gifted to find missing children? Just like Jesus, prophets are rolled in frankincense. Reminiscing on the gratitude of a few people, who did listen to the Holy Spirit telling them to give the prophet whatever money that he laid on their hearts which they did, was enough for Jesus to deepen my visions. Only the perfect one can give you perfect vision. Only the perfect one can give you the gift of all the fruits of the spirit, which he did give to me. Only the perfect one can deepen the gift of love the more, after a long walk of longsuffering with him at my side.

In furtherance of this Jesus rolled me into myrrh. Jesus is showing me prisoners who are incarcerated though innocent. This gift is a branch of the same gift of discernment. Prisoners are sent to the electric chair without real proof of a murder or of a series of murders. How did Jesus prepared this gift in me? Sleeping on sidewalks as commanded by the Holy Spirit, when after an hour of sleep, Jesus would wake me up in an instant. Then he would take me through towns walking until breakfast time. Jesus will; can do it all.

Anytime Jesus applies pressure to me or on me, it is a sign that he would not relent no matter what. Jesus living in me makes determinations on anyone, regardless of how cute they look. For the love of Jesus, he prepares a body to go out into the world to do precisely what he wants the prophet to do. The triune God knows what to look for in the distance, as human beings prayed to God for him to direct their paths.

During my childhood, I could not have sung a song by myself in front of anybody other than my immediate family. I could have only sung in a group. But the Lord Jesus started grooming me for the pulpit in my late thirties, when I moved to America in 1988. In 1991, I passed the examination to become a Real Estate agent in the state of New Jersey. This profession allowed me to be more relaxed one on one in closing sales. Jesus misses nothing.

Incense is not to ward off satan, the devil together with his army of evil spirits. Incense is for the lifting up of the souls of the human race when songs of praises go up. But in these end times, Holy Spirit preachers are blessed by Jesus to lift him up in worship, Incense is no longer a requirement for the house of the Lord. Animals are no longer sacrificed for atonement of sinful mankind. Jesus is now our shepherd. Holy Spirit preachers are now given deeper anointing as well as greater gifts to combat satan in these evil times so perilous.

Jesus is bringing about a renaissance on the planet. This precludes Middle Eastern countries and their counterparts. Jesus is showing me copulation. Jesus is opening ministries to be run by young preachers to teach the big why about copulation. The university of Jesus is opening its doors where the membership is free. But after graduation, your hours will be pretty long. Even after sermons, you will be very busy going to the homes of your members to continue another service.

Pastors will be having two or three services of deliverances per week at their local church. Charismatic singers that Jesus is raising up in these times will be accompanying their pastors anywhere they go. Some buildings in close-down cities will be renovated to aide pastors in providing not just for the homeless, but for people who have to overnight.

Jesus is specifically making a statement. Jesus is saying that God proves everything. Jesus told Moses to tell Pharaoh that, I am that I am sent me. This is not a litmus test. This is a reality check. This is Jesus who deals with the absolute. Wearing a crown on your head does not necessarily make you a king. But wearing an anointing crown on your head puts you in heaven as on the earth. Jesus is never in the background throwing stones. Jesus is very visible.

Jesus carries his cross as a wounded soldier carries his fallen buddy on his shoulder. though all bloodied up Jesus still remembers who carried his cross. This gift of remembrance even in the face of death is given to all prayer warriors interceding for fallen pastors.

There are nine fruits of the spirit all interlocking each other in myrrh. If we will only pray for the eyes of Jesus, then we will be gifted to see the glory of Jesus perambulating the earth. Triumphantly we will walk. Triumphantly we will talk. Triumphantly we will be worshipping Jesus in all his splendor.

Jesus is stupendously gifted to bring about change. We often decree that a change is going to come. We have not seen anything yet. This is why the Holy Spirit has to come to well up the gift or gifts in your bellies for you to bear witness to the glory of God. Man cannot live by bread alone, but by every word that resonates from the mouth of Jesus.

The book says for there is none beside thee. Yet doubt still eat our hearts out. The humidity is high but the love of Jesus will keep us cool. The sweetness of Jesus is in his sharing of his body and his blood in the form of Holy Communion. Jesus is saying that too many people have strayed away from his sweetness.

The gift of family is seriously lacking in all fifty states of America. Family means husband, wife and child or children. The children that comes from a prayerful couple or a prayerful family will constantly persevere the road of having and keeping a family. The gift of a home is also the gift of family. Jesus has also gifted me with the gift of a home, which he did tell me in the year 2001.

The gift of tolerance which is one of the keys to building a family is seldom seen even in the workplace. Could we honestly respect each other especially when there is disagreement? As soon as someone says something that the other person does not wish to hear, then a war erupts.

The gift of a missionary is essential in church building. Coming from a Spanish background, I can help propagate Jesus with the Gospel. The world needs missionaries. You can look right; you can look left without paying attention to detail. Jesus who hides deep within, speaks to you to get on with the job at hand. Jesus is looking for a seed of obedience to fertilize its soil.

Jesus holds children dearest to his heart. Especially, those children who have lost their parents in sudden-death situations. These children live deep within themselves. They dwell in a world of utter loneliness. They trust no one. Their rooms are rather messy. Their thoughts are continuously on the last images of their parents, which they hold unto forever. Obtaining these gifts are not easy. Congregations can pray for these gifts.

Children running away from the homes of extended families. Jesus is saying that enough is enough. A referenda do not make it right. The families that go out of their way to rescue children left behind by the death of their parents in places of disasters are dearest to the heart of Jesus. Special attention should be paid to these families, as well as proper documentation should be given to them respectively.

The victory will always be his. As a child I stuttered, but praying for the sick and the shut-in allowed the love of Jesus to fill me with compassion, especially for the patients that I could not confront. Certain diseases at these institutions required the much needed grace of Jesus to strengthen me. All patients need to be prayed for anywhere the love of Jesus takes you.

You constantly ask Jesus for the desires of your heart. Satan hears all that you are asking Jesus for. Satan will come along to steal your prize. Yes, long before you are made aware of it. But the grace of Jesus which is his anointing saves you from losing the prize. Jesus takes his sweet time to nurture you. His anointing is given in small or rather tiny doses. His fire can put you to sleep.

There is a gift to know when the good Lord is calling you home. For Jesus promises long life to his faithful servants. Undoubtedly, these are the ones who would know beyond a shadow of a doubt, when Jesus is calling them home. These servants of the Lord would begin preparation for burial. These are your interceders as Jesus intercedes for us. These would not stop praying until Jesus comes to them with a gift of a promise to them.

Jesus gives abundantly to his sheep in green pastures. His sheep knows his name. His sheep will be fighting the good fight. His sheep will waver not. His sheep is up with him all night long. Through the mercies of the grave Jesus is praying for the ones that the world kicked out on the streets in their nakedness.

The timing of Jesus in his preparation is truly mysterious. His ways of sending people to you to undertake certain offices or rather ministries in the church is ingeniously gentle. Someone would come to you to ask you to join a ministry. Then Jesus allows this word to take root deep down into your soul. In this ministry that Jesus has selected for you is to develop your soul for combating the enemy. It is the smoke before the fire.

The gift of the Holy Spirit well up in me after a very long ordeal with satan. This cemented my call to the ministry. It was not too long after Jesus overtook me. In 2010, Jesus told me that he is giving me two fishes from the river Nile. This in essence means my entire journey with him throughout all America bringing hope to the downtrodden. Jesus is saying to a whole wide world that the enemy will do anything to make you believe that Jesus cannot truly live in you.

Jesus is alive. Jesus demonstrates his presence in your intercessory prayers on behalf of others. Just thinking about Jesus is not good enough. The soldiers gambling for the robe of Jesus under the cross, to this day have not stopped anyone from gambling. As a matter of fact, the gambling industry have grown into a billionaire industry. Jesus is saying that the eagles have better sense than Americans. They just stand in awe at the magnificence of an eagle gliding in the wind.

The reality is that Jesus is too much for the human race. No one man can do it all. Jesus is gifted for the absolute while being in the absolute. The family is broken as an old broken record discarded, but yet sitting on the shelf. Jesus loves order. The heavens are put together in order. The heavens are waging a war between satan, the devil, together with his evil cohorts.

Every child that enters a Christian Family becomes a

target for satan to do battle with. Every child that comes out the womb of a preacher's wife becomes a target for satan himself to do battle with one on one. Preparation of gifts become vital.

Satan is chewing out the brains of fetuses, whilst even in the womb. Doctors are petrified. Administrative bodies do not want to call on any preacher, especially one that is gifted. When Jesus walked on this planet, he healed a man born blind. This caused havoc in the society. The king sent out a decree to have Jesus arrested. The sons of satan would have you arrested for propagating the life of Jesus.

The prize is Jesus. The prize for satan is destruction of the family. When there is no head of the household this is destruction of the family. Jesus is all about family. Jesus was born into a family. One given to him from above. When we do not wait on the Lord, we allow the devil to come in to destroy the very fabric of family life. Jesus gave the example a long, long, long time ago.

Nobody supported Jesus. The hierarchy went after Jesus. Jesus is the same today, tomorrow and forever. Jesus preached against their doctrine. Today we do the same. They came after Jesus. They would come after us as well. We must lift Jesus up in order to keep the family strong. We must stand on the Word of God. We must persevere no matter what comes our way. We must give him all the glory.

The golden rule is to do unto others as they would do unto you. It is a rule that is totally misunderstood. Human beings want God to be dressed up in the way that they choose. Any other way causes rivalry. How on earth do you want Jesus to stir up your gifts in your belly? You got to change your attitude. It is all well and good to call yourself a Christian, but are you showing it in your giving to others?

Wearing a jersey saying Jesus loves me does not mean

anything to Jesus. On your face you wear a spirit of guilt everywhere you go. That guilt is a poor representation of Our Lord Jesus. You walk the streets as though you are the prominent one. You stop to get a shoe shine, because it makes you feel so good. You plague the society with tons of records, as though you have become a household name in the community, or have helped the poor of the poorest.

Jesus is reemphasizing family. Sunday mornings the family is not well represented in the house of the Living God. Most Christians are rejuvenating from alcohol. Or suffering from a drug overdose. Or afraid to come out to church because they have already spent their tithes at the gambling tables. Or suffering from a dose of amnesia until Monday morning.

Their excuses are usually all the same, they fall asleep during the service. Or my Pastor is longwinded. All these excuses add up to the same thing: destruction of the very fabric of the society, which is the family. In this case the destruction of the Christian Family.

JESUS IS TEACHING ME HOW TO USE THE GIFTS:

James 1:17 Every good gift and every perfect gift is from above, and cometh down from the Father of lights, with whom is no variableness, neither shadow of turning. In the year 2002, I was living on Pines Road, Valdosta, Georgia. The Lord Jesus woke me up to begin to teach me precisely what he had stirred up in me. Jesus took me door-to-door.

Knocking on doors was not a pleasurable journey. Introducing myself as a Minister of God working for the love of Jesus did not ease the pain of slamming doors in my face. But every once in a while someone would welcome me in to receive a Word from the Lord. The gift of perseverance kept me going.

In the beginning, I would tell a story. I would ask people to name their children, so that their parents would know what their future would be. Then they would ask me questions about a particular situation or for me to answer a burning question that is troubling their heart. Immediately, the gift of wisdom would go into effect, but the answer that I gave would not be well-received. Surely, they would ask me more questions.

The Holy Spirit would vociferously allow me to answer their questions. But more importantly, the Holy Spirit would make me stand on every answer that I gave. This made some people really uncomfortable. It is amazing how the truth circumvents the soul. It is astounding the more to see the power of Jesus come alive. Jesus is all about his father's business.

Intrinsically, God the Father, God the Son, and God the Holy Spirit is one and the same God. A mystery which some scholars interpret as a form of reincarnation. God's Word is the same today, tomorrow, next week, next thousand years, forever and into a new Heaven and a new Earth. These are two things that scholars cannot stand on. Scholars are always iffy about truth.

Jesus is the truth. The wisdom of God poured into me, as I went door knocking. Ironically, it was a time when the World Trade Center came under attack. Some Christian folk viewed me as a spy. I would sit and talk with people for hours at a time. I would take them back to their childhood to show them when the evil began in their lives. Pin pointing things by using graphic illustrations.

Jesus is taking me through the souls of the people, which he allowed me to speak to at a time of total security, amidst a Middle Eastern War. Some people would call their neighbors over to the house to hear a Word from the Lord. Jesus will faithfully astound his children through the wisdom of God. He strapped me down in a seat of blindness, and took me wherever he may go.

He will physically take me across a highway without looking left or right to tell somebody something. Jesus is nothing to be played with. One day I am sitting on a bench at a nearby park, when I heard the voice of Jesus saying power, within that instance power was given to me.

The next day, I entered a house with a woman, who had a damaged right arm that she could not use. Immediately, I raised the arm to the heavens and she was healed instantly. Jesus always preempts me. Jesus is always around me whether I see him or not.

One night just around midnight early one Saturday morning, Jesus started a conversation with me. And of course, Jesus is doing all the talking deep within me whilst I am doing all the listening. Seemingly but jokingly Jesus said to me to pull the curtain back. It was already morning with the sun shining through. Did I felt the time going? No, I did not.

Simultaneously, Jesus started to let me know that he has anointed me a prophet. It did not come as a surprise to me, because my first pastor was a preacher/prophet also taught by Jesus. Jesus is showing me the alphabet. Individual letters that took tons of time to reproduce. Today we take this for granted. Conjecturing, conjecturing, conjecturing is not Jesus. Jesus does not have to stop to think.

The entrance to heaven is not so far away. We have become like Moses. Our disobedience to God have failed us in not finding the entrance to heaven. No man, who has stood up to God to tell him like it is could ever find the entrance to heaven.

The letters of the alphabet were given to the entire world by Jesus a long, long time ago. Make no mistake about it! Jesus on the other hand, is slowing down the production of weaponry in the East Pacific Region of the world. There is a mastermind operation deep in the heart of Belgium. Whose connections are variables from at least twenty countries of the world. Their mission is to control the steel industry.

Missions do fail. But hanging out with Jesus is life eternal. At night, Jesus and I would walk for at least ten miles to the Valdosta State University. It was very relaxing. The topography in some areas reminded me of Philadelphia. Few students were seen in and out and around the campus. The atmosphere was one of calmness. On my return to my room, I was lost in the loving embrace of the arms of Jesus.

The Lord Jesus has a profound and genuine way of putting you to sleep, even when you are aware that he is putting you to sleep. It is all perfect timing. Jesus keeps you focus on the things he wants you to bear in mind. So profoundly focus are you, that the rain is falling all over you and you are not disturb by the falling rain, or the fact that it is falling on you.

The Almighty Jesus does not need any help. Jesus is allowing me, as well as you to obtain a blessing in spreading the good news. Your mission is to speak the truth wherever you go. Walking down the streets one day on the sidewalks of Pines Road, I ran into a young lady who said to me that, "Jesus has blessed me with wisdom." I greeted her in the affirmative. Smilingly, I shook my head together with Jesus for she was pretty young.

After many days of barren knocking, I encountered a preacher, whose left leg was bandaged in leather. Jesus told me exactly what to do which I did. After praying the Lord's Prayer and holding his body close to mine, in that instant, he told me that, "something had happened to him." A few weeks later, I ran into the preacher who was smiling as I drew near, only to find out that there was no leather wrapping on his left leg and that he was healed. When praises go up blessings come down, thank you Jesus.

Jesus has never stopped being about his father's business. Jesus is about sharing his love if only you would come and listen. All it takes is a single moment of your single time. Jesus truly takes his sweet time to teach you anything. Jesus is in no hurry to prove himself to anyone. The life and times of Jesus is in your heart, as you go along a lonely road to spread his message.

Crossing the railroad tracks be it day or night are dangerous, for there are no signs or blinking red lights flashing in the distance to warn you of an incoming train. This reminds me of the ill responses that I received from Christians, whose doors I knocked, as I climbed their doorsteps to let them know that Jesus is near.

My treatment in the city of Valdosta had a bizarre ending. I remembered leaving my motel-type room early that day, when the police car mounted the sidewalk. A black officer shouted at me saying that, " the telephone at the precinct is ringing off the hook, and that I must now stop door knocking, now." Immediately, Jesus told me to stop. A few days later, I was on greyhound heading for another state to continue the work of the Lord.

Jesus is showing me not just the face of the city of Valdosta. But the face of the establishment, who heads the very city in keeping out the whole truth and nothing but the truth, even in the courtrooms and Halls of Justice. The vitality of a city is in the womb of Jesus. The aspirations of a city are in the womb of Jesus. The clandestine operations of a city are in the womb of Jesus.

Wherever you go there is a mirror on the wall. That mirror is Jesus. However you tilt that mirror to see what you want to see. That mirror is Jesus. God is everywhere; so is Jesus.

In April, 2001, I was homeless in the city of Brunswick. I met a woman of God who was suffering with her womb. She was forty years old and lived with her son who was at that time 14 years old. This woman of God had to wear pampers. I told her in her living room that Jesus is telling me to tell you to eat cucumbers daily. She immediately went to the supermarket to buy a few cucumbers.

Well into the second week, I paid her a visit at her apartment, where she greeted me with the good news that she no longer have to wear any more pampers. This was the first time, that I have ever borne witness to a healing of this nature. But it was not the first time, that I have told someone to eat something for their condition. Jesus is laughing profusely. Jesus is saying that it is about time that we get it together.

Not too long after this, I stopped a young man in his mid-thirties telling him that Jesus is calling him to preach the Word. He laughed at me. Then the Holy Spirit took me in flight. I told him that, he had come from a long line of ministers to which he did not want to confirm. He abruptly ended the conversation by saying that, '' he is not accepting the call to the ministry.'' Jesus is not saddened by his non-committal attitude. Jesus is very happy. When convicted, the young preacher would lose blessings going back to the fourth generation.

There is a milestone in every person's life. There is always someone that would come along to deliver a Word from Jesus to you, which would become your milestone. Prosperity in Jesus requires the eating of the scroll. It is continuously portrayed in movies that Jesus wore white. Jesus wore black. The world is afraid of itself. What is Jesus really saying? When you die and Jesus comes to you black in black, what will you do?

Jesus is not in the compromising business. Jesus is not about wild concessions. Jesus is awakening the world with a resounding voice. Walking down the streets one day, I ran into a beautiful woman who was well into her eighties. She took a glance at me; for a moment she paused in silence and smiled. She wanted to know who I was. I told her that I am a minister. She looked at me puzzle. Her question was, ''if I believe in people seeing the dead?'' My answer to her went like this: please do not allow your very own children to doubt for a moment that you do see the dead walking the streets. Immediately, she became happy. This is Jesus.

The Holy Spirit cannot go the way you want him to go whenever you feel like it. The Holy Spirit cannot be pushed aside whenever you feel like it. The Holy Spirit cannot be surmised. We cannot closet Jesus. We have to let Jesus have his total way. It cannot be fragmented. We have been living in a wishy-washy world for too long.

The sparrows speak out to us early in the mornings. The problem is that we do not understand the language. Spring time comes; spring time goes, but yet we do not see the change. Jesus is the change. The gifts of Jesus is nothing to be played with. Once given then Jesus opens up a road for you to travel. It is not how long the road is. Could you stay the course a little longer?

I remembered a story told to me by my Bishop in 1998 as a novice. He told me about a happening a long time ago. He said to me, " that he was coming from a church meeting one night and passing by the cemetery, he encountered a spirit man. The deceased man was tall and came alongside him, whilst he made his way to his home. The Bishop was gifted to see spirits, so he was not afraid of the man that came alongside him, that night. As he came up the staircase and knocked on his door, he told the spirit man that it is time for him to go now. His aunt opened the door, so he told her the story.

Her reply was that, "the man was your uncle." There is a reason why the Lord Jesus has reiterated this story back to me after all these years. The problem with the society is that they do not want to identify themselves with the real crucified Jesus. They prefer the movie's interpretation of Jesus. The portrayal of Jesus by an actor does not give credence to the charismatic Jesus. Jesus is Holy. They filled the story with a whole lot of drama to play on your emotions.

Jesus is not about playing with your emotions. Jesus loves you. Jesus wants to reassure you, that he will not abandon you, not even for a moment. This also means that you cannot allow anyone to make you abandon Jesus. For the sweet smile of Jesus surrounds you with lots of kisses.

You the runaways. You the one about to commit suicide. You the one that believes, that the wrong that you just did, that Jesus will never forgive you that wrong. You the one in jail that nobody cares about. You that sit in bed with a terminal illness that the doctor say, "that there is no cure." You the man facing the hangman's rope, or the electric chair, or the gun pointed at your head. Jesus died for you.

The people that go through a whole lot of hell on the face of the earth are gifted with a mighty gift. Hence, the reason why satan and his cohorts came after you. When people see angels descending and ascending they too have to watch out for jealousy in their family. Even on the pulpit there is jealously amongst brothers. Sisters who are anointed in song have to be fearful from jealousy in the family.

Sometimes, I am walking in the hot, sweltering heat, then Jesus would begin to harass me saying that I have been telling someone to pick you up, but the fear of not knowing you defeats the purpose. Preachers must undoubtedly show obedience to the Holy Spirit, before they could demand attention from their own congregations. Jesus knows that a preacher's walk is not an easy walk. Satan is always after him. The congregation would always come after him, especially when he stands alone.

It is not a cake walk. It is a faith walk. Jesus has given us three mountain peaks: faith, hope and charity. We are still stuck in our faith walk. Can we love Jesus the same way that we will love our own mothers, who have brought us into this world? And equally, can we love Jesus the same way that we will love our own fathers, who have brought us into this world? The mountain of faith is not a mountainous mountain. It is only a mountain with sharp curves. Just take a look at an eagle in flight, and he will teach you, how to get around the sharp curves of a mountain.

Jesus says that when you see me you have seen the father. Many of us who have seen Jesus in his Holy Spirit have also seen the father. Our biggest misstep is that we do not take God at his every Word. Second to that, is that we do not allow Jesus to finish the sentence. Jesus is our everyday meal that we eat whenever we sit to break bread. Jesus is our daily consumption. Not our amusement park consumption.

Jesus looks for a vessel from on high, and like the eagle follows him wherever he may go to see all of what he is doing on his own free will. It is like one sunny gorgeous day; you are walking briskly in the park. In the distance you see a child playing in the wind with great enthusiasm. The sight of this child fascinated you; for some reason you have to go to see precisely what is so alarming. As you drew near, you realized that the child is doing his endeavor best to catch the wind that is blowing all around him.

You asked yourself a question. Why is he trying to catch the wind? Jesus is not about you trying to catch the wind, or you trying to chase the wind. Jesus wants that great enthusiasm that you possess to use it mightily. Jesus wants to use your soul in you. For some people, it is extremely difficult to hand over their soul in them, and to give it all to Jesus. The Holy Spirit knows you better than anyone else. Can you walk with him?

Jesus is not ordinary. Even though Jesus had to pay income tax as everybody else, this does not make him as fragile as us. The corridors of the university are filled with slime. Jesus is not happy with the teachings of its university. This university is a cathedral. Jesus is saying that his church must be swept clean long before his coming. The angel of death will be coming through to take out anyone that is not about his father's business. No more foolishness, no more, no more!

It is time to give up the practice of mortification. The beating of the body with whips to cure your shape of iniquity is grossly horrendous. Jesus is showing me his whippings on his back. Jesus paid the price for each and every human being born and unborn, when he was imprisoned for the sins of humankind. Jesus paid the price on the cross for all of us to get to heaven, so that no man could boast. We do not need to be filled with obsessions of illusions.

Jesus is already showing me, that refusal to conform to the way of the cross will be a very sad day for everyone's homecoming. Jesus is looking at them biting their nails in submission to satan's request. Everybody is hooked in their own beliefs in God to serve him in their daily prayers, whilst stuck with their monotheistic belief in God.

Jesus of Nazareth King of the Jews is his name. A name given only to his mother Mary. God does not make mistakes. Only human beings are found in error. For answering the call, Jesus takes you out into the wilderness or desert to teach you the gift of true identification. I remembered Jesus telling me no school for me. Of course in obedience I did whatever he told me to do. Surely, I got into good trouble by listening to his every Word. Jokingly, Jesus and I would have a hearty laugh.

A gift of discernment was given to me. A gift given to Prophets. Who do you say that I am? Jesus too is a Prophet. In the year 1999, Jesus gifted me in prophecy. One who delivers divine messages wherever one may go. From time to time Jesus would allow me to tell somebody something. One day sitting on a bench, I met this nice lady so the Lord was pushing me to tell her that he is going to bless her with a brand new house. Immediately, she became real excited and wanted to know more.

Jesus is saying that there are some people which will take this to mean that, why pry into my affairs? Or who do you think you are? This is the difference between the people of God, who possess the Holy Spirit, to those that do not have the Holy Spirit. Jesus is even adding much more to what is given. A people who is divided by politics in the house of the Lord, will not appreciate Jesus non-changing ways. Some of us love to be called "Christians" and believed that this would ultimately take us to heaven.

Can a rotten nose take you to heaven? No. Then why do you poke your nose into everybody's business. You claim that Jesus is your Lord and Savior. Then why are you embittered over someone's success? Your neighbor next door, you have not spoken to for years. Please tell me, how do you want to get to heaven? Your friend stop you on your way to work to ask you to lend him a $100. Your reply was a big lie. Please tell me, how do you want to get to heaven?

Jesus is showing me laughter, laughter, laughter, laughter, laughter. This is what they did to Jesus on his way to Mt. Calvary. The Jews denied him. The few Gentiles wept for him. The truth is the truth and there is nothing greater than the truth. The evil one is dwelling inside of you, but you keep on lying to yourself. You keep on believing that somebody did you something. When you have resigned to your old self.

The laughter of Jesus continues to this very day. The world did not end up in chaos. This had been prophesied some three thousand years ago. What people do not want to see is true prophecy. They believe what they want to believe until they come face to face with reality. They try to speak wisdom, but they cannot. Wisdom is a gift from God.

A walk with Jesus is a walk with fame, and a walk with

fame is a walk with his father. Jesus is walking to the mall to see what you are planning to wear over the weekend. We live in a world that we think is our own. No. This world, this whole wide world belongs to Jesus. Be careful what you do! Jesus is coming.

I am shopping at the supermarket, and I inadvertently stopped to speak to a woman. Jesus is using my tongue to say to her that she will be getting a brand new car. A few weeks later, she is showing me the brand new Mercedes Benz. You see Jesus does not make any mistakes. I did not gift myself. Jesus gifted me. One day I was shopping at a nearby mall when I heard someone said, "Prophet". I turned around and the child looked at me telling me, "that I am blessed with wisdom."

Sunday morning you were at the church looking at your neighbor with a naughty eye. Did you see Jesus looking at you? Or did your Pastor stopped by to tell you anything? Whether he did so or not, Jesus saw you first. Please do not take Jesus for granted! The stars and the moon comes up every night. We tend to forget how beautiful it is to go stargazing. The world is passing us by slowly, but surely. We keep allowing the devil to steal our joy. We worry about everything.

At the church, my job is to deliver anyone that is harboring a demonic spirit. Either satan or any member of his army. Sometimes, I am taken aback when someone comes to the church for the first time to use the gift of Jesus. Soon after the deliverance, the person never showed up at another service. Jesus remembers. The same thing they did to Jesus, is the same thing they would do to all preachers, prophets, and prophetesses as well. Jesus is watching.

At another service, a member of the church came forward with an impediment in his intestines. After the deliverance, he came into some money, but sad to say, he never gave the church his ten per cent. I remembered delivering the Word, when I confronted a woman who had harbored forgiveness for some forty years. It was someone that I knew for eight years. Her husband was one of the deacons at the church.

The question of forgiveness is something that I have preached on at the very same church. God has mandated me to come out of the Book of Revelation. This has caused me to stumble in many churches. Who are you to speak out from this book? The anointing of Jesus opens up doors in areas that I am not looking at or rather paying close attention to his workings. Yes, Jesus talks to me. But that too is also a suffering.

Jesus keeps me focus all day long. Forgiveness is not an easy subject. Because the real subject is forgetfulness. Jesus said on the cross Father forgive them for they know not what they do. Jesus is also the father. So how could the father forgive the whole wide world when they have also crucified him too on the cross. Jesus gave up the Ghost. Which is also the father. It is an embodiment of the Truth. Truth forgives; Truth forgets.

We all need Jesus to dwell in our bellies in order to forget the wrong that others have done to us in our lifetime. Crime is committed every second of the day in someone's home. It begins with the immediate family as it did with Cain and Abel. The prophet Abel went directly to heaven. A man of God, that was always pleasing to his heavenly father. God can stop anything, but our problem is that we love to question our heavenly father. Jesus is saying too much, too much.

Too much talk on his pulpit. Too much talk in his evangelical schools. Too much talk in his universities' classrooms. Too much talk in preachers' conferences. Jesus is not going around in a circle. Jesus knows that the cure is forgiving others, before they could even think of forgiving you. It is easy for someone to tell a lie on a minister of the Lord. The minister must not show disapproval, when he meets that person anywhere. It is not how tall you walk as a minister. It is who you represent as a minister.

The carnage will be real one day. The rising tide is drawing nigh. The birds of the air will know of the coming of Jesus, even before mankind. Jesus teaches his birds how to fly. Jesus is like a swan in the air, when he comes alongside his birds. His animals, his precious children in his garden of the mountains will know of the coming of Jesus, even before mankind. The fishes of the sea will know of the coming of Jesus, even before mankind.

One Sunday morning before I left the service, my Pastor told me that another Pastor is on her way to the church to see me. The Holy Spirit must not be provoked. As I made my way out of the church, here she came out of her car. Jesus allowed me to embrace her. Immediately, my entire body felt cold. Whatever spirit cohabitated her embraced me also. Precious Jesus moved me into prayer, so that the evil would not enter my body. Smilingly, she thanked me and left.

Jesus is constantly provoked by some preachers because he has allowed some women to become not just preachers but pastors also. Interpretation of the Word of God belongs solely to Jesus. And Jesus does not care who you are. Especially, when you have called yourself, as so many of you have done to propagate the gospel.

Yes Jesus harasses his Sons of the House. If you are not anointed, Jesus will not harass you. His anointing is to let you know that he is with you always. You have to know that Jesus is with you even in the grave. Whereas others may fault you into disbelief that Jesus really and truly have anointed you to go out into the world to preach his Word, Jesus will show up.

Everyone wants to be like Jesus but nobody wants to read their Bible. It is extremely wonderful when Jesus overtakes you in the reading of the Bible. It was six o'clock that evening, when Jesus and I read the Bible until six the next morning. Jesus did me that to show me precisely, who he is in power. All sleep was erased from my eyes all night long.

Jesus is saying that the world is still asleep. It is time to wake up and not slumber. All day long, we sit to think about how the world will end without having a direct conversation with Jesus. Wishful thinking by human beings would not get the job done. Making movies about the end of the world does not mean a thing to Jesus. It goes to show that man will go to any lengths to satisfy his own ego.

Justifiably so, the Prophet Daniel said all of this in his writings. All this was prophesied some two thousand years ago, before the birth of our Lord Jesus. It is written that man cannot live by bread alone. Why the gold rush? Jesus is recording the many sides of the world that man has allowed the entry of the devil. Make no mistake about the timings of Jesus! In retrospect, David killed Goliath.

This is a prime example of Jesus killing satan. No one knows the hour or the time of the actual end. God the Father is the only one that knows. Did God the Father ever spoke to you? Yes he did. At least one time in our lifetime. But Jesus which hath become Holy Spirit speaks to us often. Until we can appreciate the love of God in our hearts, we will not see the face of God the Father. The river runs deep, but the ocean runs deeper.

There are many people, who are mentally disturb owing to the atrocities of life. For this reason and this reason alone, they have become victims in unbelief. Does this mean that Jesus will blame them for things that they cannot comprehend? Jesus is not foolhardy. Jesus knows everyone's heart. Jesus knows everyone's sincerity. Jesus knows everyone's integrity.

Yes, God is everywhere. Sometimes, we allow satan to get to our heads quicker than Jesus can get to our hearts. It is not who we are going to put as our next pastor. It is allowing the entire church body to fast for at least one week. Then Jesus will come in to make a determination. Or at the service, the entire church body prays for a release of the Holy Spirit, who will use the elders to make a determination.

Jesus is about examining our conscious. We must be aware of our own existence and our environment. Keep it clean! We spend too much time faking it to make it rather than cleaning up our surroundings. We as a people are not supportive of each other by helping one another in keeping our districts clean. Jesus is saying that cleanliness is one of the keys to happiness.

I remembered walking the streets of New York City, where the sidewalks were filled with broken crushed bottles. My first impression was an air of violence or gang warfare in the city. Some residents would literally break a bottle on the sidewalk, just to show their arrogance against the establishment. This too is noted in other states like New Jersey, Chicago, parts of San Francisco and so on.

One night I am sitting on a bench in the great city of the melting pot reading my Bible. For some reason, I fell asleep. At three in the morning, the Lord awoke me only to find out that someone placed a dollar in my Bible. Yes, the great city of New York is filled of many surprises owing to the existence of beautiful people which are immigrants. Jesus is very much aware of the biasness of citizens against immigrants.

Their tongue would from time to time put them in trouble. Assuredly, you have been blessed by Jesus to have been borne in America. What are you giving back to Jesus for this great blessing? It is the freest country in all the world. It is a gift from God. It is one of the gifts which human beings take for granted. Love thy neighbor as thyself. We do this sometimes. Jesus wants all Americans to do this: love thy neighbor as thyself every single day of your lives.

The more you give is the more you would receive. This too is taken for granted by all Americans. Building bombers by the tens and twenties would not save America. Giving to the needy; giving to the blind; giving to the deaf; giving to the nations which were robbed by tyrants. We ought to spear head the latter.

The world is overwhelmed by too much poverty. We can no longer sit back and blindfold ourselves in believing that everything is alright. Jesus is recording a play by play documentary. One day Jesus will be playing an entire episode on national television.

Winters in the melting pot are not easy for the homeless. The temperature could be 30 degrees Fahrenheit and two hours later below zero degree. Jesus, who is the almighty, sees everything. There are too many people living in the inner cities of New York with warm basements. It is not too much to ask God the Father, God the Son, and God the Holy Spirit for you to house someone or a family in your basement. The saving of your soul is worth more than your keeping a clean basement.

The job or work of a preacher is to save souls. The whole of the heavens rejoice as one soul is saved. The rich loves to cast aspersions on the impoverished. Jesus loves to meet rich folk. They can always tell you or show you how to become rich. They would never say by whose design. Jesus wants you to pick up your cross and follow him. Jesus does not care about your present situation inclusive of your financial woes. Jesus is your provider.

Jesus loves the kaleidoscope of colors worn by the people of Los Angeles, California. Its impact with the sun surely shows up the beauty and the serenity of his environment. The people of this great city are not just giving of their resources. They are giving of their time and efforts, in areas that some ministers of God, have departed from, a long time ago. It is real and it is true. Jesus did not only bless the people of California. Jesus did bless all Americans at the same time.

Jesus is showing me the state of affairs in all of America. Too much food is thrown away daily. The time is now for stock taking. There are needy countries all over the world. There are hungry bellies in countries that are not friendly but mean to us. Jesus is saying love them anyway. Go with Jesus to these hostile countries without fear of anyone! You say that Jesus is your Lord and Savior. Then go in the name of Jesus.

Some of these countries are experiencing severe droughts. Be kind to your fellowmen! There will be animosity. There will be racial slurs .There will be death threats. Jesus is saying that when the eye of the needle becomes a true reality, the evil one submits.

No one can really face up to the wiles of the devil, except you have been strengthened by Jesus, through his anointing. To clean yourself from past sinfulness, one has to take a deep breath and swallow your pride to begin to run the race as never before. Time waits on no one. Jesus is not timing you.

We take walks at night through lonely streets. We are hoping that nothing will ever happen to us. Jesus is right there waiting for you to acknowledge him by praying a simple prayer. Most times, we miss the moment. Other times we treat it as trivial. Then once we are making money, everything that went wrong matters no more.

We need the light of Jesus shining brightly in our eyes to

keep us fully awake at all times, especially in these mean times. Yes, friends are few. You cannot trust yourself and yourself alone. There must be someone in the whole wide world that you can put your trust in. Find him or her! Now let Jesus in to sew the seed of trust. We often wonder why nothing is coming our way. That is a trust factor.

Trust Jesus! There is no other name under heaven. Jesus is the light of the world. God knows how to make an impact. The Magi which is the three wise kings, who travelled with gifts following as a guide the brilliant light of the star that led them to the baby Jesus. These were three obedient kings that did everything God the Father mandated them to do. They did not play hide and seek with the Word of God.

The same light is the gift of a prophet, which he uses to see satan anywhere or in any place, that he wishes to hide. This discerning spirit is a gift of light. Some of us are born with this light that Jesus uses in our hands to heal someone, which the Lord wishes to touch. Some of us are scolded for having this gift of light by our own parents. And as time passes by the unused gift now turns into a torment in our very own lives.

Is not what you say matters; is what you do! We got to be careful and watch what we say. Not because the children are looking, but the Almighty Jesus is right here. Jesus shows his entry with light; the light is here with us. We have to find the light.

Some of us have lost our homes to satan. We firmly believe that we have lost the battle. In no way under the sun, that someone can come along to change our minds. Jesus is that someone. All you lost was a fight. Now the battle begins. You needed Jesus. The very most loving person in the whole wide world. Even Jesus was mocked, because they knew that Joseph was not his real daddy.

They also knew that God the Father was not his daddy. How can God create a Son through a woman? Even to this day this question is beating up the minds of unbelievers. God the Father, God the Son, and God the Holy Spirit are all one and the same God. It is a mystery of Faith.

Human beings would go to the mall to shop. They shall touch everything that they like or not like. Jesus touches you. Jesus touch does not feel the same way, as when you touch something or someone. A simple touch by Jesus heals you. We personally want Jesus to graphically teach us how this is done so that we can learn from the maestro of all things.

We tend to forget that Jesus is Holy. There was a time, when the angels of heaven visited humankind. Equally, there was a time that Jesus visited his twelve disciples, as well as his close friends after his resurrection. No one could have hugged him. Surely we cannot hug light be it day or night. Even the light created by human hands we to this day cannot hug. Further proof that Jesus is the light.

At night, as I strolled the streets doing the will of the Lord, if the area was covered with darkness, I would have to carefully watch every step I made. For the result would be disastrous. It is like a blind person tapping on the edges of the sidewalk as he passes by. Jesus teaches his form of light in a totally different way to humans.

That particular night, the streets were well lit-up, and I heard my name called. Smilingly, I crossed the street to approach the gentleman, whom I knew staying at the shelter. He said, "prophet, I have a very bad headache." Immediately, the Lord Jesus raised up my hand and placed it on his forehead. He quickly pull back his head saying, "hey prophet that fire was very hot." Praise the Lord, he was healed. Thank you Jesus.

Jesus is lamenting for those persons that have regrets. The

many souls that have gone beyond, without an answer from Jesus, as to where they are? Firstly, they are where you have planted them in the graveyard. Secondly, they are not to be used as mediators. Making intercessions with deceased relatives and friends does damage to your very souls. At the graveside, you lay flowers and you pray.

Lighted candles are not the light that Jesus is. The light of a candle are as false as the representation of satan. Jesus knows that a whole lot of people will not like this. Jesus does not care. Look up in the heavens; tell me what do you see! Real light. If Jesus wanted you to light up your grave, he would have put real heavenly light around your grave.

In God there is order. Jesus is celestial. Our bodies cannot exist in the heavens for we are earthly. Everything that man touches will one day come to an end. Yet the heavenly light will be here forever. Jesus is your heavenly light. He created you for a very special place, which is heaven.

A place where no one has to get up early every morning to turn the lights on. That is why Jesus is taking his sweet time to roll you into him. You got to be beaten into shape. This has nothing to do with your earthly size or figure. Every turn is like a football player doing everything to make a touchdown. Or like a baseball batter making a home run.

We have to produce order for Jesus to come and bless. Without order there is confusion. Too many favorites. Too many people to strikeout. Too many ideas. Too many views without a vertebral column. The brain is as complex as you want to perceive it to be. Yet who made the brain. Jesus. Does Jesus knows that he really and truly made the brain? Yes he does. Does Jesus knows that he really and truly made the heavens and the earth? Yes he does. Does Jesus need help? No he does not.

The light does not need help from anyone to keep it from

diffusing. Because Jesus is the light. The earthly light needs everyone's attention. The light goes out at the house; we need a new bulb. The headlights go out as we are driving at night, we can all get into an accident and die. The lights at the railroad tracks go out, we have a very serious traffic jam. Chaos.

Bewilderment is a serious and unnecessary evil that human beings have created. Once it is funded, nobody cares. Jesus is in control. He has been alive from day one and is still going strong. There is no question that Jesus cannot answer. Jesus wants his children to know that he is who he is eternally. God the Father, God the Son, and God the Holy Spirit sees all things.

Talk shows on national television will one day come to an end. Jesus is saying too much foolishness .The advertisers do not care once they get a return on their investments. Jesus of Nazareth, King of the Jews does care about his children's Bethlehem. The love of Jesus is pouring all over his children to save them from this predicament. Attention must be paid at all times to his precious ones.

You think that it is cute to rub soot on the light bulb, so that it will emit less light. Think again. Jesus is coming. The sky is blue, when the sky is cloudless. The light of the day goes away in the evening time, to prepare for the light of the stars and the moon. There is freedom up above. Few mountain peaks penetrate the clouds. The eagle is the only bird that enjoys the beauty and the freedom of the sky. Where will you like to be? In the sky or on the earth.

Jesus showed up one day when I was talking to my brother preacher, who lived in Baton Rouge, Louisiana. The revelation came that he is diabetic. The Lord Jesus told me to tell him to eat "cabbage" as often as he could. Often times, the Lord Jesus would allow me to call him on my cell phone, to remind him to eat cabbage the more. This continued for quite a few months. Until one day, calling from Shreveport, Louisiana to let him know that Jesus says that he is now healed from diabetes.

The tears rolled down his face as he spoke to me on his cell phone. There he was, as I could see him in the distance of some 300 miles, weeping in the morning sunlight confirming everything. Thank you Jesus .The diabetes had swollen his white feet. And as a country boy, he loved to walk barefooted.

Jesus is truly the light. Jesus works only if you will let go of your disbelief. Jesus is not driving around in a Cadillac without power. Jesus is not driving around in a Lexus without power. Jesus is not driving around in a Mercedes Benz without power. Jesus is not driving around in a Lincoln without power. Jesus wants everyone to call on him right now. Jesus is the only real superpower.

It is sweet of you to weep for the love of Jesus. Please be reminded that Jesus wept too! Jesus wants to permeate your whole body with his light. You have been running for your supervisors far too long. You have been tailgating every car you see that is in front of you for far too long. You have been side stepping Jesus for far too long. Jesus is not in the distance. Jesus is right here standing at your side.

You run the risk of losing Jesus, when you do not fellowship. You shall at all times maintain a friendly relationship, especially with your immediate neighbors. God the Father, God the Son, and God the Holy Spirit is everywhere. You love those sun- roof cars, so that you can stick your head out to stir up trouble. Be reminded that the light of Jesus is seeing you in the distance!

The babies of the children of the light will be seeing seraphim and teraphim worldwide. Miracles will be on the increase before the year 2050. One day a woman in

Shreveport, stopped me to let me know that her mother is diabetic. The Lord Jesus allowed me to say to her, "that your mother should be eating steam onions." She immediately started to laugh and said, " that her mother loves onions and she would be very happy to eat them."

Three weeks later while I was walking down the street, I kept hearing a car horn blowing. My friend was doing everything to get my attention. At the traffic signals, she got my attention. She pulled over in the parking lot to share the good news with me, that her mother is now healed from diabetes. Thank you Jesus. The light of Jesus never stops shining.

The light of Jesus is awesome. Jesus is continuously flowing through his elements up above. His configuration of stars are not up there to adorn the heavens. Jesus is using his stars as God used the star for the direction of his three wise kings. There is nothing old or new under the sun. Jesus houses all the ingredients, for human beings, to stay the course no matter what.

Jesus is teaching the whole world the power of the light, that he has created in the heavens for you to enjoy both day and night. Jesus is teaching all aspects of the power of the light. We tend to fall away from the truth easily. Some things we acknowledge and others we brush aside. Some things we do not want to be told or to be reminded about. Jesus is not about making concessions with the devil on behalf of man. Jesus wants you to know that he loves you with his whole heart.

Jesus, who is teaching me how to use his gifts has not stopped yet. It flows like the River Nile. Practically everyday there is something new. Jesus is showing me his transfiguration. Proof that he wore black. Jesus was transfigured from black to white. The light of God encircled him. Jesus is the glory of God.

Our ultimate goal is to Worship Jesus. Yes we say that we love him. Yes we say that we adore him. Yes we say that we worship him. We just lied to ourselves. These words have become commonplace in our homes. We have failed to realize that word got meaning. We treat word the same way, as when we order our daily breakfast. It is commonplace in the very fabric of our society.

We walk the streets everyday. Greeting our friends as we walk by with the same words. Yes Jesus was good to me this morning. Yes Jesus gave me back every penny that they stole from me. Yes Jesus this; yes Jesus that. Yes this morning, I woke up with a bad feeling believing to myself that this day will be my last day. And for some reason by the Grace of God, I am still alive.

As you are rising in the morning, Jesus comes to you and put his arms around you and he begins to speak to you. After listening attentively, you turn to do precisely what Jesus says to you. This is a testimony that is lacking throughout the house of the Lord. Are you and Jesus having a conversation, whilst you are listening? Humorously he smiles and you smile too. This is worship.

The Pastor does not have to have a choir to sing before he preaches. No, he does not. Jesus had no choir to sing hymns of praise, and worship, before he had delivered the Word in those earthly days. Jesus wants his worship. We need to cut out the running around to tend to the business of the Lord.

We say that we adore him. Do we greatly love him? Then why are we putting gods before him? We pay homage to other peoples" gods. We traveled the world to the shrines of Vishnu, the Hindu goddess. We go visit the Bhudhist monasteries feeding the rats and spirits with milk and rice. Yet we say that we love Jesus greatly. We attend festivities to these gods annually. Who do we think we are?

We go to West Africa to participate in blood-drinking ceremonies. Where they wound the animal to fill a bucket of blood for their worshippers. We believe that this is true worship. We attend the home of a medium for him to do a job for you to be successful. You bear witness to him drinking blood before he tells you anything. Yet we still maintain that we greatly love Jesus.

Jesus does not need any of these witchcraft ceremonies to enter or bear fruit in the house of the Lord. We give honor to mounted rings worn on the fingers of some ministers. We do this by kissing the rings of priests and kings during their ceremonies. Jesus was never wedded, so he had no need of a ring. Jesus wore no gold earrings rings, chains or bracelets on his body. It is a sign for us to know that he is rolled in gold.

We have parties in honor of Jesus. Why must alcohol be served? Then we wonder why our children becomes addicts. We could believe as much as we want to believe that Jesus drank wine, alcoholic wine. These misconceptions are prime examples of an intoxicated world. Everything is alright. Go have a drink! My son just graduated with a degree. Go have a drink! My daughter just won a gold medal at the World Games. Go have a drink! My son just gave birth to our first grandson. Go have a drink!

It is a pity when we have to use Jesus as a scapegoat. You could end up in hell by not watching your mouth. When we use or abuse the name of Jesus any kind of way that we feel justified in so doing, be careful! When in doubt take nothing or do nothing. Your soul is a mighty precious gift that you do not want to fool around with. Be extremely careful! For narrow is the way to heaven which few take.

Jesus is saying that we need to fast. The pillars of Jesus are crying out each and every single second of the day. Some of us have never fasted. Some of us really do not know how to fast. Albeit this may be the case, we shall owe it to ourselves to get to heaven at all cost. This is why we pray.

Praying and fasting is like your arms and your legs telling the heart that they can write or run with these limbs. Jesus knows that the church is suffering from the lack of fervent prayer. Passionate prayer takes you to worship. This is prayer without ceasing. You have made up your mind that you will die at all cost for the love of Jesus. Though none go with you yet will I follow you. Jesus, I know that you did not give me everything that I have asked you for, but I will follow you no matter what. Quit bargaining with Jesus! For one day, he will come to you to show you the nails in his hands and the nails in his feet.

PROPHECIES HAVE ENDED AND THAT YOU ARE EVIL:

Matthew 13:54-57 And when he was come into his own country, he taught them in their synagogue, insomuch that they were astonished, and said, Whence hath this man this wisdom, and these mighty works?

55 Is not this the carpenter's son? is not his mother called Mary? and his brethren, James, and Jo-ses, and Simon, and Judas?

56 And his sisters, are they not all with us? Whence then hath this *man* all these things?

57 And they were offended in him. But Jesus said unto them. A prophet is not without honour, save in his own country, and in his own house.

Jesus is saying that a prophet will not ever have honor in his own country. I recalled one day, I was visiting a church in company with one of my previous pastors. It was a Sunday and he was taking me to any church that would be opened that late evening. He introduced me to another pastor, who was the pastor of four churches in the state of Texas.

I introduced myself to him as a preacher and prophet of the Lord. Immediately he responded to me saying, '' there are no longer anymore prophets.'' These very same words were said to Jesus all during his walk with his heavenly father. Solomon said in the book of Chronicles 7:14 If my people, shall humble themselves. This is what we are missing on this planet. We all want to love God without first obtaining the gift of humility.

The gift of a prophet is a mighty gift. Any preacher that does not wear your hat as a prophet will forever abase you. Satan will use anyone to lower your rank. The entire book of Revelation is all prophecy. It will take a prophet to disclose and unravel this prophetic Word of God. It will take the almighty hand of Jesus to break every bone in the body of satan.

One day, in the summer of 2005, I was living in the tiny town of Vivian, Louisiana, when a group of preachers told me to get out of Vivian whilst I am still alive. It was told to me that the people of this vicinity kill prophets. This small group of preachers did everything to convince me that my life would soon come to an end, if I did not leave now. The Holy Spirit did not allow me to leave the town of Vivian.

My life in the neighborhood continued as usual. Until one day I was threatened by one of my brother preachers, who did everything to deny me the right of prophecy. He would send members of his congregation to tell me that I was a false prophet and that whatever I was saying to people was false. But the people kept on coming anyhow. They would tell me that he did not like the fact that I preached out of the book of Revelation with authority.

Some people would tell me, that he told them to tell me to go back to Trinidad, and that nobody wanted to hear my interpretation of the Word. Smilingly, I kept the peace in obedience to the Holy Spirit. As time passed by, my then

Pastor, who always took me around with him, took me to one of the nearby churches that poisoned me that late Sunday evening at their repast.

Jesus is saying that the blood spilled by the beheading of his Sons is a sign of a ruthless world. Human beings would stop at nothing to avert the truth that is coming upon the earth. Truth nobody wants. Christians want to hear from whoever they put in office, rather than whomever Jesus has prepared and sent.

Jesus is not a political party, where everyone selects a person to represent them in their vicinity. Jesus is not a Board of Directors, whose job, is to seek the company's interest. Jesus is not a scientific project, where everyone is invited to participate by sending their ideas. Jesus is not a monarchy that dictates to everyone in an atmosphere of hostility. Jesus is teaching everyone, that the Living Word of God is the whole truth, and nothing but the truth.

A prophet will never have honor in his own country because of Jesus, who has already lay claim to the title of King of Kings and Lord of Lords. Jesus opening sentence at the synagogue was to tell everybody, who he is and what he is about to do, which is preach the Word of God. Jesus is the pioneer of Christianity. Jesus is the archetype of truth.

Daniel 12:5 Then I Daniel looked, and, behold, there stood other two, the one on this side of the bank of the river, and the other on that side of the bank of the river.

6 And *one* said to the man clothed in linen, which *was* upon the waters of the river, How long *shall it be to* the end of these wonders?

7 And I heard the man clothed in linen, which *was* upon the waters of the river, when he held up his right hand and his left hand unto heaven, and sware by him that liveth for

ever that *it shall be* for a time, times, and an half; and when he shall have accomplished to scatter the power of the holy people, all these things shall be finished.

8 And I heard, but I understood not: then said I, O my Lord, what *shall* be the end of these things?

9 And he said, Go thy way, Daniel: for the words are closed up and sealed till the time of the end. Jesus is saying that this prophetic word is already unfolding for the past two thousand years. Whereas Abraham, the Patriarch whose blessing of his seed will continue by the Grace of God the Father, and the Son, and the Holy Spirit, which is bearing witness right now.

The gentiles, who are scattered all over the world are and will from time to time be held in strongholds, because the evil one follows the good closely. Jesus is making this abundantly clear, especially to his stewards of the Word, to take a look at yourself before you hold others accountable.

How many preachers are doing everything that Jesus tells them to do? Jesus is saying that the time is now for you to come to the throne of Grace, which is the feet of Jesus, which is the throne of God footstool in heaven. Many have walked crookedly in churches, and to this day, are held in the highest esteem by its members of the church. These men of God have also held top positions in the hierarchy.

A country like Mexico, who sits on the arms of America, and as it were is run by a President. Jesus is not happy with the slums which have been there for centuries, and are still present to this day. All these things were prophesied under the umbrella of the Word of Jesus given to Daniel. Human beings do not want to be told what is right or what is wrong from anyone that is truly a representative of Jesus.

They look at where you come from, before they pay

attention to Jesus's every Word that comes out of the mouth of his Sons on the earth. They look at his background. If his father was not a statesman, they would never ever listen to his report. Whereas his father is or was a statesman, and now his book, or his letters gets printed by the most prestigious company in the world.

The universities take his report and they make text books out of his writings. Students from all over the world come to these colleges to study something that Jesus never intended to be published. But because it is a man of high standing no one questions his thesis. Does Jesus hide this evil? Of course not. Look again! Jesus did not hide the sin of Eve and Adam.

Jesus hides nobody weaknesses period. He did not hide his brother Adam sin, who was made by the hands of God his Father out of the dust of the earth. He did not hide his sister Eve sin, who was made from a rib of Adam by the hands of God the Father. He did not hide any of these evil things Yet the world goes around killing the seeds of Adam, no matter what.

Jesus knows of all these great companies that have employed his brothers and sisters and children of God. Jesus knows precisely what is going on in today's world that had already been prophesied. Companies employing children to **wo**rk for little or not pay at all. This is not happening in all America. But the stewards of America know about this happening even as Jesus speaks. Turning a blind eye to things of this magnitude does not free you from serious sin or sinfulness. Not because it is not happening on American soil, free you from the stain of evil doing.

Jesus is our Savior. Our job is to be an example in the household first, before being an example anywhere else. Jesus is the only one worthy to be praised! There is no other.

Isaiah 9:7 Of the increase of *his government and peace there shall be no end,* upon the throne of David, and upon his kingdom, to order it, and to establish it with judgment and with justice from henceforth even for ever. The zeal of the Lord of hosts will perform this. Jesus is emphasizing the fact that there will be no peace on earth. Why? The world must know, that they have killed the only begotten Son of the True Living God.

The world must know about the rivalry between the children of the promise, and those of Hagar, the Egyptian maiden and servant of Sarah. You cannot replace order when broken by jealousy. A jealous lover according to human philosophy has nothing to do with the jealousy of Jesus. The whole of heaven was destroyed by the jealousy of satan. Jesus is not about repairing the damage done by the devil and his cohorts.

Jesus is still talking about the vast number of slums all across South America, a place that he has single out for riches and wealth. Countries like Brazil and Argentina. These are two countries with lots of gold, silver tin, copper to name a few. Where does all the wealth go? No one else pockets but the filthy rich. Is Jesus happy about this? No Sir. Well then, what do you expect Jesus to do? Lay down and cry, of course not.

Jesus is about empowerment. And this is where Jesus places his Sons and keep on sending his Sons for you the evil one to destroy. Jesus hears the cries of his suffering sons who have been targeted everyday of their lives by the very power structure. Yes evil are in high places. God the Father, God the Son, and God the Holy Spirit allows the flow of the river of evil.

Jesus told Adam that the day you eat the fruit of the Tree of Life you will surely die is still reminiscent to this day. The immutable law of God, who is Jesus is unchanging. The slums of Brazil are very much shameful to say the least.

Words really and truly cannot describe the filth, and the stench that the children of Jesus have to endure each day of their lives. Jesus cares.

Yes Jesus knows that the years been tremendous. Yes God the Father knows that the years been tremendous. Yes the Holy Spirit knows that the years been tremendous. The atrocities of the slums of Brazil are tremendously inhuman. Of course, none of this is printed, or will ever be printed by any prestigious newspaper company. And anyone that prints, and show these slums graphically or otherwise would be beheaded.

All through my earthly life, I have borne witness to squalor. Houses without doors, windows, and bathrooms, that were occupied not just by single people, but by families. The naked eye speaks all truth. The stench makes you vomit. The rats are seen gnawing on the dead. The roaches are biting on the feet of human beings. The flies are very busy buzzing around. Disease is everywhere.

The faithful reporters, though few in number, would always be ignored. Followers of Jesus of Nazareth, King of the Jews will forever be the footprints of His Majesty the King.

Ecclesiastes 3:11 He hath made every *thing* beautiful in his time: also he hath set the world in their heart, so that no man can find out the work that God maketh from the beginning to the end. Jesus is showing me that, whereas proof is given as humankind increases on the face of the earth, to the surprise of the abundance of food, still evil convinces the heart of man.

The wiles of the devil takes you wherever you have been offered up to be, especially by your parents that sought the devil for your future. Thus making you a victim of circumstance. Parents who sought sorcerers throughout the length and breath of the land are the blind spots in children's lives. They do their evil without telling their children anything about it during their lifetimes.

Jesus in his masterpiece of creativity gives each individual a measure of faith. This range that Jesus places in our souls will take us in the right direction. But your very parents knowingly knowing that Jesus is going to take his sweet time, for them to benefit financially from your birth, now then impulsively seek sorcerers to bring about riches quickly. There is always a bad seed in the family. This is the one that they will seek throughout their lifetime. Even though they are Christians, they will flout the law of Jesus.

It is easy to blame curiosity. Instead blame yourself! Jesus uniquely takes his time and fashions us carefully into a measure of faith. This spirit of perfection works himself through us. This work of the genius cannot be replicated. The world is indeed a beautiful place, but, are we keeping its true magnificence? Callously, we go around breaking and destroying anything and everything because, we have to bend those knees to Almighty Jesus.

Seriously, we do not want to take Jesus at his Word. It behooves us to do everything within our power, to prove that, no one man could have created this universe. Until we are filled with the Holy Spirit, we would not be able to ascertain the mystery of faith. God the Father, God the Son, and God the Holy Spirit will from time to time be that highway in our lives to take us to heaven.

Jesus is showing me the miracle of the five loaves and a few little fishes. Jesus is saying that in these modern times and now in these end times no one is believing in that miracle. People are checking out the slot machines, and the ATM machines for instant cash. This is absolutely what the world wants, instant cash. People all over the world wants to get money from their account or anyone's account now.

They must not work for it. They must not show anything for it. They must have it all now and forever.

God the Father, God the Son, and God the Holy Spirit made this world. The Pagans would say, "No he did not." The pagans would go about building and making effigies out of anything, that they could put their hands on to create an image. Why an image? Why a likeness of what has already been created? Why not lay claim to something that is totally different? The pagans are non-believers in the existence of God the Father, God the Son, and God the Holy Spirit.

Jesus says it best. Let the blind lead the blind. You are walking down the street, and you decide to stop at the park and take a picture of a statue. Standing in front of you is a man speaking and gesticulating at the statue. We see this displayed everyday of our lives, wherever there is a statue or not. But do we really see satan, the devil in the midst of it all. No sir.

Jesus says that a clean hand and a pure heart shall see God. Could we look at everyone's hands and select the dirty hands from the clean hands? Then why question Jesus, who shows you proof after proof each day. Jesus is not stupid; that is why he has given you beautiful parents. Wise people, who would teach you how to climb every mountain. Wise people, who would take you by the hand, and teach you what is right and what is wrong. Wise people, who would teach you by example: by reading all the literature they could read in front of your very eyes.

Your pagans are your leeches that would cling to your hearts, so that they could teach you all the ways of a despondent. .Every time a new born baby comes into the world, that baby would remember his past, present and future. No one could tell him what he saw or bear witness to excluding his contemporaries. Dates and figures might be inaccurate, but the juice of the heart of Jesus would forever linger on in his seed.

The mountains that beam from the eyes of your father and the hills that permeate your mother lips are sufficient to fuel you for the rest of your life. The heathens would come and go and build effigies throughout the world, but Jesus will always be your standard bearer. It is not our job to satisfy the bellies of the unbelievers. Jesus fed thousands of people with the miracle of the five loaves and a few little fishes. Yet we are still crying for those, who have turned their backs on our sweet Lord Jesus.

Some of us had the pleasure of growing up in a big family. Some of us have had a mother who did everything in the kitchen without help. In today's world, why has this love disappeared? What are we really thinking about? Who has become your master? Is it the job?

Luke !:33 And he shall reign over the house of Jacob for ever; and of his kingdom there shall be no end. God the Father, God the Son, and God the Holy Spirit will reign over the entire universe for all eternity. This is a world without an end. Jesus is Prophecy. Jesus is the name that the atheist would have to bend those knees to, when they are sentenced to hell.

It is not what the world thinks that matters to God. There was only one family that was saved in the whole world, which was Noah and his household. This eight in number represented the family of a just man. God is like some of our earthly parents, who when they say something, they meant every bit of that word. The Lord is my shepherd. Really. Then why are you being swayed by an atheist?

Jesus is walking briskly in front of me, whilst simultaneously showing me an unprepared world, whose desire for richness is as meager as slime. The prophetic Jesus is saying that this is unfolding and unfolding and unfolding right at this very moment in time. How can people say that prophecies have ended, when things are unfolding before the very eyes?

We live in a narcissistic world. People have become lovers of themselves. Jesus reminds us about Abraham and his cousin Lot. The place that Lot chose to reside in was called Sodom and Gomorrah. In this great place of corruption with men and women becoming attracted to their own selves moved God the Father to destroy these two cities. Jesus reminds us that his stepfather Joseph had a wife called Mary.

So when two persons of the same sex want to become intimate with each other this is an abomination in the sight of The Almighty God the Father, God the Son, and God the Holy Spirit. Jesus is not playing church. Jesus is not hiding behind the fence and throwing stones at you, when you pass by along the sidewalk. Jesus is making it plain everyday, that it is still an abomination in the sight of Almighty God.

There is no justification for evil. Whereas laws have been changed in some states of America, to make this a national anthem in all America, Jesus is not sleeping. The world could go around in a merry-go-round enjoying their vomit as they regurgitate their word full of spite.

They opened clubs in every district, town, and city. Whereby they would begin to buy up all real estate in these neighborhoods to convert them to homosexual districts. This they would do wherever they go to build strongholds. These are your powerhouses of devil worshippers. These satanic groups of people go on to form and open up new towns with the money that the evil one quickly disbursed to them.

Go to California and you would see, how much real estate they own! Go to Louisiana and you would see, how much real estate they own! Go to Texas and you would see, how much real estate they own! Go to New York and you would see, how much real estate they own! Go to Washington and you would see, how much real estate they own! When you get tired, go to Europe and see how much real estate they own!

God the Father, God the Son, and God the Holy Spirit shows his patience and long suffering, to his creatures that show him everyday that they do not love him. They use and abuse Jesus summers to march throughout his land in protest to God that he made them this way. Jesus says take a good look at yourself and that is who you are. You have male organs then you are male. You have female organs then you are female.

Stop the lies! Defeat the devil at every arm length! Then leave the rest to Jesus. Visiting the Doctors to have a sex change would not alter the situation. Listening to successful people, who are everything like you and becoming a follower, would not alter the situation. Jesus does not compromise. Jesus is not about to auction anybody off to the devil without a fight. Our duty is to let go and give Jesus the fight. Are we really listening or are we waiting for another? God the Father, God the Son, and God the Holy Spirit loves you.

Look at the stars up above! Could you count them? Jesus can. Jesus is saying that these LGBTQ strongholds were already painted in the books of the prophets. God misses nothing. Jesus preached the Beatitudes from a mountain top. This sermon was all about prophecy. Jesus is reiterating that blessed are his prophets, when they do as Jesus says do.

For prophets will at all times be persecuted even by their very own. The LGBTQ organization would stop at nothing to do the will of the devil. The openly gay movement has attacked Christian churches all across America for not agreeing with their philosophy. They would go to extreme lengths, and place their placards on the steps of the house of

God, in protest to the law of Jesus.

Every year, the slime of the earth would hold rallies, in great cities showing their nakedness to everyone, no matter what. They would literally walk the streets naked in support of their political policies. Their agenda means nothing to Jesus. The rocks of the earth would cry out in support of Jesus. To think of a people who blasphemes Jesus daily would turn away from the evil one, for God to relent, and turn their sorrow into joy forevermore.

The worshippers of the devil must bear in mind, that the act of sodomy by male partners are an abomination in the sight of God. The destruction of Sodom and Gomorrah by fire was not just a passing thing. An entire twin cities were utterly destroyed by fire by Almighty God the Father for sodomy and lesbianism. Two women being intimate with each other. And in today's world are getting married. Also two homosexual men are getting married.

Then the slime of these couples are given children to raise by the society. This is called the extended family. Preachers of the Word of God have an obligation to Jesus to preach the word in season and out of season. The world wants this terrible sin to go away, whilst the preachers must keep their mouths shut. Jesus is not about keeping his mouth shut.

The slime of homosexuality and lesbianism are totally wrong. For those of us who have family members that choose to live this way; that is their choice. Christians that are true followers of Jesus have already been spoken to by Jesus, long before the coming of this very sad and erroneous time in the history of mankind. Prophets have been singing like the nightingale of the night for God the Father, God the Son, and God the Holy Spirit.

The song is all about Jesus. This song is to turn the hearts of the children of Jesus away from the enemies of God. For we are very conscious, that satan comes around like a roaring lion, looking to devour the souls of the children of Jesus. The devil is very much aware that his time is drawing nigh. His boundaries have already been shortened by Jesus. Satan is unaware of time, because of his fall from heaven.

Needless to say, that the slime would continue to enter sanctuaries, convents, and kindergartens. Pastors who are men and women of God disappointedly heads the list. These gay pastors get married to women and continue to have an intimate relation with another man. Thus hiding their homosexuality. The lesbian pastors do the same. Then some do otherwise.

The homosexual church leaders compound it by employing gay ministers of music. The congregations are very much aware of this nastiness. Even some church leaders would go to hell saying that nothing is absolutely wrong with this behavior. These congregations in these churches would be pack out in capacity: nobody really cares about the gospel. All these church leaders care about are money, money, money. That is their god.

In all America we have the most prisons worldwide. These prisons are packed to capacity. Sometimes thirty or forty people to one cell. Is this humane? Yes we pray for miracles from these very cell walls, but the blame is on society. In the beginning was the Word and the Word was with God and the Word was God. Are we doing everything to tempt Jesus? This is sacrilegious.

Jesus sent Moses to do a great work. The people stoned him for the very slime of the earth. When a human being has to become intimate with the dead: this is slime of the earth. When a human being has to become intimate with the idols: this is slime of the earth. When a human being has to sleep in the grave with the decease: this is slime of the earth.

Jesus told all these stories and was slammed dunk by the slime of the earth. Be reminded that Jesus came to fulfill the law! The unchanging fingers of Jesus makes the evil one tremble at every turn. The earth is the Lord's and everything therein. These breeding grounds of the slime will continue until Jesus comes again. Hell is real.

1 Peter 1:9-10 Receiving the end of your faith, *even* the salvation of *your* souls.

10 Of which salvation the prophets have enquired and searched diligently, who prophesied of the grace *that should come* unto you: which we are experiencing right now in these end times. To construct and conceive in the mind: which is having the mind of Jesus. Eyes have not seen and ears have not heard the true beauty of Jesus. Satan have taken our eyes off Jesus.

We have not seen Jesus walking on water even in the distance. We have not seen Jesus changing and multiplying the fishes in the seas and the oceans .We have not seen the cherubim walking up the staircase of heaven in broad daylight. We have not seen Jesus walking upside down in the rainbow. We have not seen Jesus rising in the morning with the sun sitting on the top of his head. We have not seen and heard the voice of God saying this is my beloved Son hear him.

The mind of God is upon us. Proof of his existence is slowly on its way. Could we hold on? For those of us, who live on the outskirts of the city of San Francisco and have had the pleasure of viewing the Golden Gate Bridge: this is a glimpse of Heaven on earth. God does not make any mistakes. This peninsula was not just founded. This came directly from heaven open doors. There are no accidents in heaven.

Take a good look at yourself! Jesus does not make junk.

The beauty of Jesus flows over you. A reflection of yourself is a perfect picture of heaven on earth, when a picture is taken as you see yourself in the flowing river. The saints cry out for you every time you stumble and fall. The alleluias crescendo when someone gets baptized in the name of Jesus. Yes one day, we will see and hear all these great things that Jesus will perform before our very eyes.

The angels have not thrown in the towel. They are continuously praising Jesus at the throne of Grace. There sits God the Father, God the Son, and God the Holy Spirit. How excellent is thy name in all the earth? We have not seen anything yet, but we are about to quit. There is a dance coming down from heaven to the earth which everyone will be involve. Stay!

Malachi 3;4 Remember ye the law of Moses my servant, which I commanded unto him in Horeb for all Israel, with the statutes and judgments.

5 Behold, I will send you Elijah the prophet before the coming of the great and dreadful day of the Lord:

6 And he shall turn the heart of the fathers to the children, and the heart of the children to their fathers, lest I come and smite the earth with a curse. There is a very serious danger in this Word. For many have come and gone believing that this had already taken place. Yes, the Book of Jude precedes the Book of Revelation but this is not the criterion to use in unraveling prophecy. Jesus is the key to everything. From the beginning of the Bible to the very end. It is all about one man, his name is Jesus.

The only person that remembered the law of Moses to this day is Moses himself. To date the prophet Elijah has not made another entry into the world. Yes, he is to come. Jesus is the truth. The whole wide world has to see Elijah, when he returns to the face of the earth. God the Father, God the Son, and God the Holy Spirit will accompany him. Jesus will have a full movie house on that beautiful day. There will be no room, not even standing room, on that great and beautiful day.

Remember Jesus was transfigured! It will be a day of many miracles. The heavens will be rejoicing both in song and in dance. The ripple effect will be from East to West and from North to South. There is no theatrical production on the earth to be its equal. Keep praying and remain constant in prayer! The novelty of the day will be your entry into heaven.

It is easy to assume that Jesus was the one who came as Elijah, but Elijah is not the perfect one. Elijah did not and would not come to spend 33 years on the face of the earth. His coming will be like a serial movie. Where each appearance will be told, so that the people will get there at the appointed time. It is like the star that led the three wise men, directly to the birthplace of Jesus.

To this day, some people are still waiting for the first coming of Our Lord Jesus. Jesus is not Elijah. Jesus is the True Living Son of the Almighty God the Father. Obedience is greater than sacrifice. Jesus came to fulfill this word. Yet everybody still believe in sacrificing animals for whatever their agenda may be. Walk the streets of Haiti and please tell me what do you see?

Pay a visit to West Africa, and pay close attention to the vast number of animals they sacrifice on a daily basis, just to get rich! Jesus is the crucify one and there is no other. How many buffaloes must be slaughtered? Stop the blood drinking! Yes Jesus is coming. But Elijah has to precede him.

Yes I know that your New Testament preachers do not believe in the Old Testament, where everything emanated from. Jesus belongs to everyone. And that is why he is the color of olive oil. No other man has walked on water, before the coming of Jesus and after the coming of Jesus. Moses said that an eye for an eye to this day people are still digging the eyes out of one another.

The coming of Jesus meant the end of all these heinous crimes. People who are lovers of these laws would never put an end to them, whether Jesus returns or not. Each and everyday, they take the law into their own hands. The same goes with the laws of slavery. It has ended since in the 18th Century; it is still in effect today. Human beings would tell a lie for anything. There is no good reason for one to tell a lie.

Infidelity to Jesus is perpetuated by non-Christians world over. The Bible in one hand and the gun in the other. This is the number one reason why Elijah has to return, to show the world that reincarnation is a myth. Jesus is not a myth. God the Father, God the Son, and God the Holy Spirit is a mystery of faith. The Trojans wars were all about myths and legends. The coming of Jesus sparked off wars, wherever Jesus placed his feet. They came looking for Jesus everywhere he went to see who is this man, this colored man, preaching the good news.

The saga of Hercules had been and still is a Greek myth. The troubled human race loves fiction immensely. The truth about Jesus that Jesus himself left behind is now scattered because of legend. Statutes adorned the public squares of Greece. Even some Christian Churches have statues of Jesus, which Jesus never told them to erect. Circumcision is in the heart, and not in the sight of people to go feel and touch. Jesus is not about drama. Jesus is real.

So by lying to the people and saying that Elijah had already come is nonsensical. A blatant lie. Biblical scholars which are not for Jesus, would paint any pictures to draw the masses. Amy doubts and fears, that you harbor in your hearts about the reality and existence of Our Lord Jesus, would overpower you to the other side. Any events and periods in time, that were purposely left out purely because of evil, would obviously have you second guessing. Where is the movie of Elijah's coming?

Jesus is not stupid. Would not his coming be plastered all over the world? The front page of every newspaper world over would have run this prophetic story. Flashes of lights and beams of earthly thunder would have consumed the entire planet. Human beings would have remembered and passed this on from generation to generation. If you sweep your yard clean on a daily basis, when you raise your head you will see Jesus.

Job 8:7-9 Though thy beginning was small, yet thy latter end should greatly increase.

8 For enquire, I pray thee, of the former age, and prepare thyself to the search of their fathers:

9 For we *are but of* yesterday, and know nothing, because our days upon earth *are* a shadow: Of course our days upon the earth is a small fraction of the years of Adam and his wife Eve. But what is this prophetic word all about; pertaining to these dangerous times? Everything in the Bible is all about Jesus. Be reminded that the world was made for Jesus! This prophecy is like a river that appears to have ended, but it flows hundreds of feet under the earth, and continues its course in a totally different direction.

People keep judging the man of God that Jesus sent with a message to his children. Only to find out, that because the prophets of Jesus showed up empty handed: bias comments were swirled at the Sons of God because, they were not lettered. Jesus will always be your latter end. Generally speaking by and large, we all want to be born rich and die rich without having a brawl with satan, the devil.

Jesus is speaking from the highest mountain top that you

could have ever imagined. His is an impending situation. How could one justify a world without anything, that one man takes in his hand together with his Son and transform that emptiness into greatness? Where are these witnesses? Why must anyone believe in this one man? Jesus goes on to tell the story about a rich man.

How many people that you have been to school with in your lifetime that were born rich? Could you count them? Are they all Sons and Daughters of King Jesus? No, they are not. For Jesus to increase in you, you must decrease. The wisdom of God is enormously awesome. Human beings make predictions that falls by the wayside. Somebody could have, should have or would have done something. The room gets quiet as soon as Jesus makes his entry.

Jesus has the tools in his hand to give to us to be successful in anything and everything. Yet we would from time to time go the way of our fathers. Every time we put something together satan comes along and takes it away. We never really get started. The years pile up and now we are gone. We see this in our very own families. Jesus is the rich man standing there, waiting for a man of wisdom, to come along to show the others something.

Jesus is saying to press on with all of your might in seeking heaven open doors. Once you are seeking and not finding, that means that you are not giving up on your tomorrow. As soon as, you have made up your mind to find heaven, satan will find someone, someone close to you, to stop you at all cost. You must not achieve anything greater than that someone. The evil has made you go off in tantrums, on everybody, be it verbal or otherwise, who you deem your enemy.

You have gone to work patiently plodding your next victim. You begin to believe in your deliberations; believing to yourself that you got satan and not the other way around.

Satan already knew that he got you: becomes silent even in the absolute. Some of us would know all of this and would still go and play games with the devil. Jesus emanates all power. Until we come to realize this absolutely, the enemy would not run away from us anyhow.

Have you ever noticed that as soon as someone did something wrong, a whole flock of people were there to see, and pay close attention to what the accused one looked like? The reverse is utterly ridiculous. When Jesus started to preach the Word; they started throwing stones at him. Who do you think you are, the son of a carpenter? What did Jesus do? Continued his preaching!

The last word that Jesus heard on the cross at Calvary's Hill was and still is crucify him. Jesus does not care about your long skirts and your hidden bodies under linen.

God decides the way one shall go on the face of the earth. Abraham did speak about Jesus, because he knew him face to face. When the going gets rough the tough gets going. Jesus is the answer in every book. Discarding him in one book means hell: the burning fire that will annihilate your soul. There will be no party for you in heaven. There will be no standing ovation for you in heaven. There will be no remembrance of your loved ones for you in heaven.

Jesus gave Abraham, not just a new name, but everything. It is to show that Jesus will give you everything, plus an overflow. Jesus is the only seed of his heavenly father. There is no one else beginning from Adam to this present day, that can boast of this phenomenon, but Jesus. Adam was made from the dust of the earth. His wife Eve came out of his body molded by Jesus from a rib. Everything was fashioned from the very dust of the earth.

Jesus loves the proving business. The river of uniqueness is continuously flowing and flowing as the result of Jesus.

The promise made to Abraham that his seed is numbered as the stars above and the sands of the seashore below equal the same--prove me! Jesus is coming on a black horse, way out in the distant, riding the winds of the heavenly floors. Jesus is not about the math.

Jesus says that nothing is impossible with God. Jesus also says that when you see me you have seen the father. Jesus also says once again, that when you see the face of God you will surely die. Jesus is simply saying: be on watch every single day of your life! You cannot allow the enemy to bait you with his subtleness. The enemy is conscious that you want to walk lofty. Your job is to ignore him.

The straight and narrow road is easy to find. Things must from time to time go our way. Especially now that we live in a time of instant cash. We taught that instant coffee was top of the line. With a credit card in hand you can buy almost anything. Jesus is not the creator of this new way of life. Some of us do not like to hear the truth. This we ignore daily. Jesus knows that a whole lot of people including his own do not have any control over such things anyhow. But the truth is still the truth.

Some people no longer receive cash or check on their job. They have no choice but to accept a credit card. But the truth is still the truth. Jesus is very much more so, than ever present. We shall know the truth from Jesus at every turn. All these things were already prophesied when Jesus says that I will break down the walls of Jericho. At that time Caesar ruled the world.

This is the 21st Century and we still have not seen anything yet. To say that prophecy has ended, when the entire Book of Revelation is now unfolding its roots, whilst simultaneously the prophets of old, songs have not been completed. It is easy to tie a horse and leave and go away, than to tie a donkey and do the same. The world is your donkey, and the few prophets that are feverishly doing the will of Jesus will be caught standing.

The innocence of the law is in the eyes of the children. The world does not care on every side, what they do in front of those innocent lambs. Prophecy is sublime: Isaiah the prophet foretold of the coming of Our Lord Jesus. Jesus entry into the world took 500 hundred years. God the Father, God the Son, and God the Holy Spirit is speaking to the world, but the planet keeps counting the cost. Jesus is not and will not be counting the cost.

Isaiah 9:7 Of the increase of *his* government and peace *there shall be* no end, upon the throne of David, and upon his kingdom, to order it, and to establish it with judgment and with justice from henceforth even for ever. The zeal of the Lord of hosts will perform this. There will be no peace on earth. The coming of Jesus on the face of the earth, marked the beginning and ending of the Rule of heaven on the earth. Nobody wants the seed of Abraham to rule over them, as David ruled the house of Israel.

Look around you and see precisely what you got. Governments all over the world trying to bring about World Peace. Conventions after conventions holding meetings among nations to resolve peace around the globe. Down through the years of centuries of peace talks the matter remained the same. Even though there were instances of peace between and among a few nations, these peace treaties when signed by the respective leaders only last for a season.

God the Father, God the Son, and God the Holy Spirit will triumph to the very end. Whatever mankind does against Jesus will only last but for a short time Peace talks are not just for the Middle East. Peace talks are not just for your own political gain. Peace talks are not just for a hand shake and smiling faces. Peace talks are not just for the News Media. Peace talks must have the Prince of Peace present at all times.

Jesus is his name.

It is not how many books that came out of a scholar that counts. It is not how many skyscrapers one has built around the world that counts. It is not how fat your pay check is in any given one year that counts. It is not how many cars that you have built and sold worldwide that counts. It is not how many airplanes that you have built and sold around the world that counts. It is not how many ships that you have built around the world that counts. Jesus died to save us from a bomb that is greater and more devastating than Heroshima and Madagaski. Thank you sweet Jesus.

The plots of the enemy are varied. An imposter working for the enemy is not easily detected. It takes time to catch him in the act. Whatever you are missing in your goodness and kindness, that is the mark of the enemy. Jesus has a very huge heart. He is forever giving somebody something, until an imposter comes along to show him something else.

You are off to the supermarket with the exact amount of money needed. On your way on foot, you observe a crowd of people looking at a fist fight. As you stop to take a look, the crowd push you to the ground and all your money too. Did you see the imposter? Of course not. Jesus is the head of my life. What about you? To gain the whole world and lose your soul is on you.

Today's establishment would from time to time put their heads in the sand. They would do everything to subvert the true course of the way, the truth and the life. Some churches are raised up purely as a business to make money. Some churches are put together as a family church. Some churches have been erected purely to save taxes. The seed of the imposter is plastered everywhere.

When you propagate for Jesus by giving out tracts, this is not a guarantee that your soul is going to heaven. When you stand on the corner telling everybody that you are blessed, this is not a guarantee that your soul is going to heaven. Missionaries around the world have to be very careful going on trips that Jesus never commanded them to undertake.

The zeal of Jesus is in his building a new heaven and a new earth. The zeal of Jesus is in transforming you into a new creature. The zeal of Jesus is in his production of beautiful mansions. In my Father's house are many mansions. All our loved ones are waiting patiently for us in heaven, so that we can all give thanks and praise to a risen Lord.

JESUS TAKES YOU THROUGH THE HOUR OF NEED:

Matthew 11:28-30 Come unto me, all ye that labour and are heavy laden, and I will give you rest.

29 Take my yoke upon you, and learn of me; for I am meek and lowly in heart and ye shall find rest unto your souls.

30 For my yoke is easy, and my burden is light. Jesus is saying that there is too much going on in the world, but first seek his face. Throughout the history of mankind, the devil from time to time, would come along in an attempt to provoke and to fervently disrupt, the congeniality of the brethren of Abraham. The question begs, where is the original citadel of David? Destruction of the inheritance of the seed of Abraham would forever be, the cause of instability throughout the Middle East. Jesus says that my yoke is easy and my burden is light. Think about that!

It is easy to assemble people of a scholarly background. The example that Jesus gave, as he walked the streets of the world, was a nature of spiritual wisdom in his assembly of the apostles. Could you count how many scholars there were?

Were there five, four, three? Are we still counting down or do we find this amusing? Jesus is extremely modest. It is not alright to build the house, and when you have run out of money, now you are calling on Jesus.

Did Jesus turned his back on you? Well, that is exactly what the world has done to our Lord, and until now continues to do. Why keep running when there is no hiding place? His eminence is Jesus. The child that runs away from his parents did not do that to hurt his parents. This child wanted all the attention. This more than likely created an atmosphere of discord between the parents. Reality is something that the human race does not want to come face to face with; they rely on suppositions.

The lightning flashes and the thunder rolls, and the thunder rolls, and the thunder rolls. Whereas the human race wants the lightning to flash every time, before the thunder rolls. Jesus does not bring a spirit of fear. Before Jesus comes to you, he will always say do not be afraid! The devil is the one that brings a spirit of fear.

Some of us would see Jesus standing at the yield sign and drive through Jesus without looking left nor right. Some of us would never be ready to do the Lord's work. Some of us would run out of patience even at the yield sign. We go weary and gladly so because, we are not listening. If someone sees Jesus before us, we become gravely offended and paranoid by the thought. Together, we must all see Jesus first.

We cannot all see Jesus first. The immutable Jesus is unchanging. He pays a visit to whomever he chooses. Thank you, Jesus. Take my yoke! Join me and become a servant to others. Yes, the road is rough but become a servant to others. Yes, I may or may not have to go it alone, but become a servant to others. My mother says, "not to, you are my only child," but I will become a servant to others. My father stands betwixt, but I will become a servant to others. We are too reluctant to join Jesus and become a servant to others.

We have read the Word and the devil soon afterwards came and stole our joy. Too often, we become caught up within ourselves to become a knight in shining armor for Jesus. Too often, we wished for the role of leadership and was denied. Too often, we did everything right and for some unforsaken reason was turned down. Too often, we applied for the vacancy and no one ever took the time out to even give us a call. Too often, we have been literally overstepped. We must press on in spite of everything.

We left the church, and could not remember the Gospel reading, and what the Pastor said in those few minutes. The devil stole your joy. We have rehearsed the hymn repetitiously. We believed in all fairness that we have memorized our parts together. When called upon to sing the hymn some of us could not remember what we have previously rehearsed. The devil stole your joy.

We must learn to yield to the blood of Jesus. We must learn to fight for what is right. We must learn not to give up. We must learn to shut the devil out of our lives completely. Shut him down I say! Yes, Jesus commands us. Jesus is the Centurion. In a family of eight siblings, the devil would go after the one who is the apple of God's eye. Jesus in this scenario will be misunderstood. Meanwhile, the evil one is continually playing with your mind. As the days go by you become worrisome. Why me, Lord? Wherein faith is slipping away.

Jesus is the root. Your mind is like a theorem. In some instances, highly inquisitive. The enemy adopts a position in your mind to assimilate all the information coming your way. The medical doctors cannot see or discern a spirit anywhere in anyone's body. It takes an anointed man of God to pervade and spot the enemy, and cast him out of the seed and offspring of Abraham.

Sometimes, we feel left out and deserted especially, when we have to make a very important decision now, and painfully all alone. So, we refuse to put the axe to the tree, and grind through whatever it is, for as long as it takes. Time passes by. We fail to see Jesus, as he passes by to instruct us, as to what to do in situations like this. Gentle Jesus wants us to help each other in fulfilling their need at all times. When you put your head to the plough Jesus is right at your side. He is speaking to you, as the sweat flows into your eyes. The burning to the eyes is just a little fire from Jesus.

We say that we love you Lord, but are we real? Are we just giving you lip service? Then we need to make a commitment with you, right now. Jesus is always beside you. He is not in the distant, as we so often think. The anomaly in our lives needs addressing. Have you ever seen a turtle wading in the water? He can do everything, but drown. It's a mystery, how he cannot drown cast in a thick shell?

Some of us are praying right now to Jesus to become a turtle, to live freely and enjoy life as the turtle. His protection is his shell. Your protection is Jesus. You see his protection, but you cannot see Jesus as plainly as you see the turtle. We believe in our imaginative mind, that God must have done something wrong when he made us. God created the turtle, and he provides for him. Whereas, humankind has to sweat to provide for himself. Are we missing something? Yes, for all have sinned and have fall short of the Glory of God.

Psalm 38:6 I am troubled; I am bowed down greatly; I go mourning all the day long. For some of us Jesus is our last hope. We keep running and running and running. We keep avoiding him at every turn. Yet we expect affirmative action from Jesus immediately. We wait until the last moment to choose Jesus. Many times, as we are running from the Lord, we hear him echoing in the wilderness, but sadly, it is to no avail.

Vengeance is mine says the Lord. You are troubled because you take it upon yourself to go after the man that killed your mother. For on the day of the funeral, you made a promise on your deceased mother's grave that you got this one. Jesus hears everything. The keeping of the promise has become a burden for you to bear. You swore before your other siblings that you got this one. You have utterly ignored your wearisome body and the sixth commandment.

In this case, you have allowed the devil to overpower your mind in completing your way of the cross. Now, it is extremely difficult for anyone to talk some sense into your head. As the days, and weeks, and months, and years go by, your mind has become all torn up, like the shoes on your feet. Your black hair has already turned grey. Your youth has turned to wrinkles. Your family and friends could hardly recognize you.

Jesus is saying to everybody, be still! I created you to be a conqueror. I am that I am has made you to be somebody. Anything that goes wrong or right, I allow. There are situations that people end up in, because of the weakness of their loved ones in their life. Trouble is everywhere. You do not have to go look for trouble, for trouble to find you.

You could be at the coffee shop having a hot cup of coffee as you sit all alone, and here comes trouble. You could be at the house in bed sleeping all safe and sound, and all wrapped up in the sheet, and all alone, and here comes trouble. You could be out walking your dog in the park, in broad daylight, and here comes trouble. You could be at the hairdresser's shop curling your hair, and here comes trouble.

I am troubled, since I have my husband, who was incarcerated and was found guilty for a murder, which I knew that he would have never done, so help me God. Jesus knows your pain and Jesus knows your sorrow. Pastor had been shot dead, whilst preaching the Word of God on the pulpit. Where was Jesus? O Sing unto the Lord a new Song. God the Father, God the Son, and God the Holy Spirit is the Victory.

Satan would try anything to stop you from receiving a double anointing. Stay strong! Stay strong! Stay strong! Jesus is saying this obsequiously. Your husband did not do anything wrong to stand accused. His being found guilty by the system does not make it right. What makes it right is that Jesus is Lord of all. The evidence though appealing does not make it right. He being found at the scene of the crime does not make his conviction right at all.

When parents gave birth to identical twins, the mother would know all the differences in her two boys. Anything that is said about those two boys, she would know exactly, which one did the wrong. She would not ever be wrong. Did the wife of the husband, who has been convicted for murder knew her husband? Yes she did. In the same way, that the mother of the twin boys knew her sons.

Jesus is showing without a shadow of a doubt that the church was given to pastor as well as his wife from the mouth of the convicted one. As soon as, Jesus designates a wife to a husband of the cloth jealousy even in the congregation would raise his ugly head. Yes, we say that we love Jesus, but the truth, we cannot stand. It was true that the pastor was set up by the jealous one. It is equally true that the evidence was hidden by the jealous one.

Jesus says victory is mine. After twenty years, the case is now reopened. A new lawyer called by Jesus to become a lawyer is given the hot seat. The people took offence. He is too young they say. He has no experience. His mother cleans patients at the city hospital. Pastor's wife would not listen to any report. Why she is carrying Jesus deep within her being. The young man did discover the murder weapon, in the closet of the Senior Deacon's Office.

Subsequently, the Pastor, who had been killed, whilst preaching from the pulpit made some people thought for a moment, where was Jesus? Jesus is and will always be victorious. The evil one would from time to time play tricks with your mind. The pastor is preaching on Sunday morning at the usual 11 a.m. service. Judas the gunman came through the door and shot pastor with his pistol and fled.

Why all the flowers? Jesus is showing the world that he does not have any favorites. Men of God, anointed by Jesus, to preach the Word is not promised how their end would be determined. The obedient ones are those that walk blindly. They go any and everywhere the spirit of the Lord leads them. They ask no questions. On the contrary, everyone else questions Jesus vehemently.

Faith is the substance of things hoped for and the evidence of things not seen. Fifty per cent of the human race are unbelievers; they would not ever see Jesus. Fifty percent of the planet do not believe that they would go to heaven. As far as they are concerned, they have already convicted themselves because they have sinned against Jesus grievously. In no way, they would ever allow Jesus to come to them to sentence them to hell.

The preacher has to deliver the Word in the light, in the darkness and under any grave circumstance. Whereas, the congregation would look at things through their own mind set. Jesus is constantly working on the Sons of God, thus bringing them to perfection, though none of them would become as perfect as Jesus. Why all the marching?

The celebration of the death of a pastor must not be used for political gain. There is no death to be compared to the crucified one. There is nothing to be compared to the crowning with thorns. There is no likeness to the whipping of Jesus with the cat-o-nine tail. There is no similarity to the constant mocking and tormenting by the crowd, who too tried to deny Jesus of his Kingship. We do not want Jesus of Nazareth. We want Barabas they shouted.

Assassinations cannot be compared to the crucifixion of our Lord Jesus.. To murder a prominent person by secret or sudden attack is a heinous crime. But this in no way could be compared to the one that never, ever did one wrong thing in his universal life. Jesus is awesome. Holy is his name.

The assassination of a President or a Prime Minister or a King would and could live on in anyone's life especially, when they had borne witness to the day, hour and precise occasion of this horrendous act. Whether viewed on national television or heard on the radio or saw a photograph on the front page of a newspaper. Be it as it may; it is not a good feeling.

Some people might have hated the man. But in that moment of sadness love took over and move you into a tear drop. The flashing of lights and the constant scene playing over and over again hypnotized us to a frenzy. It is unbelievable. Nobody cares but Jesus. In that moment everyone is caught dead on the telephone. Talking and talking and talking and talking; lost in the wilderness of hope.

On the sidewalks people got together in small groups conversing on the death of someone they hardly knew, but now, have known through the media a whole lot more about the deceased. The atmosphere was dense. as Jesus slowly passed by to heal the hearts of those lost in grief. The dumbfounded would be the ones that would be hurt deeper than the others. They would appear to be bewildered, though speechless, sudden death pierced their heart intensely.

Those who are prayer warriors would be moved into the singing of hymns, all night long. Even though they knew him not. The saints of Jesus, whose lives are mirrored by a closer walk with Jesus, would also be in prayer, for the bereaved family of the loved one.

The plane had crashed into the jagged mountains killing hundreds of passengers aboard, including both pilots and crew and husbands and their wives and children. Trouble everywhere. Where was Jesus? God the Father, God the Son, and God the Holy Spirit is indeed everywhere. Did these families or these passengers gave their souls to the devil? No. They all had breakfast before they boarded the flight. They hugged and kissed their friends and families before they took their seats on the aircraft.

Jesus is saying that we have all sinned and fall short of the Glory of God. We are all sinners. In my Father's House are many mansions. I go to prepare a place for you. Jesus knew that his hour had come, so he asked his eleven disciples to stay up with him all night long in prayer. They all fell asleep. Jesus was all alone in prayer. The families and friends and brothers and sisters are presently mourning for their deceased loved ones, that had passed on into new life. Jesus had already paid the price.

As soon as, tragedy comes into our lives, we allow the devil to take over our beings, and put into our minds wild imaginations. All of a sudden, we forget Jesus, and what he just did for us not even 24 hours ago. Questions and questions and questions are thrown left and right to the Holy One. Conclusions are already formed in the hearts and minds of people that Jesus is not alive.

The car crashes into a steel bridge the immediate family is burnt to cinders. Where was Jesus? In the sermon on the mount, Jesus says that when they say all manner of evil things against you for my name sake, your blessings will be a hundred fold. True followers of Jesus would have these questions thrown to them by their better halves, to take them away from the road of the mustard seed.

The smallest seed in the planet; yet grows the largest tree. David the smallest boy in eight-boy children; yet became king of Israel. His son Solomon, who did not asked Jesus to build or erect a church for the True Living God was given the prize of the apple of David's eyes. These few things make Jesus synonymous in a world, he had created. The moving vehicle is Jesus. The outstretched arm of the mustard tree is Jesus. The rainbow that emits out of the tree is Jesus. The joyful singing of the birds in the tree is Jesus. The speaking of many languages in the tree is Jesus. The cloud descending on the top of the tree is Jesus.

The brothers and sisters of the bereaved couple would from to time be told by evil neighbors, that the couple gave their souls to the devil and that was why they and their children were burnt to death. Astonishingly, this is precisely, what comes out of the mouth of dogs. When we are mourning for our loved ones, there are languages of the vernacular, that we would shun at the hour of our need.

When people curse you with a curse whether they mean it or not, they too would be forever be cursed. Jesus does not say these things to anyone. Jesus says love your brother no matter what harm he has done you. Jesus says love your sister, who bad talks you both day and night, even at family gatherings. Jesus says do not return evil for evil. Jesus says do good to your neighbor.

Your husband had to report for duty in a rush, and for some reason he left behind his favorite sandwich, which you his loving wife had prepared and his favorite orange juice. This bothered you for a while, but in an instant, you let it go. You fell asleep and had a vision of the angels and the saints praising Jesus in heaven. The telephone is ringing off the hook but you are overpowered by this vision. Suddenly, your brother woke you up with the news, that your husband responding to the call ran straight into a pole and was pronounced dead on arrival at the hospital. Where was Jesus?

Obedience is greater than sacrifice. We fail each and everyday in being punctual at our jobs. We do as we like on these jobs forgetting that, Jesus is the one responsible for our employment. We abuse the sick days that is given to us each year. During our break periods, we would find or adopt any excuse, to make us go over what has been allotted to us, even by the unions.

This beautiful and wonderful woman of God is one of the most perfect examples of a faithful wife. Something that is lacking very much in our society. A dutiful wife gets up and prepares a meal for her handsome husband. She knew something was about to happen, but Jesus preceded her directly to heaven to show her the beautiful mansion which God had prepared for her in heaven.

How many people in the earth could say boldly, that they know for sure that they are going to heaven? Jesus shows his nails in his hands and his nails in his feet and the wound at his side to the Apostle Thomas, who demanded, that he must see Jesus for himself, after everyone already told him that Jesus is risen and have seen him. Must we see everything first, before we believe?

We believe that being lazy are a glorious sight in the Lord. We believe our unwillingness to work on the job site in an effort to finish on time are a glorious sight in the Lord. We believe that withholding, the virtues of punctuality and regularity are a glorious sight in the Lord. We believe that complaining and fussing over petty things are a glorious sight in the Lord.

The train derailed at winter time killing dozens of passengers and injuring hundreds. Where was Jesus? The tempest is Jesus. God gives life and takes lives. Jesus in his humility, one of the fruits of the spirit, is doing his father's will. Jesus is likewise showing all of the fruits of the spirit. Love is perfection summed up in glory. Jesus is right there tending to everyone simultaneously.

Jesus is at the morgue. Jesus is at the hospital. Jesus is at the sight teaching and showing togetherness by everyone's efforts. Jesus is there in songs of hymns. Jesus is there in the flower, or flowers, or bouquet of flowers that adorned the casket. Jesus is with the Doctors and the Nurses and the Police Officers and Fire Officers and the drivers. Jesus does not run away.

Miracles are happening at the hospital. The faithful are healed rapidly, as they are brought into the hospital. Resuscitators are removed quickly from patients. Families are not all in despair. Jesus is working with the hands of the doctors. Jesus is keeping up the nurses at watch at night. Jesus is leading the prayers offered at that time into worship.

The School Bus had crashed into an oil tanker. that left an oil slick on the highway. Thus killing the driver and twenty children, whose bodies were charred to death by the flames. There were no survivors. Where was Jesus? Human beings blame God for everything. If it snows in summertime the blame would fall on Jesus. If the sun shines at nighttime, the blame would fall on Jesus. The school bus driver has nothing to do with the death of these poor innocent souls. Jesus is innocent and is innocence.

These souls are happily resting with Jesus in heaven. The death of children is dearest to the heart of Our Lord Jesus. Jesus remembers his own childhood days, playing with his brothers and his sisters. Something that Jesus will not ever forget. I say will not because Jesus is forever in his innocence. The spinning wheel of time is a mystery. The adage time waits on no man is something that, earthly people cannot put together, as Jesus slowly passes by.

We oftentimes forget that human beings like Adam and his descendants once lived for 1,000 years on the face of the earth. Today we totally disregard this as fallacy or myth. But a lie we quickly believe. To say that, these fatalities are not now resting in the loving arms of Jesus are deceptive as the former. The mind of Jesus is as innocent as, a new born baby.

Jesus knows that every parent wants their children to bury them and not the other way around. Jesus knows the grief. Jesus knows the agony. Jesus knows the torment. Jesus knows the sleepless nights. Jesus knows the screams in the midnight hour. Jesus knows the staying up all night long, wondering and wondering and wondering, whether or not my baby is really and truly with Jesus. Jesus knows the driving all night long by some mothers, thinking and thinking and thinking about the death of their children. Jesus knows the visits they pay at the riverside, or the waterfront or the beach wondering, whether Jesus is real. Jesus knows the agony and the pain.

Yes, it is a struggle. Yes, it is a fight. Yes, it is a struggle. Yes, it is a fight. We must hold on to the loving arms of Jesus. We must hold on to his birth, when thousands of babies were killed about the time of his birth. For Pharaoh had sought his death, because he knew of the coming of the King of Kings and the Lord of Lords. The mother of Jesus had felt the pain and bore it all in her soul. Did Mary, the mother of Jesus, ever envisaged this genocide? No, no, no.

The mother of six was taking her baby across the street in a stroller. Crossing in the crosswalk at a Red Light, an SUV running the red light killed her and her only baby son. Where was Jesus? When anyone ran a red light, who had already slept, but have a problem with relationships would ultimately be a prime vessel for satan. In this case, the devil made him do it.

Jesus is not responsible for any relationship that is not doing good. Jesus is not weeping for the one that killed the mother and her baby. Whereas, Jesus is weeping tearfully for the mother and her darling son, as well as, the other children that were left behind. The other children would from time to time remember that sad and lonely day. This is a time that family has to bury the hatchet. The children should not be separated not even for a moment. Grief could last for a lifetime.

The pastor and his wife have to keep them constantly in prayer. The teachers at the schools have to pay special attention to these children. For the road is narrow and few is with Jesus on this journey. The prayer warriors in the neighborhood should remain vigilant for these children, until Jesus comes home to roost.

All across the country people are losing their jobs, because of too much crime in the neighborhoods of inner cities. Where is Jesus? Jesus is not going to come into your house, when you must learn to clean out your own house. Crime is in the inner cities, because the people or the residents of these neighborhoods want the very evil in their backyards. At every corner, there is something sinister or illegal happening. Drive-by shoot outs occur daily.

The business sector in the community is grossly fed up. Owners of small businesses in the area have to at all times be armed. On any given day, there is or will be a robbery. Store clerks are threatened constantly by the hoodlums. Store managers are harassed by some shoppers, with their deal or no deal tactics, to force the manger's hand on the mark-up price.

Unions are no longer seeking the interests of the workers. Everything now is purely for political gain. Unions leaders are now vying to become Mayors and Assistant Mayors or sit on the board of Teachers. The people not only pay their dues, but their dues are given to politicians solely for a seat at the round table. The workers' voices are now stifled and are stiffed by the officers of the unions.

Jesus is presently showing me not only all America, but the whole world, using and abusing workers' dues by union officials for any gain whatsoever. It stinks in the nostrils of Jesus. Jesus is saying, I have supplied the planet including the seas, and under the seas with luscious food for your very souls. I have heard your prayers. I have felt your pain. Do not forget for one moment that hell is real!

Why are people weeping, when they have heard that their beloved ones are admitted to the ICU Ward? What are all the tears about? Jesus is always available. Too often the human race goes into cardiac arrest unhearing bad news from the doctor. Who is the doctor? Jesus is the doctor. We go to church Sunday after Sunday, praying and praying, and paying our tithes and offerings. Yet as soon as something happens, we go into cardiac arrest.

We are angry with Jesus. We have already given up on Our Lord and Savior. We start making funeral arrangements. We walk the streets everyday singing hymns. Well now is the time to really sing them hymns. We finally got something to shout about and Jesus is his name. Where is your faith? The lights in the Intensive Care Unit are running to a low each day. Jesus has not even got started. Our fuse goes out quickly, as the fuse in the light bulb.

Composure! Composure! Composure! This is what we need. Some of us would go to the park, and sit on the bench reading a book. All we would hear is the fluttering of the breeze in our ears. This is Jesus in his tranquility. Jesus keeps us calm. We got to be determined. We got to be settled in our minds to fight satan through and through. Whenever there is a blessing to receive satan stands at the door. His job is to take it away from you, after all that you have done.

The devil's job is to accuse you in front of your heavenly father over and over again. He would bring up past sins that Jesus had already forgiven you. He would add things that you had never done before the heavenly father. He is a liar and God allows him to put forward his case. Meanwhile, we are standing and praying, and praying and praying, because we do not have the last word. Jesus delivers the last word.

We got to hold on to God the Father, and God the Son, and God the Holy Spirit. We got to allow Jesus to sing a new song. We shall overcome. We got to show our children, who got the power at the ICU ward. We got to show them that when the doctors have failed to heal, it is not over. The children have to see more patients leaving the intensive care unit healed by Jesus. That is why we pray.

The fight is not over until a healing has taken place. The Glory is not received by Jesus, until we have grown to waiting, until our love ones leave the hospital singing and dancing in the name of Jesus. We cannot throw in the towel, because we feel that, we have past our limit in prayer. We cannot say that we have been praying for the past six hours, whilst our beloved is still motionless on his sick bed.

Time now is obsolete. Prayer takes over. Jesus is in charge. We got to push the devil over the same mountain that he takes refuge. We got to burn the devil with the fire of the Holy Spirit. That is why, we shall not give up, until a healing has taken place. We got to plead the blood of Jesus It is not how old our best friend is? It is not how much wealth the person possesses? Or what is bereaved to us at the point of death? It is about the love that we have for Our Lord Jesus.

We have stayed up all night long at the gambling casinos placing our bets. We have been seen with the rent money, at the side of the table of the three-card game on 34th street. We have been seen throwing dice all night long on the street corners of Chicago. Are we listening to the voice of Jesus? Or are we putting our fingers in our ears? Jesus is the Son of the True Living God.

We have seen or have known or have heard of people, who have been incarcerated wrongfully by the Justice system. Some of these good people would not see daylight between 15 years to 30 years or even for the rest of their lives. There is surely a preponderance of evidence, that is used by the judges in sentencing someone to prison. Jesus is showing me, the many bribes, given to judges to rule in favor of the rich, and the wealthy in the society as a whole.

For too long the bench has been abused by Judges seeking financial reward. For too long the bench has been destroyed by the rats, who called themselves men of integrity, to fill the highest offices on earth. These men of great distinction walk flamboyantly in conceitedness. They walk tall in their courtrooms. Human beings tremble before them.

Needless to say, that that too is one of the reasons, why there is a pile up of work on the desks of the clerks. The world is spinning on its axis yet nothing in the absolute gets done. Why nothing good happens each day? Why is it all bad on the news media? Jesus did say that we are living in perilous times. Is not this accurate? Are not these times very dange rous? Sometimes, we cannot trust our own shadows. But the world keeps moving on.

God is not satisfied with the astute of this world. Judges, whom are called by Jesus, and are placed in these precarious positions of great esteem have to be impartial. But do we see this unbiased behavior displayed in any courthouse world over. The results are clearly seen by the vast number of prisons being built to breed more crime in inner cities. This has become a crisis. You cannot treat the children of Jesus in this manner.

There is no restitution given to families, when their sons

and their daughters are wrongfully arrested. Then not are they wrongfully arrested, but they are beaten up whilst sitting in the cells of the precincts. Jesus sees everything. Jesus knows everything. The sky is blue and the cloud is white: the color never changes? The leaves on the trees are green: the color never changes? Jesus shows you what to do, but you are and have become too illustrious now. The children of Jesus are not to be served by you.

Families go into disarray, especially when the bread winner is incarcerated. The wife or mother or woman of the house becomes all upset and most times does not know what to do. Depending on the situation, monies have to be gotten right now, to stop the wound from hemorrhaging. The bailsman must be paid. Another sore thumb in the society.

Then he returns to work only to find out that, he no longer has a job. These are the same systems, that were put in place during the days of slavery. They are put there to keep you in bondage. Instead of your name you are given a social security number. This is based on the same slavery system. Certain numbers must identify certain ethnic groups of people. India has a caste system. America has a glorified caste system.

We cannot find a workable or feasible manner of doing things, because we are biased. We lack the tenacity. We lack the spirit of comeliness. When judges are tippy-toed by satan, they have to learn to admit to themselves that they too are imperfect. That they too are not above the law. That they too must not be naive. For the house of the simple is full. And yes, the court house is full of the ignorant.

Jesus did not bless you the judge, to show off on the ignorant. He blessed you to be patient and kind and loving in understanding that that too could have been you as the ignorant. Until you see that you should have defrocked yourself. Yes, you do not see that because you feel so called to height. Your father was a judge. His father was a judge also. His father who was your great grandfather wore the judge's robe. Do not take Jesus for granted! Hell is nearer than you think.

The ignorant did not make himself one lacking comprehension. There is a reason why he is out of touch sometimes. The reason is not always what you have already concluded. If you love your wife, who has fallen sick one day, and now could no longer return to work, you would take your sweet time to give her the kind of bath you know in all honesty, that she would enjoy.

The gavel is not a tool to play with when you are seated on the bench. You do not need to bring attention by striking the table more than one time. Most judges are blessed with good wives, so why the animosity? If your wife was present in the courthouse we already know that your behavior would be one of excellence.

At the Children's Cancer Hospital they are at the hour of need. Some parents are blamed vociferously for bringing into the world a child born with cancer. It is a disease caused by a malignant tumor, that invades healthy tissue and spreads to other areas. Jesus shows a few of these parents what to do in situations like this. The few chosen parents would from time to time do everything to get in touch with other parents, who are experiencing the very same thing.

The question is patience, patience, patience. Because generally people do not have patience. Jesus do not want you to bury your patience into the sand. Jesus wants you to tarry with him a little longer. There is something to learn from this or any sickness that comes your way. Be calm! So that you can focus on Jesus. Cancer is like the clouds in the sky, when suddenly the white turns to grey and there is a downpour of rain.

Jesus knows that you want your child healthy and strong for the rest of his or her life. Jesus knows that the parent would blame themselves first, for the cause of this tumor. Jesus knows that the parent would tell the child to think positive. Jesus really, really, really want you guys to relax. Jesus is fast asleep on the boat with his disciples. there was thunder and lightning and very rough and high waves. Jesus is asleep. The disciple's teeth started to shatter and they became so afraid; what must we do?

They woke up Jesus, who was calm and focus on his heavenly father than the storm. Jesus spoke a word and the storm disappeared. How many cancer patients have parents which are servants of Our Lord Jesus? How many of you have been kind and loving to other cancer patients? How many of you believed, that your family have been cursed with a curse, or witchcraft or voodoo been poured all over the family. We could always believe, what somebody have said to us.

Did Jesus tell you that? Then why believe a fool, who is dressed up in priestly robe? Jesus does not care how many churches have been given to him by Jesus. All Jesus cares about is did you hear from Jesus? Jesus is patient. Could we be patient with patience, when we are struggling with unbelief? When the parents are scared, then they put the same fear into their children.

From the time the doctor tells the parent that the child has cancer here comes unbelief. Few parents go to another hospital to seek another answer. Still few parents would go to yet another hospital to seek another answer. Jesus is showing, that Jesus himself is put on the backburner, when something or anything does not suffice. As soon as, we wake up in the morning feeling drowsy, our first impulse is that we need to see the doctor.

When you are a child of Jesus and you fall sick Jesus comes

to you to let you know the condition of your body, and to tell you precisely what to do, to make your body healthy again. This is the Grace of God. Where there is grace there is mercy. Jesus knows all his children. A father would know his son by looking out into the distance. A father already knows to prepare for his son's homecoming.

The evil one does not know anything about Jesus's sons homecoming. The evil one did not know that, Mary the mother of Jesus was full of grace. The evil one did not know that, Mary the mother of Jesus, was filled with all the fruits of the spirit. That is why her conception was immaculate. Presently, in this world there are but few people, that are endowed with all the fruits of the Holy Spirit.

In these end times, few people want to acquiesce with the Word of God. They still prefer to hear from last day preachers. They have all become afraid of the revealing Word of Jesus. They do not want to know, what is to come. They feel that Jesus is very much unfair. They must have a say in telling Jesus what to do in our world of the future. Because that new world becomes our world and not the world of Jesus, who is our eldest brother. God is wrong to be always in control.

Leukemia patients are at the hour of need. It is a fatal disease of the blood where white blood cells multiply in vast numbers. This deadly disease is responsible for some people not attending any church whatsoever. It is like a volcanic eruption where the hot molten falls on you and disfigures you beyond repair. The blood of Jesus cleanses any impurities from the blood.

Satan knows how to hide in your bloodstream. At night, he will come out of your body, to put everything, that you have put together in your bedroom, just hours after you fell asleep. When you have awoken, you are wondering, if you did or did not fix this room properly, before you went to bed. And quite naturally, you would doubt yourself and blame yourself for your blatant forgetfulness.

You would nickname yourself "Scoundrel". You would always be making excuses for your knave attitude. There is no one that Jesus did not give a mountain to remove in their quest for glory. To feel sorry for yourself is not the answer, for those that have placed you on the pedestal. Being successful in life, and now here comes this sickness, that have toppled you in the grave, is not a pleasant memory to leave behind. Far too often, these are the last images of the deceased.

Jesus had to put up with a great deal of insults from the enemy, as he brought sight to the blind and healed every disease on the planet. It is easy for you to tell your child, that he has to make it to the top. Did you make it to the top? Pressure breeds leukemia. Children, who are gifted are under the most pressure to succeed. The arrows of life are waiting to pierce their very souls. Some people would say, that all they want out of life is a one bedroom house, with a large garage to park their luxury car. Their own family would take offense for that statement.

Aspirations put a whole lot of people in trouble with the enemy. and like a tree with many branches, so the enemy can confound the little wisdom that you possess. Jesus is allowing the sun burns on your faces to dry up before fall season. We shall pay close attention to little details, when walking barefooted in the park. Quit assuming! Since we are aware that the enemy is doing his utmost best to get you, why play into his hands? His only weapon is his mind versus yours.

Satan cannot win you in your heart and soul. Stop playing mind games! Jesus is not and will not provoke you in your mind. Sometimes, we wish that the apple tree can bear grapes. Sometimes, we wish that the mango tree can bear guavas. Sometimes, we wish that every fruit can be borne on one tree. But does this really exist. Of course, not. Did anyone try to prove Jesus wrong? Many did.

Some of you came from a good seed, and act as though you came from a bad seed. You do everything to prove Dad wrong. You would never forget what he did to your Mother. Right or wrong, Dad would forever be the wrong person. Jesus knows your daily thoughts. So does Satan. Jesus does not make you forget. Satan does. Jesus does not rearrange your bedroom. Satan does. Jesus does not stand in your way of progress. Satan does.

People suffering from muscular dystrophy are at the hour of need. This is one of the diseases that confuses many fine doctors world over. These patients are wheel-chair bound. There is no heads or tails with this one. The doctors cannot just go cutting. Many a gifted doctor have tried working with another gifted doctor to detect and stabilize muscle. The clashing of nerves entwined and woven into muscle, thus allowing blood to flow as though normal inhibits the hands of a doctor.

Could God gift a doctor, who has no faith? No. The doctor shall have faith to move the mountain. The higher the mountain, the deeper the gift. Self-will would not get you up this mountain. The grind up this steep mountain is tremendous as we walk hand in hand to discover Jesus in his wealth of suffering by bearing all burdens. Many a time we fail to achieve great height simply because, we would not defiantly love our neighbor as ourselves. We prefer that our neighbor love us first with greater love.

Most families with patients of muscular dystrophy avoid going to their homes. Does their homes need cleaning out? Yes. Bedrooms need vacuuming. Sheets need changing. Curtains need changing. Wash basin, bathtubs, and commodes need cleaning. They pretend to their friends, that they love their blood relatives. Liars.

At the hour of need, we have unsolved murders. A young man had left his home in the middle of the night sleep walking, and has never returned home. It has been twenty years now. Unsolved murders always take on an image of mystery. But is it really? The Sons of God are made aware of any happenings, before the actual hour. They are so programmed by Jesus to speak into the hearts of man.

When a mother or father or both parents have to suffer the loss of a child in this fashion, where no one could say or could give or could shed any light on the situation, then something grossly had occurred. We are all striving to be happy, then why this sudden sadness? It is like we had found the only seed and happily planted it, in the right soil, and tended to it, and did all the right things, and whatsoever we did, the seed never grew. No roots.

We sat there thinking. The tears are flowing like a river because, we are still assuming that, we must have done something wrong to Jesus. Assumptions are thoughts of the devil. Once stuck there, you would be there for the next hundred years. We have to clear that exit to ascend to an entrance. Because Jesus has to come to show you the gifted one, the trail that your child took, before he was stabbed to death and thrown over the precipice. Unsolved murders are crimes of rivalry between brothers and sisters, or first cousins or fathers and sons or husbands and wives.

These crimes oftentimes would have a paid accomplice. The bribe constitutes millions of dollars and merging of businesses. This marriage is like unto Jesus--unconditional. Satan enjoys trying to keep up with the magnificent one. Something ought to be pursued at all cost. The result being great success at pursuit of happiness. Ice skating up and down ridged mountains might look very easy to viewers, until disaster occurs.

Kidnapping children and murdering them for unpaid

ransom, need much more attention from various governments that is given world over. The search for these hoodlums should not be stopped by anyone to say the least. These cold-blooded killers must be captured at all cost. Jesus knows all these hiding places around the world. A ransom is a bribe.

Kidnappers are your drug lords. As soon as, you had turned them in to the police or to any authority; here comes evil. If not your child, your wife. And the threats on your life begins or on the immediate family, for a ransom. Or for a return of someone that you have imprisoned. Jesus is saying to the families in need, that Jesus was sold out by his disciple Judas Iscariot for 30 pieces of silver.

You cannot surrender to the evil one. You cannot go along with their demands. You cannot lose faith. There job is to stop you from doing the will of the Lord Jesus. The people that accepts bribes would be those, which had never ever been to prison. They would sit in high places. They would never turn the other cheek. They would have parties at their palaces every year. They would stand aloof.

In the business sector, they would be seen cutting ribbons to open a new business or to promote a new product or to win you over with some commercial rhetoric. The paid price of 30 pieces of silver for the death of Jesus should at all times be a pillowcase, for business people, who are doing business with strangers from other countries. You should not allow the enemy to beat you to the door of your next blessing.

To seize and hold a person unlawfully, regardless of the circumstances, is an abomination in the sight of Our Lord Jesus. To detain someone for more than 24 hours is the same as kidnapping. This kind of behavior has become commonplace, even with the taking of your grandchildren, without first consulting the mother or the father. Brothers abducting their brothers or their sisters' children, without their consent is the same as kidnapping.

Sickle cell is an abnormal red blood cell. These persons, who are born with this malady, often turn away from the loving heart of Jesus. At their hour of need, they would feel abandoned for no apparent reason. They feel better today and worst tomorrow. They are like a juggler. Their blindness to the obvious, allows the evil one, to trespass against them at the hour of need.

Jesus is ever present at the hour of everyone's need. No matter the situation. No matter the condition. No matter whether you have thought that Jesus heard you or not, keep on praying! Jesus loves you.

HE HAS DEEPEN MINE ANOINTING:

Psalm 89:20-24 I have found David my servant; with my holy oil have I anointed him:

21 With whom my hand shall be established: mine arm also shall strengthen him.

22 The enemy shall not exact upon him; nor the son of wickedness afflict him.

23 And I will beat down his foes before his face, and plague them that hate him.

24 But my faithfulness and my mercy *shall be* with him: and in my name shall his horn be exalted. Jesus is saying that every anointed Son of God would be viciously attacked whilst doing the work of Our Lord Jesus. During the winter months of January and February of 2000, my good friend Robert, whom I came to have a great deal of respect for his obedience to the voice of Jesus.

In these cold months as a vagrant in New York City, Manhattan, he would ride the E-train all night long to keep him warm. The E-train final stop was at the then World Trade Center, before the horrendous attacks by the Radical Muslim Islamic people. Occasionally he would meet and speak a word of wisdom to a fellow homeless man, or woman on the train.

The homeless population grew each night, as each carriage were filled up as the time went by until six o'clock in the morning. The stench made breathing very difficult. At times, coming off the train to catch your breath, the temperature could drop to below zero. This is frost bitten temperature. And it could take another hour before the train returned to your stop. During the night, the only train that operated after midnight on this side of the city was the E-train. It did stop at every stop going and coming.

Jesus calls your name out aloud for you to hear his voice, and go do what he wants you to do for him. It is that simple. We make it difficult by trying to differentiate between his voice and the voice of the enemy. We want to interpret the Word the way we see it, and not the way of Jesus. So the fight begins. To follow Jesus one must learn to give way to all his teachings and his promptings. Here in lies perfect understanding.

One night at the stroke of midnight, Robert was taken by Jesus to the outside staircase of the Twin Towers. As he ascended to the top of the stairs, there was a man sleeping between the revolving doors on that cold, naked ground. Immediately, Our Lord Jesus opened his Bible to a passage which was read for that poor soul. Was it cold? Tremendously cold. And reading without gloves was painful. Was there a hat on his head, as he read the scriptures? No.

Jesus is showing that the great city of Manhattan, New York does not treat his children first overall. With all the wealth that Jesus have given to the great state of New York, where was their love? With all the immigrants that I, Jesus have sent to this state to make it the greatest state and city in the whole wide world, where was your love? My children whom you have called destitute, vagrants, bombs and of like ilk. Names that I have never called you. Names that I have never associated with you. Names that I have never sewn into your hearts. Who do you think you are?

I, Jesus have found you naked in the 1930s and have clothed you. I, Jesus have given you a name above all names. I, Jesus have put all your enemies under your feet. I, Jesus have made you into a melting pot, that now you boast about without boasting about me, Jesus.

Robert's second trip to the World Trade Center was about the same time, climbing stairways, to look for Jesus's children left on the outside to die. As the very cold breeze tear through the clothing of my good friend's clothing, I could see his eyes watering, to see and find human beings stuck at doors' entrances and exits, seeking survival of the fittest.

Stop taking Jesus for granted! We take our parents for granted. We take our brothers for granted. We take our sisters for granted. We take our wives for granted. We take our husbands for granted. We take our Pastors for granted. We take our teachers for granted. We take our elders for granted. We take anyone that have done something for our benefit for granted. Stop taking Jesus for granted!

The Jesus in you is greater than the dreams that you have cultivated in and carved out for yourselves. This is what we fight against each day of our lives to get a glimpse of heaven deep within. The beauty of Jesus is seen in the eyes of the forgotten children of Our Lord Jesus. If they need ten cents to add to the cost of the hamburger, they would honestly ask you for ten cents. And that smile is for sure a glimpse of heaven on earth. It is a smile of sincerity.

The population of the homeless grows every 36 hours, as each day passes by. At night, the A-train which stops at every stop throughout the entire city, inclusive of the Brooklyn area, is not heated as the E-train. For those who could stand the cold weather, and enjoyed the sights, and the sudden cold air, when the doors are opened at every stop to Coney Island, hats off to them.

The cold nights represented systematic slavery in Germany, where the nefarious ex Chancellor Adolf Hitler, had created the Volkswagen for war during World War II. The Beetle was built by the Jewish slaves during the Holocaust. These people of color were shipped off to those plants, to build these cars to carry the bombs up and down treacherous mountain terrain, for the soldiers to plant in mountains tops. These children were the seed of Abraham, descendants of Isaac, descendants of Jacob born of the promise.

The descendants of the promise are your homeless people in any society worldwide. We would forever be the target for the Sons of satan. Jesus looks at everything. The experiences of Robert, one of the Sons of Our Lord Jesus, was not quite what he really wanted to do for the Lord. But, when Jesus has called you to undertake a mission for him, he anoints you deeper, as the day goes by to strengthen you for what is up ahead.

Breakfast was reading the Word on the A-train, whilst Jesus put him to sleep. Lunchtime was a chicken burger or two at any fast food outlet with nothing to drink. Robert read the Word from cover to cover. He read all 66 Books. Robert tried to cram verses of scripture, but Jesus would not let him. On occasion Robert would go to the largest library in the world on 34th Street to read whatever literature Jesus puts before him. The Public Library housed nine floors of reading material from around the globe.

The Public Library opened their doors around 9 a.m.to almost midnight. Even on Sundays they are opened. It is like the sun rising early in the morning and setting in the evening, but who is minding the store. Is the library crowded on the inside? No. Jesus sees everything and knows everything. Wonderful is his name. Jesus rent his clothes in disgust.

New York is a state built on a hill top. The hill top is Jesus. People from all over the entire world flock to New York for a face lift, only to find out that the wretchedness that they had left behind, came back to haunt them all the days of their lives. They had made promises to Jesus that when they got their safely, they would make every effort to become somebody in this evil and God forsaken world.

No jobs. Yes, there are. Racist! Prejudice! This is what you see everyday in the so-called beloved city of Manhattan. Insults slurred at you! Go back home! Foreigner! This is how they treat Jesus in the hearts of people of peace. They gave up everything. What did you give up? They saved every penny to get to the state of New York. Now they have become homeless, because you have hate in your heart for people of another country.

Yes, the road is tough for one to become successful. But you have made it much more difficult. Robert like most foreign people have to keep their mouths shut to stay alive. It is bitterly cold, but wear a smile on your face. Yes, I have a green card; no I do not have a green card--same treatment, no jobs. What about the statue of Liberty? After a while, one does not know what day of the week it is. The blocks in Manhattan, though the largest blocks in all the world seemed longer as you perambulate, especially on a cold frigid day.

Skyscrapers adorned each step, as far as your eyes could see. Excellent! Magnificent! Everywhere he turned his head was wealth. Limousines, stretch-limousines. The city known as the "Big Apple". Peradventure if there will be ten, will you destroy the city of New York. Words of Abraham to Our Lord Jesus. Yes, there are angels walking the streets of New York daily.

The stench on the trains when a bomb or vagrant or homeless person enters, will not be near stink, as the stench in Hell. There is no city that is booming and booning, that Jesus is not at this time blessing. It shows that Jesus is still in the blessing business. Right in the midst of 34th Street is your big screen TV. It shows the power Jesus gives to his people. Riches plastered everywhere. Technology on the increase, another sign of power and riches and Jesus, who is our Glory.

When the temperature drops below zero, it would not take long before a body part has become frostbitten. In this case, Robert's big toe lost all feelings. God the Father, God the Son, and God the Holy Spirit does not tell you or guarantee you, life or death, as you walk a closer walk with His Royal Highness. Jesus shows off his wealth to his Sons, especially when he is deepening their anointing.

The subways are not heated. Some trains are not heated. The blowing wind seemed like knives cutting off your ears. Your nose becomes frozen and your lips are all busted up and peeling from that dry cold air. Your complexion gets lighter and lighter until summertime. Survival depends on Jesus. Every now and again, Robert had to stick his hand out to beg someone for money to purchase a meal.

These are times that satan, the devil, uses to insult your integrity. Shame! Chagrin, humiliation, abashment, disgrace, mortification, dishonor, ignominy, embarrassment, disrepute, odium, mortify, humiliate, abash, humble. These are the gifts that satan and his cohorts cannot possess. Your trousers keep falling only to realize, that you have lost two more inches. People look askance, when they see you coming their way. As soon as you get in the line, people step backwards to avoid any body contact.

In the wilderness, you grow to hold on to your only best friend, Jesus. Jesus keeps you focus on the hours in the day.

Your weatherman becomes Jesus. He teaches you how to dress, as the days go by. In this way you do not overdress. You learn to share your meal with a fellow soldier. This reminded me about Robert's mother. One sweet or candy would be divided among ten people including herself. Excellent! A sight seldom envisaged.

Jesus teaches you, the who you are. The extravagance of the greatest city is utterly displayed in Manhattan. Shows are advertised on that large TV screen. Lines of people are seen gathering, with chairs in hand, overnight to get their tickets. Fortunately for some, you would get two tickets for the price of one, when the temperature drops. Theatres are packed out from the daily influx of tourists from all over the world.

The yellow cabs blow their horns as soon as you enter the sidewalk. In the middle of these happenings, you would have the pickpocketers walking alongside you to trespass against you. On the crowded sidewalks, you could lose anything that you had once possessed. The streets of heaven are paved in gold; not the streets of New York.

Immediately, as you entered the super market you could feel the uneasiness in your body as you would do your endeavor best to obtain the product and pay for the item swiftly. Because before you have taken notice, the police officer would be call in to escort you out of the vicinity. Whereas your biggest thieves are your three-piece suited guys and gals. But of course, nobody would ever take notice of the well-groomed. Jesus is not going to take your kindness for weakness.

The snow piles up on the sidewalks, as the temperature drops below 30 degrees. Newspapers stands get snowed in as the air is filled with thick snow falling everywhere. These conditions make it very difficult for Robert to walk those very slippery sidewalks. More dangerous are the entrances to trains to ride the subways, Jesus is showing the ungrateful side of a city, that he has made most abundant in every respect of the word.

Why show favoritism for certain peoples in your community? Why must the Italians occupy a certain area of the community? Why must the Germans occupy a certain area of the community? Why must the French occupy a certain area of the community? Why could not we all live in unison as Jesus emphasized in his Word? How is it so hard to love thy neighbor as thyself? Jesus says Father forgive them for they know not what they do.

Jesus is non-negotiable. A walk with Jesus is not like a walk in the park. The tourists for the most part are steered to places not frequented by the homeless. The tour guide is often knowledgeable of his city. Jesus is showing that the tour guide is bought and sold out by the city. Is the city in the house of Jesus? I think not. When Our Lord Jesus has adopted you as his own, he takes you out daily regardless of the conditions of the town, or city, or parish.

Jesus keeps you duly informed not just about the environment, but more about heavenly things, and not just heavenly things, but earthly heavenly things, and not just earthly heavenly things, but keeps you up all night long. All these are signs that Jesus has deepened your anointing. Robert remembered one day, as he was working the grave yard shift in the second largest chicken facility in all America, a young lady came up to him, pulling him in tears, to pray for her because Jesus told her that he is one of the Sons of God.

From time to time people would see Robert and give him money, while they listened to the voice of Jesus. The Christmas shows in Manhattan, took on the image of a narration of the Nativity. Buildings were all dressed up in green and red and trees were decorated with a golden star at the top, as lights of all colors filled the trees. Was this Christmas real? No.

Jesus is showing that he did leave his disciples with this new commandment: you love one another as I have loved you. This commandment should at all times be the motto in great cities. There is nobody in this whole wide world, that came on the earth, bringing with them anything. Jesus created everything. God the Father, and God the Son, and God the Holy Spirit is not going to get tired from your disobedience. No sir. You would get awfully tired, even for being disobedient.

The sudden show of giving since it is Christmas is stupid. In these times, the human race should stop and think, and show more gratitude to others, since they have been through all the trickeries of life. The stores opened until midnight had nothing to do with the death and resurrection of Jesus. The expensive toys sold at hangman prices, have nothing to do with the birth of Jesus. The exchanging of gifts at this season of goodwill had nothing to do with killings of babies born around the birth of Jesus. The advertisements on Cable, during this time of giving, had nothing to do with the star at Bethlehem.

The tricks of satan comes out each year around this beautiful season of giving and loving. Do not fall for lies! All these stupid inventions at this time had nothing to do with Jesus. Children are the dearest ones to the heart of Jesus. Stop lying to them! The Lion of the tribe of Juda will get them in the future. The stories being told by the followers of Jesus, during the season are all true to keep your feet firmly on the ground.

A wealthy city did not become wealthy without the Word coming out of the mouth of Jesus. The city should not allow the enemy to take over their city at anytime. The city owes Jesus repayment for the damage done to his Christian country. A city without lights is a dead city. The season of the coming of the child Jesus, takes place in every Christian country under the sun.

It is a time for families to get together in one place to pray, and to give thanks to God the Father, and God the Son, and God the holy Spirit. It is a time of deep anointing, especially for soldiers outside of their countries doing everything to protect Christian countries, during their celebrations. It is a time to remind all peoples of the peace of Jesus, when he walked the face of the earth bearing the peace sign deep in his soul.

When God the Father, God the Son, and God the Holy Spirit blesses you with a ministry he would not ever allow satan, the devil, to cast it into the sea of nothingness. How could a city that Jesus had blessed with Fame become cynical? How could anyone in authority, allow any perverted person, to break the second and greatest commandment of the law? Jesus would not relent until you have learnt to love thy neighbor as thyself.

The great city of Manhattan is one of the wonders of the world. There is no city that is not represented by a member of ethnicity like Manhattan. There is no man, but the resurrected Jesus to have given this city a new beginning. Why built shelters without the consent of the crucified one? Why are lies told to the best of the people only and solely to squeeze money from their pockets? When the church did this evil, did Jesus knew about the wrong? Yes, Jesus did. Jesus says do not spare the rod to spoil the child.

Surely, Jesus knows what to do. And that had given the open door of the attacks by the Radical Islamic movement towards the World Trade Center in Manhattan, New York on September 11, 2001. On that day, Robert was in Georgia watching the terrible site on someone's TV. His body was in deep pain and anguish, just before he was led by the Holy

Spirit to view this ordeal.

A walk with Jesus is a novelty. The Holy Spirit can take you anywhere in a matter of seconds. Viewing this burning of the Twin Towers live on TV from the living room of a faithful servant of God in Valdosta, Georgia, whilst remembering the word of Jesus to love your neighbor as yourself overwhelmed Robert. The utter destruction of the Twin Towers was not by accident. The death total though huge could have been much more, because thousands of people frequented those towers on a daily basis.

People from all over the world came to ascend the elevator of 110 floors to the roof top to take a view of the surroundings inclusive of the Empire State Building. This ascension took a few minutes. God the Father, God the Son, and God the Holy Spirit does not adore evil. The towering inferno of September,11 was the result of intolerance done to his children, who slept on the naked streets of winter.

Jesus is not going to allow bigots to destroy his blessed city, for the sake of more than ten just people, in the entire city of Manhattan. Jesus had already blessed the state of New York, moreover, the city of Manhattan, before the very foundations of the world. Whereas the people of the good state of New York may or may not agree with the Word of God, Jesus shows everything through their bigotry lives.

The people of this great state must give an account to the One True Living God, and his Only Begotten Son, Jesus. Jesus has blessed the city with enormous riches, so that nobody wherever they had come from would not become desolate. The chains of bondage had been denied from colored people, because of His Omnipotence. The city of New York and the state of New York are not a sanctuary place. Jesus is your sanctuary.

Make no mistake about who and what Jesus is to the

great city of New York, Manhattan. When you have never lost everything you definitely could not feel the pain of destitution. Utterly impoverished might or might not be a better word. You have gotten nothing. Jesus is the Word of God. The same destitute is the only people praising Jesus. They thank him everyday for waking them up this morning. They thank him for the free breakfast at the breakfast shed. They thank him for their daily baths. They thank him for the people, who left their clothes behind for them to wear. They thank him when someone stopped by and gave them money.

Yes, you have seen them pushing the grocery carts full of cans and bottles. They are by and large cleaning up the city. They have been keeping the city clean for more than twenty years. Did the city ever gave them anything? Of course not. Yet, as soon as, there is a crime in the area the very same vagrants would be incarcerated. Why? Because they are homeless.

Jesus is saying that it is wrong for any city, town or parish to lay blame on anyone ethnic group of people simply because, they are vagrants. Is this a reason for society to pass judgment? Is this a reason for anyone to pass judgment on anybody? Jesus is saying, that there is no society on the face of the earth, that dictates to the owner and the creator of Heaven and Earth.

Referenda are not the criteria for passing judgment on the destitute. There is no rich man, who would let anyone park their car in his garage. There is a price to pay. Jesus had already paid the price. It is grossly unfair for someone to come to your house and dirty it. It is grossly unfair for someone to leave their homeland, bound for New York, taking everything with them including Jesus and received the blows from the imps of satan.

If you would have made the Lord's Prayer, your daily

prayer, then you would have been on the road to loving your neighbor as thyself. Yes, Jesus is standing right there beside you; he has not left your side. When a stranger comes to your house, you shall treat him with a very warm welcome. You shall share your meal with him. You shall be hospitable. Do kindness without expectancy!

From this vantage point, Jesus will now make you his own. The church is not a circus. The church is not to be used for entertainment. It is Jesus's secret place. The Jesus in you have to become like unto Jesus. This requires a deep anointing. The evil one loves to imitate Jesus. The enemy knows when Jesus is about to deepen your anointing. Then he accompanies you to the football game to scream and shout your head off. Meanwhile, Jesus had already told you not to go to the game on that night. But in disobedience, you made it your duty to attend the game.

The new World Trade Center has nothing to do with creating an atmosphere of peace. The doors of the state of New York must never be shut to immigrants. The windows of homes must not be used to throw garbage, onto the heads of the homeless, as they are passing by. The rivers of water that flows all through the city will now become, as dry and as arid as the Sahara Desert. Out of the mouths of babes and sucklings wisdom will flow.

It is a pity, when a homeless woman goes to the doctor and is found to be pregnant, the ugliness of the society wears her out. Automatically, she is held in contempt. She is already maligned. Why maligned her twice? The evil names echoes, as she passed by. Who made you? Yes, God made you. Who made the homeless woman? Yes, God made her also.

Jesus made Eve from a rib out of Adam. And because of this great miracle, the woman must be looked up to in the image and likeness of the first female human being. Jesus is Lord of everyone. Am I my brother's keeper? Sure do. God the Father, God the Son, and God the Holy Spirit is and will always be is forevermore. We too, are the authors of our own sinful behavior. This is one of the reasons for your ugliness.

The Almighty Jesus judges every single human being on the face of the earth. Likewise, it is a pity, when a homeless man has to be taken to the doctor. Why all these experiments? Why use him as a guinea pig? Why give him all these drugs to take? Have not you use Jesus's children enough? Well, the game is over. Jesus is now your traffic signals.

Until you get in line with God the Father, and God the Son, and God the Holy Spirit you shall not enter the kingdom of heaven. The greater the gift, the greater the penalty. The higher the office, the deeper the fall. In the wilderness there are many doors that look like Jesus. Pray God that you will open the right one! Pray God that when you have entered, Jesus in his humility will open and keep the door open for others.

For too long, the children of Jesus had to suffer immensely for the sins of their forefathers. For too long, the children of immigrants in the state of New York, had to sit at the side of the road, in the cold weather to wait for their names to be called, thus flouting the warnings of the prophets. For too long, the people who were put in charge stole the moneys, which were placed aside for the handicap.

Woe onto you so-called brothers and sisters, which were given the best seat in the house of the Lord! Woe onto you dumber than you think believing that Jesus would not ever find out how stupid you are! Woe onto you defiant of the laws of Abraham, Isaac, and Jacob! Woe onto you defiant of the laws of Jesus the only one True Son of the Living God! Woe onto you boastful city of Manhattan, New York!

Yes, the handicap, they who need much more than parking spaces nearest the doors of any building. For the love of

Jesus, you can do more for the love of your fellowmen. The isotopes in the lives of the handicap prevent the blood flow to the brain. If only the doctors would humble themselves and sit under the cross of Jesus, the world will be a show piece for Jesus. But Jesus already knows that the majority of people will be defiant.

The handicap are also people who have lost their way. They had been faithful during the good times of a robust economy. But as soon as, the Twin Towers fell, they closed up shops and tuck their heads in like a turtle. Jesus is not about hypocrisy. The roads of the state of New York are wide and varied. The roads of heaven are narrow and curled at the top. Becoming a hoarder might look pretty, as you hide what you deemed valuable.

Look up at the buildings, as you walked the streets, I dared you for you canst see the top. That is why some of you fall crippled in your old age. Before you had come to a great city, you washed your clothes by hand. You waited until it was dried, and then you iron your clothes without an electric iron. The coal pot had five irons sitting. Jesus knows from thus you came. The clothes you migrated with could not fill the suitcase. Anyone could see that you believed that you have arrived.

Some people are handicapped in their hearts. They truly believe that everyone is going to heaven. They look at everything black and white. You are either good or bad. They believed with great passion that the earth would not be destroyed by fire. They also believe in luck and magic. Why go to church, just because your boss goes to that particular religious church?

Is Jesus really listening to the echoes of the souls not found to be buried at a local cemetery? Are the families believing that one day they would meet again? is there truly life after death? All these questions Jesus hears from up on high. The attacks by the, Radical Islamic Terrorists, to this day are very much alive in the minds, and hearts, and souls of those, who have lost loved ones.

Must Jesus leave Heaven to go to each member of the bereaved families to tell them, how sorry he is to have allowed their deaths? is this a new World Order? Is this a sign that the World is coming to an end? Far from the truth! The world is too busy trying to bring about their own revelation. We walk in too many different directions. We foolishly believe that Jesus is hiding something.

We need Jesus to deepen our anointing. We need Jesus to deepen our wisdom and understanding. We need to ignore what we hear from our surroundings. It is not right to turn a deaf ear to something of real importance. It is not right to entertain negative thoughts towards your fellowmen. When you dislike them befriend them. When it gets to hating foreign people call on Jesus both day and night.

Some of us need a fresh anointing. We have come to a dead-end and nothing more is happening. We see a lot of smoke and no fire. We keep calling on Jesus and Jesus is not answering. We keep not letting go of everything that is evil. We keep not living a life of holiness. We keep not praying and fasting. We keep not paying our tithes and offerings. We keep holding on to the same old friends that Jesus had warned us about. We keep avoiding to press on no matter what.

Forbearing the right ways of life would result in any anointing. Jesus being able to withstand the snares of the devil, was able to now pour his Holy Spirit in us. Jesus is showing the entire municipality that he is Lord of all. The Holy Spirit owes no one an apology in the destruction of the Twin Towers on that evil day. God the Father, God the Son, and God the Holy Spirit will be with the families that stood their ground believing in the One True Triune God. Their anointing Jesus had already deepened in the gift of deeper wisdom and understanding.

The twelve apostles never had it easy, since they have laid their eyes on the real Jesus. So will you be tested from time to time by Our Lord and Savior Jesus, as you walk with him on the narrow road to heaven. Peradventure, Jesus is the way, the truth and the life. No one comes to the Father except through me. This Word had caused a great swing in the minds and hearts and souls of the human race. To the extent of great damage to the Twin Towers in Manhattan, New York.

Jesus is talking about the statutes that decorate the city. Much too much emphasis are placed on other celebrations that have no bearing on the sweet name of Jesus, and what he has done for the planet. Nobody celebrates the name of Jesus by going to church just once a year. Nobody celebrates the name of Jesus by going to church twice a year. People should have learnt after the disaster, that they need to lift up the name of Jesus everyday of their speared lives.

You do not need to march for gun rights. No one gets a deeper anointing for marching the streets on any occasion, except for the death and resurrection of Our Lord Jesus. No one gets a deeper anointing for marching the streets for LGBTQ Rights. No one gets a deeper anointing for marching the streets for the disposal of the New President. No one gets a deeper anointing for marching the streets to lift the ban on vetting immigrants.

We lift the wrong things up, are like lifting, the dress up of a new born baby doll. We would forever believe that Jesus is hiding something from us. We have become too old-fashioned, even in the way, we are now giving thanks to his blessed name. The streets are growing naked with prostitution even after our darkest moment. Jesus wants you to lift up the flood gates of heaven, for him to pour out a new blessing unto the city.

A new blessing means a new day for the people to make a conscious effort to rally for the handicap. Robert has seen clearly that the handicap is handicapped in their soul. Your soul is fed too much with pollution of the spirit of darkness. In every store there is a symbol of darkness with someone in uniform waiting to take you to prison for shoplifting. There are also undercover police officers walking the streets of the city of Jesus. This spirit of darkness is spreading throughout the four corners of the state.

And as soon as, the season of Jesus's celebration comes around there are police officers' vehicles, including buses parked in Manhattan to cart off the homeless to prison, for walking out the shoe store with a pair of brand new shoes. Jesus is saying that all these happenings are the cause of the wrong doings of the society as a whole. Moreover, 90 per cent of the people are doubting the love of Jesus, since September, 11.

The spirit of darkness had come to the city long before that tragic day, of a memorial, that nobody really wished for. Consequently, the rest of the non-Christian world rejoiced over the wounded city. This gave them more power to advocate their beliefs in a monotheistic God. They did not care for the sufferings of millions of people, which inhabited the city of the brave.

The spirit of darkness would remain over the city, until the people of God the Father, God the Son, and God the Holy Spirit return their faces back to him. There was a time when things were beautiful, and everyone took great interest in each other. People from around the world flooded the city to enjoy the shows at Broadway, and at Radio City, and the Palladium, and the World Famous Madison Square Garden.

At the age of 120 years old, Moses had perfect vision. An

absolute example of a deeper anointing. How many people are aspiring to duplicate the conscious awareness of this miracle? Yes, the enemy had thrown us under the bus. It would take a pressing to the mark of Jesus by everyone, to do right until thy kingdom come. In these perilous times, Jesus is showing me that some human beings will be living past 120 years.

This is proof that the precious little ones must see to encourage them in their walk with Our Lord Jesus. It is a blessing for a man of God, to attain that milestone in good health and power and love. It is a blessing for a man of God, to have a walk with Jesus both day and night. It is a blessing for a man of God, to have a face to face conversation with Our Lord Jesus.

Has anybody seen the serpent crawling through the city of New York, that dark and lonely night? Since your answer is no, then you are absolutely in the distant doing everything that you know that you would not be doing in heaven. It is grossly unfair, when a multitude of people flock to a land only because, the serpent took them there to be destructive. And as diabolical as it might be, the world took little notice of the marching to and fro by the LGBTQ group in the city of Manhattan. The word SERPENT MEANS LGBTQ.

There is no human being, that would leave their country for another knowing full well, that there would be thugs and vagabonds and notorious people, where he and his wife would be sojourning. Yes, the thugs, would do anything to destroy, not just the beauty of the city, but would vandalized and strip the name of Jesus out of the heart of decent folks. Suffice it to say, that the serpent in his wisdom just does not get it.

The laws of Jesus are not hard to follow, if you would only seek his face day and night. The hoodlums would from time to time, put pressure on you for you to become one in likeness to them. They would teach you how to rob, steal and vandalized people's property. They would make you believe that the Bible is written by the hand of man, and not by the inspired Word of God.

The serpent would continually seek you to provoke you into damnation. He would talk to you in your ears to go do something evil, even when you know right from wrong. Jesus is not in the provocation business. Jesus is with you especially, at the time you wholeheartedly believe, that he is not there. The serpent would tell you to go put graffiti on the walls of buildings, public buildings, subway trains, buses and old cars left on the roadsides.

You see these drawings even in the city of Brooklyn. The evil from the eye of the serpent is looking at you for he is very much aware that his boundaries are slowly shortening as time goes by. Now that he has failed to destroy the great city of Manhattan, he would proceed to ultimately destroy the melting pot of Brooklyn. The serpent would be crawling through the canals at night looking for a soul to devour.

The serpent is unnoticeably hidden in your wallets to prevent you from giving to the poor and the homeless. Giving is not only at Christmas time. Giving is something you ought to do quite naturally. The more you give, the more Jesus will return to you and your siblings and your siblings, siblings, a blessing from heaven. Jesus wants you to bear this in mind. It is not how much work that you have done for Jesus that counts. Jesus gave his life for everyone. To give to someone you do not know anything about becomes a deeper blessing that Jesus will return to you.

Jesus does not forget your giving. Always give with a smile. Do it quickly! For when you stop to think about it or to whom you are giving, the serpent would come to steal your blessing. And now you are right back or even further back, than where you have first begun. It does not take a whole day in your giving for Jesus to come bless you. It does not take a whole day to prepare to return a blessing. It does not take a saving account to remember the goodness of Jesus.

The Almighty Jesus holds all the doctorates in his giving. They did him wrong, yet he has forgiven them. The streets of New York are now covered with slime. Only Jesus can come to rescue you from the hands of the enemies. Only Jesus is qualified to do this work for his heavenly Father.

The serpent knows how to play hide and seek in your mind. Robert's experiences have taught him to ignore the variables of Manhattan. A city that does not sleep. A city, that the world has come to accept as one of beauty and kindness and blessing that has dwindled into the jaws of the enemy. Samson, one of the Judges of Israel, was told by his parents through an angel, that alcohol must not enter his mouth. Though gifted greatly, he became disobedient and lost his beautiful eyes.

In this modern hip-hop world, the youths believe that they are invincible. They put the word of Jesus in their songs and their raps and their jazz and their rhythm and blues without the word from Jesus. Samson, who was one of the greatest Judges that ever has embraced this earth, paid a high price, which resulted in his death. We must learn to wait on Jesus, to give us the all clear, before you go do whatever you feel that is so right to go do.

The business community of Wall Street, which is in the heart of Manhattan, is not of Jesus. Jesus says that he will supply all your need. The infernal one loves to imitate Jesus. When the heart and soul of all America become Wall Street, once again the serpent shows his ugly head. The world or the New World could not ever be run by brutal billionaires. All these billionaires were not made by the clean hands of Jesus. How many of them go to any church come Sunday

Mprning? How many of them stand at the head of any food line, in the naked cold, to feed the homeless? How many of them stand anywhere to give out warm leather coats to the homeless? I know of one.

The damnable follows Jesus in order to make a fool of the elect. The deeper your anointing the more you would be able to discern the abominable one in your visions. The children of Jesus should at all times not bend their knees and walk in the direction of Balaam. The children of Jesus do not need to burn candles at any church. Jesus does not need your flame. You need the fire of the Holy Spirit. You do not need novenas. You need the fire of the Holy Spirit. You do not need the rosary. You need the fire of the Holy Spirit. You do not need to geneflect in front of idols or statutes. You need the fire of the Holy Spirit.

The serpent crawls through the streets of the financial sector of Wall Street. Everyone passes you in suit and tie and expensive dresses, when you have found yourself homeless on Wall Street. The perfume they wear day after day by the workers on this side of town are very expensive. After a while, Robert came to the understanding that in this part of town, he has to be really careful being seen in the area. Robert sometimes wonder, where is everybody?

The money, which is black gold, flows through the streets of Manhattan, like diamonds in the sky. The greatest diamond collection one can find is in the center of Manhattan. Where is everybody? Everybody is looking at each other to see which one is going to do the Will of the Almighty God. Needless to say, the milking of the cow is over. What seemed to be comfort will now be grief.

Worshipping the serpent through the psychic hot line 24/7 is one of the downfalls of this great city. Turning the eyes of the serpent into soap operas are another one of the downfalls of this great city. Money laundering from Wall Street to all across the globe is another one of the downfalls of this great city. The valley of iniquitous living among human beings is another one of the downfalls of this great city. Much too much in the adoration of self.

Since the poor is mistreated by the great wealth of Manhattan, then Jesus must defend the poor of the poorest. The defense of Jesus towards the most vulnerable in the society is greatly profound. Jesus is continuously showing all over the world, that the poor will always be with us, is also very profound. Turn again and you would see for yourselves, that the majority of rich people in the world have given their souls to the serpent.

The making of parts for machines worldwide and their distribution especially in the aeronautics division are erroneously corruptible. Insurance companies have been seen bribing politicians in their quest for favors. Wall Street is fast becoming like Egypt in the days of Moses. Great thinkers are being paid large sums of money to sign off on any plan, that would benefit the cartels. The eyes of satan are all over the financial sector of Wall Street. There are no boundaries to greed, which are connected to all the streets that pivots off Wall Street. They used to say that 42nd Street is the most and now was the most corrupt street in all America--look out Wall Street.

The eyes of the serpent are now filled with glaucoma, as Jesus keeps up the pressure on Wall Street. Jesus is saying that there will be no turning of the sod of the mountain of guilt that stands atop of the financial sector. Jesus knows precisely what affects so-called main stream media. It is not flattery when the truth is being spoken. It is not remorse, when you come into a world that boasts about: you can be anything you want to become. Philosophy: the logical study of the nature and source of human knowledge or human values; the set of values, opinions, and ideas of a group or individual. Jesus is not about your philosophy. Jesus is about his philosophy.

In order to obtain a deeper anointing as life evolves, one has to carry out all commands given to you by Jesus. The Almighty Jesus is not going to listen to you after he has laid down his life for you. Robert recalled that he has never had to dust his shoes off from any state in America that he has visited. You cannot inherit a deeper anointing. The more ministries Jesus gives to you the deeper is your anointing.

Some preachers want to serve God and mammoth. You cannot go to school to learn evil to fight or deliver evil from anyone. That is like hiding your head in the sand. Yes, Jesus created both the good and the evil. Jesus gives everyone a choice. There was a time when animals were used as sacrificial lambs in atonement of sins. Jesus is the lamb who takes away the sins of the world. But some people had not given up blood sacrifices.

This in turn allow even their children unborn to inherit evil in their lives. Thus giving their children epilepsy, seizures, tuberculosis, diphtheria and of such the children of Jesus will not bear. This provocation of the Holy Spirit did not just begun, because for centuries the practice of voodoo and witchcraft have dominated two-thirds of the world. This evil some people refer to as good. There is no such thing as good witches.

These two religious groups have spread worldwide. And have started churches all across America Anointed preachers of Jesus carry within them the Holy Spirit. Whereas they carry the spirit of beelzebub. They too are the authors of magic. A so-called phenomenon. Jesus who is the one that is to come is waiting for his heavenly father's word. Jesus is teaching all creation the importance of word.

The word was made flesh and dwelt among us. This is

Jesus. The degree of anointing is far too much for any human being to behold. Jesus rose from the grave. Jesus ascended into heaven. The deeper the anointing, the greater the work. The deeper the anointing, the longer you shall live. Why? There is work to be done in the vineyard. The deeper the anointing, the greater your love for the people of Jesus.

The serpent is threading the needle whilst you are serving two masters. The deeper the anointing ultimately result in the breaking of bread. Jesus showed this to two preachers on their way to Damascus. They only recognized him after the breaking of the bread. Jesus is clearly giving us every opportunity to walk with him closer. We become too much afraid even with our close walk with Jesus.

Jesus really wants to double and triple and quadriple your anointing, but we allow flesh to get in the way of the Lord. There is a comfort in our walk with Jesus. From the time everything is going alright, we become lazy in the spirit. We got more than we had asked for and now we relent. We must realize that there is much more work in our Father's vineyard. We cannot allow the enemy any ground to further his obsession with lust.

For as long as we are alive there would be a battle with the lustful one. We at no time must let the walk with Jesus to become too comfortable. Jesus does not need anyone; all Jesus wants to do is to deepen our anointing. Be grateful for the little things! Sow seeds if you must! But for heaven sake do it in the name of Jesus. Sometimes it is good to take a walk; to stroll around the shopping center, but we cannot allow the serpent to intrude our private and brief moments with Jesus.

A walk with Jesus is only lengthened by the will of Jesus. A talk with Jesus is an excellent moment and an excellent conversation to have bearing in mind that you have to do all the listening. It is a mystery of beauty, when you can continue the conversation, even in the twilight and much more as you sleep. A soft gentle loving voice is the voice of Our Lord Jesus.

His anointing is wiser than the serpent, which crawls on his belly, to peep at you in order to frighten you in your walk with Jesus. Jesus says fear not the one who can kill the body, but fear the one who can kill both body and soul.

THE ANGELS FEED YOU DAILY:

ISAIAH 65:25 The wolf and the lamb shall feed together, and the lion shall eat straw like the bullock: and dust *shall be* the serpent's meat. They shall not hurt nor destroy in all my holy mountain, saith the Lord. Jesus is saying that man's wisdom does not excel him in proportion to the meat, that is laid before him. We pray everyday with little or no result at the end of the day. We believe that something is very wrong with the prayers we mumble below our breath. Suffice it to say, that there is something missing on the road to Mt. Calvary.

Some people make the same mistake over and over again throughout their lives. They depend too much on themselves in choosing a discipline that will take them to their mountain on high. You have paid your tithes and your offerings and still there is that dark cloud of debt in your life. You have made every excuse not to bother your pastor, or your prophet or prophetess to help you find your path in life. Jesus have put these men and women of God, to help you to remove the dark cloud in your life.

We cannot do it alone. And when you cannot trust someone then your foolish pride gets in the way of progress and prevent you from lifting Jesus up and not yourselves.

How can you love Jesus when you cannot love and trust someone? The principal has sent for you to tell you about your child; you ignore him completely. The teacher has implored on you to get with you and your child for the well-being of his future. Meanwhile, you like most parents did not want to be bothered by the teacher. You believed with all your heart, that there is something sinister about this teacher. You firmly believed that you have no need for Jesus.

Be reminded of the bandage on your left leg, as you are hopping around the city, looking for someone to heal the wound on your broken body! At no time could you separate yourself from the lamb of God. It is unfortunate, when Jesus provides help and we ignore the love of Jesus. During your lunch hour, go visit someone at the Hospital! Or just follow someone in the elevator to visit their loved one. You would quickly find out after a while, that you need Jesus all of the time and not some of the time.

Of course, the wolf and the lamb shall feed together because Jesus says that he will provide for all of us, since we have all been chosen to dwell on this very earth. But those of us, who have lost the way by seeking other houses of worship to obtain quicker success and an end to poverty should acquiesce and bow out of this theory, before it is too late. For the things that we are constantly running from would become our greatest strength, if only we would listen to the thundering voice of Jesus.

It is impossible to count the stars in the sky at night. So it is not easy to remove the bandage from the left leg. We have all fall short of the glory of the Lord. All we have are the promises of Jesus to heal our broken bodies, whenever we fall prey to the ways of the evil one. From time to time, there would be collision courses on our way to success, especially in fields, that Jesus must be sought out with all our might to achieve great success. Until we have become one with our blessed Lord, the serpent would trick us out of our blessing.

Some of us have given up hope, that no member of our family would ever become a super star in the movie world. Have we ever asked Jesus to bless us with a special someone? Or all we ever think about is to lift up ourselves. Have we ever prayed and fasted as a family to achieve such a gifted someone? And have we sought the prayers of the pastor or the prophets or prophetesses to bring about such a great and special blessing? Jesus says ask and you shall receive.

We love to boast about great athletes in our debates. We love to talk about them everywhere we go. Are any of these great ones a member of our family? We love to cheer on our favorites. Are any of our favorites family? We love to imitate great singers. Are any of these great singers family? Jesus is still saying ask and you shall receive. For our uniqueness have made us special in the sight of God the Father, God the Son, and God the Holy Spirit. Worship him and him alone! Adore him and him alone! Put him and him alone on a pedestal! Love him with all of our mind, heart and soul. Leave nothing to chance! The enemy with his bag of tricks, call magic, would be there to entice us to lose our blessings.

The wolf and the lamb shall feed together are not an anomaly. It is not the choices we make. To follow Jesus is to follow him blindly. Avoid life's nakedness at all cost! We go to the movies and we see or envisage personalities that we believe we should have inherited. Does not the rose garden tell all the other flowers in the world, Am I not the most beautiful flower in all the world? Jesus is the most beautiful flower in all the world.

Jesus is showing me a walrus. A large marine mammal with ivory tusks and a tough body. Some of us would like to be a walrus because of its tusks and its hide. But could the walrus survive in hot weather. No. Moses said an eye for an eye, a tooth for a tooth. Jesus, who came to fulfill the law, says turn the other cheek. Some people put a sign outside of their homes to take your shoes off before entering their house. This sign is really for the other people and not for family and friends.

There are signs, especially in rich neighborhoods, to keep your feet off the grass. Moses was told by Jesus to take your shoes off, because your feet are on sacred ground. We flout the laws of Jesus faster than an ATM machine. And as soon as, we are caught in the lions' den, now we are on bended knees begging Jesus please let me off the hook and I would return to pastor the amplifier that I stole out of his church.

Some people have made promises to Jesus and to this very day have broken all of their promises. There is no man on the earth that can beat Jesus in giving. But when you have made a promise to Jesus, you must not allow the enemy to stand in the way. There are absolutely no excuses for breaking any promise that you have made to Jesus. You were much better off when you had never made a promise to Jesus.

Jesus is very busy taking care of you and your family, quicker than your brain could conceive. The prophets which came long before the birth of Jesus proclaimed the coming of Jesus. They were jailed for just mentioning his birth. Some of them were stoned by the general public for their boldness. Some of them their homes were burnt down by the officers of Pharaoh. And then some of them were beheaded for the Word.

Jesus keeps showing me a very stubborn people. Their hands are always out begging, when Jesus had already paid the price. All Christians have been taught this from inception to be assertive. You must defend with your life the sweet name of Jesus. Jesus have placed the Bible into your hands for you to read the best way you can. Most of the time, where is the Bible? On your dash board in your car. Or at the house brand new and was never opened. Yet you cry all day long for Jesus.

Jesus have allowed you the gift of reading. You read the newspapers first thing in the morning. You read your novel last thing at night. And the precious name of Jesus is shut up in your closet. The gift of reading that was given to you will in the pursuing years will leave you because of your stubborn behavior towards your Lord. Jesus does not have to come to you to let you know of your sinful behavior.

At birth Jesus gave you perfect vision. A gift of sight. Jesus in his goodness allows you to go to kindergarten to develop the gift of reading. Something that he had paid the price for with his life. Consequently, Jesus takes you literally by the hand and steer you through elementary school, and Middle school, and High school, and College, and University. Jesus is sitting and waiting for you to begin reading from Genesis to Revelation.

Meanwhile you are too busy boasting about yourself. Whilst the men of God are going through fire for you, to feed you, come Sunday morning. Men of God, who are anointed by Jesus to bring his Word do have the greater burden. Jesus never told you not to boast, but boast about sweet Jesus and what he has done for you.

Some of you have been healed by Jesus in your youth. Where is your Bible? You have never taken the time to go buy the True Living Word of God. During the intervening time, you are fast becoming a basketball star. And now you are depending on self-will. Clearly you have given the gift of sight to other things, that mean absolutely nothing to Jesus, but of course means a great deal to you. Jesus is sitting and waiting for you to set your priorities right.

Some of you have been healed at death's door and have attended church, but for only a few weeks. Where is your Bible? On your bed head as you perused the pages of favorite passages of scripture. Jesus is showing me his mercy towards you and his ever saving grace towards your loved ones, who did everything to bring you through.

Jesus is reading his Word and the lion shall eat straw like the bullock. Isn't it expensive to live in this world right now? I remembered as a child, when a pound of sugar cost one cent, which in America would be one penny. Today that same pound of sugar cost $2.00 plus tax. It is a shame, that even though there are people, who had lived in those days and are here with us today are not using social media to speak the truth. For the truth must be spoken at all times. Jesus is the truth.

For some reason the human race has become so egocentric. Pride is the evil crown on satan's head. A piece of which is given to followers of the bride of satan. Some of us have become shopaholics over the years. Who take pride in visiting any or every store to purchase something, that they have already bought before. Jesus has a way in sending someone to deliver a word to them about the situation. Pray warriors would come to them over a period of time, to tell them to form a prayer line, or join them in their prayer line.

How many dresses could you wear in any given day? How many hats could you wear in any given day? How many shoes could you wear in any given day? It is very painful, when you see clothes stacked on each other with tags, and no breathing space in the closet. Hats in boxes that have never been worn, and they are out there peradventure shopping for more hats. Shoes stacked in boxes one on top of the other with tags touching the ceiling. Even Solomon in all his glory was not robed like this.

One cold rainy day, there is a knock on your door, and at that time, you were expecting someone. So you rushed to the door and quite naturally you quickly opened it. Surprisingly, a young woman about your size all soaked with water, beseeched your intelligence. Jesus is now turning you to the closet. Though speechless, under your breath, you asked her for her name, as you go through countless dresses to give her one.

Jesus keeps popping up to let you know, that it is wrong to have clothes in your closet, that have not been used. Likewise, the congregation could not allow the First Lady to do everything for them. Respect is the word. Jesus keeps rolling out the red carpet. Intermittently, the congregation is not following the footsteps of Jesus. Because they have fixed their eyes on Mary, the mother of Jesus, more than on the King of Kings and Lord of Lords.

Jesus is reading his Word and the lion shall eat straw like the bullock. In these perilous times, Jesus have seen fit to anoint women preachers. And for some reason, so-called Bible scholars are vehemently not allowing women to get on with the business of our heavenly Father. Far too often, they have fell short of some directive that Jesus had given to them to do, but have failed in their duty. If the pulpit would only speak the truth then too, the mercy of Jesus will move and flow as the river Nile.

Jesus is waiting patiently for these so-called Christians to be an example of a true representative of Jesus. The work of the Lord is indeed tremendous. Interpretation of the Word of God is absolutely Jesus business and not ours. Children, who are called to preach the Word of God, are held back simply because of jealousy, in the house of the Lord. How could people follow the man of God, when he too is indeed disobedient to his heavenly Father?

Children are not to be made deacons, when they are called to preach the Word. Children are very precious in the sight of Jesus. Children are not to be told that they are not ready for the congregation. Children are not to be coached by the pastor, as to what to say and how to say or bring the Word of

God. This is not show time. This is not entertainment time. This is Jesus time.

The rock is Jesus. Out of the rock comes abundant resources. Children are your abundant resources. Jesus will electrify his anointed precious ones to do wonders in a corruptible world. Their innocence will be their strength. Their tongues will set the whole world on fire. Please do not try to embarrass these precious little ones! Please do not mimic their presentations!

The preachers, who are anointed by Jesus, and have cared less about women preachers have been castrated even in the Word of God. The Book of Revelation would not be given to them to prophesy in the name of Jesus. Jesus knows everything and is about showing the world everything that is to come. How could you be so judgmental? You either heard from Jesus or you did not.

Jesus is showing me children, who are called to preach, and are threatened by their parents not to tell the pastor. Some parents are of the belief, that their children should not surpassed them in life. Some preachers which are beholden to the scriptures, and would not deviate to Jesus's interpretation of Word, are the very same preachers, which avoids children from ascending their pulpits.

Jesus begs the question. who do you say I am? Peter the Apostle spoke up and said that you are the Son of the Living God. Jesus answers him and says, that the spirit of the Living God, which is the Holy Ghost, gives you the answer. What is of flesh is flesh and what is of spirit is spirit. Every church has a Bible scholar, and every Bible scholar would not agree with the other person.

One person had the answer out of twelve as to the question, who do you say I am? Jesus math surpasses all physics. As soon as Jesus does not speak to you individually, all hell breaks loose. Where is your faithfulness? There are steps that lead to heaven. And only one person will take you there.

Jesus is saying and dust shall be the serpent's meat. Who wants to be caught dead in their tracks, stealing the Word of God? Jesus is the one that the world is created for. The rivalry between Jesus and the serpent began, when God made the world for His only Begotten Son, Jesus. The fall of the serpent and his fallen angels from heaven to the earth created such a tempest of dust, that the dust became the food for the devil.

This rivalry is liken unto the castrated bullock, which is unable to have children. So too are the rivalry between castrated men and Jesus, and castrated women and Jesus, because they could not bear children. This hatred is the dust which is the food for the serpent. This behavior of hostility and animosity could be seen in the eyes of the enemy. The crawling serpent gathers dust on his body, as he makes his way into the hearts of men and women.

We see this clearly in the Garden of Eden, when as soon as God formed Eve from a rib of Adam, here comes the serpent to display his prowess. The devil cannot be creative. His subtleness, which comes in the form of trickery, and his persistency will wear you out once you start listening. Jesus is the great I am who have sent you.

To preach the Word, wherever He has directed your path. To go boldly into the world armed with your sword. Jesus is showing me choppy waters. Adam and Eve had no written Bible to read and follow the way of Jesus. After they were banished from the Garden of Eden, for their disobedience in breaking the law, the only law, not to eat of the fruit of that tree: burning swords surrounded the Garden of Eden.

At the very entrance, there is an angel, that is put there by Jesus to keep watch. No angel falls asleep. But yes, the fallen angels do fall asleep. Their hours of destruction are from midnight to three o'clock in the morning. During these hours the serpent and his cohorts are extremely dangerous The angel of God, that keeps watch over the children of God, also keeps watch over the children of Adam and Eve,

The eagle follows the coastline of the seashore to catch its prey in the midnight hour. Its camouflage feathers are not seen by the eyes of its prey. Adam and Eve had to listen to one voice, that one voice was the voice of Jesus. During these dangerous times, we too have to listen to that same voice, the voice of Jesus. Jesus is silently listening to the voice of many waters, as Jesus keeps watch over his precious little ones.

The eagle ascends with his catch for his young ones to feast on all night long. Whereas, the serpent is rolling in the dust keeping his eyes on the changing times, as each change bears his sign of the mark of the beast. His number 666 will now become a sign for his earthly followers.

Jesus is saying and dust shall be the serpent's meat. The scientists believed that the earth is millions of years old. This is preposterous. In like manner, they too believed that the serpent's meat was not dust. In furtherance of this, they too believed that once the earth was square and not round. Jesus does not make any mistakes. Half the time, their earthly predictions are totally wrong. Just take a look at the world today.

Sanctions are put into place by countries world over, when they are not conforming to the ways and means committee. Force is not the answer to bring about friendship. This is like driving with a full tank of gas, but the needle is on empty. The animosity is increased and nobody cares about Jesus precious little ones. Nobody cares about the root of David. Nobody cares about the crucifixion of Our Lord and Savior Jesus. Nobody cares about the poaching of Jesus's animals.

Every scientist cares about the cross-breeding of animals, to bring about other castrated animals world over.

To this day the mule, a product of cross-breeding a horse and a donkey, is still not considered a failure in the eyes of the scientists, whose prize are to prove the Bible, the true Word of God, wrong. Jesus will not be moved by the tricks of the enemy. Sanctions though unanimously agreed to are not in agreement with the Word of God. Jesus came to tear down walls, when he walked the face of the earth. The planet is too busy rebuilding the very same walls, that the Lord had already torn down.

In the time of Noah, Jesus saved one family. In today's world nobody believed this truth. The scientists have been working feverishly to renounce this truth. Articles appear in their periodicals about the Garden of Eden and where it is located. Where is the location of the birth of Jesus? Where is the location of the foster father Joseph and his wife Mary? Where is the location of the tomb that Jesus laid in? Belief is not enough.

Who are you to place a penalty on any country? Who are you to put your beliefs in the minds, hearts and souls of anyone? Only Jesus is authorized to do this. Socrates was poisoned and his books were all burnt. Nobody is marching the streets of America for freedom of the press. Reporters are killed by the serpent's followers, when he broadcast the whole truth and nothing but the truth. Where are the scientists?

Jesus did not impose any sanctions on the serpent. Satan, the devil, is seen roaming the whole earth looking for souls to devour. The angels in heaven are instructed not to touch the serpent. Then why are countries getting together to impose sanctions on any one country? The owner of the universe is God the Father, and God the Son, and God the Holy Spirit; the owner is not you.

To every seed a plant grows. The bird of the air would pick up a seed, and take it to a land for Jesus to nurture for his children. Sometimes countries are in a deadlock to bring about sanctions. Sometimes countries go along with their partisans to pass sanctions, either way it is totally wrong. Sanctions do not come out of the heart of man, sanctions come out of the mind of man. Jesus forbids mind games. Jesus says love God with all of your mind, heart and soul. Jesus never says love God with all of your mind.

Sanctions are the serpent's game. And the enemy knows how to play with the minds of the human race. Take a good look at the TV! There are no sanctions put in place to control the freedom of homosexuality. What was in the closet years ago has become prime time in today's world. Whereas, some religious denominations support the LGBTQ. Jesus does not support the serpent.

Talk show hosts flamboyantly parade themselves on Cable TV, as though it is a God given right to speak about their attendance at a gay marriage. And surely they have the audacity to show the so-called couple cuddling on cable vision. And now they have taken front seat in virtually every movie. It is now a big hit in all America. Jesus created male and female to bring about his precious little ones.

Scientists are working long hours to bring about two males giving birth to a child. The serpent is right there in the minds of these scientists, who have already given their souls to eat the dust as the serpent does. He would take you to fulfill all of your ambitions.

And dusts shall be the serpent's meat, when you allow Jesus to strike him on the head. Some Christians believed with all their hearts that they must go after the serpent. They watched the movies and idolized the scene, where the horseman came upon a snake, and the horse became startled, and rise up with its front legs raised high, and the horseman took his gun out and killed the snake. These Christians believed that the serpent and the snake is the same. No it is not.

The United Nations are famous for imposing sanctions across the board. To this day, what great achievements have they done towards real unity. The united nations were formed in 1945, to promote security, economic development, and peace. What security? They did not alert Americans on the September 11, 2001 blow up of the then World Trade Center. Why is everybody shielding the UN?

Jesus is saying that evil nations should not be working together with Christian Nations. Evil is evil. Good is good. A country like America could not be attacked without internal help. This internal help came from high places. Diplomatic immunity is foolishness in the sight of Jesus. Money laundering is the biggest crime in the UN. Hoarding up stacks of cash in safes are the way of life of these so-called important people. Jesus is shaking off the dust from his shoes. Jesus knows how to start a volcanic rumbling at the UN.

Good intentions are not good enough for Jesus. Sanctions are like wrestling with the serpent's bride in the dust. Nothing would ever get done at the UN. Some people would go to the beach and would never go further than waist high. Tempers flare up at meetings both inside the UN and outside the UN. The preponderance of evidence is not enough for Jesus. The slothfulness of courtrooms is the answer for the attitudes of Heads of Governments in each and every nation on the planet.

The disappearance of evidence given to UN Heads, that overseer the Charter of each and every nation under God, thus misleading people of color in their quest of a new beginning. Each country is not obliged to worship and adore another country. God the Father, God the Son, and God the

Holy Spirit is the only one to be adored and worshipped. Empty promises are the dusts that fill the serpent's belly.

To God be the Glory great things he has done. The military are the eyes of every country. Officers are hand-made by Jesus to become leaders of men and women. These soldiers of the army of the military of God, are quite aware of their walk with Jesus. For they sleep not in dangerous places knowing that Jesus is keeping them up all night long. There is homeland security, but where are the eyes between midnight and five in the morning?

Jesus is repeating himself by saying that the United Nations are America's biggest enemy. They always turn against you quietly and silently and walk away with a big smile on their faces. They euphemistically use word when texting their fellowmen on their ipads. They communicate in languages that draw on your emotions, but at the same time keeping their focus on the changing lanes.

The beauty of the sky is that there is no changing lanes. The beauty of the sky is that there is no traffic signals. The beauty of the sky is that there is no hills and valleys. The beauty of the sky is that there is no subways. The beauty of the sky is that there is no hotels. The beauty of the sky is that there is no hiding place for the serpent. Jesus is not about bringing the world to an end. Jesus is about bringing his children home.

Economic sanctions do not guarantee safety for Jesus's children. The wealth of any country would not ever be dictated or overseered by a foreign entity. Jesus's natural products should flow without stoppage on the Pacific Ocean and the Atlantic Ocean. These two corridors are your main arteries which are branches of the river Nile.

It is easy to buy a skipping rope and go skipping around the park in your neighborhood. Nobody would stop you, because you are a representative or a resident of the said neighborhood. Likewise, economic sanctions would only work well in their own neighborhoods.

But partisan governments would not see the light shining from deep within their bellies; giving them sight to draw a straight line perpendicular from their mouths directly to the heavens. There is nothing wrong with Heads of Government doing everything to help their fellowmen rise up out of poverty. Jesus is saying do it with love.

And dusts shall be the serpent's meat. The wealth of any rich country should not be allowed to be used against poor neighboring countries, thereby, subjecting them to the whims and fancies of a dictator. It's like a family of twelve, ten boys and girls and their parents. The last boy out of five brothers became very wealthy. He owned 1,000 square miles of rich land. The estate came with waterfalls, several lakes and springs, and coastline by the Pacific Ocean.

Two-thirds of the territory comprised of lime stone, marble, and gravel, and granite. The other third was beautiful beach front, together with rich soil for plants and vegetables. A few years later, tin was discovered in abundance in the foothills of the only mountain on the estate. Consequently, his brothers and his sisters decided that they would slow poison him with acid periodically.

It is the same thing big countries did and are justifiably doing to their neighbors. Intrinsically, Jesus is showing the rest of the world, how important it is to hold on to the Word of Jesus, until Jesus completes the sentence. Too many countries have become leaders in both the cartel industry, and the money laundering industry. Jesus is not pleased with the carnage of dead bodies found floating on the Ocean floors.

Nothing gets past Jesus. The tears of Jesus are in the eyes

of little baby bears left behind, after poachers killed and strip their parents of their fur. Footprints of blood would lead you to the actual site. The devastation of rain forest and the searching and killing of everything in sight, as the tears of Jesus flow into the river Nile. Notwithstanding the disruption of people's property and their livelihood.

The bird standing on one leg used to be a notable sight. The calf cuddling under its mother elephant would have been a gorgeous picture on the front page of the National Geographic Magazine. The licking of the young horse by its mother would have been next. Gone were the days, when the animals ran wild in their surroundings. Jesus is showing me these visions, as he takes me through a troubled world.

The harpooning of crocodiles and alligators for their hide, and the destruction of swamps for mans' selfishness and utter disregard for the environment; and the chaff he will burn with unquenchable fire. Every creature on the face of the earth had been created before human beings. Yet humankind is liken unto Jesus, but is the human race really, doing our heavenly Father's will?

The fishes of the sea do not debate Jesus. They go about their business multiplying to put food on the table for disobedient man. Yet human beings are liken unto Jesus. We love to walk in the mud near rivers and lakes, or sometimes create mud in our own backyards to walk in and wrestle in, but are we sure of its outcome? Jesus wore shoes on his feet wherever he went. His unchanged garments, he would wash at the riverside by hand. Jesus sleeping time was just one hour daily.

Jesus turned to his disciples and said to them to stay awake with me for my hour has come. Jesus already knew that, he was going to be arrested and be crucified. His disciples had all fallen asleep, except Judas Iscariot, the one who betrayed him for 30 pieces of silver. Each leader of a country has the responsibility to Our Lord Jesus to take care of his environs.

From time to time there is evil planted under the bridge. The serpent is wise, but Jesus is omnipotent. The betrayal of Jesus is not to be taken lightly. Heads of governments should be expecting someone to sell them out for 30 pieces of silver. It should not be a surprise, when the obvious is obvious. It should not be a surprise, when they lie and cheat and steal from you, as the Head of government.

Jesus does not like to repeat himself, when he says that the serpent is wise, but Jesus is omnipotent. The devastation of swamps to be developed by Real Estate Housing Developers, to feed the serpent with the dusts of the remains of the dead are sacrilegious in the eyes of Jesus. Real estate developers do not care about the Lord Jesus. They would with justification convince the state, that the piece of land that the swamps are located at, are more beneficial to the hierarchy than to the environs.

And dusts shall be the serpent's meat. Marble that is created by Jesus is fast becoming the meat for the serpent. Magnificent edifices inclusive of Cathedrals are adorned with marble floors. The irregular crystals are drawn by the hand of Jesus. The mobs or gangsters in all America have been burying bodies of Priests and the laity in the floors of the Cathedrals. Jesus says gold and silver have I not, but what I have is far greater than these two elements. At least forty people had seen Jesus rising, and going straight up into heaven.

The irregular crystals are made up of the very same material which will be used for our new earth. Jesus is saying that this new earth will be a permanent earth that will not be dug into by our modern-day equipment. The light of heaven will be our new light and not the sun and the moon. For rain there will be a beautiful mist in the form of rainbows, which we can reach out and touch.

Some people whose bodies have been shot up, wounded in battle, amputated by car accidents, burnt beyond repair, beheaded and stoned for his name sake will be remodeled in the likeness of Jesus. Jesus is saying I come to give life more abundantly. I am building a new heaven and a new earth. Keep this in your mind, heart, and soul! When anybody has anything negative to say to you; repeat those immortal words deep in your soul!

Jesus is at the podium looking in the distant to see who is on their way to heaven. This is you and I waiting for our loved one to show up at the appointed hour. Some of us have attended more than seven funerals in one given year. We have heard the word and we could recite the word verbatim. This is not the dusts for the serpent's meat. Take a good look at yourself! Annihilation of yourself would be the serpent's meat.

The actor is given a role to play, and sometimes more than often becomes the villain in everyone's mouth. It is very much disturbing for the actor to continue shooting, when this is brought to his attention. Whereas, once everyone loves the role that is played by the actor, now everyone gives him high fives. Jesus is saying I come to give life more abundantly. Because your constant annoyance of the actor will be interpreted as dusts shall be the serpent's meat.

We live and we learn. Do we? The jail houses are filled and overflowing. Sentences are far too long. Yes, he did wrong. No one is disputing that. Take a glass of water and throw it in someone's face! The fight is on. Take a gun and put it to someone's head and pull the trigger! The person is dead and there is no fight. This is what you have done to those, who are given long sentences.

Ask a question? And accept the answer that the person gives and use it to turn that someone around. If he has never loved someone, then he has been abused. Please do not continue the abuse! His shifty eyes and constant talking to himself are not signs of wantonness. The constant pounding on the walls and bars are not just for attention, but rather for Jesus to come and comfort the incarcerated one. The visiting time needs to be extended. Housing needs to be provided especially after long sentences.

God the Father, God the Son, and God the Holy Spirit is seeing how the enemy uses the people in authority, one by one down the road of an iniquitous life. The incarcerated one male or female has to sell the idea or thought to the Warden in order to buy his freedom from bondage. Institutionalized slavery is precisely what American prisons have become.

This particular form of slavery is meat for the serpent. These men and women shall be treated with dignity, thus saith the Lord. Their individual body is the temple of Jesus. Whether they have done wrong or right, it is not the office of the Warden and his associates to use and abuse their bodies as dusts for meat for the serpent. Jesus is right there looking on at the mess of the Justice system.

There is absolutely no respect by officers of the Prisons for the inmates. Programs that were approved by the state and local government take a long time for the wheel of justice to spin. Some riots are intentionally started by the prisons' officers. These of course, are never found out to be true. Some prisoners' doors are intentionally left open for them to make a run for it. Urine is put in the food for the disobedient ones.

The Institute for the Mentally ill is also one of the places for abuse. Patients are given far too much drugs, that are recommended by the Doctors. Families do not really know the severity of the prescribed drugs. Jesus is saying that families need to press on in prayer, and more visits to hospitals to be with their loved ones. Keep a listening ear, and always double check! The serpent's head is very high with power both in the rooms and corridors of these hospitals. Do not give up on your loved ones, no matter what the doctors say!

For the families, who have their loved ones staying at their homes and enduring that spirit of torment, Jesus is saluting you, and will keep you holding on, to bear witness to the miracle of deliverance, and a sweet-familiar odor of the love of Jesus. How great is the name of Jesus in all the earth? When loved ones could not hold on for a miracle of the restoration of someone's mind, that is the dusts of the serpent's meat. To love God is to hate the serpent. The miracle, of the loaves and the fishes, is not admired in this day and age.

It is not pleasant for anyone to have to bear the sufferings of a patient, who has lost his or her mind. People are cruel to their fellowmen, who have to bear the cross of a loved one. People would call them all kinds of names, that no one in their right minds would ever want to repeat. Jesus is showing me his crucifixion. Some people at the sight thought, that Jesus had lost his mind. For it was not a pretty view. Jesus is standing with one foot in the water and one foot on the sand.

And dusts shall be the serpent's meat. Jesus is saying that the enormity of crime in all the earth, especially, missing children in America, leaves one to think, what is the world coming to? Some missing children are discovered buried in unmark graves. Some parents are distraught over the fact that no one in the city did not see anything. Pictures are posted in subways, at train stations, at supermarkets, at the bus stop or at convenient stores. Still no word. Also in the lobbies of the local libraries.

Jesus is saying that what goes around will one day come to dusts as meat for the serpent. Jesus sees everything. This great evil that threatens the very fabric of any society would not go unpunished. Some missing children are brutally killed and taken to the hospital to be dismembered, and their organs are used to benefit other patients. Whereas, others are used as prostitutes on the world market. Very, very few have found someone to really take good care of them. Jesus is not about how the world sees it. Jesus is all about how he sees the murdering and the raping of innocence.

The police officers should not be blamed for such great cruelty that left parents utterly distraught. Weeping mothers, whose lives have been shattered by the disappearance of their girl children, are held in their right minds by Jesus. Though some parents have offered monetary rewards for the return of the children.

In these perilous times, there are cameras in all the familiar places, yet the discoveries are like night and day. Cars are still allowed to tint their windows in all America. One thing is sure is that money talks. The serpent's head is riding high at an all-time high for the great increase in the number of missing children. It is indeed a ruthless world. Jesus is showing me a bundle of snakes all wrapped up together.

And dusts shall be the serpent's meat. Some children are abducted and sold to couples for a handsome price. As soon as a child resembles one that is deceased of a rich family, the hunt begins. It is like the perfect swap. Some of these children attend schools overseas. Some of these children would not ever return to America.

And yes, there are some planning their every escape to return to their loved ones. Jesus is saying that the parents must not give up and to keep prayer alive. There are some women who cannot have a baby, and have gone to extremes to kidnap a child, or have paid money to have one abducted. Either way it is evil and wicked, as the serpent goes around like a roaring lion to steal. kill, destroy, and torment the children of Jesus.

Photographs of missing children plastered on the walls of Wal-Mart in big cities are just too much to handle. They are like broken glass pane windows shattered on the floors of buildings in run down cities. Have you ever seen, clouds touching the grass as you walked silently in the night? It is a sign from Jesus speaking to his children from on high, that you should not be taken blindly by the tricks of the serpent.

Sports commentators love to describe anything that looked beyond the norm as magic. It is all well and good that you believe that you have to speak in flamboyant rhetoric, but you ought to be really, really careful with your tongue. Magic is evil. Did Jesus give you that office? Jesus is saying beware of false prophets. People are fascinated by commentators, who could hold their interest during a sporting event. And surely they would repeat exactly what you have said verbatim. The use of language is very important--word has meaning.

Sportswriters, whose articles are widely read all across the ocean floors, should be extremely cautious in their delivery of word. Their use of the vernacular in their writings must not be entertained by the spirit of the serpent. The very letter of the word is food for the serpent. The enemy would from time to time, come to you and demand that you write the article this way and not that way.

Pay attention to colloquialism! When you want to be a great sportswriter, you must first have Jesus on the inside in the form of the Holy Spirit. Secondly, you must be faithful to the Word of God. Thirdly, you must die for his Word. Your writings shall be pure and fresh. God the Father, God the Son, and God the Holy Spirit is the only one who is perfect in everything.

Jesus wept for Lazarus. Would Jesus weep for sportswriters? Peradventure, if there are ten sportswriters that is doing the will of Jesus, I will not destroy their holy office. So were Sodom and Gomorrah utterly destroyed; so too will their offices be annihilated. Jesus is not playing the waiting game. The truth is not spoken in their writings. And dusts shall be the serpent's meat.

Jesus has no favorites. The athlete that is grinding in the gut that nobody pays attention to is truly a man of God. It is not about statistics. It is about who will endure to the very bitter end. Jesus is saying that also there is no rule of thumb. The message that Jesus is sending, is that the hour has come for sportswriters to put an end to their foolishness.

No sportswriter shall have a favorite. If you do, keep it to yourself. The roses in your yards might blossom every year, but until you have come face to face with Jesus, your writings would become the dusts, as meat for the serpent. No sportswriter should be entertained in the locker room. No athlete has any right to say to any sportswriter, what took place in the locker room. No coaches have any right to say or tell what was said in the locker room. Jesus is saying enough is enough.

Sports personalities should not be accepting moneys under the table from sportswriters. Likewise, coaches. It is about time that the owners of both the NFL and the NBA team up together to stamp out corruption in sports. Essentially though it may seem, the Presidents of both divisions need to be much more vigilant. It takes one to know one is somehow fitting in this conversation.

People do not want to lose respect for the athletes, who are not taking bribes to fuel the argument. But Jesus is a fine one to debate with. Jesus is coming. Yes, he is. He is putting together his anointed ones, that will do his will and only his will. He is continually sending his messengers, throughout the media, to allow everyone to stop and take a personal view of oneself.

Jesus is slowly pulling in his sheep, so as to allow others to observe, a change in the life of the one who he is bringing home. Jesus is taking his sweet time to turn the tide around.

At present, he is already using children from around the world, to speak a word of wisdom, that ho one have ever heard before. The innocence of children touches the heart of a true man of God, who will eventually turn his life around by trusting in the name of Jesus. God the Father, God the Son, and God the Holy Spirit is faithful to the end of time.

And dusts shall be the serpent's meat. Jesus is showing me, what humans do before every meal, they wash their hands. Do that make them really clean? No. Jesus says that clean hands and pure hearts shall see the kingdom of heaven. The laity have to understand precisely what Jesus is saying from up on high.

Hands and feet, without them we are nothing. Then why are the laity giving their hands to the serpent to receive blood money? Nice car. Did Jesus give you that nice car? No. Wednesday evening at church, you are giving your testimony and saying that Jesus gave you that nice car. Did Jesus ever told you that, he will one day bless you with a nice car? No he did not. Well, why allow satan to bring you to church to glorify the name of satan? These are the things that the laity do at churches on Wednesdays all across America.

Jesus says that one has to worship me in spirit and in truth. When you are serving both mammoth and Jesus, you are considered lukewarm. Conversely, you are abiding with satan. And what does satan do? Return the favor by sending you to the store, to purchase all the articles that one must use to anoint the home. The result is dirty hands.

Christians are fooled by these dirty-handed people. The trick of the enemy is making a fast dollar. At nighttime, the enemy would put you to sleep, and give you a number, that you would not forget when you awake from your slumber. The result was that the very next day, you did hit the jackpot and won $500. Now your life of pleasure has begun. Every

Thursday, Friday, Saturday and Sunday you are at the club.

Satan already knows that he got you. Now you would meet someone to take you up another level. The drug life has become your solace and your private secret place. The deal was since you have begun to owe the drug dealer money, now let us make a deal. At the club you are selling drugs whilst you are high on crack coke. What goes in must come out. The more money you make; the more money you spend. And now satan is speaking to you.

You have arrived. You have now become another drug dealer. Nice car. You have ten people working for you and this includes your wife. The house that you have once rented, have become your permanent home, lock, stock and barrel. You have purchased the house. In ten years, you have bought half of the block on the other side of the street. Life is great.

As time goes by the police whom you could not bribe, would one day have a showdown. The bullet proof vest that the enemy gave you for protection, have been riddled with bullets, and now you have gone to hell to be annihilated like satan. Meanwhile, your widowed wife is seeking the help of the Pastor in the neighborhood with blood money to save her soul.

The wise Pastor would not accept the offer, for he is a true man of God. Jesus is saying that the flesh of the couple would become dusts as meat for the serpent. The children that are left behind are not curse with a curse. Thank you Jesus. The sins of the parents did not fall on them children. Your sinful life belongs to you and you alone. That is why you are unique.

The angels feed you daily with life's happenings, as you take your strides through the mirrors that surrounds you. The galloping horses around the track or on the streets of your towns and cities are a constant reminder of Jesus's investment of his horses which show no fear. Jesus is always welcoming his children back home by allowing them to come face to face with the truths of life.

The family of Jesus had to put up with the doubts and the fears of cousins and nephews and uncles and aunts of both Joseph and his mother Mary. Jesus keeps saying that he knows, what you have encountered, because he too had family struggling with the wiles of satan. He too had relatives that did not want to accept him as Lord of All. He too had aunts that did not want to pay homage to his good name.

Jesus is saying that one of these great days, angels will appear at your side windows showing what Jesus is doing in heaven. Jesus wants you to know that he will not desert you, or abandon you, wherever you are in this world. Just remember that the more you give the more you shall receive.

PREPARATION FROM EARTH TO HEAVEN:

1 Corinthians 2:9 But as it is written, Eye hath not seen, nor ear heard, neither have entered into the heart of man, the things which God hath prepared for them that love him.

10. But God hath revealed *them* unto us by his Spirit: for the Spirit searcheth all things, yea, the deep things of God.

11. For what man knoweth the things of a man, save the spirit of man which is in him? even so the things of God knoweth no man, but the Spirit of God.

12. Now we have received, not the spirit of the world, but the spirit which is of God; that we might know the things that are freely given to us of God.

13. Which things also we speak, not in the words which man's wisdom teacheth, but which the Holy Ghost teacheth; comparing spiritual things with spiritual.

14. But the natural man receiveth not the things of the Spirit of God: for they are foolishness unto him: neither can he know *them*, because they are spiritually discerned.

15. But he that is spiritual judgeth all things, yet he himself is judged of no man.

16. For who hath known the mind of the Lord, that he may instruct him? But we have the mind of Christ.

But as it is written, Eye hath no seen. Today we have opened the Book of Revelation and now eye is seeing the Glory of Jesus in all its splendor. Jesus is saying that from earth to heaven is like an ice skater standing on one spot and spinning like a top and nobody knows what the end will be.

We had Jacob and his twelve sons, which formed the twelve tribes of Israel, giving us a true picture of the struggle of man from earth to heaven. Jesus knows how to start a fight. Joseph, who is Benjamin's elder brother, but is the eleyenth child in number had a dream. Yet still a lad, and lacking in much wisdom told his brothers and his father the vision.

Jesus is the vision. Jesus is revealing to Joseph what will become of him in the future. In the vision Jesus shows Joseph, one of the Sons of the house His Glory. The child awoke his father and brothers all excited, because he saw everybody bowing down their heads before him. His father being the wisest really could not deliver the word in spirit and in truth. So what did he do, gave him a coat so radiant that they all jealous their brother.

Consequently, they all decided from the mouth of the eldest to kill him. But the love of Jesus in their heart changed their minds, and then they decided to kill an animal, and soaked the beautiful jacket in the blood, and took it home to Dad. Jacob wept for his lost son. But the truth was that they had sold him into slavery.

God the Father, God the Son, and God the Holy Spirit decides for Joseph to be incarcerated by the Great King of Egypt. In this dungeon of suffering and torment of the spirit, Jesus is transforming Joseph into a mighty man of God. One meal a day. A loaf of bread was all that he can have. The Glory of God in his true magnificence is about to open up the true meaning of the coming of the Messiah.

Jesus is taking center stage. Twelve gates will adorn the new heaven. Three gates in the East; three gates in the North; three gates in the West; three gates in the South. The number 144,000 thousand people are the fullest of the Womb of Jesus. The name of each family is already recorded in the Book of Life. Jesus is not about the measuring rod that is used by statisticians. Jesus is about the Holy of Holies.

And the dove descended upon the head of Our Lord Jesus saying from heaven that this is my beloved Son in whom I am well pleased. Jesus is saying that this very Holy of Holies is still blasphemed around the world. The Holy Ghost is God the Father. How could you worship one without the other? Theology is the Word of God. Obedience to God overshadows everything else. God will come to you and he will tell you what to do. There is always a witness.

The Prophet John, the son of Elizabeth, the cousin of Mary, the mother of Jesus, all bore witness to this phenomenon. The angels who are ever present with Jesus, bore witness to the Word of God. Jesus is showing me his right hand, as he directs his chosen ones to heaven. How many of you in this world are truly under the directions of Our Lord and Savior?

The sun and the moon will be no more. The alphabet and the way we speak will be no more. People will be speaking only one language. Our food will be manna. The pendulum swings both back and forward, as the earth begins to shrink to nothingness. Boundaries will now be shortened. Land masses will suddenly disappear. The overcast clouds will be no more.

Famous ski resorts will one day come to an end. The meteorologists will not be able to forecast the weather anymore. Sudden darkness will appear everywhere almost simultaneously. Jesus cousin Prophet John said to Jesus that no one could tie his shoe lace. As a child I struggled to learn how to tie a shoe lace. Jesus speaks in parables, so did John.

A whole wide world has grown to tie their own shoe laces. What are John and Jesus really saying? Eye hath not seen, nor ear heard. It took two thousand years for the Book of Revelation to be disclosed. There is no one that would ever be like Jesus. So quit looking for another one! There is no one that would ever be like Jesus. So quit trying to replicate him! There is no one that would ever be like Jesus. So quit lying on Jesus!

Jesus keeps showing the whole world how great is the name Jesus. Some parents from the Latino culture have named their children Jesus, and to this day they are totally the opposite. Adoption of his name does not bring power. Jesus keeps showing up at the river Jordan. No longer a place of worship and adoration. The memory of the baptism of Jesus is no longer sacred.

Pilgrimages of people from all around the world had been marred by extreme violence. Everybody fighting for the wealth that the name Jesus brought to the land. The threats by the Muslim world, to stop Christians from visiting one of the wonders of the world, had been enormous. The bloodshed was equal to the war in Iraq. Prophets were beheaded for following the name of Jesus over Mohammed. Churches were burnt down for erecting a cross, either inside or outside of the church premises.

Christianity suffered one of its biggest lost on the borders of the river Jordan. Anointed men and women of God were hunted down and burnt on stakes. Eyes were gutted out of their sockets. Pilgrims lost their feet, when caught with a Bible. Bibles were taken out of churches and burnt in the eyes of Christians. Jesus will not forget. You will reap what you sow, thus saith the Lord.

Bodies hacked and not have the true Christian burial rites still haunts the people of God. Bodies thrown into cesspits and ravines and flush down toilets would make a man puke out of his guts. Flies covered these naked bodies everywhere. There were not enough covers to go around.

Mercenaries from different countries had to be sent in to stop the carnage. Where was the footage? Burnt. Jesus is bending the tree to show the world that nothing is ever hidden. The eucalyptus plant was used to cover open wounds, as the sick lay in wait to see the only visible doctor. Jesus is about unwinding the clock that nobody wanted to go back into, because they believed that it is all over now. Jesus death on the cross is indeed a mockery in Jerusalem. Jesus who gave sight to the blind man, the first ever done by anyone on the planet, has now become sacrilegious.

Graves of famous people, who had died for the love of Jesus were desecrated. Christians schools were all burnt down. Orphanages were under attacked by the savages of monotheistic gods. Women of faith were raped and sodomized. Children were fed to crocodiles, as the genocide wore the ugly head of 666. Jesus is always present with his angels to bear witness to the cruelty done to Christians.

The robe of satan changes its color as time goes by, as a sign that his power is fading. Jesus color is always constant. In the business community, very little prices end in 00. Why the continual changes? Why should the last two digits be a reflection of the same number? Why is the business community, so enthralled with the craftiness of the devil? Jesus is coming.

In an effort to save the consciousness of mankind, countries from the West decided to bury the dead by sending special burial boxes to the actual burial sites. Whatever humans do to please themselves are not enough for the Lord Jesus. There will always be a dark cloud hovering above the site of those that lost their lives for the love of Jesus. Presidents would come and go to try to heal the wound from the lance that pierced Jesus on the cross. Jesus will not forget.

The blood of the lambs that were slaughtered for the love of Jesus is unforgiveable. The desecration of human beings by urine also is unforgiveable. Jesus came to breakdown the walls of indignation, but the enemy felt as though he deserved the victory. Jesus is saying that no stone will be left unturned. Jesus is saying that, there is no fight that Jesus had ever lost, would ever lost and will ever lost.

On the cross, Jesus said that it is finished. Immortal words have no end. Whereas, the world would forever hold an opinion. Jesus does not care about folks' opinions. The New Jerusalem is already built, because the birds of the air will keep disappearing one by one. The cities of great countries and towns of great countries will keep disappearing one by one.

Life is not full of expectancies. But the Maple tree gives us wood to build furniture, and sap from its fruit that produces, the world's best Maple syrup. Jesus is showing me the world at its best, which is now at its worst. The tears of children wailing and utterly terrified are not going to go away naturally. The mountains cry out, for the children whose bellies were ripped out and fed to the crocodiles. Their feet were decapitated and fed to the lions. The hairs of girl children were sold to companies to fabricate wigs. Jesus will not forget.

On the cross Jesus was given hissop to drink. How many Christians were ever poisoned for the love of Jesus? The wars between Christians and Muslims were even older than Abraham. Jesus, the Nazarene, had to educate the scholars of the time, who were worshipping the stars and composing the zodiac. It is interesting to note, that they had never listened to the voice of the Lord.

Jesus is showing me himself looking directly at me. The persecution of Christians is not truly covered by any form of media. The sensational side of life is equivalent to the number 666. The serpent, who is the devil loves his role given to him by God the Father, God the Son, and God the Holy Spirit. A slave does not know what his master is doing. Needless to say that the society is enjoying the footage.

Too much time is spent on world politics. Too much time is spent on attacking each other in matters of trivialities. Too much time is spent on making things right without the wisdom of Jesus. Jesus entered Solomon, the son of David, king of Israel. Jesus speaks to his heavenly Father about his anointed one, who felt oppressed by the ignorance of his people.

God the Father is moved by the acceptance of his son Solomon to bear the cross of suffrage. And because Solomon did not ask for silver and gold, the love of God gives him more wisdom than any earthly king would ever attain. This great blessing infuriated the very serpent, who fought him night and day with the spirit of torment. Eventually, a whirlwind of angels came to his rescue.

Jesus is the same today, tomorrow and forever more. Jesus is not going to bend as social media bends to the whims and fancies of their peers. How many times must Jesus send Prophets to these networks? The word says touch not mine anointed, and do my Prophets no harm. It does not matter whether you are a Bible scholar or not. Ignorance to the Word of God is no excuse. Obedience is heaven first law.

The Prophet had been told by Jesus after he had healed the king with the withered hand, do not eat bread from anyone on your way back home! The Prophet did not do what Jesus commanded him to go do. Another Prophet met him on his way back and invited him for a meal, which he accepted. The lion which is satan ate him up.

Jesus is showing me the seven stars in his right hand. The first church is Ephesus. A church that is situated on the island of Patmos. Jesus is speaking about things to come that eye hath not seen, nor ear heard, neither have entered into the heart of man, the things which God hath prepared for them that love him. The church of Ephesus in its beginnings loved the Lord Jesus. This is just like us human beings, when we have so-called fallen in love. But as time goes by, we begin to become jealous.

Jesus who is the church is truly our first love which we have departed from, as soon as we have fallen in love with someone else. The serpent never gives up for he is willfully doing his tricks to draw attention. Jesus appearance changes in the midst of the seven golden candlesticks.

Our eyes are vehemently glued to the TV. This happens everyday from the time we wake up in the morning, to the time we fall asleep, and still the television set is running all night long until sunrise. Jesus is saying, where is your first love? No one found time to pray to their first love. In the mornings, we race out the house to purchase a breakfast and off to work. No prayers. At lunchtime, we jump into our cars to purchase a meal. No prayers. Where is our first love?

The architect of our lives must be Jesus. No second guessing. Take a look at the mountains! They go up and down and sometimes deep down. Could you tell how deep down you are after falling off the cliff? No. Well Jesus, who is Holy Spirit, who is the Lamb of God, that takes away the sins of the world, is not waiting on the world to play catch up. That is why his eyes are flaming red and his feet are like fiery brass.

Human beings love to tell people what to do. Human beings love to push people around. Human beings love to hear the sound of their own voice. You see it displayed in front of you everyday. Expressions like nobody can tell me what to do, and who do you think you are, are commonplace in the society. Already, you have denied your first love. On Sunday mornings, your eyes are trapped watching the football game.

The disciples were asked by Jesus, who do you say I am? The very same question is posed to you. If you love me you will keep my commandments. Jesus is showing me himself kneeling on one knee. This is what you do, when you want to have things your way. You procrastinate. Meanwhile, Jesus has turned away and left. And until Jesus decides to intercede for you, here comes a storm.

Could you survive a famine? David did. David never left his first love. David had a repentant spirit. Just saying sorry is not good enough. Just saying please forgive me, is not good enough. Just saying father for I have sinned against my neighbor is not good enough. Just saying five our fathers, five hail marys, and one I believe in God are not good enough. Just lighting candles and offering prayers to statutes are not good enough.

Your wife tells you that she loves you over and over again. Your wife shows you that she loves you over and over again. Your wife makes sacrifices for you over and over again. Your wife cooks for you over and over again. Your wife tells you everything on her mind over and over again. Your wife forgives you over and over again. After all of this, you still treat her as a fool over and over again. How can you love Jesus whom you do not see and hate your loving wife who you see?

Being perfect in one thing does not let you off the hook. For all have sinned and fell short of the Glory of God. When you went to the interview to get the job, you took it for granted, that because someone is praying for you, that you would get the job. This was never the case. Yes, it is a good thing to have someone praying for you even in a prayer chain. But where are your knees?

All churches do not carry kneelers. This should not prevent you from kneeling on the floor. Likewise your homes, learn to put them two knees on the bare floor sometimes! Isn't it ridiculous, after all this time that people are of the belief that Apostles or the making of Apostles are over? Jesus is not the last Apostle. Where is your faith? Too many times you believe that you can move the mountain. Twenty years later the mountain grew much bigger.

Arithmetic, Algebra and Geometry are not mastered by everyone. The rate of failures have been ridiculous for too long.. Small wonders why, Americans boast about their Physics, which are far greater to master than Math. Have you ever seen a real vision of Jesus? If not, then you should ask yourself why. Jesus is showing me churches building up by hands that are not clean. And then these houses of Worship are used for gambling. How dare you petition Jesus over and over again?

Casinos have become a way of life in America. Christian folks petition Jesus as soon as they have placed a bet on any number. They would be uttering the name Jesus in colorful language, especially when they have won at the gambling table. As soon as, they have collected their winnings, they would go to the Pastor to give him their ten per cent. Dreadfully Wrong!

The feet of Jesus are lit up with fine brass, as if burned in a furnace. Simultaneously, Jesus is showing me his fiery eyes. Because they have lost their first love. When Jesus is giving you something he tells you long in advance. Consequently, he strengthens you for the journey of faith. So the passing years will always seem like yesterday. Then one day the blessing comes in a way that is totally different to your great expectations.

Until you have given up the ghost, your blessing would be hanging in the distance. A postmortem is what you are asking Jesus to commit to after your death. You have given up on your first love, just like the people, that had borne witness to Jesus's crucifixion on the cross. When their thoughts cascaded in all directions, for Jesus to come down from the cross, to prove to them that he is, who he says he is.

The second church is Smyrna. Jesus is saying I am the first and the last, which was dead and is alive. Jesus is saying that the world has to endure great tribulation, because of religious denominations' sinful ways over years of domination. The candlesticks are your churches whose doctrine had encompassed lighted candles on their altars. This evil creates generations of curses.

You see this displayed daily in churches that open everyday during the week. Parishioners and non-members purchase these wax or tallow-made candles, to be lit and prayers offered up for deceased loved ones, or prayers offered up for success in some endeavor or discipline. Jesus never taught that to his disciples, whilst he lived on the face of the earth.

Jesus never laid out playing cards on a table for people to choose a card and then talk about their future. These practices still exist in denominational churches. At the cemeteries, you would see families gathered for prayers with lighted candles, to hear from their deceased loved one. The High Priest of these churches and cemeteries world over calls himself the Pope. A name that Jesus never called him, or give to him. Are you really following in the footsteps of Our Lord Jesus?

Other churches have picked up this candlelight form of so-called worship. Thus spreading the disease of generational curses throughout every town, city, province, and state in America. Suffice it to say, this trickle off into other reservoirs of churches which are not denominational. The poverty in spirit soon follows into the classrooms of elementary schools, middle schools, high schools, and colleges, and universities.

Prayers to the saints for jobs, cars, houses, business ventures, inventions, scholastic achievements to name a few are a curse whether you are successful or not. This curse or curses are not visible to the naked eye. The serpent, who is the devil, would take you along the road of glitter and glamour. These places would always bring you good luck, one of satan's favorite words. Words that you blatantly use that are commonplace.

Poverty in spirit is like a vine that everyone sees climbing the walls of houses. Does this protect the family in any way, shape or form from the evil of the world? Moses had been told by Jesus to paint the houses with blood from the animals that were sacrificed. This was their protection from death by the angel of death. The result being all the Egyptians firstborn males were killed by the angel of death. Whereas, the first born males of the Jewish people survived the outcry of death.

You do need a pair of binoculars to see into the distance. But do you need a pair of binoculars to show you the way? You definitely need Jesus. There is a long line outside the church door of Jesus. Can you see it? If not keep pressing on until you see that line. Do not try to change the world, for the world would overpower you and change you into itself?

When Jesus lived on the face of the earth, he had numerous encounters with the devil. His climax came, when he fasted for forty days and forty nights. During this time, God the Father burnt his feet, thus preparing him for his ascension into heaven. Jesus is saying that the world owes God everything. God the Father, God the Son, and God the Holy Spirit is not playing church.

The synagogue of Satan had already been formed, since the

beginning of Communism. They would from time to time threaten your beliefs to the point of death. When you visit their country, they would not allow you to walk freely and go wherever you would want to go. How about the respect that you gave to them over and above your own Christian brothers and sisters? This is not fellowshipping.

Hate is unseen in the heart of man. The lance in the ground is seen by everyone. Is Jesus really making a point or are you expecting another one? The synagogue of satan is not expecting another one, then why are you not doing the will of your blessed Lord? Jesus is saying, that it is easy to wear the shirt on the other side, than to prop yourself up on your own ladder to hear from the Lord.

You want to wear a crown on your head. Well then get to work! Is Paris burning? We often look at being incarcerated as not a good thing, even though, Jesus too was incarcerated and did nothing wrong.. Your mother, who was incarcerated for just standing on the corner, is a good example of one standing for Jesus. Your sister, who was incarcerated for just passing by a scene of a crime, is a good example of one standing for Jesus. Your brother, who was incarcerated for just being in a white neighborhood after midnight, is a good example of one standing for Jesus.

He that overcometh shall not be hurt of the second death. Jesus is saying that for those who loved Jesus in spite of their being born into a religious denomination, due to their upbringing will through the mercy of Jesus, escape the fires of hell. Everyone would not have been a recipient of the Holy Spirit, even when the good Lord Jesus returns. Parents will be having children in that very hour. Children will be having children in that very hour. Weddings will be taking place in that very hour.

People in hiding from persecution will be drawn out by the voice of Jesus. The trumpet will sound before Jesus makes his entry. The deaf will be healed from the sound of the trumpet. The blind will see Jesus with open eyes. The lame will put away their crutches at the sight of Jesus. The downtrodden will wear a smile from earth to heaven.

The third church is Pergamos. Jesus is saying that the one which hath the sharp sword with two edges is still sharpening the sword on both sides of the altar. Let it be known that Our Lord Jesus is presently witnessing blood sacrifices on his altars throughout the land! Heads of chickens are bitten off and the blood are drunk in the spirit of evil. The whole world is increasing in the spirit of Beelzebub, satan's right-hand man.

This new wave of water, rolling up on the shores and into the land distributing its length and breadth in a diabolical way, is already damaging the souls of the planet. Jesus is looking at the spirit of Beelzebub who is beating his breasts on the walls of churches and using his horns to tear up altars that venerate the slain martyr. Antipas was a true representative of Jesus.

Antipas recorded everything in his publication that took the form of a scroll. His message was poignant. Though highly respected by his peers, he too never held back on speaking about the hierarchy's participation in blood sacrifices. His persistency drew the attention of the Pharaoh that ordered his death. Speaking out gets you in trouble. Pastors that would have their church members with them, giving out church literature at a mall, would not invite trouble.

Jesus is raining down stones from heaven. False prophets had encouraged people at houses of worship to become intimate with satan and his fallen angels, whilst they the prophets drank blood from sacrificial sheep, that were slaughtered on the altars. This practice is presently going on today. Women also are used as sacrificial sheep. The three Cardinal Virtues are Faith, Hope and Charity. 99.99 per cent of the world are placidly lukewarm in faith.

In Japan, there are some Christian folks, who are held hostage for their strong beliefs. Meanwhile, the hierarchy downplays the freedom of the press. Jesus is wearing his two-edge sword to show the rest of the world, that there is no easy passage into heaven. One percent of a billion is well over 144,000.

The twelve tribes of Israel had been forewarned by God the Father, not to pack your baskets with manna, that you would not eat the very same day. Moses was the chosen Prophet to speak such a word. The people began to complain that they could not have chicken on their plate everyday. Today, chicken is eaten by everyone in almost every household on a daily basis.

The view of Jesus is way past the clouds in the sky. Human beings view are at eye level. Some families pledged to have a get together at least once a month. Before they meet, they would call each other to decide on a dish, so that they all would not bring chicken. Jesus says that we shall confess one to another. Jesus says do not lie to one another.

You hate God the Father, God the Son, and God the Holy Spirit, when you do not pay your tithes and offerings. The laborer is worthy of his reward. As soon as you stump your toe, against the sidewalk, the pain is instantaneous. But, this is no comparison to the nails that they pierced in the hands and feet of Jesus. The crown of thorns that they pierced in his soft, tender scalp, whilst in prison, is a sign for believers to hug each other tenderly. Jesus died for our sins, when he himself had never ever committed a sin.

Jesus is saying it loud. The promises that he had made before the foundations of the world are yours only when you repent. There are no plea bargains in the house of the Lord. The law is the law. The crown for your head is already designed by the greatest superstar in the universe. His name is Jesus. Your name is already inscribed on the crown.

The fourth church is Thyatira. The vision for this church has never been kept. Jesus promised the Pastor, that he will give him the morning star, once he had completed his job. Some Pastors are not given that honor to know and see precisely what the Lord is actually giving them. Or, in prescient, to receive exactly what they had asked Jesus for in the interim. The vision was to build a Cathedral and take the church to worship, honor, glory, riches, and to cast out all demonic spirits from the house of the Lord.

The morning star is a planet seen in the eastern part of the sky just before sunrise or at sunrise. Astrologers love to get together or to agree on any given theory that they want to forge into the bosom of Jesus. At 14, Jesus had an audience with astrologers, that took him all night long to prove to them that what they saw in the distance could be anything else, but the morning star. Can satan paint a beautiful picture in the distance? Yes, he can. Human beings should learn to tread the sky with their eyes cautiously.

The gifted scientific people, who have fallen away from their first love, love to tell people what to do. These pioneers had become the founders of Scientology Churches all across the world. And like satan would paint an excellent picture. They are the same people, who would use magic on their pulpits, when delivering the word. God the Father, God the Son, and God the Holy Spirit is allowing the evil to flow like a river.

Astrology: which is the study of how the moon, sun, planets, and stars are supposedly related to life and events on the Earth. This theory, that had been forged in the minds of astrologers to influence human beings in accepting their false beliefs, that the stars and the planets in the sky influence events on Earth, is highly preposterous. Jesus is in control.

Jesus is standing.

The fall of the beautiful false prophetess Jezebel came when she gave herself to satan. After becoming his bride, he entered her and made her a queen of the city. Her job was to entertain all dignitaries from the city and all around the world. Her intimacy with high officials was enormous and her name Jezebel became famous on the planet. These acts of fornication as well as fornication with idols were an abomination in the sight of God.

Jezebel's way of life had lasted forty years. It is a pity to see someone, that is given the beauty of Jesus, misrepresent his good name. God the Father, God the Son, and God the Holy Spirit is showing the human race, his compassion towards Jezebel by asking her to repent. And of course, like satan, she too held on to her evil ways. Evil likes company. Father forgive them for I have sinned, this is two months since my last confession. This form of confession is a travesty in the eyes of Jesus.

The church of Thyatira was going somewhere, until the Pastor became intimate with Jezebel. Her beauty swept the feet off the pastor of this great church. This pastor had everything going his way, when his telephone rang with Jezebel on the other end of the line. Her beautiful seductive voice overpowered the man of God, so much so, that he dated her within a heartbeat. Jezebel reassured the pastor, that she would not touch the anointed man of God. In furtherance, she had promised him, that they would not be alone, when he came to her house.

Jesus is saying that the pastor of this great church fell. As well as his ministerial pulpit. For the love of the flesh was worth more to them than the love of Jesus. Warnings came to them by other travelling prophets to change their rotten ways and repent. This they never did.

The fifth church is Sardis. Jesus is saying vehemently and without reservations, that this church hath livest and art now dead. Repent, repent, repent! Have you ever noticed when you look out into the distance you could automatically draw a straight line. Then you smile to yourself on discovering this wonderful sight. Did not your mind work a trick on you?

Whimsical is a driving force that could wreck and split a church into many unequal parts. Jesus is showing me the steps to the top of the pulpit. Every church that is given to a pastor to build from the ground up, would not have the same design, or hold the same number of people. Oftentimes you struggle and wrestle with the Holy Spirit. You have heard what Jesus said, but you could not come to terms with reality and truth.

For some reason human beings have this undying belief, that they could be perfect as their heavenly Father is perfect. The devil loves this kind of thinking. Because here it was, that this Pastor of this great Cathedral shared the same belief as the devil. The devil loves to mimic Jesus. The wedge, which you have given to the devil, would result in a long life of grief and sorrow.

Jesus shows up at the beginning of your fall. Why? So that he can have the victory. Your telephone has been ringing at the church's office all night long, until you got there. You have visited all the sick and sick non-members of your Parish. You have fed the poor breakfast, lunch and dinner at your shelter obliquely opposite the Parish. The fatherless children you have provided shirts, pants, socks and shoes at the beginning of every school year. You accepted monetary favors from everyone.

Once a year, you would have someone tie you up and whip you with a cat-o-nine tail, so that you would become as perfect as your eldest brother, Jesus. You would not accept or eat the scroll. Whereas, Jesus keeps showing his pastors that he is the only perfect one. Why keep changing doctrine to patronize the members of your church? Holy Communion is simply bread and grape juice.

When Jesus looks at you directly into your eyes that is your first warning. The paintings on the walls of the interior of the Cathedral, should not be there, to create weeping by church members, for the love of Jesus. Children must be with their parents or guardians whilst in church. It is imperative that they hear the Word of God.

The white garments of Jesus are synonymous with his purity of mind and heart and soul. The completion of the transformation of Our Lord Jesus ended before Jesus met his cousin John. Jesus kept the pastor of this great church who repented. The prophets and prophetesses that came to his church, to warn him over and over again, and had to dust their shoes and leave and go for the love of Jesus, also will be dressed in white like unto Jesus.

People overcome a few things in their lifetimes. Whereas anointed men and women of God have a steep mountain or mountains to climb in their walk with Jesus. The greater the gift: the steeper the mountains. It is nice to say or think that you want to be like Jesus, could you climb those steep mountains? Jesus's *thirty-three years* was not a walk in the park.

Satan and his subjects delightedly lived an exorbitant life without a sweat. But now, their rivalry towards Jesus made them all ugly. All anointed men and women of the Lord always looked more beautiful, and like the roses, scented of the sweetest perfume. For the word begins with the letter "a" which also stands for Alpha. The white garments of Jesus are not for sale in any clothing store. The white garments of Jesus are not visible in any painting on the walls of any earthly church. The white garments of Jesus are his treasure and his alone.

The building of churches in the name of Jesus for ludicrous means, and wantonness, have become so commonplace in societies world over. This shows up the strongholds of the people of Jesus. They would settle for anything: a mouse on a mousetrap.

The sixth church is Philadelphia. The Pastor of this great church had never given up. Young, and bright, and full of energy was his name. His church sat on the banks of the River Nile. Floods of children would stop by to greet this charismatic and beautiful man of God. His choir though small filled the air with melodious sound of hymns. His wife was full of joy and childlike. The doors of his church opened an hour before the service began each Sunday morning.

His gifts of healing kept him very busy. The steep steps of his mountain were like the Living Word of God. The word Philadelphia means love everybody. This great man of God has to bear all the mumblings and grumblings of his people throughout the life of his ministry. He must wield with a very firm hand. His electrifying body comes from the outpouring of the Holy Spirit. This great man of God of the church of Philadelphia must have the Word of God sewn in his heart, sewn in his mind, and sewn in his soul.

The Pastor of any great church would always be under attack. The very fact that he is doing a great work for the Lord, awakens satan and his minions. Any step that Pastor makes will be accompanied by a step from satan. Any man that resides near a river of water will never run out of food, and silver and gold. Jesus is beside him watering and replenishing his cup. The branches of the fruit trees will bend and swing with the weight of the sound of songs.

I know thy works: behold, I have set before thee an open door, and no man can shut it: for thou hast a little strength, and hast kept my word, and hast not denied my name.

The soldiers that have given their lives in the service of their country are the pillars that Jesus is talking about. These soldiers will be branded with the name of the heavenly church The New Jerusalem. This will be an insignia as the wounds of Jesus. Long lines of soldiers will be honored in heaven. Their commandant will be God the Father, God the Son, and God the Holy Spirit. Their jewel will be their national anthem.

The seventh church is Laodiceans. The Pastor of this great church fell to the greed and lavish living of members of his congregation. The First Lady was the queen among queens. The church needed nothing. The pastor and his wife and children had breakfast at one family mansion. The pastor had a golden tongue. Every Sunday he had three services.

People of wealth must not be told what to do. Jesus is showing me a wealthy fortress. A place of wealth that nobody had ever seen in their entire life. A treasure of everything that one could imagine, together with the pearls and diamonds of heaven. Human beings in their formative years, though tearful, love to fantasize what the Glory of God looks like. The unseen will always be immaculate. The side dishes, one will not be able to delight in, in our flesh. This is why our bodies have to be redesigned by the careful-pure hands of Jesus.

The doctors, the lawyers, the architects and engineers of this world, in their conceitedness and bias attitude, would not accept the word from any pastor. A weak pastor would ultimately become lukewarm. Jesus is saying that you are neither cold or hot because of your transgressions. Jesus is the limit. How many times must Jesus say that he loves you? Human beings from time to time, grow weary in waiting upon the Lord. Meanwhile the devil had already placed his bread in the basket even at communion.

As soon as you have eaten the devil's bread, which is your

exceeding limit, he is most delighted with his smile. Rich people waste everything. Rich people count every penny. Rich people care only about themselves. Rich people believe that God owes them something. It is futile to think that Jesus owes you something, when you basically had no input.

Who made you? Jesus did. You are lukewarm since you cannot have your own way. You go out into the world with your money in your hand to buy friends. Your wife would also be rich. Your cars would also be flamboyant. Your children would also be precious, no matter what they did. Your sons and daughters must be held in high esteem. Are the rich too prestigious? Yes they are.

How many times should the world hear about your past achievements? Jesus evolves. Jesus is building a brand new heaven and a brand new earth. The newspapers are the biggest culprits in their featured stories. They are known for resurrecting the past. The newspapers strive on rhetoric of important people and their reruns. The rich are repeatedly written about anywhere they go.

How about those business deals that nobody ever hears about? The merging of companies just to get commodities at a cheaper price. And the devaluation of the dollar by countries around the world, to so-called bring in business. Then one devaluation leads to another devaluation. The disparity between the rich and the poor is widening, as the days go by. The sudden slump in the eurodollar is gradually slipping for their lost of interest in Jesus.

The world is lukewarm as the church of Laodiceans. The world takes everything for granted, as Jesus looks at the living wage .Jesus says I will spue thee out of my mouth, because you are lukewarm. For those of you that overcometh will have a seat at the Throne of Grace. Jesus is sending kisses to those, who are ready to fight the great fight to the bitter end.

The picture had been painted by prophets and prophetesses long before the coming of Jesus. Their generations have not seen the light, as you are seeing the light of the day. At this hour revealing things are taking place, as a wakeup call early in the morning from a cock in the yard, and the flapping of his wings.

Jesus is showing me people running from unfair practices. The world knows exactly what Jesus is talking about. Force never works! The Throne of Jesus is illuminated everywhere. His Grace is sufficient for everyone to have an overflow. It is easy to say, "let us go," but is the light of Jesus taking us there? God the Father, God the Son, and God the Holy Spirit is here to take you to the Throne of Grace.

THY KINGDOM COME:

2 Timothy 4:18 And the Lord shall deliver me from every evil work, and will preserve *me* unto his heavenly kingdom: to whom *be* glory for ever and ever. Amen. Jesus is setting his time on the clock. A forbidding task is rolled up into one's amazing grace. Some people would go around painting fences in red paint with the word HELL in large bold capital letters. These demonstrative signs are no more than an attack of satan.

We live in a world of lettering. In a monotype case where letters are placed in an individual box the letter "e" occupies the largest box. The letter "e" is used by far in volume to every other letter in a monotype case. Jesus is saying that one letter shall not be dominant over and above the others. If you stand on the beach and lookout straight ahead of you, and focus on one thing only, your eyes would not be able to hold on. Could you hold on to the threshing floor of Jesus?

Jesus says and the Lord shall deliver me from every evil work. Evil is everywhere. Jesus is showing me himself on a ladder. Families placed themselves on a ladder, and use the actual step that they have made it too, and then judge the world from where they stand. They use the ladder as a measuring tool. Everybody would not make it to the top. Because everybody would not find Jesus in their nick of time. Different walks of life and different cultures across the globe produce different results.

Your mind is a mighty and powerful weapon given to you by God the Father, God the Son, and God the Holy Spirit to wrestle with the serpent and his third of fallen angels. They would all come to get you even in the womb. It is a treasure when a baby is in the womb and its mama is praying or reading the Word of God. This is seldom seen anywhere. If the mother, who is carrying her baby has not come face to face with her blessed Lord Jesus, then the fight between the serpent's household and the mother shall begin, until thy kingdom come.

This is how quickly the enemy works. He loves to imitate Jesus who is faster than light. Jesus was offered up as a child by the preacher, who had been spoken to by God the Father to do the blessing. Christians are not seeking clean hands and a pure heart to do the blessing of their precious little ones. Christians shall bear in mind, that when they are pregnant their job are to find Jesus on bended knees. Your child needs Jesus much more than you can ever imagine.

Jesus is not coming to you on roller skaters because you have become pregnant. There are no excuses when you did not find him. The love of Jesus does not have a price. Whereas, everything in the super market is marked up with a price, that you cannot afford with the living wage that you receive; and now here comes a baby. The serpent would, from time to time, come to encourage you to put up your child for adoption. The enemy would sought your embarrassing mother, who did not want a grandchild out of wedlock. Meanwhile your beloved father has taken the side of his wife.

Jesus is saying hold on to unchanging hands. Take the foolishness of your parents! Jesus will not abandon you. Nine out of ten times your mama has thrown away babies in her teenage years. PRIDE! And your father paid the doctor bills. Lift your head high! JESUS LOVES YOU! Jesus will not forsake you not ever in a million years. Consequently, return to school to complete your degree and watch how Jesus will lift you up.

Too many beautiful young ladies, from inner cities, have taken to the streets, and fled, and have miscarriages because of the bias standards in the society. Some of them though pregnant have been raped, whilst sleeping at the homes of so-called good Samaritans. Some of them would be making continual phone calls to their parents and loved ones, only to be blamed for their own misdeeds.

Judgment is passed on these beautiful young ladies for giving birth to the sons and daughters of Our Lord Jesus, whilst living in abject poverty. God the Father, God the Son, and God the Holy Spirit had given the earth laws directly from above, which are not carried out, or put into practice, even at this very hour.

In today's world, brothers are marrying their sisters without the accused finger. Uncles are marrying aunties without the accused finger. Fathers are marrying their daughters without the accused finger. Business owners are marrying business owners' children without the accused finger. Professors and marrying professors without the accused finger. Billionaires are marrying billionaires without the accused finger.

Some miscarriages have resulted in the lost of their wombs. Whilst others, have lost their minds to the extent that they have forgotten their own names. Runaways have become an epidemic. The streets of New York are painted with the feet of these precious-innocent ones. Children hugging children at night: with each passing day looking like their last day. Children stealing food out of super markets putting themselves at risk of being incarcerated. Children hopelessly walking over train lines day and night not knowing where to go.

The voice of a mother crying in the wilderness is always heard by God the Father, God the Son, and God the Holy Spirit. The City of Troy, which had been one of the great cities of Rome: their people would use runaway children under their feet to keep them warm at wintertime. As the fruits of the fig tree fall to the ground, those feet of the people of Troy, would have been crushed by a passing train on entering hell.

The screenwriters are all obsessed with the way in which the world have turned for the worst. They perpetuate sin like if it is an honor or a right in the eyes of Jesus to do wrong. Do we have to form groups or picket lines to get to heaven? Where are the applause for good behavior? Jesus supposes that this has ended. Screenwriters need to be bold and robust. Screenwriters need to consult Jesus first. Screenwriters need not be bothered with the emptiness of this world. Screenwriters need to be focus on the raven in the sky.

Pasteurization is the process of killing disease-producing microorganisms by heating the liquid to a high temperature for a period of time. It is a pity with all this knowledge that humankind could not find a cure for Ebola. Microorganisms are simply microscopic in size. There is no fire on the face of the earth, that could eradicate any curse, that God the Father, God the Son, and God the Holy Spirit have allowed to enter.

Jesus always says that he will come like a thief in the night, then why are you probing? It is about time, that the whole world stop and pickup, where they have left their first love, the good Lord Jesus. Poliomyelitis has been around for centuries.

Jesus is accepting new applications for the job you want, and the job you do not want to do. You love Jesus, but you are scared of the devil. How could you love somebody and at the same time be afraid of that very person? Especially Jesus! The human race is willfully calling all so-called incurable diseases, curses. When a man is in an accident head on and wakes up in the emergency ward unaware of his condition, how dare you comment that, "it is good for you?" Jesus died for you.

Jesus is looking at the itching fingers of the medical profession. The type of credit cards that the hospitals would like to see, before they approve an operation. Jesus is sitting at the bedsides of patients, and listening to the conversations and the verbal comments of angry patients. The nurses on the floor are seen tiptoeing in the middle of the night, so as not to disturb her patients. Whilst on the other hand, there are doctors, who are on the job for one reason and for one only, money.

Societies are constantly changing the world. They tear down walls; they tear down buildings; they tear down blocks to get their people together. Then they use Jesus as a smoke screen. On the sidewalks, when they are giving out their bible tracts they would repeatedly say, "that they are saved, sanctified and filled with the Holy Spirit." How could you become that assertive, when you have failed in the giving of your tithes and offerings?

Jesus says lie not to one another. Which Bible are you reading? If you are not reading the Holy Bible, Authorized King James Version by Thomas Nelson, please remember that there are over 500 different versions! It is all well and good to say, that you are a Christian man, or lady or woman. But, what have you done lately for Jesus? The last time you have paid a visit, to any sick member of the family, was years and years ago.

The birds of the air would be seen heading out in a totally new direction, before the storm strikes. The human planet would forever be caught in total blindness of any storm.

Joseph, the stepfather of Jesus, was told by God the Father to put his pregnant wife on the back of a donkey and head towards the mountains. Over 99.99 percent of the people in this world would have put Mary, the mother of Jesus on a horse, or a mule, or an elephant, or a camel.

Jesus says I look to the hills from where cometh my help. Since man had discovered things and new places not clearly mentioned in the Bible, he has taken upon himself to eat the bread, that the devil knead. God the Father, God the son, and God the Holy Spirit speaks in parables and Word written on rocks and clay mountains. Of course, you need wisdom to unfold these writings.

The word ancient is not a word created by Our Lord Jesus. Because the human race is made in the image and likeness of our creator, God the Father, God the Son, and God the Holy Spirit. Adam lived to 1,000 years. Was he in a wheelchair, or on crutches, or used a walking stick? No. At that age Adam was ascending mountains. The scientists are misleading the whole wide world in believing that the earth had been here for millions of years.

The subtitles of motion pictures need much to be desired. Moreso, foreign languages interpretations to English. In documentaries, one does not have to show the nudity of both men and women. Animals in mating season do not need to be recorded and shown. Their privacy need not be invaded by scientists and shown to the general public. Jesus is showing me molten mountains, which the scientists hide their cameras in order to record and write, a so-called documentary about the work of Our Lord Jesus.

God the Father, God the Son, and God the Holy Spirit is not interested in the misguided information by the scientists. The cameras are not equipped to truly record the hands of Jesus at his handiwork. The angels that keep watch at the four corners of the world, are not seen by any scientific invention. The building of the roads, thus providing a new earth, are virtually unseen by cameras and by the human eye.

Astrology: the study of the supposed influences of the stars, and their movements and positions on human affairs are all conjecture. This is a wake-up call for the world. The breaking of the ice on the ocean floor will all be melted, before the stars fall to the earth. Jesus is the only one to give directives, for the earth will become smaller than you think. Presently the earth is shrinking as the tide goes out.

The atmosphere is becoming less misty than usual. Condensed vapor will disappear, as the boundaries of countries will not be visible on maps anymore. All these early signs will be writings in the minds of Christians, that the earth will be folded, as a book in the sunset. Horses, which are the most graceful creatures on the planet, are tremendously abused by owners and trainers around the globe. These creatures of elegance and charm, add mist and fog to the surroundings.

Jesus is using this hour to unmask a dubious world, which is filled with unanswered questions, before they act on the Word of God, which is the only impeccable Word. It is easy to climb a coconut tree, than to ascend a perpendicular mountain without slopes. This climbing becomes more crucial on a foggy day and night.

Jesus is moving around by standing in the midst of his people, yet no one sees him. The truth will be unfolded for everyone to see and bear witness. One by one will be removed from the lies of the serpent. The sword has already been shown by the right hand of Jesus. The blade still glitters even in the night.

Human beings that had been living inside of mountains and caves are now receiving the Word of God in multitudes, because Jesus knows how to draw people to the light of God. Their appetites are enormously opened for the Word, which is the revelation of Jesus. Their children cling to the voice of the Lord. The Emmanuel of Jesus is ripened and is falling from a seed, that had been planted a long, long, long time ago.

Jesus is showing me his sword glittering at noontime. Which in essence means that Jesus is in the distance coming. The coming of Jesus will be his climax. Everyone will not be around to see that great, and beautiful, and stupendous, and glorious, and phenomenal occasion. But for those of you that will be around, one will be taken, whereas one will remain. There will be no festivities in honor of the risen King. There will be no palms in the hands of people to place on the ground for the risen King.

For the world will always want a celebration of sorts. At this time, all the misconceptions will be no more. But before his great coming, Jesus is giving the human planet time to requite. His Grace is still flowing, as the two fishes from the River Nile, go skiing through the cold winter that freezes both hands and feet.

The four beasts had each of them six wings about him. These celestial beings know nothing about earth. Their whole lives are spent in adoration to God the Father, God the Son, and God the Holy Spirit. Jesus is sending this message out to everyone, who is fed up with just one thing. The Triune God has gifted the human race with so much things to do, and places to go, and what is the world doing, absolutely nothing. They sit and tap their feet each day, expecting that things are going to change without first consulting Jesus.

Hosanna is what the crowds shouted to honor Our Lord Jesus. The four beasts created a crescendo by saying Holy, Holy, Holy to the Triune God. Jesus is showing me the children at orphanages in every capital city, of every country, here on earth. Children left behind owing to the death of their parents. Some of these children have aunties, uncles, brothers, sisters, and grandparents. A few of these children have relatives, who are very well off but, scoff at them. Derision is a curse.

These children are seldom seen in public. There are no graduations at the end of their school years. At six in the evening, they retire to bed to see another day. At birthdays, there are no cameras, or cell phones, or gifts, to record their special occasions. No balloons hanging from the ceilings, or happy birthday cards are visible. Yet the world does not want to be bothered.

Jesus is showing me children with dirty hands. Which means that the governments in these countries are not Christian people. When the four beasts whose faces are different saying Holy, Holy, Holy to the Triune God, and they are full of eyes within: they are seeing everything. Dirty hands and dirty feet. Jesus does not need any human being to explain to him anything. Poverty in any country is not an excuse for abuse. Children are seen wearing no shoes, no socks, or no slippers. Hand-me-down clothes fit any size.

The books that are given to the orphanages by the good Samaritans of the world: these people of God are not held in high esteem. The children, who are leaving these institutions, when they have become adults, are not given any assistance by the hierarchy. How could they survive in a ruthless world? The four beasts, that are ever in the presence of the Triune God, see everything and communicate to Jesus and his four angels, which are posted in the four corners of the world.

These four angels do not have to wait on Jesus's command to bring forth an earthquake. Philanthropists travel to countries of poverty to lend a helping hand by visiting first, these monotheistic governments, to beseech them the privilege in honoring Jesus. By and large, freedom is not given to these charitable people of Jesus. These few laborers of Our Lord Jesus are often met with threats of hostility and violence.

The scars of horrendous behavior are phlegmatic. Too many times, the sky had been enveloped in flames owing to severe earthquakes and visibility had been poor. Jesus had to call off the angel not to hurt the earth no more. The four beasts, which are older than the earth, look so radiant and beautiful when seen in the light of God.

The beast that is like a flying eagle has tremendous power like the element uranium. Scores of countries would have liked to be blessed with this powerful element. Overall the few countries that are blessed with the highest tonnage of this electro-magnetic radiation are controlled by the hands of God.

Jesus is the author of the Bible and he will not allow no more abuse of his elements in the future. Storms will come and storms will go. Typhoons will be no more. Jesus says that the earth will not be ending by water, as it did on the last occasion, because he is the ultimate end. The beast, who is like a flying eagle, will one day show himself to the planet.

God the Father is showing me his back, as he stands erect facing his new world, as he spreads his vision for the future. God the Father is clearly painting not just a new world, but one that will never be as the one that we so want him to keep. God the Father hears all the bickers of the false prophets, that this present earth will undoubtedly be the new heaven and earth.

God the Father is moving on in the spirit of his love, rolling back the mountains, and the seas, and the hills, and the islands, which he will throw in the sea of nothingness. All these things will take the image of a new catalyst, to be filled up with new creation of abundance of his loveliness. God the Father is showing me a starving world. A world that is without any direction. A scattered world.

The order of the world is one of disorder. The triumphs of this world are all wrapped up in selfishness. The human race succeeds by trial and error. God the Father triumphs on perfection. All the more reason why, he can and will boast alone on building a new heaven and a new earth. The trees, and the seas, and the lakes, and the rivers, and the fountains of water will be no more. God the Father does not have to go to the doctor, or to the dentist for an extraction, or for sparkling white teeth.

Presently, we go for liposuctions. The bridges that we have created, and the pitfalls of life that we have spun into a web, have had an enormous effect and will have a tremendous effect in the future. God the Father is looking at the web, whilst simultaneously opening up new roads with the hope, that the children of God find these paths to heaven. God the Father provides someone to guide his children to the light. Surely, there is a church door open to everyone somewhere.

The King of Kings and the Lord of Lords has to keep his lakes of fire burning. One of his beasts is like a lion. This particular beast will one day show himself. God the Father knows, that the world would like to see into their Father's house, if even, it is at least once in a blue moon. The character of God the Father is not about his fortitude. His character is built-in every single element of the universe.

Every creature was created and is created for his pleasure. Though the earth is filled with animals that were put together by human hands, families have become worried about their pets making it to heaven. Two of these pets namely cats and dogs are sometimes buried with their loved ones in the very same casket. God the Father is saying that families do not have to bury their cats, and their dogs in their burial plots.

God the Father prefers that these two pets are buried in their own back yards.

The world is already misguided in so many ways, thus creating somewhat of a frenzy, among the children of God. The scientists claim that the cat originally came from *Miacis*. This is not true. Likewise some 50 million years ago. Outrageous! Cats and dogs are a great wonder of the world. The bodies of human beings are sacred and therefore cannot be buried together with animals.

The world today is an-anything-go planet. Each individual must be convicted by God the Father, otherwise, he or she would not quit doing wrong. Now wrong is right and right is wrong. God the Father has seen this great wrong and will one day do something about it. The planet is trying to sleep with one eye open and one eye close. The beast that is liken to a lion will not be sleeping at all.

One day, this same beast will sound the alarm to the whole wide world in an effort to get their attention, before it is too late. Families are doing everything to bring their relatives under the same banner. Some families are buying up churches and making their own relatives pastors of these great churches. The beast that is like a lion will one day pay these houses of worship a visit. Anyone caught adding to the Word of God will be taken out from the Book of Life. Anyone caught substracting from the Word of God will be eliminated from the Book of Life.

Jesus is saying that the time of the rod of iron is now. For the world keeps dipping its feet in multitudes of dusts as footprints on the wooden floors of well-polished mahogany. God the Father does not need a hearing aid. God the Father does not need to be reminded. God the Father does not need to ask a favor. God the Father does not need in memory of.

The beast with the face like a man is saying: beware,

beware. Every athlete on the planet be it soccer, cricket, football, hockey, baseball and basketball, why must your body be tattooed? Jesus the supreme master of all talked about the piercing of the skin. The drawing of blood by skin piercing and exchanging of needles between each other are forbidden in the Ten Commandments. The pencil markings and drawings on the skin are a duplicate of the Egyptians' warriors.

God the Father will not be stationed anywhere on the battle field. The prize of the New Jerusalem, which is the bride of Jesus, is the main reason for the downfall of the serpent. If we ask God the Father for a red Cadillac, we do expect a red Cadillac. But can God the Father give us something that exceeds the quality of the red Cadillac? Yes he can. So then, why hold God the Father hostage for a red Cadillac? God the Father knows what's best for everyone.

Christians often question God the Father on the life hereafter. Jesus sheds his light on the heavenly bliss by saying I am the light of the world. And indeed he is. God the Father promises that heaven will have no moon and no stars. The light of Jesus will be the only light, to light up heaven. Babylon is fallen, is fallen and has become the wine of the wrath of God. The twelve pillars of heaven, which will be named after the twelve apostles, did not come about by the drop of a hat.

The blood of Jesus, as he stood hanging on a wooden cross, is rolled into the twelve pillars of heaven. The white garments of the twenty-four elders that stand before the throne of Grace are not just lily white; they are rolled into the blood of Jesus. Talking about Jesus would not get you into heaven. Are you willing to die for the love of Jesus?

Jesus has twelve fruits on the tree of life. And each month one fruit is borne. And it begins with the first commandment: Thou shalt have no other Gods before me. And the second fruit will be: Thou shalt not make unto thee any graven images. And the third fruit will be: Thou shalt not take the name of the Lord thy God in vain. And the fourth fruit will be: Remember the Sabbath Day to keep it holy. And the fifth fruit will be: Honor thy Father and thy Mother. And the sixth fruit will be: Thou shalt not kill. And the seventh fruit will be: Thou shalt not commit adultery. And the eighth fruit will be: Thou shalt not steal. And the ninth fruit will be: Thou shalt not bear false witness. And the tenth fruit will be: Thou shalt not covet. And the eleventh fruit will be: Love the Lord your God with all your heart and with all your soul and with all your mind. And the twelfth fruit will be: Love your neighbor as yourself.

The love of Jesus is expressed more and exceedingly more in worship. But how many people are really accepting the beast with the face like a man in the consummation of the Bible? The fifth commandment says honor thy father and thy mother for thy days will be long in the land of the living is totally ignored by a disrespectful people of God. How can you love Jesus and in the same breath be disrespectful to your neighbor? How can you say that you venerate Jesus yet you steal god's money by putting less in the offering?

God the Father has his way of dealing with his earthly pleasures. The trend today is to videotape any happening and send it off to social media or *Facebook*. God the Father has his way in showing himself undisturbed. When a man of God who has become a multibillionaire and never says that Jesus gave him this business then why are you messing with this man?

Singers would say when interviewed on the radio or television network that God has inspired their rendition. This means that these artists are giving God the praise and the glory. This means that you who have professed to be a Christian should be singing this song or hymn without a doubt. But then what do we do? We ignore the truth because we prefer the song, or the social network, over God the Father. We are overpowered by the music, or acting, or the singing, or the beauty of the artist.

And because we do not see the face of the King of king and Lord of lords, who is God the Father, then we believed, with all our mind that God the Father truly does not love us. The Word says that if we see his face we will surely die. We ultimately do not accept God the Father at his very Word. We dare him to show his face, before we pay homage and adoration to his Good Name.

God the Father is not going to bow down to any human being that he has created with his son Jesus. Every living creature has been created for the pleasure of God the Father, God the Son, and God the Holy Spirit. God the Father is saying that Babylon is fallen, is fallen.

The beast with the face like a man is who sees with eyes within and without is walking on water like Jesus, because earthly people still would not accept this great phenomenon of the many things that Jesus had done. Evil is Evil no matter what or how human beings choose to justify their own misdeeds. It is easy to justify a line of molten single type in a stick, than to blatantly do everything to make wrong right.

God the Father takes you to the supermarket and after shopping, he takes you back to the vegetable section to buy a sack of onions to eat each one raw. Reluctantly, you purchased the sack of onions. At dinnertime, you blatantly refuse to eat the whole onion raw, but you choose to eat it steamed. Did you do the right thing? In your mind, yes. Why? Because you ate the onion.

God the Father does not say in your mind. God the Father says to do precisely what his Son and his only Begotten Son will do is to eat the onion raw. In disrespect to God the

Father you would say that, "God is Crazy." Were you there when God the Father, God the Son, and God the Holy Spirit created the stars up above? Your earthly father gave you his life story from beginning to end throughout the years he had spent with you. Upon his death, you came to the realization, that the pastor knew some things that you had never heard before, plus others from his siblings.

In God the Father and God the Son, and God the Holy Spirit absolutely nothing is left out or is a surprise. Isn't that wonderful? Then why question him. Truth walks a very thin line, which few will ever accompany Jesus. Thy kingdom come is in the Lord's Prayer. Yet the whole Muslim world follows their so-called prophet mohammed, who did nothing and absolutely nothing in all of creation. Jesus is your masterpiece.

It is easy to lift the curtains to see out the window clearly. It is easy to close your eyes and fall asleep. Did you see Jesus on those two occasions? Then why question him. Jesus is in everything. Whether a kind word is said to you or not Jesus is in everything. Your neighbor passed you by without saying, "Good Morning to you," leave it alone! Jesus is in everything. Your birthday came and you had nothing to eat. Jesus loves you.

At the restaurant, you ordered a meal and for some remote reason you ordered a large slice of chocolate cake, and chocolate ice cream. You yelled at the waiter several times, because you have finished and you wanted to leave but he paid you no attention. Happily, he stopped by to let you know, that your meal has been paid for by one of your best friends with a handsome tip.

God the Father did not allow you to see who did what was required for him to do. In furtherance, his blessing is greater for never ever telling you what he had done. Then why question God. God the Father gives you favor. You left the house in a hurry and you had left your wallet sitting on the window sill. Already late for work, you discovered no wallet. You turned and asked the first person that you saw for the passage, but the words could not come out from your mouth. The recipient, a fellow traveler, hears from Jesus to give you the passage with a tip.

With his fist folded, he gave you the passage, which resulted in $100. Turning from the cashier's window to say thanks, he disappeared in the crowd never to be seen again. Jesus is saying that, we must not allow our minds to rule over us. Thy kingdom come must be worn in your minds at all times. Some people are prone to prayer, as quickly as the breeze flutters the leaves on the trees.

Crimson red is not only a purplish red or like a vivid red, for it is the true color of the Robe of Jesus. A color highly disgraced by public officials in ceremonies around the world. Respect for God the Father, God the Son, and God the Holy Spirit is at its lowest, since Noah had begun to build the ark. God the Father is always reminding his people to hold on to the Word of God.

The Jesus in you is the same today, yesterday and tomorrow. The neighbors that you had shunned, since you have moved into your new house, are the same light of Jesus that you have been running from, even from within. God the Father is not pleased by Christians, who walk on their knees, thus paying homage to his wonderful name. God the Father is not pleased by the constant reminder of his blood, which was shed on Mt. Calvary, for the forgiveness of sins by priestesses.

Remote control is not the answer to earthly human wisdom. The touch of a button is not going to bring Jesus to your given call. Jesus is as ready as you are ready. To be ready is to be found waiting. The world stands in line without ever noticing. The world takes its cue from the mouth of Jesus.

God the Father does not care how anybody feels about his Word. For his Word is like the feet of Jesus, which is and which was and is presently flaming and burning, as the fire of coals in a coal pot.

The feet of Jesus are like the color of brass that lights up at nighttime to show you the way to heaven. The world will shrug their shoulders in utter disbelief, as the feet of Jesus is seen from up above. With the four beasts: singing and chanting their Holy, Holy, Holy to their Lord and Savior of the Universe, in thanksgiving for what he has done. God the Father is dressed in military-kingly attire, as he stands before a prism of light.

Jesus is seen with a two-edge sword in his mouth, as he stands before his beloved apostle John. The Son of God is dressed in battle array. The Son of God is reassuring his people of the many promises he had made during his earthly life. The Ten Commandments that Jesus gave to Moses, the prophet and deliverer, of the twelve tribes of Israel on Mt. Sanai. These commandments are flouted each and everyday by a ruthless and self-centered people. Their manner of worship and glorification of the Supreme God need much to be desired.

How many times must Jesus say I am? How many window panes must your child break in the neighborhood, before he is chastised by you the parent? How many red lights must you run through late at night, before you do the right thing? God the Father is still holding the sign up, to let you know, that Jesus died and rose again, for you to have a seat at the right hand of the throne of God.

It is easy to believe that the rain that keeps wetting you on your head is coming from above. Then, why worry about everything? The whole wide world goes to the supermarket and purchases all the food and drink on the shelves, yet these producers of fine wheat and drink no one has ever met. Forgetting that, the Jesus in you is far greater than any producer on the earth.

The airlines crowd the runways of busy airports around the world. Everyone has a passport to show on entry in and out of any foreign country. Jesus is saying that his airport will not be crowded as Kennedy Airport. Jesus is saying that his sword in his mouth is getting sharper and sharper as the days go by. Babylon is fallen is fallen and has become a cage for every hateful bird.

People of God do not want this book to be disclosed in every way. People of God must not be told of coming events that their loving Father will be destroying everything to dust. They feel that God the Father, God the Son, and God the Holy Spirit shall abstain and change his mind, his heart and his soul. The truth is something that the people of God cannot handle. But Jesus is saying that right is right and wrong is wrong. Jesus also is saying that the changing of the guards even in the four corners of the earth will not ever take place.

A slain preacher that had preached the Word of God to the ends of the earth, and someone beheaded him just because he is preaching about the Son of God will not be taken lightly by God the Father. This slain man of God was about his father's business. This slain man of God was about doing the will of his Almighty Father. This slain man of God was winning souls for Jesus. This slain man of God gave up his life to preach the Word in Spirit and in Truth. God the Father's Word cannot be compromised.

The house of satan, the devil, the serpent, the dragon will all come a tumbling down with the point of the very sharp two-edge sword. The Son of God is not about having a repeat of sinfulness and squalor and lasciviousness in heaven. Jesus is not about holding back his arm, when he thinks about his twelve apostles, who went out into a dying world, that was hungry for truth.

Jesus is saying that when a war is raged against his Father's kingdom, God the Father, and God the Son, and God the Holy Spirit does not really care. Yes God the Father created both good and evil. He did that to give mankind a choice between good and evil. The choice is now yours. The battle is an ongoing battle, until the Lord Jesus gets the order from his heavenly Father to end all of the foolishness.

There are windows in the sky for Jesus and his heavenly beings to have a peripheral view from heaven. So high and distant are the angels, that the greatest inventions of mankind cannot see the glory of Our Lord Jesus. Jesus from his heavenly couch radiates so much light that even the angels cannot see his beautiful face. All they see is a sketch. And as he draws near the angels will see his garments. His trousers cover his ankles and is fastened throughout with white gold.

Jesus is dressed in lily white from his neck to his ankles. His twenty-four elders also were dressed in white. These are your twenty-four Prophets who were beheaded for the Gospel of the Good News. Some of these prophets were not named in the Bible. Jesus is saying that these prophets were on their Father's business, when God the Father allowed their decapitation. For the love of Jesus, John the beloved, stood and wept under the cross of Jesus.

God the Father's ways are not easily perceived by members of the family for fear of the serpent. Jesus will send someone to put their heart at rest in the understanding of his Word. These saints of God form his choirs in heaven. Jesus is assembling pillars to erect buildings in his new heaven. This new way of life will not be experienced by all humanity. Jesus says during his earthly life that when someone strikes you, you must turn the other cheek.

Jesus even supposes that he was only talking to himself. We are living in very aggressive times; so wicked, that the cries of abusive children could be heard in heaven. God the Father remembers the cries of his children, and yes, the islands will one day disappear, but the fire and brimstone, the evil ones will not escape. His wrath is here to stay. There will be more wars coming and there will be rumors of wars.

The two-edge sword in the mouth of Jesus signifies heinous crimes and blasphemies from the mouths of totalitarians. There will be a constant rise of very wicked leaders across the globe. More churches preaching the blood of Jesus will be cursed by the mouths of evil followers. More churches will be burnt to the ground and evil signs will be erected on those sites. More churches will be painted with blood from the steps to the front door. More disruptions of church services will take place in popular cities too numerous to mention.

The cries of the sentences of the 1,000 years that satan and his followers once endured will be heard in streets throughout the lands of Christian peoples. People will be putting cotton in their ears, as they make their way to their homes. These shouts of pain and agony in the groin will be the first signs of satan's realization, that his time is coming to an end. His power will begin to weaken as the sun's power weakens at nightfall.

The blood of Jesus will be blasphemed by followers of satan in spite of what they will bear witness to. This is a message to the disobedient followers of Jesus that evil does not change no matter what. A trick that some members of Christian families use against their own to get them to become a follower of satan. You do this for me and I do this for you is and still is a tit for tat comprise.

How many times must your mother and your father say, "Do not speak to strangers!" Some of us grow as adults and is continually doing exactly the opposite to the given Word. Moses said an eye for an eye and a tooth for a tooth. This adage has become a paradigm in these modern times. Jesus has already fulfilled that law to turn the other cheek. Christians must pay close attention to the Word of God, which is the Word of Jesus. Do not repay evil for evil!

God the Father is the only one to avenge. No man under the sun has no God given right to go after another human being. The blood of Jesus on the crucifix is enough to heal all wounds. Satan the enemy of God will constantly be around you to push you into leaning to your own understanding.

Of course, Jesus heard you that is why the Word of God still lingers in your heart. You got to stop pleasing your mind. If you would let Jesus in then you would not ever have second thoughts. The commands of Jesus are easy. Christians make it hard by debating and questioning Jesus. Jesus told his disciples to follow him! A command! So Jesus is telling the whole wide world to follow him! Jesus also says that the road will not be easy and he will not be making it any easier for his preachers.

Babylon is fallen, is fallen and is become a habitation of foul devils. Vultures will be on the increase before the coming of the Lord Jesus to devour the carrion of human beings, after that great and dreadful day. God the Father is increasing their birth rate over a span of three scores and ten. Jesus the High Priest will be making his appearances to countries around the globe with his two-edge sward in his mouth. Firstly, these appearances will be seen by his little innocent children.

God the Father is not about making his people afraid. For the Word fear not will be heard by the children, before the trumpet is blown for the children to focus on what Jesus is showing them. Yes Jesus will be speaking in their native tongue. Jesus is the creator of all languages: the voice of many waters. Children will not be afraid of the Glory of the Lord Jesus. Jesus will always be alone. Jesus does not need anyone. The face of Jesus will be sunless to his darling little children.

God the Father will not be accompanying his son. Everything has already been put in place by God the Father. Even the waters on the Atlantic Ocean, the second largest body of water on the earth will be really, really, really calm. The terrorists that plague nations by night are your drive-by killers. These gangs are seldom seen and often show up in neighborhoods that are not their own. Jesus is showing that these foul spirits are on their way to hell.

When people park their cars to go shopping, or to attend a function, or to see a friend, God the Father knows that the eyes of the evil ones are hidden sometimes in other parked vehicles. These vagabonds roam the streets both day and night stealing fancy cars, and turning them into the hands of ruthless millionaires. This nomadic way of life is expressed in affluent cities.

Any member of a gang who swears to kill police officers or high-ranking officials, as they journey from their homes and from their offices or work stations are among these foul devils. God the Father is not plea-bargaining with anyone whose name is not mentioned in the Book of Life. God the Father is holding everyone responsible for his own conduct. God the Father is sightseeing, as he plucks the eyes out of the heads of thieves that dismember bodies even in the graves.

The sanctity of the bereaved and the sanctity of the dead is uppermost in the singing of the four beasts Holy, Holy, Holy to the Glory of the risen Jesus. God the Father knew, that the death of his own Son, would have provoked the wicked kings to sabotage and desecrate the body of Jesus. The angels of heaven, which are your four beasts, came down to protect the sanctity of the Blessed Lord.

This transition from heaven to earth caused a mighty wind to roll the stone away, which blocked the door of the sepulcher. This huge stone weighed 2 tons. Acid was poured all over the stone enough to burn your hands to crimson. No human hands could have rolled this stone away. Jesus redemptive mystery was displayed at the sight of a new and wholesome tomb. The women of God that came to the tomb were told by an angel all dressed in white, which is one of the twenty-four elders, that Jesus is risen indeed he is.

Then God the Father spoke through the very angel and say to the women that Jesus will meet all of you in the upper room. Behold the true Man of God came and met with his loved ones as well as his disciples. Jesus is risen and is waiting for Word from his heavenly Father. The man with the two-edge sword in his mouth is looking at blood diseases like cancer, diabetes, sickle-cell anemia.

These blood diseases are sometimes misunderstood as Jesus defines its true definition. Some people of God are given food to eat from the hands of an evil person and because they are weak in faith these diseases show up in their lives. The mercy of God always says fear not the one that can kill the body but fear the one that can kill both body and soul.

Jesus always wins the battle even in the grave. Rest assured that if you had lost a loved one caught in the subtleness of the serpent, that Jesus had already won the victory. This abstruse attitude that possesses fallen peoples of God, that satan uses to dim the light of good people, as if to say surely that person is going to hell must be disregarded at **all cost.**

Satan plays with everyone's feelings and emotions. Jesus does not. Jesus keeps you focus right from the very beginning. The New Jerusalem, the bride of Jesus, has already been built. Jesus is dancing for his bride which is the great Holy City, the New Jerusalem. God the Father is sharing his Word among his preachers to form the roots of the tree of life.

God the Father says that if you make him your first love you will eat of the tree of life. Jesus is saying that the river that flows out of the New Jerusalem to nourish the tree of life is giving its fruits in due season. These twelve fruits and the leaves are the prizes that the saints will receive as they enter heaven. God the Father is breaking down walls of the cities of Turkey for their utter disregard of the messiah. The root of David, of the tribe of Juda will prevail over their religious beliefs.

Jesus is and was and is the groom of the great city, the New Jerusalem. There is no equal on the earth or in heaven. The rivers of water will flow through the throne of God the Father, God the Son, and God the Holy Spirt. You must reap, what you sew. The merchants of the earth, who have fornicated with the harlot, and have drunk of her wine, and have committed adultery, and have blasphemed against the Holy Spirit, will be thrown into the lake of fire. It is not alright to lie to your children and tell them about your successes. It is not alright to cheat to make it to the top.

God the Father together with his Son will always be building new things in heaven for his people, beyond our wildest imaginations. The beast like the flying eagle is a tremendous sign of hope to fallen people under the yoke of witchcraft embedded in the souls of generations of family curses. Jesus who is rivers of waters is stemming the tide and breaking these strongholds of great evil.

For families who have found out the truth of their past generations, Jesus is saying thank you to you, for now you will be able to rest in the soul of Jesus. Longer life will be given to you, so that you will be and will become a light that will burn for generations to come. The memories of innocence far outweigh the torments of this world. The love of Jesus grows deeper in your bellies, as your sufferings increase.

To families who have to take their loved ones to and from hospitals, because they have lost limbs, Jesus is saying your fruit from the tree of life awaits you. The pain of love that is shared in homes that do everything to the limit of the love of Jesus in setting higher standards, your fruit from the tree of life awaits you. Your prayers may not have been answered in the time that you desired, but your fruit from the tree of life awaits you.

The blessings of Jesus though rich and powerful will not elude you because of pitfalls. An impassioned heart is a fervent heart. To wear the face of an eagle, as the beast that stands before the throne of God saying Holy, Holy, Holy is to have tremendous power on the face of the earth. This gift will be one of great miracles, which have never been seen, since the habitation of Our Lord Jesus.

The Glory of Jesus, whose garments were dipped in his blood by the Holy Ghost will be worn by him on his return to the earth. The coming of Jesus will be fierce.

The author: Prophet Allyson Michael D'Espyne

www.ingramcontent.com/pod-product-compliance
Lightning Source LLC
Chambersburg PA
CBHW071213210726
48293CB00002B/406